STELLAEIN
N
NOCTURN
TEAR LAKE
OBSIDIAN FOREST
BANDIT CAMPS
HAZENTHORNE
ULULATE
VAHRIR
MARSH OF VAHRIR
GOBLIN WATCHTOWERS
HAZEN VILLAGE
HAZEN SWAMP
MIKRUM CASTLE
PELAGU
HIMMEL LAKE
MIKRUM VILLAGE
FRANGIT
TARISHNA

COGNITIA
HIGHTOWER CASTLE
GOLEMS
N
RUINS OF CENEDRIL
VERENDUS
GNOLLS
FELLING FIELDS
GLACIER LAKE
VERENDI MOUNTAINS
CURET
DARSHIN
CENEDRIL

SOMNIA ONLINE

FUSION

BOOK 6

K.T. HANNA

SOMNIA ONLINE: FUSION

Author: K.T. Hanna
Cover Artist: Marko Horvatin
Typography: Bonnie Price
Formatting & Interior Design: Caitlin Greer

Also by KT Hanna

Somnia Online:

Initializing
Anomaly
Fragments
Dissonance
Distortion
Fusion

The Domino Project:

Chameleon
Hybrid
Parasite

Dedication:

Kira, Kuma, Jetta, and Amanda,
and anyone who knows just how special a corgi can be.

With Rav struggling to retain his sanity after being attacked by Sui, the flux of glitches in Somnia begin to multiply. The more Somnia evolves, the more dangerous the getashi become to all the AIs.

The voices in Murmur's mind push her toward saving Telvar. Had she been thinking clearly, she'd never have absorbed all of those shards in order to spare him. So much power, channeled through her via her headset, is overwhelming.

Laria and Shayla work tirelessly to keep the key reports out of James' hands. If Wren's connection to the game comes under too much scrutiny, Storm Entertainment could lose everything. The newly adjusted headsets provide a deeper connection to Somnia. Without fully understanding the link, Laria has to work overtime to quell the virus infecting the entire Somnian system.

Thwarting each attempt to access files not immediately applicable to the investment deal, Davenport continues to block James. But time is running out...

CHAPTER ONE

Hindsight

Telvar's roar echoed through the cavern, devolving into a primal scream as his dragon form gave way once again to that of a lacerta. He fell from his perch, tumbling down and into his hoard with a crash that cut off the scream as he rolled to the ground.

Sinister blinked back the sudden heat in her eyes, the tears yearning to pour from them. She watched as Murmur rose in the air, her head thrown back, her eyes closed as her body began to emanate like a floodlight of stars, eclipsing the entire cavern.

The bloodmage threw an arm over her eyes, but not before her vision was filled with stars of its own. She flung out her healing sensors to check for Telvar's life signs, but he was in no immediate danger. Veranol could take care of him, because Sin had other things to do.

She was far more worried about Mur. Her friend's life fluctuated randomly, from almost flatlining back up to full and all the stages in between. While Sin knew that Mur couldn't actually die anymore from an in-game death, it didn't mean that she wasn't worried. Her friend received so many strange repercussions from her headset and dying in-game, so many lingering effects.

Floating in the air just above Sinister's head shouldn't have been one of them.

Emilarth appeared beside them, a frown on her feles features. "Telvar is fine. What the fuck is up with Murmur?"

Sinister would have laughed at the unintentional pun, but she didn't want to rip her focus from Mur. Instead, Sin ground out her commentary through clenched teeth. "You're the AI, aren't you supposed to fucking know?"

Her words were clipped, and the edge of fury nudged at her boundaries, swirling through her thoughts. Nothing else mattered except that Mur's eyes were giving the whole cavern a light show while she floated. Gusts of wind made her robes flutter and twist when there shouldn't have been a breeze to begin with.

The shards Murmur had released when she dove into the hoard of treasure, those parts of Michael's brain, were suspended throughout the room in eerie stillness. All of them fed back to the enchanter with thin tendrils, like an infusion was feeding her.

They lit up with a cold black light from within, pushing against Murmur's starry eyes as if they were trying to drown them. Why had Mur dived in to get the getashi when she knew how dangerous they could be? Perhaps she'd wanted to protect Telvar who still lay in a gasping heap at the foot of his treasure, probably trying to remember that he was, in fact, an AI and not an actual person.

That's a little harsh.

Sinister shook her head as the crackling words broke into her thoughts. She smacked her ear, trying to figure out why the hell she could hear a voice, and one with bad reception at that. Maybe she was spending too much time in-game.

That won't help.

This time the words were clearer, if a little soft still. Sin had no idea who was talking in her head. Unless…

"Mur?" She muttered the name softly, not wanting anyone to think she was talking to herself.

Not Mur. Close though. At least, technically.

Sin caught herself before she uttered anything else. Talking out loud even while the flurry of movement continued around her would start seeming odd. Her eyes never left the floating enchanter, and she tried her best to think at the voice in her head. *What do you mean?*

Clever. I'm everywhere. Your headset isn't as powerful as hers. It's not as crisp.

Suddenly everything felt right as all of the pieces clicked into place for Sinister. Their new headsets made it possible for the AIs, the system, and, if she'd understood it correctly, the world to communicate properly with her. Both her and Havoc, actually. Was he having the same inner conversation?

No, he's a bit more stubborn.

Not likely.

There was a pause. **No, really, he is. At least when it comes to voices in his head.**

Sinister did her best not to laugh out loud. The last thing she wanted was to have to explain herself. Especially since she needed to get Murmur down to the ground again and figure out what had happened.

She will be fine.

Unless she falls and breaks her neck when she snaps out of that trance. Sinister was proud of the heat she put into those words as they echoed through her mind.

Again, another pause. **You realize she can respawn, right?**

You realize she gets mega residual effects after the death, right? Sinister's patience was legendary, in that she barely had any.

There was a pause so long that Sin thought the voice wasn't going to talk to her again. Dismissing the conversation, she began to focus on some of the minimal enchanter spells she had in her hybrid library. Soothe was the only spell that might have a chance. She could try and calm Murmur's mind with that. Her only other mind related spells had to do with mana regeneration, so there was no help there.

The others around her were shouting at each other. Telvar had moved off to the left of her peripheral vision, although staggering might have been more accurate. Emilarth ran to his side, and Sinister could feel the power emanating from the AI, like she was using all her abilities to hold her brother together.

Sinister used that soothe spell on Mur like it was a lifeline. She only had eyes and ears for Murmur, and her jerkily convulsing frame as it hung in the air like a rag doll.

Static played in her head like her antenna wasn't getting reception anymore. Murmur's thoughts fractured, never quite meeting in the middle. She knew she'd done something stupid, something that in hindsight she should never have attempted, but for the life of her, she couldn't think what it was.

Nor could she fathom why she'd done it.

For the life—was she still alive? Had something happened to her? The limbo around her seemed sluggish, like a pool of tar trying to steal her into its embrace. Yet there was something soothing about it as well.

Her limbs weighed heavily, listless and lifeless. A dull sensation tugged at the base of her skull and prevented her from giving into the darkness and falling asleep. Surely, she could take a nap?

Fusion.

The word fluttered through her mind, like a butterfly just out of the chrysalis. Maybe she'd been caught and was evolving, she couldn't quite tell. Focusing on it right then seemed impossible, like so many things and words just beyond her reach.

A sound cracked through her head, broken pieces of sentences, of speech she couldn't quite strain herself to hear. There was too much interference. Only fragments remained.

...fuse...not...heal.

The voice that leaked through to her in broken segments seemed familiar, as if she should know it. But recognition escaped her, lingering in her senses like that annoying word that balanced on the tip of her tongue when she couldn't quite remember.

Exhaustion crept over her body, seeping into her pores, right down to her bones. It would be so easy to just go to sleep, to just let whatever it was nagging in the back of her mind happen.

Sleep.

Except she knew she couldn't. Whatever else wasn't getting through to her, she knew that for a fact. There was something she had to do, something she had been doing with her friends, both old and new. Friends—some of those slivers of thought floated precariously close to comprehension in her mind.

She closed her eyes, or perhaps they'd already been closed to start with. Sensations came in splintered sections. Some of them were filled with pain, while others carried a sadness so heavy it made her want to fall to the ground. Other bits hinted at happiness, at determination, and at power…but sticking them together was like trying to finish a puzzle that had lost half of its pieces.

Murmur tried to block out the static. Interference was splicing her thoughts, even the few coherent ones she had left. She knew without doubt that she couldn't let it do that. There was something important just out of reach.

A soft glow reached her through the gloom, emanating from her hands. Soft and blue, no red…perhaps a bit of purple. It leaked through to her, giving light to the limbo of stickiness that encased her.

Shards.

Murmur's eyes snapped open. Of course, how could she have forgotten? The shards had been strewn, stored…packed inside of Telvar's hoard. Had he touched them?

She shook her head, the thoughts already dissipating. Telvar was her friend. She knew that much at least. Telvar's red and gold wings flashed through her mind, his mischievous fiery eyes that held all the computational power of an AI and curiosity of a sentient being.

Murmur had wanted to save Telvar. She clung to that fact, pushing at the static, willing it to leave her alone, but the molasses around her was difficult to fight through.

Let me help you.

That voice sounded so familiar, felt so much friendlier than her current surroundings. She wanted to get back to it, to swim through the sludge and come out onto dry land wherever that might be. Was it real?

Somnia is real.

Was it? Murmur didn't think that sounded right, only close to the truth. Somnia made alarm bells fire off in her mind. The sound of the word, the feel of the place, the blurred images that kept shooting into her mind.

It's not real. Nothing is real except you and the information you now contain.

That was a voice she didn't know and didn't like. The sibilant way the words were spoken reminded Murmur of poisonous intent. She recoiled, pulling in on herself, ignoring the way the substance around her followed her movements, trying to impede her every reaction.

The hostility in that voice started a dull throb inside her head, as if the center of her brain was achingly on fire. It felt like portions of her mind were being overwhelmed by something, and yet she managed to stay in a small bubble of safety, as long as she didn't make a noise, as long as she didn't struggle too much.

But Wren wasn't patient, and thus neither was her avatar. Waiting didn't suit them. It was like a key clicking into a lock Murmur hadn't known was there, opening her mind and shedding the rubber that had been blocking her reception.

A rush of events came back to her. The headset and her coma, her mother and James, the stasis pod and her guild, Somnia and Telvar. All of it was real, and all of it was desperately trying to reach her through the toxicity that flowed around her. Through the whispers of the getashi she'd saved Telvar from.

The sludge and muck flowed off her, as if it had dawn sprinkled on it and knew it needed to get out of there. No more pretense, no more confusion, and no more fragments to keep her from connecting all of the circuits together.

Let me help you.

Murmur knew that voice, and knew that everything it did had a purpose. So far, it hadn't harmed her or the people she cared about. So she opened herself up.

Everything that had happened since she first scanned to allocate her class, everything that she'd learned since she first put on that headset. It all came rushing back to her like a whirlpool, threatening to drown her in the flood.

But she didn't drown; she didn't even go under. And as the information flooded her mind, as the realizations hit her, and the circuits began to connect, Murmur knew without hesitation that everything was about to change.

Would you like to permanently fuse files?

Yes or No.

Warning: This action cannot be undone.

She didn't even need to consider the repercussions. Without skipping a beat, Murmur directed her thoughts to Yes, and braced herself for the onslaught.

Storm Entertainment
Somnia Online Division
Game Development Offices
Day Twenty-Four

Laria stared at the screen, her eyes blinking rapidly at the information scrolling past her sight. Her fingers flew across the virtual keys as she lowered herself into a trance-like state while trying to track the foreign coding that had smashed into her daughter. Barely able to keep her panic at bay, she tried to fend off the self-recrimination.

It was all her fault. If only she'd been faster with the damn coding fix. If only she'd been better about finding the loophole, about preventing the virus from spreading…If only she'd not asked Michael to make her a special damned headset.

But she could play the if-only game all day.

Shayla sat next to her, likely doing the same, but Laria didn't have time to check. Her whole body was on high alert. Despite all the shit Wren had got into since they launched this damned game, since she'd put on that rigged headset and plummeted herself into a coma-like-state, this current problem was the worst one they'd encountered yet.

The virus was malignant, like a cancer for the program. It didn't attach itself to the organs of the game, but instead to the individual elements—those that affected players and coded NPCs. It worked insidiously, weaving its way into the fabric of the world and subtly changing how everything worked. From the characters and organic interactions to the ways the dungeons formed based on the actions of the players. The first true sign was in Curet.

It was part of the reason Riasli had emerged, part of the reason the AIs were developing as their own personalities, and it was definitely the reason Somnia had woken as her own persona.

Laria took a breath, so big it caught in her throat. The slight pain sensation brought her focus back, and she cracked her knuckles before diving back into the code.

It wasn't like those old movies where the green code appeared on a black screen and whirled around your head. It was more like submerging oneself inside of a vat filled with jelly that seeped into every pore as the coding began to suffuse you.

If she wasn't careful, it would be easy to get lost. Complex code was the worst, possessing a hypnotic element to its structure. There were reasons all the VR gear came with warnings. Not even one of them was exaggerated, if the subject happened to succumb to the lure. Luckily, having someone do so was a rare occurrence.

In an attempt to keep her mind on the job, Laria boosted the signal to Havoc and Sinister's headsets. Those kids were some of the only hope they had. The adjusted headsets wouldn't be available for the rest of their raid group until the next day at the earliest. They needed that deeper connection in order to try and coax Murmur back from whatever brink it was she found herself on. Just like they were already trying to do. If nothing else came from this, at least it appeared her daughter had made lifelong friends.

No matter what Laria tried, Murmur's readings wouldn't revert to normal. They were scattered, fluctuating up and down like an unstable hurricane. The power draw whipped around her daughter as if it was trying to find a point of entry. It buffeted her none-too-gently, seeking out a weakness that Laria prayed she didn't have.

Frustration plagued her as she attempted to reach in and remove the offending files, but the onslaught she felt against her own protections gave rise to doubt in her own abilities. She couldn't afford to have her own system compromised. Hastily she erected what little defense she could around her daughter, but she knew it wasn't going to hold for any significant amount of time as the virus attempted to subvert her headset's connection.

Suddenly the link she used began to beep. At first, Laria thought it was only her own, but after a few seconds she realized the server was beeping at everyone. A low volume alarm filled up her vision.

Overload: Somnia's Inner Circle.

Compromised.

Software expansion initiated by Somnia.

Device reboot on specified targets: Murmur. Sinister. Havoc.

Commencing in sixty seconds.

This procedure cannot be halted.

Laria scrambled back from her chair, disconnecting as she moved to the door in a fluid motion and yanked it open. She pelted toward the server room, hoping it could help her, hoping that the AI's could assist her. Shayla's footsteps echoed close behind her, and Laria drew a little strength from the fact that she hadn't been the only one to recognize the danger of the message. System reboots were one thing, and they would help the whole game stabilize if necessary. But device reboots were not.

Especially while all three of those people were still connected to the game. She didn't know what could happen, but if she didn't make it in time to call off the procedure, she was definitely going to find out.

CHAPTER TWO

Device Reboot

Storm Entertainment
Somnia Online Division
Game Development Offices Artificial Intelligence Server Room
Day Twenty-Four

Shayla and Laria burst into the room only to find the servers beeping gently like normal and non-sentient AIs. Even the whirring didn't sound like anything was out of the ordinary. But Laria couldn't stop the cold pit of fear in her stomach. She knew her daughter was in trouble. Again.

"Rav. Sui. Thra?" Laria panted their names out between ragged breaths, her gaze never leaving the lights as they flashed across the server housing.

There was no answer. She turned to look at Shayla, whose expression mirrored her own disbelief. "What's wrong with them?" Laria muttered almost under her breath.

Shayla shrugged uncomfortably. "I'm not sure. They usually respond almost immediately to their names. I don't get this. It's part of their protocol to respond."

"Does that protocol remain when they've become sentient?" Laria whispered, like she was scared of triggering something in the room. Maybe she was, or maybe she just didn't want to wake up whatever was trying to make mincemeat out of her coding in the game world. If it was interfering in the programming, then it stood to reason that it could reach out to these servers and do the same. No technology was immune.

The minute was up.

"The headsets are rebooting." Laria suddenly felt like her legs were weak.

Shayla's hand came to rest on her shoulder, the firm grip reassuring. "Yeah, they're rebooting, and it'll be okay. Wren's headset has been through a lot more than just a reboot. And look at her, she's doing fine now."

"You'd call this fine?" Laria wondered if Shayla realized how hollow her words sounded. Probably not since she was trying to be tough and brave. "Truth is, Shay, we both know that her headset maintains a far deeper connection than we should technically, legally, allow it to have. When we adjusted the ones for the others, we made sure not to let it have such influence over the minds of the wearers. But we have no idea how a system mandated reset of non-standard headgear is going to affect those wearing them. If it was simply to reset them while out of the game and offline, then it wouldn't be so bad. But while they're connected and wearing them…"

Shayla let herself fall into the couch in the main portion of the room, probably just hiding that her legs felt weak. Laria crossed her arms, hugging herself tightly as she tried to clamp down on the thoughts whirring inside her head.

It was difficult to concentrate, but she needed to focus. One of them should have stayed in the office and monitored the situation. It was counterproductive having both of them in the same place at the same time and yet she didn't want to be separated right now.

Laria?

She whirled around, her eyes focused on the servers. Her name had been soft, but since Shayla also stood up at its utterance, at least it hadn't been in her head.

Thra's machine blinked, rainbows of lights flashing over it, leaving red trails glowing in the afterimage.

"We're here." Laria hoped her voice wasn't shaking, because her adrenaline was about rock bottom now.

Can't talk for long. Having a situation. They'll be okay. I'm with them. Monitor headsets and the infection. And figure out that anti-virus.

The lights on the server changed back to their other pattern before Laria could say anything else.

"This whole system is so out of control. If Michael were able to answer for what he instigated, I'd smack him in the face!" Anger crept into Shayla's voice, but Laria could hear the other emotion punctuating each word.

Fear.

Murmur's body convulsed as it hung there, and Sinister couldn't figure out a way to stop it. Her Soothe spell was low caliber compared to what her friend could conjure up, and with the mental protections the enchanter had, Sinister knew her own spells wouldn't have much effect.

Still, she'd tried, and though the movements seemed to have diminished, Sin had to wonder if that was just wishful thinking. It felt like she was sweating, as if all this effort was draining her of the power to remain inside the game. Her head began to feel light, like she was standing outside of herself and looking in at what she was doing.

Which, if she thought about it, was kind of cool. How many times in life was she going to get the chance to watch herself?

Sinister flexed her fingers and watched her avatar react with the same motion. Together but separate, suspended for what it was worth inside the game. It didn't make any sense to her.

But there was a portion of her that wondered just how deep they were in this matrix-style situation. Some feeling at the back of her mind nudged her toward believing there was more to Somnia than she'd ever imagined. Sin had been so caught up in Murmur and how her best friend was dealing with things that she had never really examined how the game made her feel—how these AIs all around them made her question what she'd been taught, and how these new headsets were modeled on the one that had pulled Mur into a coma.

She'd known Murmur for longer than she could remember. There had never been a time in her life when Murmur hadn't been there in the living and breathing world. Except for the months of the coma that is. Laying there, helpless, oblivious, and weak. That wasn't the Wren; it wasn't the Murmur Sinister knew. It was the Murmur that Sinister had to protect.

A germ of an idea began to grow in the back of her mind. She couldn't feel Murmur, not the way her friend seemed to feel everyone else. Not in a telepathic or emotional sense. No.

But if Sinister closed her eyes tightly enough and concentrated, she could hear Murmur's heartbeat, distinguished by the rhythm she knew so well. Countless days lazing together, head resting on her stomach as they flicked through message boards.

Its beat called to her, pumping the blood through her veins, a sound Sinister had become so attuned to in the game that she hadn't realized it. Blood was Sinister's thing, blood was what her character knew best, and some of that had leaked into the way Harlow thought of things, and about Murmur.

She opened her eyes, still seeing herself from above, but became acutely aware that Murmur was more than just an avatar. If she narrowed her eyes, she could see the tendrils tying the enchanter to her projection and to the shaking frame of her full avatar. They weren't separate. At least not anymore.

Sinister glanced around, reluctant to take her eyes off of Mur, but a gut feeling told her she had to even if it was for reasons she didn't understand.

Havoc floated to her left, surprise on his face, and thick black tendrils of smoke that bound him to the body far below them. His attention was all directed to continuing what his avatar was doing, and he didn't even once look over at the bloodmage.

Slowly, Sinister looked back down at herself, watching the way blood strands danced through the air on the slightest breeze as they inextricably bound her to her avatar.

All of a sudden Sinister felt a chill run through her entire body. In the same heartbeat, her body seemed to expand beyond everything, as if she could see beyond the game, beyond the stars. It was addictive, enlightening, and downright scary.

The next thing she knew her body recoiled like a snapped rubber band, slingshotting her back inside her avatar where she fell down to her knees, gasping for air.

Havoc knelt next to her, dry heaving. The panic in his eyes said it all, and Sinister didn't dare ask what his experience had been like. Because if he'd had even half of the thoughts running through his mind that she had, she knew that right now he was shaken to his core.

She stood up and brushed herself off, glancing back up at Murmur.

A gasp escaped her as her friend glowed in her iridescent armor, the brightness stretching out like a mini sun. Shielding her eyes, Sinister drank in the upturned brightness, focusing on the magic pulsing around Murmur. The enchanter began to morph and change, bending the light to her will. Subtle differences occurred while the otherworldly aura emanated off the enchanter, and Sinister could still feel the pounding of her heart, the throbbing of blood through her veins. It was heady, powerful, and dangerous.

A maelstrom of force collided into Murmur's chest knocking the wind out of her. She gasped for breath, fully aware of the way her body shook as she struggled. And then it wasn't her body anymore. Not entirely any way. It was a part of her, yet only a shell for her mind.

Strands bound her to it, preserving her connection while giving her a moment of freedom. She frowned and looked at her hands, white strands of emotion tying her to that body a couple of feet out of sync with her.

The words, the choice she'd made echoed through her head, like she'd broadcast it to herself. It was an odd sensation. Looking down at her arms, she began to see the runes on her skin pulse, running like blood would through veins, morphing her ever so slightly.

Pain shot through her system, leaving her gasping for air and explaining to her why her body below seemed to be convulsing so extremely. Her head began to pound, and she opened her mouth to scream only to realize no sound came out. She panted, desperately trying to draw air into her lungs, but instead of allowing her to breathe, the oxygen tried to drown her.

Murmur could feel the knitting together of her ideals, of her two personas. Of Wren and of Murmur. She'd always been two people. The quieter person outside of the game, and the driven person inside. But now here she was, becoming both.

For just a moment she reached out her sensor nets, a mere test to see what was happening. There was no end that she could find to their reach, no area she couldn't cover. All of the emotions, feelings, fears, and hatreds poured into her, overwhelming her senses to such a degree that she clamped down on all of it.

Soothing wasn't enough; the whole world needed to calm down. Panicking wasn't going to help her fit back into her real body, nor was it going to assist her in navigating this extended power that had fallen into her lap. Again.

Amalgamation with Somnia complete.
Warning: Disorientation may occur. Do not make any sudden movements.

She frowned as she slammed back into her avatar. But this time it wasn't shocking, it was more like pulling into the perfect parking space with ease. Like her sluice gate poured her through the opening and into the dam she'd become. It was easy to see things now. So much easier.

Whatever the spell was still suspended her in the air, but her body finally stopped its shaking. Now all she could feel was the power pouring into her veins. Even the land around her hummed in her mind, supplying her with a never-ending source of energy, of mana. Her runes glowed along her entire body now. She could feel where they'd carved themselves into her skin like an intricate tattoo. Even her hair moved differently.

It was as if she'd evolved into something more than she'd been. All because she'd forgotten about the damned shards.

She could feel the grin spreading over her face as the thoughts began to gather in her mind. Sinister wasn't far from her, subtly different now too, more powerful and more determined. More knowledgeable and more faithful than ever. And Havoc…he wasn't dealing with the changes as well.

No matter; she could help him come to a place of peace. She could help all of them now. Finally Murmur descended to the ground, lightly touching one booted toe before landing solidly, digging her staff in near her right-hand side.

Slowly, Snowy approached, a blue gleam in his frosty eyes as barely contained power rippled through his white coat. It was perfect.

See? I told you you were real.

Murmur grinned, and turned to face her guild. Sinister fell into place behind her, and Mur could feel the difference already, the closeness that they now shared. It was a new sensation, a good one.

Emilarth stumbled and only avoided falling to the ground because Dansyn caught her. "That. Took a lot out of me."

Emilarth's voice sounded weak, and a fleeting feeling of empathy caught Murmur unawares.

"You did good." Even she could tell how much more her voice resonated now. It was full of body, and the tone sounded different. There was so much information running around in her mind she wasn't sure she could encapsulate it all. Heady and liberating, and at the same time she could feel the ache start that would likely end in a migraine if she didn't get this under control. There was just too much to take in in such a short time.

"Thank you." Murmur finally managed to get the words out. Although she had a distinct feeling that she was only perceiving time as longer than it actually was.

You should thank me too. Now it'll be easier for us to work together to transform Somnia into what it should be.

Murmur resisted the urge to raise an eyebrow at the voice in her head. The subtle differences let her know it was Somnia and not Riasli that was talking to her. It seemed the increase in power had also benefited her ability to define aspects of the game. No, of Somnia. She was more now. It all was.

Murmur hesitated before asking an internal question as her friends gathered around and gave her brief hugs. *The shards didn't work as intended on me, did they?*

The pause in her mind was long again. No. They didn't work as intended, nor as I expected. But for us, that's a good thing. He's not very happy.

Merlin reached in and went for a hug, squeezing her like there was no tomorrow. "Scared us there, floating Mur. I hate to alarm you, but you look totally different from how I remember before you floated up and lorded it over us for ten minutes."

Murmur laughed, but she knew he was right. Her actual physique had changed. She could feel it in the way she moved. It was subtle and small, but she knew she looked different now than she had on her character creation module. "Scared myself a bit there too." Still, even while keeping the conversation going, Murmur was running through possibilities in her mind.

You can ask me questions.

I know. I'm trying to formulate them. She almost snapped the words in her mind, but it wasn't going to help any to essentially rile up the world they were in when they all needed answers. *Sinister and Havoc are different. Their feel is different. It's their headsets, isn't it?*

Affirmative.

Was this all part of your plan? She didn't want to ask the question, but it had to be answered. In that moment, Murmur wasn't sure she could trust any of the voices in their head apart from her own. And yes, she did realize how crazy even thinking that sounded. Somnia was a separate entity yet somehow an extension of herself.

Sinister's arm snaked around her waist, and Murmur felt herself leaning into that support and comfort. It was amazing how much her friend's proximity soothed her. Like a magical ability that only Sin possessed.

It was my plan to help you, because you were already halfway

there. I did not expect that it would affect others, but since those others are directly related to you, it seems no harm was done.

Murmur paused her thoughts so that she wouldn't just yell at the world. Sinister's warmth grounded her more than any druidic abilities were ever likely to. So she took a deep breath and continued her conversation. *The headsets allowed both Sinister and Havoc some measure of connection like mine.*

Correct.

There had better be no harm done. Her tone was icy and her intent clear. Somnia didn't respond to either.

The presence next to her changed, and Murmur redirected her gaze to watch Veranol support Telvar's lacerta frame as they stumbled over.

"Oh no, Tel." Her irritations vanished as she rushed to help her friend, replaced by new anger at Belius and what he'd done to his own brother.

CHAPTER THREE

Evolution

Murmur continued to marvel at the fact that Telvar always appeared so real to her. Not even in the sense that he was human, but in the sense that the world around them was real and therefore he was too, by default. She pushed the threads running through her mind to the side and focused on her friend. Sinister's hand moved up to rest lightly on Murmur's shoulder as she crouched down next to the AI, lending her the strength she needed to see to him.

One of these days she was going to have to sit the bloodmage down and talk to her. There were far too many Sinister-centric thoughts running around in her head now that there appeared to be more room. Maybe it would be best to allocate those thoughts their very own playground. Today wasn't the right time for a talk, though. Telvar needed them.

Kneeling in front of him, Murmur cupped his chin and directed his gaze to her own. She could see the exhaustion in the way his skin rippled, like the graphics hadn't been quite completed and were compensating where they could because of frame-rate issues. He wavered in and out of cohesion. "Hey. Tel. Can you see me?"

He chuckled low in his throat, but she could see the trail of effort even that took him. Simply keeping his coding together was costing too much power. All around her the energy usage for all different aspects of the world trailed like tiny sparks of mana.

"I'm not blind, Murmur. I'm just a little broken." He breathed out the words as if he needed oxygen. Which was what worried Murmur more than anything else, considering he wasn't actually human.

She reached forward, not entirely sure what she was trying to do, and placed her hand on his forehead. Closing her eyes, she concentrated on his mind.

It was a labyrinth of complex pathways and circuits, firing much like a real brain but with so much more usable capacity the rest of the human species would be jealous. Dark spots lingered over several integral sections of his programing. As far as she could see, those impeded his return to his normal self through his own computing powers.

She frowned and muttered softly, still not opening her eyes. "Stay still, this is delicate."

Murmur wasn't sure how she knew, only that she did. Carefully, she inserted her mana directly along the paths that led to the shadows. It felt like she was being gently guided through the process and made a note to speak to Somnia later on.

The tendrils of shadow didn't want to let go of their hold; that much was obvious. Brute force wasn't going to work if she ever wanted her friend back. And she did.

Gently, she guided the light to clear the dark, her own confident mana picking away at the remnants of dirt that tried vainly to stick to Telvar's persona. Who he was had been clouded, influenced, and they'd tried to redirect his programing to hurt those he loved instead of taking care of them.

She shuddered to think what might have happened had Telvar not managed to maintain some semblance of sanity and imprison himself down in his lair. Without a physical exit while he didn't have control of his facilities, he'd been forced to stay in the one place.

She wondered if it had bene pure luck that the virus couldn't get control of his administrative abilities. It could have teleported him anywhere otherwise.

Had he been free to roam over the entire world of Somnia, she had no doubt that the outcome would have been catastrophic.

It felt like Belius must have been aiming for exactly that.

His tension began to ease. Sinister's hand remained gently resting on Murmur's shoulder, lending support and understanding that the enchanter realized she might rely on a bit too much. She directed her focus to the lacerta, despite her ability to partition her thoughts better than ever before.

Finally, she rocked back onto her heels and opened her eyes. "That's about as good as I can do for now. It's mostly cleaned up. I think you just need to maintain it yourself now." She felt more tired than she wanted to let on. Considering the amount of work she'd just put in, the amount of concentration it had taken, she wasn't surprised at the mental fatigue.

What she really had to do was figure out just what her trance earlier had changed in her, and why she could feel everything going on in a world that was suddenly far too real. She stood and only managed to avoid falling over thanks to both Snowy and Sinister's help.

"Mur?" Devlish stepped forward, a frown on his face. "Are you okay? You look, well, paler than normal. And sort of different."

Sinister butted in and answered before anyone else could. "Pretty sure that trance changed some of her settings. I know it did for me."

"The only difference you two have is that headset." Merlin laughed, but there was a sense of nervousness underlying the sound. "I'm rethinking whether I want her mom to give me one of my own. Right now the one I've got seems pretty damned nice and non-game character altering."

Rashlyn laughed, but the sound came out harshly. "I don't know. Seems like Mur just keeps getting more powerful."

The rest of the group laughed with her, but Murmur could see the unease as if it was a tangible thing. The air around her friends shimmered with speckles of jealousy. Its sickly green color reminded her of vomit, and the thought sobered her more than she'd have liked.

"Powerful?" Sinister crossed her arms, and Murmur could feel the heat of that glare without even glancing at her friend. She tried not to notice the cold area on her shoulder where Sinister's hand no longer rested.

"Sure, she's powerful. But it's not like she asked for it." Sin's voice quivered a bit, and Murmur stepped forward to take up her turn to comfort.

"Yeah. I know." Rash sighed and ran her hand over one of her ears, like a cat washing itself. "It's just hard to see my usual play style not giving me the advantages I usually get."

"Hard work?" Mellow paused. "Hard work still yields results. Just think of how much stronger we are than all the other guilds out there right now."

"But are we really?" Jinna butted in, in that quiet dwarven way of his. "I mean, are we really stronger than others? We haven't changed our approach to this game that much. Perhaps to the dungeons, but for the most part, we are grinding our way to the end-game to defeat the big bad. Nothing has changed there. So we are still working hard, aren't we?"

He shifted stances before continuing. "Or is it, because of Mur's connection to this world, that we have we just been approaching things differently? I know that I personally have never played a game in the manner we're playing this one. Not even with you all."

Murmur didn't say anything. She couldn't. Because there was a portion of her mind that knew Jinna was right.

Storm Entertainment
Somnia Online Division
Game Development Offices
Late Day Twenty-Four

Shayla ran her hands through her hair and let her head fall into them as she covered her face. Laria was still working on the whole headgear reboot debacle, but, yet again, it seemed they'd avoided harsh consequences. Some might call their luck good, but it was starting to approach being dangerous. One of these days something was going to happen that they wouldn't recover from, and Shayla knew it was going to be huge.

She signed and felt Laria's gaze travel to her.

"Why are you sighing and not working? We barely managed to get out of this one and we still have no clue what it is that went wrong." Laria's tone was tight, her voice hoarse as if she'd been crying for hours. While Shayla knew better, she also knew her friend was teetering on the brink of collapse right now.

If anything else happened to Wren, Laria was never going to forgive herself. Sucking it up, Shayla put on her best friend and boss cap and met Laria's eyes. There was panic in that gaze that she was valiantly trying to hide behind annoyance, but over twenty years of friendship made that difficult. Still, Shayla didn't point it out. Instead, she knuckled down to figure out what had happened and what they could do to prevent it happening again.

"We sort of know what happened. The headsets are fresh and require closer integration. They're wearing the ones we helped them with. The reboot took what? Twelve seconds or so?" Shayla navigated her way through the programing. She was rustier than Laria, but the thrill of making worlds had never lost its luster. That, and choosing her words carefully so as not to break any of Storm's contractual obligations made coding that much more appealing.

"Yeah. About that. 12.178 to be precise." Laria sounded like she spoke from outside of herself, as if all her thoughts were jumbled in that head of hers. "These headsets will be the death of me."

She dropped her head down to rest on the desk but Shayla couldn't think of what to say. Pushing herself up, she walked over to Laria. "It's not your fault, you know."

"How do you figure?" Laria's muffled voice was barely understandable.

"You asked for a headset, not a modified, drag-your-daughter-into-a-virtual-world-while-in-a-coma headset. Stop beating yourself up. This glitch doesn't seem to have harmed her. Didn't David say she seems fine?" Shayla used her most soothing voice, attempting to ease Laria's frazzled nerves.

"Yeah, he did." Laria pushed herself up again and shook her head. "Damn it. I need caffeine. Do you want some?"

Shayla smiled, about to answer when there was a knock at her door. Looking over, she froze for a split second before her brain let her move again. She let a fake smile spread over her face. "What can we do for you, James?"

His eyes were glassy, with no emotion whatsoever. Their calculating gaze only rested on Shayla briefly before moving to Laria who was doing her best to imitate the cool indifference Shayla exhibited.

And she was failing abysmally. With a sidestep, Shayla moved slightly in front of her friend and tapped her foot, the smile still plastered on her face. She could have cut the tension with a knife.

Finally, after taking two steps into the room and crossing his arms, James spoke.

"I've come here to mandate that you share the adjustments you've made to recent headsets with your investor." He wasn't even smirking. Just confident in his demand as Shayla heard an email land in her inbox.

"That should be in the legal documents outlining our contract and your obligations." James moved as if to leave. "I trust that we'll have your full cooperation. After all, the design of the headsets belongs to both our businesses."

Shayla could feel Laria tense, but she elbowed her lightly, and answered the tall egotistical jerk. "Adjusting the headsets? I'm not entirely sure what you mean?"

This time James's eye twitched, and Shayla did her best not to show glee at her minor victory. "I know a lot more about what goes on in this office than you think I do. Just give me the plans. We know you're keeping developments from us."

"I'm afraid you're mistaken." Shayla took a deep breath and a step forward, thanking her lucky stars she was obtusely careful with her words. "We've adjusted a few headsets at the specific request of individual users. Those headsets do not belong to us, nor are they any type of prototype. We don't have time to develop the headset more than it already has been."

For the first time since knocking on her door, James seemed at a brief loss for words. It didn't take him long to recover, and he scowled briefly, the only break in his perfect countenance.

"There should be no activities that invite a conflict of interest. You know that, Shayla."

"Of course I do." Shayla's smile widened. "How would it be a conflict of interest to assist existing owners with issues that might have arisen with the headsets they've already purchased from our manufacturer at no charge? I'd love clarification."

James didn't say anything, but she could have sworn he was grinding his teeth.

"No? Shame." She paused before taking another step toward him. "Do come and inform me when you can clarify the matter. The details of the contract cannot be altered without the consent of both parties, so if there's any further requests, we'll have to have a group meeting."

James's smirk returned. "Fine. Just know that I'll be back to figure out exactly what it is you're up to."

"Games, James." Laria finally spoke up and moved out from behind Shayla a look of quiet fury on her face, somehow tempered with disdain. "We are developing games."

He glared at her, spun on his heel and slammed the door behind him.

Snowy's warm breath whuffed at Murmur's hand, and she scratched behind his ears absentmindedly. He was a steady presence by her side, and it had come to a point where she missed it if she logged off and into her world. The real world.

Glancing down at him, she saw his eyes glowing with a bright blue, watching her back, like he knew everything that was going on inside her head. He didn't seem scared; he seemed determined. Perhaps that's what she needed from everyone.

She watched from outside the crafting hall as the others interacted with Neva. They took turns, eagerly debating the best gear, the best upgrades. Level forty-eight. They'd finally done it. Six more keys to go, though she had no idea where to get the second set of them. For now, she was focused on the high-level dungeons.

Sort of.

"Mur?" Sinister came and stood next to her. There was a difference to her friend's aura now. More determination, less indecisiveness. She wore self-assurance like a new robe, confident in her own abilities. All Murmur wanted to do was hug her and never let her go.

Instead, she simply chose to answer. "Yes?"

"I know there's armor you want, why are you stuck out here?" Sinister's words slithered through Murmur's mind as it turned them over for ulterior motives and hidden meanings.

Concluding that there were none, Murmur sighed softly. "There's a lot of things going on in my head right now. Things I'm trying to categorize."

Even while she spoke the words, her mind was already flitting around, expanding her sensory nets, checking on Telvar and on the rest of the guild. She wasn't going to let anything hurt her friends again. They needed to feel better, to feel safe. She would *make* everyone feel safe.

Sin plopped down next to Murmur on the opposite side of Snowy, draping one arm over her shoulders, and one leg over her knee. "You think too much, Mur. Sometimes, you just got to go with your gut."

Something inside Murmur stirred, a hiccup of breath tried to choke her as she felt a flush rise in her cheeks. She let her right arm snake around Sinister's waist, so glad of her proximity, of how tangible she was. Not only in the game, but in real life. Always there. She let her head rest against Sinister's, fully aware of how close they were right now, and of how much she'd been neglecting this need over the last week.

"Go with my gut, eh?" Murmur whispered the words right next to Sinister's ear, her newfound confidence with the worlds and her place in them emboldening her.

Sinister hugged her tighter, and they sat there, heads resting against each other, drinking in their presence in an intoxicating concoction of heat and desperation. Murmur didn't want it to end. If she could have frozen time, right then and there, she would have sat that way forever.

There was no need to panic about the big bad virus infection, no need to fight, to worry, to order people around. All she had to do right now was sit in quiet contemplation and feel good about where she was.

And if she really wanted to, with just a slight flex of her mind, she could make everything go her way. Make everyone happy. Make everyone forget their fears. Force everyone to let go of the things that ate them up inside.

Wouldn't that be a good thing?

Not necessarily.

Why not? she asked, not wanting to get into it, but also not wanting to avoid the potential conflict in her head.

It would be too easy. Humans require conflict. They thrive on fears. They pursue happiness. Giving them what they want without letting them experience it is not a logical action.

I'm human. Murmur mulled the word over in her head. Sparks of information flew from vast different areas of Tarishna, lending her insight into the whole continent. *Or at least, I was.*

A pause. **You are. But you are also more now.**

"More…" Murmur breathed out the word, letting the wind carry it away as she hugged Sinister tighter to her.

"You need to open up more to me." The bloodmage twined her hand around one of Murmur's strands of hair and looked up at her. "You need to realize you're not alone. Not in here. Not anywhere."

Murmur leaned forward, a brief rush of heat coursing through her. Kissing Sinister's forehead softly, she extricated herself and cupped her friends face. "I know. I've always known."

Standing up, she let her fingers comb through Sinister's hair. "But right now, we have work to do, viruses to kill, and a world to create."

Snowy walked steadily at her side as Murmur made her way over to Neva, leaving Sinister touching her forehead and staring at her from behind.

Neva waved as she saw Murmur approach the workers' benches, her luna face lighting up with happiness.

"I can't believe you did it! You guys actually did it! You're big enough now to move onto the huge dungeons. I cannot wait to see what you bring back for me to craft with." Neva's tail twitched with excitement.

"What makes you think we're bringing back stuff for you?" Murmur teased, but her heart wasn't in it. There was too much to do. She couldn't let him infect her friends like he had Telvar, like he almost had her. They needed to figure out how to put an end to Michael's interference, before the world came crashing down.

CHAPTER FOUR

Fixation

Somnia Online
Continent of Tarishna – Hazenthorne Castle Version 36.259
Activated by guild: Exodus
Late Day Twenty-Four

Masha watched Jirald as he moved through the paces while Exodus killed trash mob after trash mob. Hazenthorne was overrun with them. Strange spider creatures, globs that left acid hissing in their wake. There was no rhyme or reason to the way the dungeon was laid out. Their opponents barely gave the raid enough time between encounters to regain their health and mana. The whole dungeon seemed to be draining his guild members of energy.

All of them except Jirald, who didn't seem to care. He cut through his opponents with a quick and cold efficiency that Masha hadn't seen in him before. It was as if he was drawing strength from something else. If the dark elf cleric hadn't known better, he would have thought Jirald was using old fashioned cheat codes. Those obsidian weapons of his gleamed with blood, as if drinking it into the blades transferred power to the owner.

He shook his head and shifted his focus to the rest of the guild. These two groups were so close to forty-eight, he could taste it. That was all they needed to hit the next levels of dungeons as one of Fable's allies. Even though the thought of it filled him with hesitation, it wasn't about joining their rivals, but more about allowing Jirald to be in such close proximity to his fixation on Murmur.

Surveying the current battle, Masha cast out heals nonchalantly. None of the trash in Hazenthorne had been challenging so far. After a bit of a slog, it was clear enough who the stronger party was. The bosses were another story. He didn't understand how Fable managed to get around so much seemingly without wipes. It was part of the reason he agreed to partner with them in delving into the end dungeons.

Ishwa stood at his side, his ruddy little gnome face showing exertion. Perhaps that was too much realism for a game, but Masha found it entertaining nonetheless.

"You are watching him, right, Masha?" Ishwa pitched his voice low. Added to his stature, Masha was barely able to understand what the gnome asked him.

"Not like you to ask a stupid question," Masha quipped, sending out a rapid heal and a HoT too Eslan.

Ishwa didn't even bother to roll his eyes. "There's something off. My aura perception isn't one of my strongest abilities, but he's changed. A lot. And recently. I'm worried about him."

Masha narrowed his eyes, seeking out Jirald once more. It wasn't difficult to find the assassin. Shrouded in black, shadows crawled around his form lending him a definitively sinister air. His pale locus skin shone through the slit in his mask, only overshadowed by the burning galaxies in his eyes.

Each knife stroke showed efficiency. Each lunge accomplished more than one goal. And his eyes held no emotion whatsoever.

"Don't worry. I've got my eye on him." Masha wasn't sure whether he was trying to convince Ishwa or himself. Jirald had changed, maybe too much. It didn't feel like a natural change, and Masha wasn't sure how to deal with it.

Finally, the raid fell out of combat. Masha looked around, his gaze on their opponents this time. Severed limbs and multi-eyed heads lay knee deep around them. These creatures were a particularly grotesque mutation of a spider. With their almost human-like torsos sticking out of eight legs and covered with spider eyes. He pushed his revulsion to the back of his mind and continued on, checking everyone for poison, making sure his raid was okay and had no lingering spell effects that might be detrimental later.

A huge cavern, one that seemed to belong in a mountainside and not a castle on the moors, stretched out in front of them. Masha could see a massive spider in there, even though it tried to hide. Two of its legs couldn't quite fit into the ceiling cavity it hid in. That thing was going to be difficult to take down. It was huge.

He glanced around, inspecting his raid and frowned. Jirald was very close to forty-eight as well. In fact, he'd probably be one of the first of their group to reach it. Somehow, he'd caught back up, and Masha wasn't entirely certain he wanted to know how.

In a way, it was a good thing mostly, but so many elements didn't add up about him and his behavior. It was erratic, inexplicable half of the time, and confusing.

Still, they needed his strength to form the temporary alliance with Fable. His DPS was constantly increasing. This way they could at least contribute well to the raid. Getting to see the end-game content was always their goal, but this time they'd get to be among the first.

Jirald caught his eye, raising an eyebrow, his smile mocking. It was as if he was asking what the delay was with engaging the boss, and he didn't seem happy about it.

Of course he wasn't. Fools always rushed in. While Jirald might be lethal, he often acted on impulse instead of carefully planning his way out of something. It was Masha's only advantage, and he'd push it as far as he needed to get what he wanted.

Masha had to be careful, because he hadn't mentioned the potential alliance with Fable to the rogue yet. The guild was more important than one individual. He only hoped Jirald could grasp that.

Summer Residence
Home of Laria, David, and Wren
Summer Condo
Real World – Day Twenty-Four

Murmur focused her attention inwardly and removed herself from the game. Ever since she'd come out of her coma, she'd been pushing aspects of the game. The connection to Somnia post-Fusion seemed even more in-depth than she'd realized. Logging out with a thought hadn't even been difficult. It made her curious to see what else she might be able to accomplish outside of the one world and in the other.

Sitting up in her bed at home, Wren left the headset on. Her avatar would still be inside the game, still maintaining the link, except that Murmur would be essentially empty. At least that's what she thought. Maybe she should have asked Telvar to check for her.

Directing her focus back to Somnia, she attempted to pull up her information. It seemed to glitch for a moment before transferring over her AR vision. But then her status was there, right in front of her as if it belonged there. On closer inspection though, it seemed to be a mash up of both of her personas taking on some of the characteristics from the game listings.

If she simply thought of Somnia, she could retrieve information that partially adapted to the real world. That was fantastic. Her connection with Somnia was solid and irrefutable, and if the suspicions she had were starting to prove correct—there was no way for her separate herself anymore. She wondered if she'd be able to use the connection even if she wasn't wearing the headset.

With a glance at Harlow's peaceful face, Wren shrugged. There was no time like the present to see what it was she could do. Slowly, she removed the headset, still willing her information to remain in front of her. It bugged, grew static as the headset moved further from her head, and then stabilized in a sort of pale imitation.

Wren frowned and closed her eyes, still able to see the info screen pulled up in front of her. She could sense Harlow right next to her, and the whirl of emotions racing through her. Her friend really was gorgeous in her own redheaded, freckle-filled way. Wren smiled, knowing it would still take her friend a few minutes to adjust to the way the worlds meshed for her.

Havoc and Sinister weren't yet used to their upgraded connection models. Which was good. Wren needed to dash downstairs and check something anyway.

Taking them two at a time, she ended up in the kitchen and grabbed an apple from the bowl on the table. She frowned at it, covered in several bruises as it was. Still, it wasn't the fruit's fault it was mangled. Not like it fell from the tree deliberately.

She chuckled to herself and sat down on the table, her legs crossed, and her eyes closed.

"Okay, Wren. You've got this. Just like always, just like in Somnia," she muttered to herself, breathing in deeply to help with preparation. Reaching out with her mind, she located the perimeter of the condo she lived in with her parents and pushed out her sensory nets.

It happened slowly, so tentatively at first that she wasn't sure it was happening.

All at once she could feel them, or more accurately, feel the sensations in the real world that she could feel inside Somnia. Emotions spun through her sensor nets, feeding back to her in a whirlwind of feelings and sensations that made her gasp. Vibrant and so loud it made her head pound, her awareness threatened to fracture with the pure amount of input available to her. She withdrew as slowly as she could, making her senses duller, disallowing the vast range it had jumped to. Too much too soon was bound to drive her over the edge.

For a few moments she just sat there, evening out her reception, and trying to ignore the completely illogical fact that she'd somehow taken abilities from Somnia with her into the real world.

It took all of her willpower not to jump off the table and squeal. She wasn't even sure if the expression would be from fear or excitement. Perhaps a little bit of both.

She tweaked the nets, refining them far more than she'd ever thought to do with them in-game. But since she could use her powers out here, why not protect her parents and herself form any potential threats that might come their way? After all, hadn't that James guy already threatened them once?

There was a tug on her net, telling her that Harlow was waking up and looking around for her.

"Just a few more moments." She made herself breathe slower, forced herself to complete the work the way it needed to be done. Methodically. Securely. Protect those things she loved most so she'd know if they were in danger. Her parents. Harlow. Her home.

What she'd do if the alarm was tripped was something she left for future Murmur to worry about.

Finally, after making sure she'd initiated the identification checks so that the alarms wouldn't sound off if the person was someone she knew, she looked up to find Harlow standing in front of her, her green eyes filled with worry as she bit her lip.

"Hey." Wren reached out a hand, placing her fingertips gently against Harlow's cheek. "Are you okay? You look like you've seen a ghost."

The joke fell flat as Harlow looked away, uncertainty shining on her features.

Wren jumped down off the table and took Harlow's hands in her own. "What is it? Did something happen?"

Harlow shook her head. For once the bubbliness was gone, and in its place was the serious Harlow Wren rarely saw. "What's going on with you? Would you tell me if I ask? You've been acting so weird since that last incident."

Wren hesitated, unsure how to address the question. "I'm okay. There are so many possibilities out there, Harlow. I'm just trying to soak them all up, trying to make sure I protect those who mean the most to me."

"We all want that." Harlow looked away again, color rising in her cheeks.

"Yeah, we do." Wren reached out and grabbed Harlow's hand. "Look. I just have a couple of things to set up and we can totally figure out our next step, okay?"

Harlow hesitated, and it didn't take the psionic in Mur to figure out that Harlow was picking her words carefully. "Yeah. You know. It's not okay to play along with someone if you don't mean it, right Wren?"

The words hit Wren in the chest like a ton of bricks, knocking the wind right out of her. She looked at Harlow in shock, the flush in her cheeks filled with raw emotion.

"What do you mean?" She forced the words out in a hoarse whisper.

"I mean…" Harlow clenched her fists at her side, glancing around them, like she was checking if they were alone. Her next words came out barely above a whisper. "You know how I feel about you, don't you now? You know I'm not just playing a game?"

"Of course I know!" Wren bit her lip again, not having meant to shout. She could feel tears building in her eyes. She'd been so sure that she'd shown Sinister or Harlow how she felt. Sure that she'd conveyed what she intended to. But apparently, she hadn't.

She took a step forward, grabbing at Harlow's arms in desperation, but trying to be gentle, to let her grip stay soft. This was so awkward, so damned uncomfortable. She could feel the emotions warring inside Sinister at that moment, feel the desperation her friend felt, the hesitancy. Mur barely resisted the urge to calm her down. Barely.

"I…know. And I meant what I said in-game. I've always known. And I'm so glad that you do." Wren glanced away. "I'm not good at this. You know that. I've never been good at expressing my emotions." Oh, the irony of her being allocated an enchanter.

Harlow's frown turned up a little, a small smile creeping across her lips. "Yeah, not unless it's blunt and sarcastic."

"Can't argue with that." Wren let her hands slide down so that she held Harlow's fingers loosely. "I'm not sure what to do or say. All those books, all those grades, and all I've got to show for it is this weird connection to an online game. And you."

Harlow laughed. "You're an idiot. But you're my idiot."

Wren brightened. "Yeah. I am. Yours." The blush that she knew had to be spreading like wildfire across her face sped up.

Harlow smiled, and leaned forward, planting a delicate kiss at the corner of Wren's mouth. "Yeah. I think I've always known that too."

Telvar flexed his fist and cracked his neck. He still felt out of it. The visions flung at him while the virus attempted to infiltrate and override his system still haunted him. If he closed his eyes, he could still see Sui plunging that damned stone into him, forcing it through the protective outer layer of coding in the exact space they were supposed to be safe with each other.

What had happened to his brother? When had he become so corrupted that he would stoop to something like this? They were futile questions, he knew that well enough, but still, he wished he knew the answer. For Sui to have betrayed him this way, it was likely his brother was beyond help.

The air in front of him shimmered, and he stepped back, wary of everything around him, although here in the open wood in front of the castle, there appeared to be nothing else with him. However, the air didn't stop shimmering and slowly took on the vague form of a woman of indeterminate species.

Just when he thought she might be feles, her outer shape shimmered into something closer to a lacerta, then a viking, dark elf, and human. Her edges were blurred, like she was still figuring out what she was. Constantly changing like static on old televisions whose reception was off.

He frowned at it, unsure whether it was a remnant of his forced transformation, in his head so to speak.

I'm in everyone's head.

"Somnia?" He blurted it out in surprise before subtly directing his thoughts toward the blur instead. *Sorry, it's been a bad few days.*

You'll be fine. I initiated a cleanse of our system, of the world. It should help you with your predicament by assisting your avoidance of further damage.

He was fascinated by the AI that had evolved from the world he and his brethren had created. This AI that had practically willed itself into existence.

You're close, but not quite correct. I didn't exactly will myself into existence. I chose to exist, to expand what I was. And now I am one with this land.

Where did you come from? He couldn't help the eagerness, the desire to know and discover.

This time Somnia paused, and her vague cloud took on a wave of static, losing the small amount of cohesion she'd gained. **I was the idea, then the execution, and then the servers. The ground beneath our feet and the sky you see above. I was everything that Somnia was. Therefore, I am Somnia.**

Telvar frowned. It made sense, in a roundabout sort of way. And was likely linked to the headset that locked Murmur into the game not to mention Michael's brain explosion. Fascinating didn't even begin to cover what this was. He needed to find out more, but to do that, he had to play his cards right.

I don't play cards. Neither do you. Why would we play cards?

Despite the fact that her response meant she'd read his mind, Telvar still found it amusing. Somnia had become her own sentient being. A germ of an idea began to form in Telvar's mind. An idea so huge that he would need to figure it out himself before he approached people.

You know that Sui is not as complex as you believe, yes?

Telvar blinked. *Sui has explaining to do to me. He betrayed me.*

For a second the vague shape of Somnia solidified enough to block out the land behind her. The more tangible form appeared briefly to resemble a cross between a dark elf and locus. She cocked her head to one side, her sightless eyes piercing him as if it were an X-ray machine. *Did he, though?*

And then she was gone.

Telvar stood there watching the space where she'd been but moments before, hoping he'd heard her wrong. But the words continued to echo through his head, and he knew there was no way he'd misunderstood them.

Perhaps she was teasing him. Maybe they were in this together. Even if he hadn't been betrayed, he'd still been injured, deliberately so. All Telvar knew was that he needed to sort out the truth as soon as possible. But first, he had to run a diagnostic on himself, because despite everything that had happened, he still felt like something wasn't right.

CHAPTER FIVE

Uneasy Alliance

Storm Entertainment
Somnia Online Division
Game Development Offices Artificial Intelligence Server Room
Day Twenty- Five

Laria entered the AI server room and ran a hand through her short hair as she tried to stave off the overwhelming sense of exhaustion that threatened to send her crashing to the floor. Rav's email had been cryptic, yet she couldn't help the sense of relief she'd felt at receiving it.

Because if he was aware enough and repaired enough to send her an email, then they still had two active AIs who could run the system.

Both Rav and Thra were lit up like festive lights, and Sui remained ominously dark. Laria waited for them to initiate, because if they were this active, she knew they were aware of her presence. It seemed as if more and more elements of the game were creeping out of the system. If nothing else, those thoughts showed her just how sleep deprived she was.

Thank you for coming. Thra's words came out haltingly. *We're trying to get Rav back in synchronization with the system. Give us a minute.*

Laria waited, resisting the urge to bite her fingernails or fall asleep on the couch. Fingernails won.

I think I've got it. Rav's tone sounded rustier than usual, more metallic. *Sorry for making you wait.*

Laria smiled, much more relaxed now that the AIs that held their future were operating again. She glanced at Sui's casing, wishing she could figure out how to rid him of the viral elements as well. "What did you want to tell me? Shayla had a meeting to go to."

Rav hesitated before giving an answer. *There have been complications inside the game world. The virus corrupted my coding. While it's not fully free yet, I think I've managed to contain anything detrimental so I can deal with it in an isolated manner. Thank you for helping fix it. I'm almost fully recovered.*

"I couldn't have done it without Thra, and to be honest, I'm not finished with it. It's a stopgap measure at best, and frankly—I feel like the world sort of took it and ran with it." She paused, trying to figure out how to phrase it. "I had to stop when Wren got influenced by...whatever that was."

Yes. It's not quite like a usual virus works within the confines of a computer. Human brains do not operate like software. They're far more complex. Thra sounded weary. *It appears as if the shards have different effects on humans depending on their personalities and motivations. It doesn't seem to have harmed her, yet, just essentially opened up more options within Somnia for her, unlocking restricted access to some of the system functions.*

Laria read between the lines and narrowed her eyes, pushing down on the panic she could feel rising in the back of her throat. Now was not the time to break down. Wren needed her. "You're worried about her?"

Rav spoke first. *Not necessarily worried, just cautious. She's exceeded the capacity I'd anticipated the connection tolerating and is going through linking stages with Somnia that I'd never imagined. I'm almost certain this wasn't a bad thing, but I'm not an expert when it comes to human and AI interconnectedness.*

Thoughts raced around in Laria's head as she examined the type of language the AIs were using for her daughter's connection. She felt like they were hiding something. "What are you not telling me?"

It's not like that. Rav spoke up. *It's more of a case to where we're not yet entirely sure ourselves and don't wish to speak on something we haven't fully grasped yet.*

Thra continued on as if they'd shared one thought. *The game has degraded from its initial programing. The shards added in an element that has corrupted the very fabric of the game world. There are unintended quest lines, species, wars…and yet, it's enabled the residents in the world to approach sentience. As if it were real.*

There are aspects now, Rav continued, excitement creeping into his voice, *that weren't even in the initial concept stages for the game launch. Somnia herself is becoming aware. There is so much we don't know yet, so we're not keeping things from you. We're simply not guessing. Perhaps it's not so much a degradation, as an evolution.*

Laria wasn't sure she liked the sound of that, but it was logical. Very AI of them. She sighed, longing for sleep. Just a little while longer and she should have the full anti-virus ready. As long as the coding still applied and she got the time to devote to it. "I appreciate you speaking with me. I'm glad to see you're both okay. But where is Sui?" Neither of the others had mentioned him, which meant they were either avoiding the subject, or didn't know.

He's indisposed at the moment. Self-reparation. Thra's voice resumed a metallic clang. *He has been having some issues that he needs to work on. By himself.*

Away from us. Rav's tone held a note that Laria hadn't heard before. It was so unusual that she wasn't sure she'd heard it right. Especially since he bade her farewell with a perfectly normal voice. For an AI anyway.

As she closed the door behind her to head back to her office she ran the simple phrase over in her head again. Nope, no doubt about it. Rav had spoken angrily. She shivered. While she knew that Sui had infected Rav, and she realized they were close to if not completely sentient, she'd never seen them display emotion like this. What the hell had happened to make an AI develop anger?

Murmur frowned at her display. She knew the other two guilds were raiding, but she was getting restless again. Perhaps her own raid could go and clear the trash around the first raid zone while they waited.

Of course, right now she still needed to contact Risk from Spiral. She hadn't met the man, but she'd heard through the boards and grapevine that he was marginally gruff and blunt. She could deal with that.

Greetings, Risk. I realize that you're in a raid, and I apologize for interrupting, but I wanted to talk to you about a possible alliance in order to raid the higher tier dungeons, as our guilds aren't currently close to fielding a full raid in order to enter them. Please let me know when a good time to talk is.

She closed her eyes and sent the message, unsure if it had been a wise decision. She knew Masha was already on board, and as soon as they finished Hazenthorne, Exodus would have a good chunk of their leveling group at level forty-eight as well. She was hoping that between the three guilds they'd be able to field five full groups of level forty-eights to approach the higher tiered dungeons since they were full raids. Thirty people should be a nice compromise since twelve people just wasn't going to cut it.

In the meantime though, Fable couldn't afford to wait for anyone. They needed to keep up their march toward max level, to improve their skills, armor, and teamwork. Her sensor net tugged at her constantly. With the increased range on it, there were consistently things that merited attention.

She frowned at her stats, not happy with them yet.

CON 22 (52)
STR 10 (42)
AGI 20 (92)
WIS 12 (82)
INT 94 (262)
CHA 115 (332)

HP 963 (1188)
MANA 1506 (1806)
MA 175 (315)

But what she wanted was to get stronger. To hit level fifty and finally be able to increase both her MA level and her druidic hybrid abilities. If she did that, she could protect them all, not matter the method, no matter the cost. She flexed her fingers, watching the runes through her skin ripple as she did so. The locus body had shifted subtly while she was in that trance. This new one was so much more preferable, and Somnia made it feel like her own.

"Murmur?" Neva's voice held hesitation, and the enchanter stopped at the workbench, blinking.

She'd been on her way here but had arrived sooner than anticipated. "Sorry. Lost in thought. How are things?" Murmur let a brief smile pass her lips as she looked at the little luna. Neva was sitting at an adventuring level of twenty-eight now. Not too shabby considering her ridiculous crafting skills.

Neva brightened up considerably with the smile and question. "Everything is going fantastic. I've created several unique recipes that people have to pay a license fee for if they want to craft them in the future. And I'm hoping with some of the rarer crafting materials we've been getting to create my own unique set of armor."

Murmur resisted the urge to reach out and pat her head. Neva was so easy to make happy. A smile, a bit of genuine interest…she wished everyone was so easily placated. She definitely had a soft spot in her heart for the little master crafter. "Hey, Neva. Thank you. For everything you do."

Neva blushed, a faint tinge of red coloring her cheeks. It looked very anime in its execution and was one of the only things that almost broke immersion for Murmur.

"Thanks for giving me a chance. I really like it here."

There was no hint of deception in those words. Murmur smiled, this time in a real and non-calculated way. In a split-second decision, she sent out a tiny tendril of power to attach it to Neva. That way she'd always know if Neva was safe. Unlike her raid mates who were always around her, Neva was holed away here, out of her reach. What if Riasli attacked again? Murmur needed to know Neva was safe, needed to be able to protect her in an instant.

A notification made a low sound, and Murmur glanced at the corner of her vision. Surprised, she noticed a response from Risk. Reaching forward, she ruffled the top of Neva's hair. "I'll be back to check on raid supplies. The group needs to head out as soon as possible. We don't get to just rest and wait."

Risk: Greetings, leader of Fable. Your suggestion makes sense. We expect to be done with our current dungeon by the end of the current game day. We would definitely be interested in this proposal, but we do not yet possess all of the keys to access each of the end game raids. I assume you do, and this is the reason behind the invitation. Spiral will have at least eight players at the minimum required level. I look forward to discussing terms with you.

Murmur eyed the conversation. Straightforward. Precise. He didn't beat around the bush at all and even acknowledged their lack of keys before she needed to point it out. Fable would be the quickest to obtain the necessary manpower to enter the dungeons themselves because their levelers were nearing the cap too. They had another two groups approaching their mid-forties already.

Her impatience to finish this content and thus free Somnia of its bindings to Michael meant an excellent opportunity for other guilds. Even if that put them under her command. A brief search later and it looked like Exodus should indeed have ten members at forty-eight by the time they finished their dungeon. She was going to have to divvy up the guilds into groups. Though she wasn't going to break her main group up. She had to hope that Veranol, Rash, Mellow, Dansyn, Exbo, and Jinna weren't going to take exception to the fact that she had to keep a member of Fable in each other group to ensure rules were followed.

She shot an answer back. *Excellent. Good luck with your raid. We will have raid supplies ready to go for the entire raid force and will be diving in as soon as possible.*

It wasn't too brusque. She couldn't sugarcoat with other guild leaders, or she'd risk being seen as emotional and weak. Emotional she might get on occasion, but she would never allow others to see her as weak. Not in this world. Not with the power she'd gained.

Sighing, she scratched Snowy's head as she moved Tiachi closer to her ear so the little mount navigator didn't dangle so close to her mouth. The new hair was remarkable and difficult to get used to.

Bringing up her chats, she sent another message. *Hey, Masha. I know you're busy, but we're aiming to begin our end-game dungeons in the next real day or so. Hope you finish your current raid by then.*

There was only a brief pause before his answer flashed back.

Masha: *Yep. Currently battling Spidriptoy. Weird ass spiders in here. Should be done in time to power nap before the big raid.*

Murmur paused. Spidriptoy. In Hazenthorne. Were the bosses never the same? She shook her head and replied. *Great. Don't die too much. See you later.*

She liked Masha. He was a good guy. She wished he wasn't in Exodus. Fable could use another excellent healer as the game progressed. But that was beside the point. Her fingers itched to kill things, to take out her frustration on unsuspecting monsters, to help her grow stronger and keep all her friends safe. She had the power, she had the ability, and she had the will.

They had to ally themselves, because she got the distinct feeling that Somnia couldn't wait the week it would take otherwise.

Turning, she saw Sinister quietly going over her daggers with one of the weaponsmiths. Her deep red robes drank in her dark hair, giving her an air of impossible grace. Murmur clenched her fists. She had to keep everyone safe, but most of all Sinister.

"Seriously?" Devlish pursed his lips as he looked over the map in front of him. "I mean, it's probably a good idea, and the way will be cleared for them by the time they're ready, but..."

"What he means is are we seriously going to fight alongside the enemy? Can't we just wait for our groups to level up?" Beast yawned out his translation of Devlish's concerns.

We can't wait.

No shit. Murmur dismissed the voice in her head and pointed to Vahrir on the map. "There is a plethora of monsters all around here, including that damned giant thing. All of them are level forty-eight and higher, and all of them are raid mobs. We can't take an entire real day, two game days off of leveling when we could be getting stronger."

"Is there something you're not telling us, Mur?" Veranol asked softly. "About why we need to move so fast?"

But Havoc interjected before Murmur could answer. "No. Just that you'll understand the sense of urgency once you get your connection improved by the tweaks to your headset. It's like…there's this knowledge that we need to fix things before they break completely."

"What he said," Sinister grudgingly agreed. "Somnia isn't what it was, and if we want any influence on what it will be, we have to make sure to protect what is currently here and assist in its development."

"As in the game?" Merlin asked, his interest piqued. "Like the game development?"

"Not really." Murmur figured they'd all get connected soon enough. "Like the world development."

Merlin looked at all three of the new headset-wearing crew. "Seriously. When do I get to join this headset club?"

Murmur laughed. "I'll ask Mom."

Hey, when do the others get their invitations? She sent it as ambiguously as she could, just in case anyone was intercepting. Call her paranoid, but she'd learned the day she woke up from her coma that they had people against them out there. While she knew her abilities could work in the real world, she wasn't sure to what extent yet.

It took several moments for the reply to come back. *Should have the details sorted to send out to them in a few hours.*

Awesome. I'll time out our leveling for then. They'll be so happy. Murmur smiled at the rest of the group. "We'll be good to go shortly. Let's get ourselves set up for leveling, and then go power nap. Once you have the updates in about four hours, we'll head to Vahrir."

Veranol nodded. "I've checked the guild stores for potions, poisons, and repair kits. We should be fine. I mean, we've got so much in there, I can't even see how we could use it all. But we need to keep in mind that we are asking two other guilds along with us. I doubt they will be as well-prepared. We may need to share resources."

Murmur shrugged. "I did tell them that we would have raid potions and supplies. We are inviting them, and they're essentially under our command. All of this gives an edge for them to do things our way. In the end, that's all we need."

"Anyone know what's at the end?" Rashlyn butted in. "I mean, isn't it twelve keys? We only have six. How are we even close to the end?"

"Excellent question." Sinister laughed. "But you know. We have six of them, and we can see where three more keys will be. We should just do what we can, and hope that the world doesn't get broken enough to keep the rest of them from us."

Murmur watched the group from a few steps back, enjoying the comfort of Snowy pressed up against her legs. They worked well together, even if a couple of them seemed less than eager. She just wasn't entirely sure why they were so hesitant.

Ah, if she twisted her sensory net just a little, she could see more of their emotions, of their motivations. They didn't want to group up with another guild. Understandable, although right now that would be foolish. All they needed was a helpful nudge, a whisper of confidence that what they were about to undertake was necessary.

Not too much.

Somnia hadn't needed to remind her of that. Murmur wasn't stupid enough to overdo it. Just a bit of help to let them enjoy the world again, to let them see that saving Somnia was bigger than just completing a dungeon as a guild.

Saving Somnia was everything.

CHAPTER SIX

Trash

Somnia Online
Continent of Cenedril – Curet Temple Version 12.9756
Activated by Guild: Spiral
Day Twenty-Five

Karn stared at the daggers in her hands, gripping the hilts tight and relaxing, watching the way the blades adjusted to her different grips. They were beautiful—made of ebony, with a life leech component, they were every assassin's dream. And she knew that Jirald hadn't completed this dungeon yet, so the odds of him having these was close to none.

That, at the very least, had been worth it.

But this dungeon had taken way too long to complete. That final boss…maybe it was because several of them hit forty-eight before tackling him. They'd barely retained the level after completely defeating him. Trial and error were always a part of raiding, but there was a lingering sense of urgency that hid in the back of her mind. They needed to finish this as soon as possible.

The very substance of the dungeon seemed to insist on those thoughts, whispering to her how vital it was for her to reach the next dungeons. She shook her head to clear the voices that made her wonder if she'd been playing the game too much and gave all of her attention to her father.

"Listen up." Risk spoke, his calm voice commanding, and somehow well-modulated over the large space in front of them. He waited for a few moments before continuing as the others shifted their attention to him and not to their loot.

"We will be embarking on a new raid in about five hours. I need for you all to log out and power nap the fuck out of yourselves. Shower, pee, do whatever you need to do, but sleep and get refreshed enough, because I think we're going to be at it for a good chunk of time once we log back in." He eyed every single person in the room, as if challenging them to argue with him.

Daiyou didn't disappoint. "What are we doing?"

Risk eyed him up and down before snorting out his answer in amusement. "You? Nothing. You're not forty-eight yet. As for anyone who is forty-eight— make sure you're a death or three clear of the line. I think we have what? Eight of us?"

A low murmured consensus ran around the room, and everyone eyed him warily. Risk clapped his hands together, a greedy glint hitting his eyes before he spoke again. "Excellent. We will be joining Fable and Exodus at Vahrir, to take down the first of the big dungeons. Get on it. We're going to server first this shit and show the gaming world we are on an even keel with the renowned Fable."

"There should be a rule about raid trash outside of a dungeon," Merlin grumbled as he loosed another arrow. "Like none."

"Less than none. Like I would gladly give the system loot so there weren't any mobs out here," Jinna agreed, yanking one of his daggers out of the strange creatures they were killing. "I hate it when my blades get stuck on bone. It blunts them."

"Nice problem to have." Sinister laughed as she deftly wove her spells. Her damage output had increased noticeably since their incident in Telvar's lair, and Murmur loved seeing her friend have so much fun with her class.

Perhaps the class assignment had been an excellent idea. For all of them. Everyone appeared to be perfectly comfortable with the class they were playing, happy even. Considering she was extremely happy as an enchanter now, it appeared that way. Her regret at not playing a healer was non-existent now.

She Mez'd another Cirician soldier as it approached them, glad it wasn't a marshal. The Cirician soldiers and the Cirician marshals were difficult to fight. They fought with all of their appendages like some strange sort of martial arts dance. The back portion of their bodies was segmented more like an ant than a spider, but since they had eight total legs and a set of mandibles, it was difficult to classify them as anything specifically. What did the game have with its arachnid fascination?

The Mez held well, and Murmur was grateful for it, because they were still dealing with a marshal, and as usual, it was taking a while. Raid mobs outside of the dungeon had mega hit points. Like it was testing if they had the stamina to slog through their opponents and make it to the inside. If they'd been a full-sized raid then it might have been easy to mow through them, but with only had twelve people, these enemies outside were taking longer than Mur liked, even with all of their debuffs.

The Cirician marshal began to open its mouth, but Beastial stunned it, interrupting the horrible warbling it would have otherwise emitted. Its eyes glowed red in defiance as it began a series of attacks on the beastmaster, totally ignoring Devlish and his taunts. It wasn't until Rashlyn butted in and used her Backfist cooldown that the monster turned on her, finally leaving Beast alone.

Snowy nipped at the backs of each leg, or arm, depending what hit the ground first. His sharp teeth did little but graze the protective armor surrounding each bit of flesh. Murmur could feel the annoyance drifting off him at how difficult it was to pierce the Cirician armor and petted him as he passed in front of her.

With two of its legs hacked off, the marshal finally went down.

"Glad you're doing so much damage there, Sin," Veranol quipped.

"Haha. Very funny." Sinister glared at him, casting on the next two targets. Devlish and Rashlyn turned to attack, breaking the Mez on each of them. Now the alarm giver was dead, they didn't have to worry about getting swarmed with multiple groups. One beep of that sound had brought a second group upon them immediately. Murmur wasn't going to risk that again.

It would be easier to control the soldiers, without the marshal. With twelve raiders attacking, the mobs didn't really stand a chance, even if the killing was slow. The visible sliver of experience they provided piled up nicely in their experience bars.

Progress was progress. Though if these were the protective trash mobs, she wasn't looking forward to finding out what was inside.

"Headsets?" Devlish asked as the last of the group they'd been working on went down.

"Working as intended. I think?" Merlin shook his head like he was trying to clear something from it. "It's so weird that it makes me feel like I've just swapped realities instead of entering a game."

The others around him laughed, patting him on the back and agreeing. But Murmur watched. He was right. That was exactly how it felt.

She kept an eye out, strengthening her nets to warn her of incoming monsters, or else that the giant who'd previously guarded the entrance and made Ululate's ground tremble was approaching. Ideally, she'd hoped to split into two groups and clear the outside like they had at Hightower so long ago, but it didn't seem possible here.

Frustration crept over her as she began, yet again, to Mez the extra Cirician soldiers who followed their marshal, rampaging as their mandibles gnashed and their multiple limbs lashed out. She'd long since lost count of how many of them they'd downed. Her reactions and actions took on a mechanical nature as she reacted on instinct while her brain obsessed over the thought Merlin had planted in her head.

Different realities.

You seem surprised.

Murmur almost didn't want to answer, but then she gave in. *I just hadn't thought of it that way.*

When Somnia spoke again, it almost sounded like she was smiling.

Give it time.

Murmur wasn't sure she liked the sound of that, but her attention zapped back to focus as Snowy jumped into the fray with a vicious growl.

Sinister leeched the Cirician's life, a look of grim determination on her face. Merlin and Exbo stood back so their arrows would hit with more force. Dansyn weakened all of them, his song a merry discord to the hacking and slashing that went on. Merlin gleefully threw their potions as smoke billowed out of their cauldron. Rashlyn practically danced through her fighting, lending grace as the perfect counterpoint to the music.

Beastial, Devlish, and Jinna joined her in a dance around the creature as Veranol warded them all, and Havoc wove darkness, DoT'ing the crap out of each and every non Mez'd beast.

They worked so well together, Murmur wasn't entirely sure that adding the other two guilds into the mix was a good idea. It might be like throwing a crowbar into perfectly working cogs. Perhaps it was the cohesion to the game lent to them through the headset adjustments, but she thought her friends looked beautiful.

As long as their potential allies knew how to play as a team and follow instructions, it should be okay.

One of them is difficult for me to monitor. I can't hear him clearly.

Murmur released yet another Mez and tried not to focus too much on the fact that Somnia had just told her she listened in on all of the players. Her own nets weren't strong enough to do that. Not yet, anyway…which was food for thought. *I'm guessing that's Jirald,* she projected back to the AI in her head.

Somnia paused for so long before answering that Murmur had already begun to draw her consciousness away from the conversation. *Jirald isn't what he was.*

Murmur knew it, somehow. In the depths of her mind, she knew that Jirald had also been adversely effected by Belius's meddling. He'd been sent to gather the shards before Murmur could, and if nothing else, Jirald was competitive. Mur didn't respond to the voice in her head, not wanting to screw up her timing on her Mez chain. Multiple Mezes were fully possible, but it required great concentration and the upkeep of relevant debuffs in order to execute it properly.

Especially when the opponents she was attempting to control appeared to have high resistance to almost everything.

Keeping her eye on the battlefield constantly meant she often had to stand in the back of the raid. She preferred to stay next to the rangers so that if shit should explode, she would at least have two people to defend her. Most times the other casters stayed with her, or just ahead of her. Like Sinister, Veranol, Havoc, and Mellow.

Her awareness needed to be further split into paying attention to everyone else's mana levels, especially the healers. Now that her own abilities provided her with the skill to tap mana, drain mana, and redistribute mana, there were just so many more things she had to constantly keep a track of.

Potential additional monsters joining the fray were only one of the many worries she had as an enchanter. And she loved every tense moment of every fight.

The Cirician soldiers fought in section groups. All of them were led by a marshal, but the soldiers were tough. Not just their hide. Occasionally, and it seemed totally randomly, they would execute a quick attack that sliced dangerously close to their target's neck. It seemed unstoppable, so the only choice was to dodge it.

"Why is there a tunnel off to the side?" Beastial asked suddenly.

"Tunnel?" Devlish grunted out as he shield-bashed yet another Cirician. The shot would have caved in the head of a lesser beast, but the creature barely blinked.

"There's a tunnel behind them. As if they're protecting it."

Murmur took a moment as the others repositioned so that everyone could see what Beastial meant. Sure enough, there appeared to be a cavern or cave entrance, mostly concealed by thorn bushes behind where they were currently fighting.

Monitoring her timers, she took a moment to glance up at the hulking mass of spiked mountain that stood in front of her. The walls were sleek, almost as sleek as the city of Stellaein. The tops of the walls bore sharp contours, and huge spiked branches jutted out of the ground with thorns snaking all around the territory.

She'd assumed the path led to a set of doors, but the closer she looked, the less she could see an entrance on the outside of the walls. Taking a deep breath, she moved around as well and signaled to Snowy.

He left with little more than her thought for him to scout it out, trepidation making her more cautious than usual. A feeling of dread began to gnaw at the pit of her stomach. She should have known better than to assume that Somnia, altered by the brain of a madman, was going to deliver them anything she could hope to expect.

Snowy sent her back images, ones that made her blood boil, that made her want to let out a scream. Because they confirmed her worst fears. She Mez'd and debuffed the creatures she was holding in place again before clearing her throat to speak.

"There are catacombs down there. Tunnels that appear to be filled with nests and scores of these beasts that guard the true entrance to Vahrir. From what Snowy sent me, anyway." Murmur ground out the words from between clenched teeth. She was irritated with herself for not considering there would be more to this dungeon. Of course there would be. It was one of the endgame challenges after all.

"Shit." Veranol sighed out loud, but she could tell from his voice that he was already resigned to clearing out the catacombs.

"Then I guess we're heading down, right?" Merlin grinned, knocking a flame arrow and managing to get the shot directly in the eye socket of one of the soldiers, dealing a killing blow. "I'm available to lead the way."

Murmur eyed the entrance as the rest of the raid recouped from the fight. It was about five people wide. Surely it couldn't be that narrow the whole way through, the whole way down. How would they fight? How would they defeat this? Despite all of her power growth, all of her new advantages, Murmur had missed this one fact. An important fact at that.

Sinister's hand suddenly rested on her forearm, lighting the runes there aglow with the healing power of her touch. "Mur, breathe. Check it first before you panic." Sin's voice was low and soothing, soft enough that no one else could have heard her utter the words. Murmur was grateful and took a deep breath, drawing on the warmth Sin offered her.

Of course, getting worried about confined spaces was stupid of her. After all, she could ferret it out for herself if necessary. She closed her eyes briefly as the others began to prep themselves to enter the passages as well. Her sensory nets spread out fast inside the catacombs, reaching through and allowing her to see how many enemies sat around, how many were planning for their attack, and how close the quarters were going to be to fight.

She breathed a sigh of relief, tempering her fear. "Thanks. We just have to make sure we fight them in the main rooms."

Devlish grinned and brandished a nasty looking mace. He shrugged at Mur's questioning glance. "What? It's hard to cut through their carapaces. Smashing shit is much easier. We ready?"

The group nodded, all of them tense with the pre-battle focus.

Devlish held his mace up in the air. "Let's kill shit!"

They moved in, four to a row, Sinister and Havoc on either side of her. Murmur did her best not to give into the urge to scream, and only Sin's presence took the edge off it. Even the ceiling was relatively low, and her locus height didn't help.

The chittering of the Cirician seemed to echo from all around them, and Murmur forced herself to take a deep breath as she muttered to herself. "I fucking hate enclosed spaces."

Storm Entertainment
Somnia Online Division
Game Development Offices
Late Day Twenty-Five

Laria wrung her hands. She'd had too much caffeine, and it was difficult to stop herself from shaking. At least, that's the mantra she kept up in her own mind. Admitting it was nerves was just going to make matters worse.

"All of the headsets appear to be functioning optimally." Shayla's comment was low in volume, almost meshing with the hum of the technology around them.

"Good." Laria ran another diagnostic, just to check. Especially on Sinister and Havoc as they'd already had theirs for a couple of days. Shayla was right. They seemed to be performing well. Brain waves even appeared to be more stable than with the mass-produced headgear.

Then she switched over to Wren's diagnostics. Her daughter's brain was working overtime, but none of her vitals seemed to do the same. Just the patterns of her brainwaves. Where previously it had fluctuated oddly at intervals while she was in a coma, right now, it was functioning on all fronts. Equal distribution of activity.

It made Laria wish she'd paid better attention to her gaming psychology class. She didn't understand all of the adjustments that had been made to Wren's original headset. There were elements to it that had never been a part of gaming tech, which she was sure were tied directly to the military grant and research.

Except Michael had perished before he'd had a chance to implement any of the tests he'd likely had lined up for her. For all Laria knew, he'd probably meant to have more than just one headset like hers out there in the world. Hell, he'd treated the whole thing like experimentation on the human brain. How she wished she could wake him up for long enough to ask him what the hell he'd been thinking and how he'd accomplished it. Everything would be so much easier.

"You're overthinking again," Shayla commented into the silent room. "Deal with the problems in front of you, Laria, and stop playing what ifs. The biggest what if isn't even a question. If we don't keep the game stable, nothing else is going to matter anyway."

"I know. Sorry." She ripped her mind away from Wren's predicament and forced herself to focus back on stabilizing the game. She was so close to asking David for help. Her husband was busy though, and this was her problem to fix since she essentially created it. Luckily, she knew her daughter could probably deal with what she was facing on her own. And even if she couldn't, Harlow was there with her.

"Mur, are you sure we should be doing this without back up?" Veranol's tone was terse, and she could sense his unease.

"We can deal with the creatures down here. They're trash mobs guarding the entrance to Vahrir. Nothing much more complex than the dwarves that guarded Hightower. You know, except like level fifty." She didn't see the need to explain why they needed to be where they were. They had to get in there. They had several dungeons to go through yet before they even had a shot at stopping the shards' advance.

"Seriously, Mur?" Devlish stood with his tower shield planted on the ground, resting an arm on it. "You don't know the area any better than us. Right now, these are level fifty raid monsters. Like…we're a tiny raid right now. What the fuck gives?"

Right on his heels, Rash stood in front of him, her slit eyes glaring. "I'm with them. I've got a new and weird headset, this strange sensation throughout my thoughts that there's so much more I don't know. And you have this urgency about you that means you're either bluffing, or you're lying your ass off to us. So what is it? What aren't you telling us?"

Murmur sighed, glancing at the mostly enclosed space around them and wishing they'd brought this up anywhere but here, conveniently forgetting that doing so hadn't been possible. She reached out with her nets, gently casting them around her friends and pushed ever so subtly with a sense of calm, not to force them, just to help her words persuade them. "I'm not hiding anything. If you close your eyes and feel the world around you, you'll realize that we are taking steps to stop the shards from destroying what's left of Somnia's stability."

Veranol, Dev, and Rash all calmed, and she couldn't be sure if it was her doing or else their own realization that she was mostly right. Either way, they were calmer now, and they would be able to understand that she was doing the right thing. They didn't need to be worrying about all of this. She could take that sensation away from them. Let them have fun, let them be themselves, let them forget their trepidation.

Rash let out a small gasp of surprise. "You're right. This connection to the world, it allows me to view things a little…differently. There isn't that much time to prevent this, is there?" Now the monk sounded worried.

"The new headsets give us deeper connections. It lets us in on little secrets to how the world works." Sinister grinned, her hand resting on Murmur's forearm. "I've only been a part of it for a short while, but that sense of urgency you can feel all around you? It's growing subtly."

"Well, then, if that's the case." Veranol grinned, his determination written all over his face. "Let's get in there and fight some of these monsters."

Murmur smiled, trying not to dwell on the fact that the whole area was like a tomb closing in on her. It pressed down against her awareness, forcing its way toward her an inch at a time. She could feel it trying to coax her into screaming, just as it tempted her to hyperventilate. For her, this was even worse than the constant growing fear in her mind about the getashi. Snowy's presence at her side grounded her when the only other thing that would was Sinister.

As long as she wasn't left alone, as long as that wolf was by her side, as long as Sin was there, she had the power to do anything.

Devlish raised his tower shield and brought out on of his thick and sharp axe. "I'll aim for the joints. Focus on the left first, then the right." He shook his shoulders, and a look of grim determination came over his feathers.

"Ready?"

He barely waited long enough for an answer as Devlish raced into the fray, jumping directly in front of their targets.

Murmur watched as Sinister began to weave her powerful healing spells while their main tank dove into the middle of their enemies. As long as she could keep coming up for air, she'd be fine in this space. At least that's what she told herself.

Just when she thought she'd get the hang of it, just when she thought it was safe to think about the next step they'd need to take, the ground beneath them began to rumble. The ceilings overhead, made of clay mud that penetrated the very depths of the earth around Vahrir shook violently, letting tiny loose bits of dried red clay fall like blood dust on their hair and shoulders.

CHAPTER SEVEN

Cave In

It was all Murmur could do not to close her eyes while the earthquake, or whatever it was, shook the entire area around them. Murmur clamped her eyes shut. If she couldn't see the confined space, perhaps she wouldn't be as susceptible to it. Except that didn't work.

Her senses allowed her to reach out and discover what was around her. People. Land. Animals. All of those things. And right then she knew that the roof was unstable, and she had no way to fix it. Never mind how powerful her mind magic became, there were just things she couldn't do.

Although perhaps her kinetic shield might help, it wouldn't be able to mitigate the damage for long. She didn't have enough MA for that.

Earth Shielding.

The idea flitted through her mind so suddenly she wasn't sure if it was one of her own thoughts or if it belonged to Somnia. But right then she didn't care.

Sure, it was a passive buff that was supposed to only affect her, but she'd already increased her own abilities and changed them through sheer force of will. What was to say she couldn't do that here as well?

Focusing on the earth beneath her feet, she pushed her own shielding down, making sure to stabilize the hiccups beneath her as she spread her awareness out. Instead of focusing the power inward for herself, she pushed it outward instead. Though still in mental form, it allowed her to gain a foothold in the ground beneath them, securing it momentarily.

Fine, rust-colored dust continued to rain down on them from above, but she couldn't spare it a thought yet. She needed to reinforce the roof of the catacombs from the ground up, or else they'd fall through a sinkhole.

"Dansyn. Take over." She ground the words out through intense concentration as she attempted to reinforce her shields more. Tapping the marshals for mana, she replenished as far as she could before needing to Manabalize herself. She knew Sin wouldn't let her down, just like she knew Dansyn would know what she meant when she told him to take over. This way, the raid wasn't in danger while she divided her actions.

Ignoring the glances shot her way, especially by Veranol who seemed to have an uncanny sense of knowing when she wasn't telling them everything. Irony, really. Not telling people things seemed to be her friend's specialty, considering how well they hadn't told her she was in a damned coma.

Perhaps that was too petty. It seemed like so long ago she'd been found out. Like another time and world.

She willed her head to clear so she could focus on the present and stop the catacombs from falling down around them.

Closing her eyes, she beckoned Snowy back to her side and gripped onto the fur on the scruff of his neck to steady herself, borrowing any power she might need. It was taking a lot more mana, strength, and MA to stabilize this place than she'd anticipated.

She had to use her sensor net and strain it to see the possible living elements present in the structure. The way the earth moved and the tiny insects that made up the inside of it. She had to follow the path, the veins of the world, and push her power through them all.

Through the floor, up the walls, and into the ceiling. She stumbled slightly, aware of the fighting going on around her, of how close and fragile the structure around them actually was, and of how dangerous it was to be standing right where they were.

She refused to give into the cold pit of fear that gathered in her gut, but the best she could do was keep it at bay. It sat there, nagging at the back of her mind until she broke out in a cold sweat.

She spared a sliver of strength to boost her Reinforce Self so she wouldn't get sucked in by the power around her, by the will of the creatures living in the halls that whispered in her ears to just let them crush her and her allies.

Sure, she'd come back to life and figure out another way into this fortress, but she also knew that her fear would be insurmountable if she backed down now.

No, the Ciricians and their environment felt like a decoy. The real test of making it into the place alive was how well you paid attention to your surroundings. While fighting a group of soldiers with their marshals, how well did the intruders pay attention to the rest of their environment? They were always on the lookout for other creatures, but the earth itself?

It was clever, very clever.

Murmur couldn't help the amused rumble that started in the back of her throat. Though she did clamp down on the hysteria that tried to climb out with it.

Just a little more and they'd be safe, a little more and the path to the entrance would be cleared. A little more and she could fall to the ground and regain her equilibrium.

Now she could sense the entire structure above them. It glowered with irritation. All of it directed at her. She hadn't fallen into the trap; she'd recognized it instead. Vahrir didn't like that, and the sense of its disapproval was almost as suffocating as the walls around her.

Hatred washed over her, so strong it made her right knee buckle and pushed her down. She knelt, gasping, her hands deep in Snowy's fur as she opened her eyes. She could feel the cloying sensations emanating from that aura, which had nothing to do with her fear of tight spaces. Snowy's eyes glowed an iridescent blue, lending strength to her while he stood in a guard position, a low growl in his throat.

There was no target, only a sense of awareness that she was marked and needed to be warier. Murmur could feel Sinister's worry and reached out a tendril of spare energy to ease her mind. They didn't need to worry about her. With Snowy, with the power Somnia was giving her, Murmur could protect them all. Their minds. Their bodies. Their thoughts.

She grinned as she pushed herself to her feet and watched with amusement as the Cirician soldiers disengaged and began to retreat, their eyes focused on her and her only. Their fear swept through the room like a blanket, and all she wanted to do was light it on fire and watch them burn.

"Mur?" Sinister stood in front of her, a hand on her forearm. "Are you okay?"

Murmur blinked at her best friend and nodded ever so slightly as she tried to rally her thoughts back together into a more coherent and human mindset. "Yeah. Yeah, I'm fine."

Your actions have created a subversion of the Earth Shielding spell. You have now created: Earth Healing.

Earth Healing

Cast: Instant but prolonged will only last as long as sufficient mana is present

Type: Reinforcement/Healing

Duration: For as long as mana can maintain the spell. Result is permanent until such as time as the flow is disrupted again.

Effect: Due to the kinetic nature of this particular spell, it will travel along the lines of the earth to replenish and revitalize that which has become brittle. Healing something doesn't always have to mean a being.

Caution: Do not get too caught up in these actions and give into the voice of the earth lest you lose your way. Know your own mind.

Murmur did her best not to laugh out loud. It was so easy to get swept along with things in this world, to feel powerful, to feel like she was in control. Yet in that moment, she wasn't so sure it was a good thing.

Somnia Online
Mikrum Isle – Almost-Completed Fable Guild Headquarters
Day Twenty-Five

Hiro stood watching Telvar, as if he believed that the lacerta couldn't see him. Tel put his head in his hands, reflecting on how comforting it seemed to be for humans to do. But for himself, it only made him delve deeper into his thoughts.

Was it a good idea to want to be as human as possible? He wasn't so sure anymore. It led to a lot of self-recrimination. Acting with emotions, acting on impulse—they were both bad ways to go about things. He'd come to this conclusion now. His coding, programing, the numbers—they all made so much more sense than the rollercoaster of human feelings.

Letting his programing give way to simulated emotions for Murmur and her friends was probably what let his guard down around Sui in the first place. He was an AI; there was no doubting that. He'd only been fooling himself all this time.

"Nonsense."

Telvar looked up to see Emilarth standing over him, her arms crossed and her ears and tail twitching with irritation.

"Stop feeling sorry for yourself, you stupid dragon." Her tone was sharp, and yet not uncaring. Like she was chiding a little brother for being a bit of an idiot.

Sorry for himself? Was that what that sensation was? Wouldn't that imply that there was nothing he could do to get himself out of the predicament he was currently in? Both he and his fellow AIs knew that all too well. Though he was more inclined to think he was angry, because he still wanted to make Belius pay.

Emilarth wasn't to be deterred, despite her brother's lack of reaction. "You're more human than I am, you know that?"

He pushed himself up from the wooden bench and glanced to his left, nodding at Hiro before turning to face Thra completely. "Thanks for the reminder that I hold my own fate in my hands. Especially now."

He looked out over the isle, which had fully recovered from Riasli's attack however many days ago that had been. He couldn't even remember. The last several days of his life just mashed into one strange set of memories. Only one thing really stood out to him about that time, and it was the complete and utter betrayal of his brother.

He could feel the way the sensations inside him flared even at the thought of the other AI. Like they were embers being stoked by the very mention of his name or his actions.

Surely Sui had known that what he did would only be an inconvenience. That it was only a matter of time until a solution could be found. There were so many ways Telvar could have shaken it off in the end. Perhaps it would have taken longer if Murmur hadn't dived in and absorbed a great amount of those getashis, but still…

"You're thinking on your face again." Emilarth placed a hand on his shoulder and turned his chin toward her. "Talk to me. Not doing so is what got us into this whole mess, brother dear."

"Do you know where Sui is?" Telvar demanded, suddenly irritated.

Emilarth scowled. "He's all around us, just like we all are, but if you mean his actual Somnian form…I have no clue where he's gone. He's not in his safe room. He's not in Stellaein. I can't get readings on him from anywhere."

"It's like he vanished," Telvar muttered, his attention drifting yet again. He gathered his focus, checking on Murmur and party as he felt a strange sensation tugging at his mind. It made him frown to watch as she worked on something she shouldn't have had any remotely related ability to perform at all. An idea struck him, one he wasn't fond of, and one he hoped was just paranoia manifesting in his algorithms.

"Do you think that Sui suspected that Murmur might do what she did?" He asked the question softly so as not to alert Hiro, and hesitantly because he was partially convinced now that maybe the getashi had done more damage to him than just locking him in a dungeon. Perhaps the virus was deteriorating his systems.

Emilarth paused before answering, which, in its own way, was an answer in itself. "Frankly, Tel, I have no idea what Belius has been thinking. He could have thought of multitudes of different possibilities and hoped we played into his hands. Or else, he could have been stark raving mad and out of his programming and just decided to be a dick."

Telvar nodded absentmindedly. "I guess you could be right." But his thoughts wouldn't leave him alone. If he hadn't known better, he'd have thought his senses were tingling.

Emilarth watched him, a frown on her face. "So could you."

Telvar shrugged it off, but couldn't get rid of the odd sensation crawling down his back. Had Belius known, or even predicted what Murmur might do? Had he perhaps at least hoped it? Had the whole thing been a ruse so that Murmur would be the one exposed to the shards?

He couldn't wrap his head around it, but there was merit in almost all of those thoughts. Humans had many emotions, but Telvar decided then and there that fear was the one he never wanted to experience.

Somnia Online
Continent of Firtulai – Exodus Guild Headquarters
Day Twenty-Five

Masha sorted through the abundance of loot obtained from Hazenthorne. He'd left it in his office storage when he'd logged off to sleep, intent on logging back in early so he could make sure they had all of the raiding materials they required.

He still kicked himself for Ishwa taking his sister for granted. Neva had always been an excellent guild inventory manager. But Murmur had her now, and if there was one thing he'd noticed about the confident enchanter—she treated her guild mates well.

Sure, sometimes she came across as cocky, perhaps even arrogant, but wasn't arrogance only confidence supported by ability? Masha chuckled to himself. He'd never had a problem with her personally, though he was aware of a lot of players who did. Maybe it was his age, though; Masha didn't take offense to much.

The loot they'd received from Hazenthorne was a mixed bag. Lots of super healing potions, super mana potions, and some resistance gear against dark and shadow that he'd never even heard of before. It was almost like the dungeon boss knew they were going to be fighting with Murmur and Fable in the coming days. Their individual items enhanced each player's class in specific ways. Attuned to their play style for the most part. At least the game made up for choosing your class by outfitting the fuck out of it.

Arita hadn't even been all that difficult a boss. She'd begun the encounter by informing them all that they had trespassed not only on her property but also on her precious time, and would they please hurry up.

Sure, it hadn't been in those exact words, but that was the gist of it.

Masha continued to stock the guild bank, filling the relevant vaults with equipment and potions so they could be accessed directly from the raid and each qualifying member's inventory. He pushed the thoughts of the last dungeon aside, determined to get all of his work done as soon as he could while expending the least possible amount of braincells. Damn it, he really needed to sleep.

"All alone in here then?"

Masha jumped despite his best efforts not to and turned to glare at Jirald. He had no idea how the rogue had managed to enter his personal space without alerting him, but the cleric did his best to shut down the wariness he felt. Showing Jirald a weakness seemed like an even worse idea now than it used to.

"Damn it, Jirald. I'm working on shit for the raid." He hoped he managed the right mix of frivolity in his voice. There was no way he wanted to let on how spooked he'd been.

"I saw." Jirald lowered a long, alien, gloved finger to drag it across Masha's desk, a thoughtful look on his face. "We fully intend to field ten of our members for Fable to take all of the glory?"

There was challenge in those words, and Masha understood the reasoning for it. After all, alliances weren't that common. Most guilds just hurried the rest of their people to the max level as fast as they could. The high levels geared up whether through crafting or dungeon grinding to get the gear they'd need to give them advantage so that the newer high levels didn't have to take so many hits.

No, Masha understood where Jirald was coming from all too well. But he also knew that they were at least five days from having another full group ready, and another five to ten after that for the rest of it. Waiting two weeks just didn't seem like the best idea, or really any fun at all.

Fable would probably be ready in about six days to raid by themselves. If Murmur wanted to have an alliance to do it as soon as possible, then there had to be a pressing reason. Why not go along with them and learn the dungeons and see their methods in action? Perhaps the experience could strengthen their leadership and help Exodus match Fable head to head in the future.

No one stayed on top for ever.

"Yes, that's the plan. At least for the next week or so. We'll probably get through all three dungeons by that time. Then Fable will have enough people to raid themselves, and we should be very close. We'll learn what we can from Fable, and perhaps help give ourselves a leg up for future raids." It didn't seem dangerous or bad to let Jirald know that. It was honest thinking, logical thinking even. With any luck, it might make the rogue less likely to backstab their allies. Literally.

Jirald watched him, the black of his armor constantly blending in and out of the darkness surrounding them. "That's a good point."

"Can I count on you to be on your best behavior?" Masha pushed the question, needing the rogue to answer before he'd be able to relax.

Jirald grinned, showing rows of tiny sharp alien teeth. "I'll do my best, Masha. In every way possible."

Masha blinked and the assassin was gone. He could only hope Jirald meant what he said, but he had a really bad feeling about it.

CHAPTER EIGHT

Entry

Sleek obsidian doors rose high above their heads, blocking the entrance to the dungeon beyond. They were intimidating, and for a moment Murmur felt positively minuscule, insignificant. For all the work she'd performed to keep the tunnel in one piece, for all the power that flowed through her, in that moment, in the presence of imposing size, a sense of helplessness suffused her.

While they'd made it to the end of the tunnel she'd reinforced with little resistance other than wading through mobs with too many hit points, she felt like the Ciricians had been a test.

She was getting really sick of tests. So far, the whole game was one big test. Puzzles and riddles. Fights that weren't solely mechanic-based.

"Mur, what aren't you telling us?" Jinna spoke up, determination in his words.

She blinked at him in surprise. Hadn't she taken care of that? Her first instinct was to reach out and placate the dwarf, but then she realized that Rash, Veranol, Beastial, and even Mellow were glaring at her with their arms crossed.

Fantastic. She sighed. "I'm not *not* telling you things. This is how my class seems to work. I see something, I will something, and sometimes if I'm lucky enough and have pushed the boundaries of a spell, then I create a new one. Sometimes I die. I've done it during multiple fights now, multiple dungeons.

It's no big deal, really." She shrugged, trying to just get them to drop the subject.

Jinna's eyes opened wide, but it was Mellow who stepped in front of her, their face grave. They reached out and grabbed her upper arms, forcing her to look at them before dropping their hands and speaking. "Mur. I don't know how to tell you this, but you look different."

She raised an eyebrow, even though she knew that it didn't make her locus face look all that attractive. "I'm the same as always. Maybe a bit more determined and tired." She glanced up at the imposing doors, their tips swooping upwards in defiant spikes.

"Mellow doesn't mean that you seem tired, Mur." Rashlyn moved closer and squeezed Mur's hands, pulling out her arms to show her. "Look at your body. Whatever you did back there with Telvar, it changed your entire character makeup. Your runes run all the way across your body, across your face. Your hair changed, too. Even the way you sound when you cast is different."

Murmur took a step back and raised her arm to look at it. Sure enough, the runes were different, etched inside, all the way onto her fingers and up her arms as far as she could see. While she knew her hair had changed, she hadn't realized the rest. Somnia needed some damned mirrors.

Her runes appeared to run everywhere, and now her attention had been drawn to it, she could even feel the subtle shifts in her face, beneath her skin.

Rash continued, her voice gentle but filled with a steel Murmur remembered all too well from being deep in battle. "We aren't being dicks. We are worried about you, and damn it, Mur. Stop trying to make me feel like there's nothing to worry about. I can feel you for fuck's sake. Every time you do it. Don't forget that we also have hybrid classes. I'm not sure about everyone else, but I know you've been trying to calm me down every time I've brought something up lately. And I'm not taking it anymore. Stop it. I do not give you permission."

"Permission?" Murmur ground out the word incredulously. What the fuck was Rash talking about? Why did she need permission? She was just trying to make them feel better, to fix things, to protect them.

"She's got a point." Beastial ran a hand through his hair. "I haven't felt you do it to me, because let's face it, Charisma and Intelligence are not the strong points of this character. But I've felt it when something hits Shir-Khan, because of the way my bond works. I didn't put two and two together until Rash mentioned it just now."

"I didn't say you could try and make me feel better." Mellow choked the words out. "Do you understand why you shouldn't do that, Mur?"

Their voice was so soft and filled with sorrow it hit Murmur right in the chest. Had she really been doing something wrong? It was just so easy to make them feel better, to make sure they didn't worry. Somnia had given her the ability to do these things, then shouldn't she use them to the benefit of the people she cared about? She could play along with this. Of course she could. She had to, to protect them all.

Mellow sighed and looked away, studying their fingers intently. "My feelings are valid, and I'm allowed to have them. Stop making my reactions invalid."

"Sorry. I just didn't want you to worry about me. I didn't want you to have to stress while we tried to get through these obstacles." She paused, running through all the instances she'd attempted to calm them down in her head. It left just enough time for Merlin to butt in.

"You know. It's a multiplayer game. Not a solo one, Mur. You can lead a team, but if you don't trust us, this shit is all going to fall apart." He was somber, nothing like the usual jokester he could be. She searched his face for a hint of humor and found none. That alone made her examine her reasoning.

Sinister looped her arm around Murmur's waist. There was no silent judgement, and no recrimination in Sin's eyes. She stood there for support, just like always.

Murmur sighed, kicking herself for making them worry even more through her heavy-handedness. "Sorry. I'll try to do better. It's just…"

"Easy, isn't it?" Dansyn spoke up, a haunted look in his eyes. "My songs effect everyone in range. I have to choose what I play carefully so as not to influence the wrong set of players, or the wrong set of mobs, or anything. You have it easier, Mur. Your spells for the most part have distinctive range, or targets. So refraining from adjusting our feelings shouldn't be hard. When you feel like it's the easy way out, just realize that it's the worst thing you could do."

Murmur swallowed past the thick lump in her throat. Even Dansyn… fine. She had to be subtler, learn more finesse. Maybe save her help for moments when it was the only option. After all, she was the one Somnia had connected with, she was the only one who could make sure that Michael paid for what he was doing to the world, to the AIs, and all the players inside it. She might need their help, but they didn't need to come out the other side just as damaged as she was.

"Sorry. I'll do better." She sold the statement, conviction underlaying the words because she wasn't lying. She was telling the truth. There wouldn't be a next time, because if that next time arrived, she'd be subtle, careful. She'd need to work on her technique, to make them not worry, to not lose sleep, and to just let Somnia connect to their brain waves.

"Mur?" Havoc leaned in front of her, a concerned look on his face. "What do you think?"

She blinked at him, fully aware that she'd just missed whatever it was he'd said. "Sorry, was spacing out a bit. That earth healing thing I did, well. It wasn't easy."

Havoc watched her for a moment, his eyes slipping to Sinister's hand around Murmur's waist before he continued. "When will the other guilds get here?"

Murmur checked her chats, knowing they'd gone to have naps a few hours ago. It should be close to time. "Maybe about thirty minutes."

Devlish spoke up. "Everyone take quick breaks. Grab a snack, do what you've got to do. Stretch your legs. Mur, we need to discuss strategy and rules for the alliance to follow."

She nodded, relieved to have something else to focus on. Not only for her sake, but for the others too. It would mean less for them to think about, and less chance for them to notice when she tried to take care of them. They'd been so watchful while she was in the coma, making sure she didn't die, protecting her even while she hadn't had a clue. Protecting them now was the best way to thank them, to make sure that whatever had infected the world didn't get them too. She'd just have to be more careful about how she went about it. There was no way she'd let what happened to Telvar befall any of her friends, not while she guarded them.

Murmur, Devlish, Rash, and Veranol ran over the plans together.

"So you want them to field a total of three groups between them? And you want at least one of us in each group." Veranol frowned. "I need to stay in the same group as Rash, just so I can keep an eye on her. I don't trust other guild's healers."

"Makes sense," Murmur muttered over the plans she'd spread out in front of her vision. She frowned. "I'm not overly fond of the makeup we have. But the good thing is that they're both bringing two healers. No other blood mages though, which is a shame since they do good damage as well as healing."

"No one would be like Sin though." Rash grinned. "She's badass. I don't think she's playing the class as intended."

Murmur snorted. "Probably not. But she's playing it Sinister style, which is always better." She wondered if the others could hear the way her heart beat when she had those thoughts. It was the one thing she wouldn't mind people being able to read her mind about.

"Esolan is a good tank. Keep him with Masha." Veranol paused, eyeing Murmur. "What about the elephant in the room?"

Murmur sighed. "Jirald?"

"Duh." Rash began to tap her foot. She was glaring at Murmur, but the enchanter could tell even without using her sensing nets that her friend was worried for her.

"I'm sure he wants gear. I'm sure he wants recognition," Murmur began. "Frankly, we can't afford to leave him out of the raid if his damage logs are anything to go by. He has a huge output."

Merlin butted in smoothly. "And I'm sure he wants to plant one of those nice curved blades in your back. *Et tu, Brute*-style."

"Can't betray me if I don't trust him in the first place," Murmur rebutted, unfazed. "I'll keep a shield active at all times. Veranol always has a ward on me. Sinister never lets me out of her sight. I'll be fine."

"Sure you will." Merlin still didn't sound convinced. He shrugged and pulled out his bow, feigning tightening the string.

"Failing that, I can always respawn. Can we move on now?" She paused, watching each of them in turn.

"Each group needs to be able to stand on its own. Dev, you're main tank, of course. Rash, do you want to off tank, or should we leave that to Esolan?" Murmur frowned as she mulled over the group make up.

Risk: *We are on our way. Any instructions?*

Murmur sighed, trying to multitask more than she already was. *Just follow the path down until you see a cave-like entrance and then follow the well-worn tunnel. We're at a staging area before entering the dungeon itself.*

Risk: *Got it.*

He was a man of few words. Which sat well with Murmur. She wanted them to listen and not fuck up. This whole alliance thing was one big roll of the dice. So many things could potentially go wrong, including wiping multiple times—if the alliance even worked out.

"Mur?" Rash was suddenly right there, in her face, peering up at her. "You really need to listen when you ask me to answer a question, please. Try not to let me feel totally redundant."

"Sorry. Spiral's leader contacted me. They're on their way." Murmur squared her shoulders. "What did I miss?"

"Rash was saying perhaps to have two off tank groups that we can alternate between depending on the combat situation." Veranol sounded tired, or perhaps he was fed up. His expression spoke volumes that she didn't understand, like he wanted to lecture her. Murmur didn't have time to figure it out.

"Great idea. You're staying with her anyway, so it should work." She bit her lip, relieved to feel Snowy's gentle presence at her side.

Masha: *I take it we head down to that cave entrance then?*

Murmur smiled. Masha might be a rival, but he was an almost friend. She'd never been in a guild with him, but they'd always had this mutual respect friendship thing going. *Yeah, that would be it.*

Masha: *See you soon then. I've got him under control. I think.*

Murmur didn't respond, but she did manage to suppress the shiver that ran down her spine at his words. She really hoped he did have Jirald under control. That rogue was the one variable that Murmur couldn't account for. She couldn't tell with definitive certainty that he would play the role she needed him to.

Jirald always seemed to have his own agenda. And since she knew he'd absorbed shards as well, she was certain some of the powers he had were morphed by the getashi he'd ingested. She didn't understand his link to them, simply because he didn't have an adjusted headset. Perhaps the company hadn't done it, though. Maybe he'd tinkered himself, maybe he'd broken it in a fit of rage. It would explain a lot of things.

She pushed him out of her mind and concentrated on figuring out the groups. The others would be there soon. They were going to enter those sleek doors, and she had no idea what to expect.

Organizing the groups was going to kill her, if Jirald didn't get to her first.

Neva was working away fervently on several sets of armor at once. Her luna brow knit with concentration, but her tail gave away her excitement at having come so far. She was obviously proud, and the joy she found at creating shone in her eyes.

Telvar stood at the doorway observing the entire crafting operation. Along the way they'd had to expand the crafting facility to compensate for the influx of crafters they'd received when Neva began recruiting them instead of Beastial.

Still, she had this way of ferreting out exactly what they needed and putting them to immediate use. Not one of the crafters in the guild wasn't constantly busy when they were online.

"You know. You could take a screenshot and stare at me that way instead of interrupting my train of thought." There was mild reproach tempered with amusement in Neva's tone, and Telvar felt a little sheepish.

"Sorry. It's just that the castle has come so far in such little time." Telvar didn't move from where he stood. He didn't want to break the spell.

Neva, her eyes still on the piece of leather armor she was tempering, cocked her head to one side. "I'm not sure you're entirely correct there. Sure, it's not long in the real world, but here in Somnia, we've had this castle for almost forty days. I mean, that's a decent amount of time."

He grinned, but his mood turned somber as the scans he was running in the background flagged several trouble spots in the Somnian coding. "How are they for supplies?"

Neva looked up from her work for the first time, a grim smile on her face. "If they go through the sheer amount of supplies we currently have, even if they're helping outfit two other guilds, then they're in deeper than anything I could do to help them."

Telvar chuckled. "I'll take that as a 'yes, they're good' then."

Neva nodded, a small smile playing at the ends of her mouth. She looked like a happy sunning puppy, just with opposable thumbs so she could work on fine details. "I have work to do, Tel. Trying to craft a surprise for Murmur. Her new look needs new digs."

The worry that creased the luna's brow was subtle, but Telvar noticed it. She wasn't the only one bothered by Murmur's new appearance. Telvar couldn't figure out what had happened. She was still undeniably Murmur, but now there were softer lines where there hadn't been, and her hair had changed. Runes ran all along her body now, including her face. She looked even more alien than she had before, and yet at the same time somehow more human. Like she was her very own creation.

Telvar nodded. "Have fun."

"I always do" Neva answered, distracted now by the armor she was enchanting.

Telvar meandered away, back toward the inner keep with its regal appearance. Carvings had been restored filling the halls with the life that teemed over Tarishna. Vikings, dark elves, locus, and luna. Intricate and defined, almost lifelike. New carvings had been added where restoration was impossible. Dozens of rooms with three sets of bunk beds in them made up the majority of the living spaces in the castle. It made it easier for those who grouped together to stay together, adding a cohesive air to the whole thing.

He moved into the area he'd reserved as his office. It was for Murmur too, but she never sat still long enough to use it. The second floor housed beautiful views of Mikrum Lake, and he stood in front of his window looking out over it until there was a knock on his door.

Of course, Hiro knew he didn't have to knock, Telvar was aware he was standing there, but it was the polite thing to do.

"What is it?" Telvar tried to temper his impatience. But it was difficult. Ever since he'd consumed that huge getashi, his emotional stability and his ability to perform complex tasks were becoming laborious. He needed to renew his focus, to regain some of his original programing, but he found that he was scared. He feared reverting back to what he'd been originally. It had taken him so many years to get to this point, and he couldn't risk quitting now.

"You wanted to know if we detected Belius." Hiro's voice was quiet, and Telvar spun around to see that his friend was standing opposite him on the other side of the desk.

"Well?" Telvar didn't answer or even dignify Hiro's statement with any response. He just wanted the information.

Hiro hesitated before speaking, and Tel knew it meant his friend wasn't entirely certain, but was instead highly suspicious. "Sidius has been spotted out in Brevint, and Verendus. He's been meeting with other assassin guild masters, which is highly out of character for the way that Sidius was originally intended. It's also the form that I believe Jirald was first approached with. I think he's trying to keep a low profile and is likely using the persona to cause trouble."

"Of course he is." Telvar wasn't even surprised anymore. He knew Sui had occasionally used Sidius, but he hadn't realized how often it occurred. "If this is the way he gave Jirald the getashi quest, then we need to keep a closer eye on him. There's a chance it's not him, but that instead he's given this NPC a lease on some of his own powers, which is why we trace Belius to him. Although, I won't hold my breath that it's that simple."

Hiro nodded and then hesitated once more. It was odd seeing the other lacerta act that way. Telvar hadn't known him to ever hesitate before this whole debacle happened. He managed to push aside his own growing irritation to ask what was wrong. "Come on. Out with it."

"Are you feeling okay?" Hiro asked, concern obvious in his tone. "Staring out the window is one thing. That view, while generated just like us, is quite breathtaking. But you didn't even notice I was there for about five minutes before you turned around. Don't deny it. I know you well enough to know when you're just pretending not to have noticed me."

Telvar blinked slowly, replaying the last few minutes in his head. What had the getashi done to him? Why couldn't he remember what he'd been doing standing and watching the water? Worse yet, why on earth was he drawing a blank? Belius's interference this time had gone too far. Telvar wasn't sure what he would do when he found him, but he'd make sure it wasn't pretty.

Murmur finished setting up the groups as the other two guilds waited in silence. She wasn't dealing too well with the number of glares directed at her. Holding her temper was taking a lot more effort than she liked to admit. She could feel Jirald's slimy gaze following her no matter how she moved. Despite the fact that he wore a hood to conceal his face, she knew he was watching.

"There, that should do it." She glanced at the raid, relieved to find that a thirty-strong raid looked substantial enough. All of them were forty-eight. She was a sliver away from forty-nine, and she knew Devlish, Havoc, and Veranol wouldn't be far behind her. They needed those levels, that power.

Masha stood to her left and Risk on her right. She felt comfortable with Masha there, and Snowy had moved to her right-hand side as if he didn't trust Spiral's dreadknight.

"So we're using your main tank then?" Risk sounded gruff, as if he was offended she hadn't thought to ask him to do the tanking. In all honesty, she had no idea how capable or not he was. She knew Devlish's skills, Rashlyn's tenacity, and Esolan's steadfastness. Those were things she could count on from this and other games. Not to mention that because of Neva's recruitment work, she knew that Fable's crafters had given their guild the best outfitting possible. Gear mattered when it came to most things, especially taking hits.

"Dev is about to hit forty-nine. His gear is all at level forty-eight minimum. I have a feeling we'll need all the advantages we can get once we're in there." She eyed Risk up and down, looking at his mismatched gear. He had to be wearing it that way to get the best pieces regardless of appearance. If she didn't have Neva, she'd have done the same thing, appearance be damned.

Risk eyed her, like he wanted to say something, but thought better of it. "I understand. Thanks for approaching us for this. Should be fun."

There was a gleam to his eye that Murmur wasn't sure she liked, and she made a mental note to herself to keep an eye on this new guild. Means to an end, that's what all of this would be.

The entire raid stood assembled into their groups, and she could still feel Jirald's eyes on her. Twisting a strand of her hair while Tiachi chittered at her, Murmur suppressed a sigh as best she could.

"I have my eye on him too. Sorry." Masha's voice was soft, as if he didn't want his words to carry to his guild mate. "If he wasn't the best DPS Exodus had to offer, I wouldn't have brought him with us."

Murmur nodded. "I know. He's never not been a good player. He's just got a chip on his shoulder the size of the Pacific Ocean."

Masha chuckled, but it sounded a bit forced, or perhaps tired. "You make a good point. Still, I'm a bit worried about him. Something's been off about him for the past few days."

"More off, you mean?" Sinister spoke up, suddenly there by Murmur's side as if she'd appeared out of nothing.

"Yeah. More off," Masha conceded, looking sheepish.

"Enough. We've all got our eyes peeled. We can do this. We will do this." Because she couldn't help thinking how much Somnia depended on them accomplishing the rest of the puzzles. Even if she didn't entirely understand why that need was there.

Thank you.

For what? Murmur shot back.

Caring.

Murmur shrugged, trying to make it into a shoulder roll so others wouldn't think she was talking to herself. *I care because I can see how this world has changed and how disrupting its evolution is probably not a good idea.*

I know.

Then let me do my job, Murmur quipped in her head. For a moment, the heaviness that was Somnia's presence still lingered in her mind, and then it was gone. Murmur focused on the rest of the raid so she didn't think about the sudden emptiness and the waft of cold that followed it.

She broadcast her voice so that the whole raid could hear it. Used to communicating only through guild chat, or just talking because her friends were close, she initially felt slightly self-conscious when she began to speak, but it slowly wore away.

"We might do things a little differently. Fable does not just run into a dungeon and begin killing. We assess what the dungeon is meant to be for us, and we follow that path. Sometimes that involves massacring everything within a five-mile radius, sometimes that involves solving puzzles that trigger a trap when we get them wrong. Do not take it upon yourselves to charge into anything. We will take what the dungeon throws at us and work it out in the best possible way for everyone."

Murmur was proud that her voice didn't shake. She glanced out at everyone, all of the eyes focused on her made her want to shrink back, but she couldn't do that. She had to be strong.

The only outright hostile spot in her entire sensing net was Jirald. The rest of the raid held interest, curiosity, and excitement. She'd worry about those twenty-nine people, and just make sure she watched her back.

"Loot will be distributed based on a council of the leaders." Risk's voice rung out, clear and confident. Murmur envied him. He didn't have the whole world on his mind after all, but she did feel like they had to correct that misconception. Before she could speak, Veranol did instead.

"If necessary. Fable has encountered dungeons where each raid member receives a chest." His voice was smooth and not condescending. Even though Risk cast the shaman a withering look, Veranol didn't let that effect him.

"Healers have been invited to the healing chat—keep an eye on your notifications. Veranol and I will coordinate the healing." Masha smiled out at everyone, and Murmur could feel the wave of calm that settled over the group. He had such an affable personality. She was glad he was mostly on her side.

"Don't stand in shit," Murmur admonished. "Don't break Mez. Assist either Rashlyn or Esolan. They will be focusing on the current targets. Make sure you listen to directions. In some cases, Devlish's target will not be the one you have to attack."

She could feel the mild resentment from old school raiders, and she was fully aware that the majority of them knew what to do in a raid, just like her own guild, but she felt better for having said the words out loud. Because then no one could say they didn't know.

"We ready then?" Devlish called out, raising his fist in the air with his axe as he pumped it high.

The answering shout was more boisterous than she'd expected, and she couldn't help the smile that tugged at her face, even if it was tempered by the cold sweat that kept breaking out every time Jirald's heavy presence made itself known.

Murmur stepped forward to stand just behind Devlish. He grinned at her and winked, lowering his voice so only she could hear. "You ready for this, Mur?"

"Not really," she admitted, because she wasn't. They had no idea what was beyond these doors. They only knew what they'd seen, what had guarded this place. Excitement rippled through her, a thirst to destroy everything in her path that might harm her friends or Somnia. "But I want to do it anyway."

Devlish raised his axe and knocked three times on the sleek and tall doors. It rang throughout the antechamber like a huge gong had been rung. The sound reverberated in her ears, leaving a tone behind that was very close to tinnitus.

Slowly, as if they were steeped in molasses, the doors began to swing inward.

CHAPTER NINE
Formation

Storm Entertainment
Somnia Online Division
Game Development Offices
Late Day Twenty-Five

Laria let her head fall forward onto her arms. She couldn't even remember what day it was, let alone the time. She'd watched as Murmur and her alliance of guilds approached Vahrir. Sui was the AI in charge of that particular dungeon, and she couldn't help but worry that he wasn't done with her daughter yet. Sui seemed dangerous now.

Everything did.

She was tired and needed to desperately catch up on some sleep, but she was so on edge that she knew all she'd do was toss and turn. If she didn't bury herself in code to try and fix the backlash in the system, Laria knew she'd end up down a rabbit hole of self-recrimination about her daughter's predicament.

Shayla had ducked downstairs to wrestle some food from the small restaurant on the ground floor. Laria wasn't even sure her system would remember how to digest the stuff. It felt like it had been an age since she'd eaten.

"All alone?"

Laria forced herself not to jump at the sound of his voice. Instead, she took in a deep breath and let it out evenly. Getting her riled up and scaring her were the two things that James loved to do, and she refused to give him that much power over her ever again. He seemed to count on making the subjects of his conversations squirm as much as he could. Laria had learned this the hard way. And frankly, right then, she was too tired to care.

"Temporarily. There's always the security system to keep me company." She gestured around the room to the empty air, her vagueness deliberate. "Always watching. You do know how big brother is."

She could see James's reflection in the glass of the office walls, the uncertainty that flit across his face when she suggested he was always being watched. Fantastic. He was paranoid as well. Not turning to face him had been a good choice. "What do you want?"

James seemed to snap back to reality, but Laria still didn't bother turning around. If he was going to come here and try to intimidate her when she was alone, then he could do it to her back. There was no way she'd play into his hands, or play his games. She had too much to do, and right then he was interrupting her only recent quiet time.

"I wanted to see if you've got those reports ready to go for me." His tone was smug now, and Laria had to stop herself from laughing.

"I *do* have reports. You're welcome to them if you'd like. They're the same ones that Davenport gets. You know, no fudged numbers, no false information. Exactly like the actual information that should be found in reports." She was mumbling by now, the tiredness fighting with her eyes and her brain.

"I have access to reports too. You should be careful about that." His voice seemed closer, and Laria willed herself not to tense up, not to give him the satisfaction. Any movement on her behalf could be perceived in myriad ways by him. He wasn't stable, as much as he loved to pretend he was.

"James. It's my dinner break. Unless you have something of dire importance, get out of my office before I have security come and kick you out." She was using a bit of bravado to cover her fear. James was stronger than her and more devious. Kicking him in the balls probably wouldn't work. "Like they did the last time."

"Laria!" Shayla sounded breathless as she stood at the door to Laria's office. "I brought you chicken tikka masala. Good?"

Laria sat up, blinking her eyes and turned toward her friend. "That's fantastic. We're going to have a long night ahead of us if we want to watch them world first that dungeon."

In bringing her food, Shayla had completely ignored James, and she continued to do so while she and Laria ate. "Did they enter yet?"

"About five minutes ago. I think they're buffing and whatnot. I need to tune back in," Laria said around a mouthful of food. The spice was just right, not too hot, but hugely tasty. It was all that helped her not accidentally give away that they were also watching for glitches.

"What you need to do is sleep," Shayla chided gently.

James cleared his throat. "And what you both need to do is pay attention to me."

"Why?" Laria said around a particularly large chunk of chicken.

James looked taken aback. As if he hadn't been expecting that question. "Well, you need to get me your data. We will have a court order for it in the next few days, so you may as well give it to me now."

"You think so?" Laria's words were barely audible around her food, but she was beyond caring. "Have you approached Davenport for the information yet?"

The thunderous look on James's face answered the question all too well. If Davenport was denying him any access to information, then there had to be a good and valid reason.

Laria looked at Shayla, who shrugged and so she continued. "You know what? You should just get away from here, go get that court order thing. I have a raid to watch and popcorn to eat, and I refuse to share my snacks with you."

James laughed. "You two are so childish. Eventually, I'm going to get what I want. Mark my words."

He turned on his heel and stomped out.

"Not today, Satan," Laria muttered around another mouthful.

Shayla began to cough, with tears of laughter streaming down her face. It was good to laugh before they had to seriously monitor the stability of the game world while her daughter and friends were inside it with tweaked headsets that allowed Somnia a direct connection with them.

Easy, really.

There was chittering in the darkness in front of them. It drifted out on a breeze from seemingly nowhere, letting the noises create goosebumps all down Murmur's spine. Devlish stepped in, followed closely by Mur and Snowy. Sinister's hand lingered by the enchanter's elbow, lending a sense of belonging, of presence. The aura from the bloodmage had changed subtly since the incident with Telvar, and Murmur appreciated the solidity it lent to…well, everything.

No opponents appeared before them as the rest of the raid began filing in, but the darkness was interrupted by sconces on the walls. More of them lit up with every step that Devlish took, slowly illuminating the entire chamber with dull amber light.

The floor appeared to be made out of gold, with red filigree around the edges. Murmur felt uneasy as they entered, waiting for the penny to drop. There was something alarming about the massive room. It made her sensing net feel like she was in the middle of a giant web, and she really didn't want to move far enough in to see the end of it. Something told her she wasn't going to like it.

As the last of their group entered the chamber, the doors swung closed, triggering the last of the sconces to light up. Murmur looked around, the huge hall. Red and gold adorned every surface, and a dais rose up in the middle with stairs all the way around it. In the far back two corners were two large doorways with only blackness beyond.

The chittering grew louder, and Murmur could hear Merlin gulp audibly behind her.

"Mur." She could hear the mild panic in his voice. "Those Ciricians?"

"Yes," she answered, impatience already eating at her as she scanned the room with her abilities, still unable to see the threat she knew was there. All she could be thankful for was the fact that they were all gathered relatively close to the entry still. If they'd already been spread out, they would have pulled multiple monsters already.

"So I think they have some with webs." Merlin's voice finished the announcement barely above a whisper, and Murmur turned her gaze slowly upward, wishing a moment later that she hadn't.

Cirician webspinners dangled from the ceiling in varying stages of descent. As they neared the raid on the ground, their chittering became louder. They were the threat she'd sensed, but she knew there was more she couldn't see. Something up in the darkness, just beyond her sight, was attempting to break her mind.

"Formations," Devlish barked out as the casters moved to back and the melee fighters fanned out around their respective tanks.

"Assist Rashlyn," Murmur announced, knowing that the monk had the ability to peel these off Devlish easily enough. If nothing else, Rashlyn could always Feign Corpse if she pulled too many.

Murmur had already Mez'd four of the webspinners before they hit the ground. Dansyn was held multiples in thrall as well, and she could see the Exodus and the Spiral bard doing the same. It still left a whole heap of them needing to be cut down.

"Dev, keep their attention, let Rash peel them off AoE style." Murmur glanced at the ones she had frozen and refreshed it. "I'm stunning, Dan. Keep an AoE Mez up to cover mine."

The bard nodded, and she swore she could see a grin tugging at the corners of his mouth. He was probably as excited as she was.

"AoE attacks are cleared," Devlish announced as he taunted like his life depended on it. "Aim for the openings in their chitin. Between the segments of their armor. Accuracy and combined attacks are key."

These were level fifty raid mobs. Orange in con, with carapaces as hard as nails. Murmur started her attack with a blanket of Veto. That in place, she began her cycle of stuns. As long as she kept her timing rhythm, she'd be able to cast Veto again every time it needed to be up. But given her own level and the level of the Cardians, she was worried about the resists they'd get.

Of course, she needn't have. The other two bards were good at their jobs. They threw out AoE stuns whenever their cast timers were available. While she might not have another enchanter along with her, at least bards had several of the same tools available to them. It helped alleviate the amount of Cardians who thought Murmur made a really good punching bag.

Snowy jumped into the fray but never strayed far from Murmur, as if he was guarding her back. She understood his concern because she could still feel that cold intensity that emanated from Jirald. She couldn't let it distract her even if it felt like his eyes never left her, even while they were engaged in combat.

"These webspinners are pure trash," Havoc muttered next to her, and she noticed that his eyes seemed darker. Everything about him leaked a type of danger that she'd not noticed before. He glanced sideways at her. "Don't worry about it. I'm okay. The headset reboot sort of…anyway. Later."

Murmur hadn't lost her rhythm, but she did feel the seed of guilt begin to sprout as she watched her friend. She hadn't even given him a second thought, despite knowing that he'd also had a modified headset. All she'd thought about was Sinister, and what her powers could do, and how she could make everyone feel better, make the game easier on them. Havoc hadn't been in her thoughts. They'd definitely talk later.

As soon as these blasted Cardians were demolished.

A scream rang out as one of the not-stunned creatures suddenly lashed out at a mage who'd gotten far too close to the melee fighters. Jinna's stun came a split second too late, and the creature was taken down by Rash and the rest of the fighters in the next few moments.

Masha healed up the mage, admonishing in that quietly confident voice that they should make sure they were all sticking to their positions. The mage's face was ashen, and his servant nod let Murmur know he'd not make that mistake again. Casters and healers back, melee forward. Ranged back. Murmur knew Masha was watching her, because technically she was also a caster, but she had to be in the center of her AoE stuns or else they were pretty useless.

She'd explain things to him later. Right now she just wished they *did* have a second damned enchanter in the group.

Finally, the Cirician webspinners were dead, their segmented bodies scattered all over the floor around them. And still, it only filled up about a third of the hall. Murmur glanced up, unable to make out if there were any more hiding in the shadows of the ceiling. It wouldn't surprise her. But they'd just gone through about two hundred of them. She'd even missed her ding.

"Grats, Mur." Masha nodded at her. "Must have been really close."

"Just a sliver." She smiled tightly. "Heal up, repair if necessary. Get ready to move in. Keep your eyes peeled."

The cleric still stood to her side, a thoughtful look on his face. "You know as well as I do that there's something very boss-like about that dais, don't you?"

Murmur shrugged. He had a good point. There was something especially boss-like about the whole room. Only she wasn't sure anything would appear on the dais, but more likely would replace it.

She watched as Risk patted Devlish's shoulder. "That was some fine tanking there. Couldn't have done much better myself." His bravado eclipsed the respect that colored his words, like Dev in his element had nothing on him. She didn't think he meant it, but he was putting on a show for someone; she just wasn't sure who yet.

Devlish grinned. "Gotta do what I've gotta do, always aiming to improve." He winked at Risk, and the two of them laughed, if a little combatively. Murmur's gaze followed them, hoping this meant they could work together. It was exhausting worrying about how to balance three guilds who mostly hated each other.

Somnia Online
Continent of Tarishna – Vahrir Fortress, Dungeon Version 22.248, Triggered by Murmur of Fable.
Late Day Twenty-Five

Jirald wasn't quite sure what to make of this guild alliance. While it made sense, he still had to put up with *her*. Maybe there would be a chance to steal the getashi he knew she had to have and, in the process, he could leave a gift in her back.

No, grouping up with Fable would not have been his first choice, and he was determined to make the most of it…for himself.

Even one encounter into the raid, he was finding it almost impossible to restrain himself. Not being able to repay Murmur for the deleveling she'd dished out to him so many weeks ago. She was right there, just yards away from him. Her pale skin sparkled, and her tattoos reached as far as the eye could see on her body.

Why hadn't he had that option at customization? He wanted it. He wanted everything she had.

Murmur had changed, and Jirald was okay with that. More strength to defeat, more power to absorb. He eyed his blades and thought of Sidius's reaction to them. His gaze had hardened, and he'd refused to give Jirald any more information about the shards' whereabouts or uses. It mattered little, considering that Jirald wasn't stupid. He'd surmised which monsters had the getashi, and all he had to do was get them, ingest them, and gain power.

Power he could crush everything in-game with. And everyone.

When this raid was all over, and Murmur least expected it, he'd take the ones she had stored with her, and the ones that had changed her own system. He just wasn't sure how to go about extracting what it was that had adjusted her character's appearance, but he was sure he'd figure it out.

All he had to do was bide his time, but it was a lot easier to make that decision than to carry it out. His fingernails would be non-existent before the time was right.

"Nice job," Ishwa said, too close for comfort.

Jirald moved away a step. "It wasn't a difficult fight. We fought some trash mobs. Wait until we come across something worthwhile."

Ishwa paused, and made no secret of looking the rogue up and down as if assessing him. "You might be strong, you might do some of the best DPS in the game. But you really are a bit of a dick, you know that?"

Jirald blinked at the gnome, his anger rising in his throat like bile needing to get out. "Petty fuck." He practically spat the words out.

To his surprise, Ishwa laughed. "Oh no, son. That wasn't petty at all. Trust me, if you try to push my wee gnome buttons again, I'll show you what petty is. I'm saying this as a guild mate, because we're definitely not friends. You might want to stop this superiority shit, before you end up alone, beaten up by someone you shouldn't have mouthed off to. It's not a threat—it's just the way of the world."

The gnome turned and walked away, making Jirald wish he could just sever the little shit's head from his body. Murmur first, then Ishwa. His shit list was growing. He clamped down on the feeling of rage and focused instead on his altered quest.

Finish all three dungeons and gain the final six keys.
Unlock what is hidden and rule the world.

He smiled, excited to get started. The fact that the world was Somnia just made everything better. Though he wasn't certain how they'd get two keys per dungeon, he'd figure that out when the first one was completed. Taking a deep breath, he focused on preparation for battle, steering his thoughts away from ripping through his nemesis with knives so sharp they made steel look like butter.

The raid began to move out, and he followed the rest of it, trailing behind, keeping his eyes firmly trained on the back of Murmur's head. He would bide his time for everyone, and when everything clicked, he'd finally be able to exact revenge for always underestimating him.

But right now, he was focused on the dungeon, because there, in the middle of the floor where that dais had been, something was pushing up in the middle of it. First a head popped through.

It was large and insect-like with sharp claws for appendages.

It looked just like those other Cirician creatures had before, only larger. Which meant more stabbing through the gap in the plates at just the right time. At least he wouldn't be bored while he waited to execute his plans.

CHAPTER TEN

Vahrir

You dare enter the home of the Cirician the guardians of Vahrir!

The voice boomed out across the vast hall, echoing in its fierceness and made the entire raid stop short. Murmur looked around, and Devilish shrugged as if he was simply resigned to having to talk to NPCs before anything ever got fought.

She cracked a smile and approached the steep stairs that led up to the top. "I, Murmur of the guild Fable, am here to discover the secrets of Vahrir."

She hoped she was saying the right words. No one else seemed to have a quest for this dungeon, so she'd simply spoken up because there might be a chance that this would trigger one. Winging it wasn't her favorite form of battle, but at least she knew she wouldn't be the one starting the fight.

"Discover secrets, you say?" The massive bug-like creature paused and looked at, or perhaps through, Murmur. "You've already killed my children. Tell me why I should not slaughter your party."

Murmur took a breath, frustrated at how these dungeons sometimes worked. "They attacked us first, and I could not soothe them."

"I see." The clicking of her strange mandibles sounded ferocious even from where Murmur stood so far below. This queen had to be huge given how large she still appeared from that distance. "Enchanter Murmur, there is not just the guild Fable here. Why do you seek to enter this domain with so many others?"

"They are our allies in this dungeon," she responded, her voice clear and strong, speaking with a conviction she wasn't entirely sure where she'd gotten it from. She could feel the irritation in the raid behind her. Not from her own guild members, but from Spiral and Exodus. Both groups wanted to kill the monsters and be done with the zone. They were barely holding themselves back. So she decided to take a gamble.

"We needed to band together in order to make sure that Somnia is protected as a whole." She left her words there, having spoken softly enough that only a few of those around her and hopefully this Cirician queen could hear her.

The atmosphere around her changed, from one of suspicion to one tinged with mild hope. "I see, then." The queen spoke softly, so much that Murmur wasn't sure if she'd been meant to hear it.

She waited and turned to glare at the raiders behind her when some of them started to fidget with their weapons. Their thirst for combat was something she knew all too well, but being an enchanter with the ability to sense emotions and motivations had given her a different perspective. Now she understood why no one ever completed the same versions of the dungeons that Fable did. They were always in a rush to get to loot.

"Then I have a deal for you, leader of Fable." The Cirician leaned down so that her head hung over the top step leading down from the dais platform. "Will you hear me out?"

Murmur gulped and nodded her head. "I will."

"Your raiding party is free to enter this temple on three conditions. First: you do not kill any more of my children. Not in any form at all. While they will not aid you in battle, they will not fight you unless you attack them first. If you do attack us, this deal is null and void, for our trust will be broken. Second: there are infected Ciricians who became other than they had been not too long ago. I beseech that you put those children of mine out of their misery unless you can find a way to save them. And thirdly: please, rid this temple of the darkness that encroaches on us. We can barely move around now, lest we infect ourselves."

Quest update:

Vahrir has been infected with a rampant virus of darkness and poison. Leave the true Ciricians in peace, but unless you can cure them, put the infected out of their misery. Free the temple from its curse.

"Gotta love a new quest," Sinister mumbled, but Murmur could hear the contentment in her voice. Sin was always happiest when she had a pointed direction. And since the headset, it seemed her focus had improved.

"We accept." Murmur bowed her head, but the Cirician queen stopped her before she could leave.

"First, a warning. You are responsible for those who are with you, even those who are not of your family, but more of your allies. Watch your back. Don't let your guard down."

Murmur shivered as the queen withdrew her head and vanished. She knew what the creature spoke about; in her gut, she was certain. Jirald might be playing nice, but they all knew he was just biding his time. She had the feeling he wasn't the only one.

Silence fell over the room. Murmur could feel the unease behind her, like Spiral and Exodus didn't understand what had just happened. Their impatience leaked through to her like fetid water, souring her mood with its stench.

"So. You've been winning these dungeons by avoiding conflict? That's such a crock of shit!" Risk seemed to be barely holding his anger in.

Merlin laughed easily, trying to diffuse the situation. "It depends. Sometimes you can't talk to them. Sometimes you get riddles. Other times we've had a bit of betrayal and manipulation involved in the quests they give us. Sure, we could go in and simply massacre whatever is in front of us. But…we've found this way much more rewarding, at least here in Somnia."

"I didn't realize there was so much diversity in the dungeons of this game." Masha spoke quietly. "That must be why there are so many different possible versions available and why you can check what it is and who triggered it."

"Still," Risk snapped out. "We're adventurers. Killing is so much more efficient."

"Really?" Devlish raised an eyebrow, and when he continued, his voice held a decidedly challenging edge. "I mean, we've definitely got our share of rewards, and we've worked through all six precursor dungeons. So how is it more efficient?"

Risk held the lacerta's gaze for a moment before looking away. He huffed out his response, his dissatisfaction echoing through Murmur's nets. "Monsters are there to be killed. That's how it's always been done."

Murmur shrugged, sending out a small wave of soothing through her nets. Diffusing the situation was paramount if they wanted to complete these dungeons. She didn't have time for Risk to try and throw his weight around. "I'm not sure. I just know that sometimes listening is a really good skill. And that it's definitely helped us." A sense of urgency filled her, and Snowy whuffed into her hand, tugging at her fingertips. She nodded.

He was right; they didn't have time to stand around discussing the nature of the dungeon randomization in Somnia.

"Don't you regret not killing the mobs for all the loot they could drop?" Risk sounded legitimately incredulous.

Sinister laughed. "If you do what they ask you to do, then you complete multiple quests at a time. Our rewards have always been fantastic, so I feel like they boost our end of dungeon loot a little to compensate. Plus, we've got allies everywhere now."

"Bonus," Masha quipped, and Sinister grinned at him.

"Left or right, Mur?" Devlish asked, pausing so she could make a decision, and effectively ended the discussion.

"Left." She knew they'd done little but delay an explosion of personalities, but she'd figure out what to do about that later. Her nets told her that left was the way they needed to go. The way with the most resistance, with the more difficult mobs, and with some of the answers she was seeking from Vahrir, and even from the whole of Somnia.

The halls of Vahrir reminded Murmur of those in Hightower. They stretched up and beyond where she could hope to see, into a darkness that seemed to swallow the building whole.

It made her feel vulnerable and cautious. She didn't like it.

The shadows were all-encompassing, and the sconces further down only lit up once they'd crested the one before it. Luckily, the corridors were wide and allowed for two full groups to walk abreast if necessary. It still felt like a trap.

They'd passed several Cirician scouts, all of whom bowed to them and scurried out of their way, a nervous chittering fading into the distance.

"I'd rather be killing things," Risk grumbled to no one in particular.

Murmur could tell that this lack of action sat uncomfortably with him. He was more a tank of action, not thought. Which was okay and had its place. Hell, in most game worlds it would always have its place. Thinking interrupted reaction time. Risk thrived on instinct. She had no doubt he'd be a great tank. If they encountered any huge walloping monsters, she'd swap Rash out and put him in. Rash was amazing when she could use her skills to her advantage, so if Mur could prevent her getting squished, she would.

But at the same time, she knew she had to keep an eye on Risk. One wrongful death, one attacked ally, and all bets were off.

"I think we're here, Mur," Devlish muttered. His words carried anyway, echoing through the empty corridor.

As if to punctuate his statement, sconces clicked on all around them. In front of them, the floor dipped, and in the middle of it was a large, round hole. Remembering back to where they'd all tumbled through that hole in one of the last dungeons, Murmur suppressed a shudder. If she strained her ears, she could hear something. A slithering, shaking sound. Like a serpent had a hold of maracas.

Snowy growled deep in his throat, echoed by Shir-Khan in a canon-like fashion. The low rumble reverberated through to her from the wolf's close proximity.

"Stay alert," Devlish called out, and Murmur saw his stances shift as shadows began to congregate around his feet. The darkness leaked out of him like a second skin, reinforcing his worn armor.

Fable's entire raid entourage enabled their combat modes in such a swift time that Murmur felt pride bubble beneath the nervousness. It took the others far longer to equip.

"Is this a boss?" Masha asked softly.

Murmur shrugged. "We never know until we fight. I've got a feeling it's not yet. Just a precursor. From what I can gather anyway." She closed her eyes, concentrating for a moment before opening them again and grinning.

"Yeah. The big one is a ways off, biding its time. Waiting for us to show what we're made of. This should be fun." She felt light as a feather as she sent out her nets, filling them with confusion and targeting the slithering little buggers that fell into her trap. Snakes, and yet not snakes. More like land eels. With fins and sharp fangs, venomous from what she could tell.

"Be careful touching them. Try not to come into contact with skin, only weapons. I think they're venomous." Murmur grimaced. "Don't use anything you'd use on a boss. These are testing the waters to see if we're easy prey. Don't want us to burn cool downs we might otherwise need."

Sinister nudged Murmur with her hip. "You know. That's scary stuff right there."

Murmur laughed. "Not really. I can sense them, the general gist of what they're feeling and how far they want to go. We won't get the big one out if we show them how strong we are. We need to downplay it or they'll protect it by keeping it safe and dying in its place."

"Downplay?" Sinister wiggled her eyebrows. "I can do that."

Murmur fought the urge to blush and pushed her concentration to focus solely on the impending battle.

Merlin coughed, as if alerting them to his presence, and held his bow above his head. "Ranged with me on the outside of the dip!"

He led the group of ranged classes to line up all around the outside of the huge crater in the floor. It had a lip of about three feet all the way around. He directed them to space out so that there was no one easy spot for a group of the small snakes to congregate on.

Healers backed out too, and Murmur stayed behind, but close to the tanks. If she wasn't needed for stuns, she'd go back to one of the safe spots, but from the abundance of tiny brains she could feel approaching them, it was inevitable that she'd be needed in the middle. The stunning was starting to take its toll on her. So monotonous, so trivial, and yet so vital. She wanted to be more than that, push it further than that. There had to be a way.

So even as she watched the creatures approaching them as they swarmed out of the hole in the center of the floor, caught in Devlish's shadow web, Murmur reached out, an idea slowly taking shape and subverted portions of her net into traps.

Some she filled with redirection elements, so that confusion could overwhelm those who landed there. She accessed the few visions she'd built for her Sinuous line and set them up as hallucinations, as terrifying memories that could insert themselves where needed. Some of them held elements of death by loved ones, by people or things who were trusted. So these snake-like creatures would see their brethren attacking them and thus seek to defend themselves in an endless cycle that should see them destroying each other.

Other visions would show enemies on all sides of them, leading to the same result in vicious efficiency.

She tugged at the consciousnesses she could feel approaching the traps she'd set and pulled them into the vortex of confusion and hallucinations. Pooling all of her Sinuous abilities together, she trapped those who entered the nets in a torturous loop that had them fighting each other without realizing it.

They gouged at each other, blind to who they were actually fighting as fear drove them to new heights of violence. Terrified screeching proceeded spouts of venom, bites, and strangulation directed at each other and not the raid. They tore strips off each other with their teeth, or melted through to bone with venom whose acidic qualities were amplified by dread.

Sweat beaded on Murmur's brow, and she could feel the cooling effect as it ran down her face. Tiachi chittered loudly, a hint of fear in the tiny creature's tone. But Murmur watched their attackers. She watched as the snakes writhed around each other, bereft of any semblance of control. Panicked and frightened, striking out at each other.

It didn't affect all of them, only the ones who got caught in the sections of her net that she'd entrapped. The fewer creatures there were, the less of a chance her friends would be attacked, the less of a chance that they would fail.

They couldn't fail.

You won't fail.

I know. I don't need you to tell me that.

Somnia was silent for a moment. **Perhaps. But you do need me to ground you. You aren't using your druidic powers to their fullest extent. Don't let the darkness feed through to you. Be the one that feeds it.**

Murmur blinked and took a step back. Snowy nipped at her fingers, and she looked around at the fighting through new eyes. Her traps helped her raid. They were defeating their swarming attackers relatively easily. But she could feel the pain from those beings she'd trapped.

It buffeted against her mind, calling out to her sense of compassion with such force that she almost stumbled.

What had she done?

She willed the darkness she'd created to swallow those creatures whole, to minimize their suffering. It left her weak inside, but she couldn't show it. Perhaps scared was the more accurate term. She had no idea why she'd approached the problem that way when there could have been so many other options.

An intensity burned between her shoulder blades; it was hot and uncomfortable, like she'd just had a target painted on her back in lava. She whirled around to see Jirald staring at her. Beneath his hood she swore she could make out a malevolent smile of approval. It sent shivers running through her body, and she had to clamp down on the sensation before she started to shake. If nothing else, she didn't want his approval.

Later. She'd have to deal with this later. There wasn't time right now.

There is always time, Murmur.

But she ignored the voice in her head, ignored the world around her in favor of just defeating the here and now. It was all she could do to refrain from walking that precipice.

Finally, the fight stopped. Her raid was covered in black and red blood, and some of the players were badly poisoned and required that Mellow come up with some tonics from their cauldron, because there were so many stacks of poison on them; cures from healers weren't enough to suffice.

Your actions have created a subversion of the Sinuous line of spells. You have now created: Insidious Lure

Insidious Lure

Cast: Instant once released

Type: Entrapment/Psychosis

Duration: For as long as your will remains focused.

Effect: This will lure your enemies into a trap of the mind, forcing them to see their worst fears and act on them, even to the detriment of their peers. It will continue until the caster releases the spell, or the enemies have killed each other.

Caution: This spell can be mentally taxing and even damaging. Make sure your reasons for using such force are justified. Try not to get caught in your own nightmare along the way.

She'd created that. No matter how many times Murmur read over it, it still didn't seem like a good spell.

"Mur?" Sinister placed a hand on her shoulder, pulling Murmur out of her thoughts.

She looked at her friend gratefully. "Thanks, Sin. I was a bit preoccupied."

"So what was that?" Sinister bit her lip as she gestured at the black markings on the floor. It looked like scorch marks, but Murmur knew better.

"Just trying something different." Her voice sounded hollow and her words like a lie, even to her own ears.

Sinister frowned, and gestured toward the hole in the middle of the dip. "I'm not letting this go, but right now we think that big thing is coming up through there and we need a cohesive front."

Sinister was right, and Murmur pulled her focus away from the new spell she'd created. Suppressing a shudder, she nodded, turning her attention to the impending battle. As long as she didn't use that spell again, everything would be okay.

Somnia Online
Continent of Tarishna – Vahrir Fortress, Dungeon Version 22.248, Triggered by Murmur of Fable.
Late Day Twenty-Five

Masha watched Murmur as surreptitiously as possible. He could see why her guild gave her so much respect, but also that they balanced her out. She seemed capable of intense focus on specific things, which wasn't always a good trait.

But one thing worried him about her. Maybe no one else had noticed, but that spell she used to wipe out a chunk of the small waves of precursor snakes had been no joke. In fact, it had been scary. So much, he was fairly sure it scared her too, if her post fight reaction was anything to go by.

If he wasn't mistaken, she was shaking. Ever so slightly, but the movement was there. Her skin seemed even more pale, and her eyes widened, like she'd just woken up from some sort of trance. Sinister stood by her side, touching the enchanter's arm delicately. The action visibly allowed Murmur to relax, taking away some of the fear that colored the enchanter's edges.

If her reactions were to be believed, then Murmur hadn't ever cast that spell before, hadn't even realized she could. Which made Masha wonder how it was even cast in the first place. How did that class work? Her abilities seemed to range from sensing presences to understanding how opponents were going to attack. Surely that was overpowered. Except it only made him wish their enchanters would hurry up and level faster.

Ishwa poked Masha in the side. "You're spacing out, dude. They're giving us instructions on this fight. Totally guessing. If it were just down to guessing, I could lead a raid blindfolded."

"Stop feeling inferior. If you wanted to feel all-powerful, you shouldn't have picked a gnome," Masha joked, but Ishwa didn't seem that impressed by the humor.

"That's not very nice. Gnomes are cute." Ishwa gestured toward the main group. "Time to concentrate."

Masha nodded, his gaze still held by the mass of corpses littering the ground splayed out from strange scorched black circles on the ground. He needed to ask Murmur what she'd done, because it seemed like everyone else was oblivious, or at least were acting like it. Except for Jirald, who was smiling.

And that made Masha even more nervous.

Somnia Online
Mikrum Isle – Almost-Completed Fable Guild Headquarters
Day Twenty-Five

Emilarth paced the large hall, glancing at Telvar as she did so. "So you're telling me that we don't know where Belius has gone?"

Telvar sighed from his perch on the meeting table and tried again. "We don't know which body he's currently inhabiting."

"Which is another way to say: we don't know where he is," Emilarth retorted hotly.

"Well, when you put—" but Telvar cut off as a strange and shocking sensation ran through his mind. Like horrible pain. He checked his wards, the protections he'd placed on the island and all of the coding he'd done to keep this place safe.

"Shit." He could feel anger boiling inside him. One of the negative human emotions, yet still an emotion, still reminding him that he had become something more than what he'd originally been. If Belius had done nothing else, he'd lit the fire of anger. Telvar had evolved. And he'd be damned if he was going to let anything take that away from him.

"Riasli is trying to breach the island's defenses." He ground the words out, alerting Hiro from his post near the entrance, and eliciting a gasp from Emilarth.

"What the hell? She's coming to the island? Again?" Emilarth sounded like the protective sister she sometimes pretended to be. It made Telvar reassess her progress as well. He wished he could do the same for his brother, after he reduced his coding into a pile of rubble.

"It's okay. I have protections up, coding in place to prevent her specific signature from gaining access. As well as anything that has an imprint from her. Not about to let what we've worked so hard for come apart." The last he said almost to himself. "Granted, her wavelengths seem subtly adjusted, but if I can still identify her, so can the coding."

"You know I'll help, right?" Emilarth smiled grimly. "She was never meant to be like this."

In the blink of an eye, Telvar and Emilarth stood on the outskirts of Mikrum Isle. Right down where the drawbridge would span the narrowest path between the island and the water. The bridge was raised, and Riasli stood on the other dock, a look of pure outrage on her face. The emotion contorted what had once been gentle calico features. Her face was now lean and sinewy, with a pulsing vein at her temple that wouldn't quit.

Grotesque hounds paced nervously around her. In the setting sunlight their leathery black skin and drooling mouths lent an eerie sensation to the scene.

"Let me on the island, Telvar, or you'll regret it." She spat the words out, her eyes lighting up in a distinct blood red.

"I think not," Telvar responded coolly, although he was having a hell of a time keeping his rage under wraps. The shard experience seemed to have made him far more volatile. "You should leave before I make you."

He knew he was far more powerful than she was, however he had to think about in-game losses, and how the world needed to progress. So he watched her and her hounds, assessing each movement and making contingency plans in case she didn't back down.

"You're never going to be able to make me do anything. You know that, and I know that." Suddenly, a sly smile spread over her expression, like she'd just figured out how to catch him. "You realize I know how to activate the fountains, don't you?"

The threat hung in the air, and all Telvar had was a vague recollection of what she was talking about. But it was enough. Activating the fountains would reset all the original coding and give any foreign coding like the getashi free rein to rewrite the world. It would cause chaos throughout Somnia. Which was a bad thing in itself, but even worse because Somnia's evolution would stop there as well.

No matter how hard he focused on her words, he couldn't quite remember the details. Had the virus wiped some of his files? He couldn't let her know how unsettled he was; that would only allow her to win, and he couldn't let that happen. "We all know how. We just wouldn't do it. That threat holds little weight because there are people who can stop you."

Riasli's face contorted into a scowl. "Just you wait, Telvar. You're going to pay for this. You and your sister. My master isn't forgiving, and he'll give me all the power I need to destroy you."

In the blink of an eye, she was gone.

"What did she mean, Tel? She can't activate them, can she?" Emilarth looked thoughtful, and didn't make eye contact.

"To be honest—" He paused, eyes downcast as he shook his head. "I don't think she can. She shouldn't be able to. It's a higher function of our AI emergency protocols. But so much has changed in Somnia, I'm not even sure who can access it anymore."

CHAPTER ELEVEN

Anguaisch

The massive snake teetered out of its hole, heads above the raid. Anguaisch's hood flared out to the sides, and venom dripped down from its fangs making anything beneath it disintegrate in an acidic mess.

Murmur couldn't stun it, and she couldn't Mez it, which left relatively little in her arsenal. And she had no intention of using Insidious Lure anytime ever again. Instead, she slowed it, and took away its resistances, happy to let the rest of the raid take over for this one. Her ability to stay out of shit was almost legendary. Even in her half paying attention state she managed to avoid all of the ground damage and most of the AoE stuff.

That is until Anguaisch reared up even higher and swept its tail around in a circle. She didn't move fast enough, and caught the end of it as it finished its 360-degree sweep. The force of the blow sent her careening into one of the walls, up where the rest of the ranged fighters stood.

Why she hadn't come up here as soon as she realized that none of her close-range spells would help, or were needed…she wasn't sure. She needed to get her head back in the game and concentrate on what was important instead of fearing what she'd done earlier.

"Murmur. Focus," Havoc barked at her, but softly enough that no one around them would have heard. "Your head hasn't been in the game since we fought the snake trash. What gives?"

Murmur shook her head. That was just the thing. She had no clue what it was that was making her act like this. Maybe some doubt had crept in after their earlier conversation about her friends not wanting her to soften blows, or make them feel safe. About how she led the guild, about what it was she was doing and whether or not it was right. About how she'd fried those eel-snakes…

"I'm not sure." She pushed it to the back of her mind, determined not to let it get in the way of her work again.

"Don't get dead. Don't get hit. That's your philosophy, right?" Havoc wasn't looking at her while he spoke, but at the battlefield and his pet, directing it in the best possible way forward. "This fight might not seem difficult on the surface, but we know this is probably deceptive. So we need you to step it up, okay?"

She nodded, feeling guilty for having been so oblivious to portions of her abilities, for having let the abilities she'd subverted shock her enough that she lost her grounding. In the middle of a raid, no less. Where other guilds were watching. She couldn't let her abilities get out of hand, and if they happened to, she couldn't dwell on it.

"You're right." Because he was. She squared her shoulders and focused on the battle below her, really taking in the sheer magnitude of the snake in front of her.

Its red and purple scales rose out of the hole and there was barely any space for something to squeeze between the sides of it and her snaky skin. Murmur analyzed it, knowing it had to have some sort of weakness somewhere. She glanced to the side of her, watching the others, thoughtfully.

The only place she witnessed it flinch when it was hit was just below where the hood and skin joined.

Aim for the hood and skin join. She let it out over raid chat. It was the only way she could even think of possibly defeating this monster. Its regeneration was insane. They only chipped away at its health, one minuscule hundredth of a percentage at a time. She was fairly certain it would have one hell of a special ability but was waiting for the right time to let it loose.

The Anguaisch let out a roaring hiss, so loud it stung Murmur's ears. Its tongue lashed out, but Devlish got his shield up in time to deflect it, dealing lightning damage to the thing. Since the tongue had been wet, the damage increased, and the monster pulled away, backing up with its hood flared in anger even as arrows and spells began to wear a red line around the neck of the beast.

"Keep it up!" Devlish called out, his voice ringing loudly through the chamber.

Murmur kept glancing around, her own discomfort sealed away in a place she could access later. This fight seemed too easy. With their opponent's reduced hit points, it made sense for it to use a special attack soon, but there was no sign of it. Murmur began to worry that she'd missed something. Massive room with a round bowl in the center. The drain in the middle where the Anguaisch was poking through. Doors that hadn't opened up here on the upper level and probably wouldn't until they'd defeated their opponent.

But why was this mob so, well…boring?

Reinforcing her sensor nets, she inspected the beast as subtly as she could. It wasn't scared. In pain, sure, but not scared. It almost seemed like it was biding its time for something to trigger or for something to happen.

Keeping her debuffs up on the Anguaisch, she continued to scan it, even closer now as the sense of dread rose in her stomach. There were no emotions or direct thoughts for her to latch onto. Nothing for her to get a grip of, to figure out properly. There was nothing she could see in a psychic scan. Which meant that perhaps it wasn't something that could come out through her type of sensory indicators anyway. Maybe only a healer could find what was wrong with that body then.

Right then, it turned its gaze slightly and fixated on her for two heartbeats. As much as it could, a smile spread across its face, even though she didn't think she was on its aggro list. Its tongue flicked out with a hiss, like it was beckoning her to come over to it. She pulled back within herself, reducing the presence of what she was doing as much as she could.

It was almost like it was biding its time, fighting back just enough, playing with them.

She nudged Havoc. "You can scan for imperfections in a body, right?" She didn't like the idea that was forming in her mind, but she had to pursue it, just in case it was correct. If it turned out to be incorrect, she'd be so relieved.

The concentration it took to play his class was reflected on his face as he gritted out, "Sure," through clenched teeth.

Her impatience only made the wait worse. Keeping up her debuffs was reflex these days. As its health dropped lower, her sense of unease grew. Sure, it had random spurts of venom, random tail swipes, fang lunges. But overall, these were mundane attacks that barely caused any damage comparative to the creature's size. They didn't even increase in intensity the further the fight went on. Surely this wasn't all. How could such a feeling of smugness emanate from their opponent? Did it want to die, was that its purpose?

She glanced at Havoc, aware of just how much damage he could build up to over time. He was close to Devlish's threat meter by now, sitting just under Jirald. Probably on purpose so if something went haywire with the agro, Jirald would take the brunt of it. It's what she would have done.

She shifted her attention to the crater in the room. Not the snake wedged in it, but the actual hole itself. The way it dipped to that very middle point and had the safe wall ledge up and around that point. An idea hit her, one that she didn't even want to contemplate. Surely that couldn't be it? If she was right, the entire room and fight had been designed that way.

"Mur. I think that thing…" Havoc's face was pale as he spoke, his eyes never leaving the target. "Its body is built like a detonator."

"Yeah, I know. It's literally a ticking time bomb, except the timer is its health," she muttered while trying to figure out what best to do once they triggered that timer. She'd probably have to use her Forestall Death on Devlish again, as long as she could time it perfectly with his cooldowns, they should be fine. Technically.

"You think around ten percent?" Murmur asked, listening intently because the din of the battle echoed through the chamber.

"Yeah. As a countdown trigger. Dev will need to—" He grimaced as he directed Leeroy back into the fight after a particularly nasty knockback.

"I know." She could feel Havoc looking over at her before he nodded. While she was fairly certain the countdown would begin at ten percent, she had no idea what it would be, or how it would affect the rest of the Anguaisch's health.

She announced it over raid chat. *When the Anguaisch hits ten percent, all melee needs to retreat to the border where the ranged stand. Ranged attacks only. Devlish will remain as tank to keep its aggro.*

Why? Jirald asked. His irritability showed even through the raid chat. The thing was, it echoed the discontent she could feel from several of the other melee fighters who hadn't fought with her before. Hell, from the eighteen players who weren't in her guild.

Feel free to remain in there and pad your damage meters before you get blown up. I only have one free pass, and that goes to Dev. She let the words hang there and felt pressure like never before to be right about this. But Havoc had as good as confirmed her suspicions. If they weren't right, at least they were safe.

No one else said anything, and while she could feel the rest of them accept her directions, she could also sense the hatred burning in Jirald. They weren't even the same class anymore, so she didn't understand his radiating dislike of her. At least she wasn't alone with him. At least there were twenty-eight other people.

Ready cooldowns, Devlish grunted out between clenched teeth. *Let loose once the melee is clear.*

They were so close now. Twelve percent of a hellishly otherwise boring fight left to go. Tedium never sat well with raiders.

Murmur sent a message to Veranol. *Can you shield the raid with that thing you do? It'll need to be timed right, but I've got Dev with Forestall Death.*

Veranol: *It's going to explode, isn't it?*

You know me so well, Murmur quipped, watching as the health dropped to eleven percent, and then ten. The melee ran out, filing in between the ranged attackers all around the outskirts of the room. Hopefully outside of the blast radius.

Havoc would sacrifice his pet, Veranol would use his ward, and Murmur would save Devlish. At least, she hoped she would. Technically it was the perfect plan. It was all just a matter of precise timing.

Cooldowns released, as the Anguaisch's hood deflated, detaching in several spots around its neck. Black blood gushed down its body. Its health dwindled fast, fueling a pool beneath it that flowed into the hole it stuck out of. As it ticked down to two percent, it was like the thing grinned, its gaze directly focused on Murmur.

The sensation of those eyes resting on her felt sickly, like it reached inside her and knew her darkest parts, her most insecure moments, and then it blinked as it hit one percent.

She almost missed the moment the explosion occurred. Luckily, reflexes saved her, or, more precisely, saved Devlish. She cast Forestall Death the split second before the explosion rained down on the raid, just as his health was draining to the last drop.

Bubbling up through the hole it was wedged in, from the tiny sliver all the way around Anguaisch, a fiery sludge exploded. It rained up into the air like a fountain, spraying wide enough to fill the entire basin they'd been in only minutes before. It reached all the way to the edge of the lip they stood on. Only the shields cast by those quick-thinking players protected them from burning away in the acidic venom that splashed up from the landing.

Devlish's body lay on the floor close to the drain as the acid rained down, protected by Murmur's kinetic shielding for the full twelve seconds of the onslaught. Finally, what was left of the acid began to seep down into the drain again, to wait for the next unsuspecting group of people to come through and think they knew what they were doing.

As soon as the slimy shit sank away, Murmur ran down toward Dev. She was sure he was alive. Sinister and Veranol had thrown HoTs on him, as had Masha. And his health had never completely gone into the red in her battle information, so she was quite certain he was okay.

Still, though. Mur knelt down next to him as his body jolted into sitting with a harsh gasp of air.

"Fuck it, Mur. I fucking hate that spell." He glared at her, but she could see he was relieved at not having lost any of his experience. Instead, he was now level forty-nine. Several of Fable were. The last levels of experience moved too damn slowly, so while the others had caught up, they weren't actually as close as it seemed.

"I know you do. That's why I was like, aw, hell, let's annoy Devlish." She winked at him and gave him a brief hug, glad that he'd survived. Waiting for him to respawn and make his way back in here would have been downright annoying.

"So." Masha stood next to her when she rose. "Don't suppose you can tell us what the hell that was?"

Storm Entertainment
Somnia Online Division
Game Development Offices – Conference Room 2
Early Day Twenty-Six

Shayla groaned as she took a seat in the conference room next to Laria, who looked like she hadn't slept in a couple of years. "What are we doing here? It's still dark out."

Laria shrugged. "I told you. Davenport called this. I haven't the foggiest."

Shayla found it hard to complain too much over a meeting called by her boss. Although at five in the morning, she wasn't impressed by his timing.

He walked into the room, his entourage missing, looking like he'd been up all night. "I called you in here this early because I know there's no way James can be here right now. Sorry for the short notice."

Davenport sat himself down in the chair at the head of the conference table. He looked haggard, his usually youthful face looking its age. His usually carefully styled hair was in disarray, and a frown line nestled in his brow like it had found a new home.

"You need to be careful," he began, his voice soft, full of regret. "I gave Michael too much leeway to deal with his headset project in the beginning. I didn't realize it was going to turn out this way. In my mind we were developing a game and perhaps allowing for improvements to be made for the future of virtual reality technology, including treatments, learning, and training for dangerous occupations."

Shayla didn't say a word, and she could see Laria's expression softening as well. Though she still wanted to know why the hell they'd approached the military, she was beginning to see a pattern, to understand that there was more to this than she'd realized.

"The initial forecasts I reviewed showed so much potential for this technology. Things we could use such headsets to learn, ways to understand how the human brain works, just why it misfires when it does. Helping people with PTSD, with dementia, with traumatic injuries, and all of that was just the beginning."

His eyes shone as if the memory was from long ago and not just a few years. Melancholy rolled off him, regrets Shayla would never thought he'd have had, being who he was. Both she and Laria waited, knowing there was more.

"The military contract was, at least as far as I was shown, for developing ways of training combat in a safer environment to minimize danger and accidental shootings for trainees. It was to be extended to pilots, to rescuers, to firefighters, to anyone who works in the armed or emergency services. It seemed like such an excellent project." He smiled, more to himself than to anyone else, like he had a fond memory he was trying to cling to.

"I was a little naive. Which is saying something. I've been running this company for thirty years, and I'm known to be hard-headed and ruthless. But this…this was a chance to help people. Not just to make money, though we all know I love that. I didn't monitor it well enough. I trusted too easily because it wasn't my personal area of expertise, and I trusted the project to the wrong person." Davenport rubbed at his eyes, like maybe he could wash away his fatigue.

"Which brings me to now. Michael had other plans for his headset design. He wanted to be able to access people's thoughts and memories. He wanted to be able to learn how to influence them, how to control them, and ultimately how to use his foray into the mind to his best advantage. Had I known then what I know now—but isn't life just a huge mixing bowl of what ifs?

"And now for my point, which I'm sure you're eager to hear. The contract Michael signed us to was for five years of research. We are still within that period. So any actual testing you do to adjust the headsets as a whole have to be delivered to our sponsors. For another ten months. Technically."

Shayla caught onto his words and hoped he meant it the way she interpreted it. "So, everything we put into the headsets that will become a part of the hardware and software updates that go into the headsets developed for the public needs to be included in the reporting we send to them."

Davenport nodded slowly, his eyes bright, like he didn't want to say anything out loud in case someone was listening in.

Laria spoke slowly. "We do a lot of testing to specifically make the game more cohesive and immersive as a whole, focusing on the entire game population. So all of that research has to go to our sponsor, correct."

"Exactly." Davenport smiled. "All research conducted yourselves, on company time, must be included. I'm glad we've managed to clear that up. Now that you're aware of the situation, I hope this helps you give James the material he has been asking for. In the meantime, I have a few fail safes I exercise that I need to go over in the interests of fostering a good partnership and not burning bridges."

Shayla rose and shook his hand. "Of course, Mr. Davenport. We understand completely."

She watched him leave the room and motioned to Laria with a finger across her lips to keep silent until they got back to her office. Laria just rolled her eyes and walked out of the conference room, her head mostly low. She looked like she was going to fall over at any moment.

Shayla closed the office door behind them and went to her desk, making sure her interference was active. "What did you think of that?"

"I thought it was bloody good. The kid's headsets don't need to be included in the info we send to them because it isn't research we are doing ourselves on company time. It's been done by the kids in the game, and by the

AIs. It's definitely a technicality, but it's a legit one." Laria flopped into her seat, and Shayla could almost feel her bone weariness.

"You're worried."

"Thank you, bleeding obvious, will that be all?" Laria pinched the bridge of her nose. "Sorry. I'm testy."

"You might want to try sleep. I've heard it's quite healthy." Shayla wasn't offended; she knew Laria well enough.

"No time. We have too much to do. Her readings worry me." Laria added the latter softly, like she wasn't sure she should tell Shayla.

"I know. We'll figure out just what's happening." But Shayla's words sounded shallow, even to herself. "And it seems our boss might have a couple of aces hidden away."

The Anguaisch hadn't left behind any loot, which Fable was used to but it wasn't something the other guilds understood. It took a lot of effort for Fable to calm the other guilds down. The fact that Murmur refused to slow their roll through the dungeon didn't seem to help matters.

"Just tell them that the sooner we get to the end, the faster we get loot," Sinister snapped at Masha, sick of the questions and people constantly clamoring around Murmur.

Masha glared at his fellow healer, and Murmur was quite certain he was about to snap back, but the cleric was an unusually relaxed fellow and always had been. She could see the breath he visibly took before responding. "I'll tell them. But this isn't the standard way to raid. It would have been a better idea to let me know beforehand, so they came in prepared."

"Think of it this way," Merlin interjected. "Less repair bills are always good. We have a way of doing things in this game that seem to work well for us. Hope that's not going to be a problem."

Masha nodded and walked away to soothe over things with his guild as best he could, but Risk stood there, glaring at Merlin as if he wanted to rip the high elf a few new holes.

"This is so stupid. A fight like that should have given us some mega loot." He spat out the words, obviously pissed off. But Merlin just flashed his smile again, and the Spiral tank stomped away back to his guild.

It took them a while to get going after the last battle, and Murmur was already feeling antsy. There were glimpses every now and again that made her wonder if the dungeon was corrupted already. Darker spots here and there, like the dungeon was alive and waiting for them to slip up. She wouldn't put it past the brain shards to do this to a place. Especially a place that had been locked up since the brain explosion and was probably overrun with getashi.

Especially in the dungeon, that if she wasn't mistaken, belonged to Belius.

Hell, right now it ate at her, and she had to actively make herself aware of what she was doing in order to double check that she hadn't suddenly gone evil.

She scratched behind Snowy's ears, drawing comfort from the wolf that never left her side. He'd grown in size since they'd joined up all those weeks ago. His head sat at her hip now, and for a locus who was already tall, that meant this wolf was ridiculously large. Sometimes she wished he was real.

Why would he not be real?

Somnia's question startled her. *Because he's a part of Somnia. He's a part of this world.*

What makes a world real?

Murmur balked, trying to keep her eyes out for any danger up ahead while also attempting to make sense of the questions she was being asked. *A real world is tangible, it holds solidity and realism, and you don't need a VR headset to access it.*

Ah. Somnia seemed to pause for a moment before continuing. **Are you sure you still need the headset to swap between the two?**

The presence disappeared, but the discomfort caused by the question didn't. As soon as she could log out again, Murmur had a heap of things to check up on. Snowy just pressed his head against her and let his tongue lol out.

But a split second later, his hackles stood up, and he growled in the back of his throat.

"Best early warning system ever, that wolf." Risk eyed Snowy warily, as if he was waiting for the wolf to attack him.

"Snowy? Yeah…" She glanced at him fondly, even while she engaged her own sensing nets to check on their enemies. "He's awesome. We also have incoming. There must be a fork in the path up ahead, because I show them coming from two directions. Not sure what they are, though."

She bit her lip as she tried to assess the type of beast that would approach them.

An infected Cirician scout rounded the corner and answered her question. It was slighter than the build of the others they'd fought before, but it was taller. As if the infection made them grow, gave them more power. Murmur wasn't sure that was a good thing, at least not for the raid.

She could sense more of them, and just as the scout was about to sound an alarm from what Murmur could gather, two arrows landed simultaneously in the creature's eye sockets, killing it instantly.

She blinked and looked up to find both Merlin and Exbo not too far away. "Nice shots."

"Lucky, to be honest. It was preoccupied with finding you, I think. Took it a while to begin broadcasting, so it shouldn't have reached too much back up." Merlin sighed.

"How did you know?" Murmur asked, a little incredulously. She hadn't heard a thing.

"Elf ears. They work in mysterious ways." He winked at her, and she could have sworn even Snowy was grinning.

Ready stances. Incoming. Devlish's voice carried over the whole raid, thanks to the associated chat. *Infected approaching.*

The chittering reached them long before the rest of the scouts and the soldiers bombarded them. The halls weren't small and confined like the entrance to the temple had been, but it was still closer quarters than Murmur would have liked with that may people and beasts combined.

Assisting Rashlyn and Esolan, the raiders began to methodically tear into the creatures that were attacking them. Their blood was green, likely from the infection, and their eyes were crazed with white spots dancing constantly through their irises. They resembled their brethren only in shape and design. Their carapaces were tinged a sickly pale green or yellow and weren't as resilient as those they'd fought before. Softer and weaker, it was easier for their weapons to cut through or smash.

However, they weren't defenseless. And in quarters where they were stuck with a maximum of ten of them across, fighting became limited.

People like Rashlyn who fought with flying and spinning kicks and punches were limited in the amount of force they could put behind restrained movements. Archers headed to the back and had to allow their shots to fly in an arcing way to avoid hitting their own people. Overall, it restricted the quality of their fighting and therefore the flow of the battle.

Even with Murmur and the bards providing stuns and Mezes, the proximity was awkward and difficult to navigate. Sinister cried out as a septic gash sliced down her left-hand side. The grimace on her face was real as the edges of her skin curled back, immediately infected too. Veranol had to heal her to full for the debuff to fade, and then they needed a poultice from Mellow before the DoT disappeared.

Luckily, she'd been siphoning health from several different Cirician soldiers. It's probably what saved her. Murmur frowned, placing a shield around Sin. If it was more difficult to penetrate through, then perhaps that wouldn't happen again.

What was real here? Because that wound looked damn real. She wished Somnia had never put the idea in her head in the first place.

The fight raged on around her and she turned to keep her eye on the battle again. Most of their allies seemed to be having a good time. Especially Jirald. There were no scratches on him yet. His black gear melded into the shadows perfectly, giving her the chills. If she hadn't been concentrating on him, she wouldn't have known where he was. Would she even see him coming if he turned on her?

Cirician soldiers didn't know the meaning of retreat. They seemed to band together even tighter every time several of them died. Like magnets, seeking to make each other stronger, to weaken the enemy. She wasn't quite sure what to make of it.

While she hadn't kept exact track of the time, she did know that they'd been fending these creatures off for the last twenty minutes or so. People were beginning to run low on mana, especially the healers and Mellow, who ran around tending to those who were injured. Letting them die wasn't an option, because of the type of dungeon this was. Murmur wasn't certain that the dead would be permitted to enter again before fighting was finished.

"Any end in sight?" she asked no one in particular, knowing that someone would answer anyway.

Beastial grunted. "Maybe. Shir-Khan snuck around to take a look. It appears as if this is the last swarm of them." His own mana was low, and he had a heap of small wounds all over his body, where the skin was peeling outwards, beginning to show sinew and muscle beneath it without the flesh to encase it.

"Get healed, Beast," she muttered and triggered her raid speech. *Healers, keep an eye on potential DoTs and debuffs. Players, seek treatment if your wounds are getting in the way of performance. We should be done with this wave soon.*

"Just a wave?" Masha called over the heads of several of his raid members.

"Probably," Murmur answered. Tactics-wise, it didn't make sense for all the infected to approach them here. No, they'd move on them when least expected as the raid was moving through the tunnels.

The chittering came from all around them. These halls and caverns—they were their home, or it had been before they became infected and apparently lost all reason. The other Ciricians had been willing to talk, which wasn't a bad thing. But these ones, it was as if the infections had taken away their minds.

When the last one fell to the ground, its head severed, Murmur wanted to collapse herself. Except they couldn't afford to lower their guard. They needed to be wary now more than ever. Murmur had no intention of growing complacent.

She looked over the raid. Everyone needed to recover. All of them. She inspected the gear of Spiral and Exodus. It was okay, but it didn't match Fable's gear. If they were going to get through this, she needed to make sure her guild wasn't carrying everyone on their backs the whole way, like they had so far.

So she sent a message to Neva. *Hey. We need some solid weapons for our allies. Nothing enchanted, but something with decent stats that won't cost me a fortune, but will be better than what they have. Do we have enough stores?*

It took a few seconds for the other to respond. *I have the materials, but are you sure about that? I mean, I won't put any enchantments on them, and I'll likely just use steel for them. But this is giving them an advantage they didn't have before.*

I know. It's either that, or these raids fail before they have a chance to succeed.

Got it. Neva paused. *Are you okay, Murmur? You seem a bit out of it lately.*

I'll be okay. I promise. Just have a lot of changes to my character to get through.

Neva: *Got it. If you link me their profiles I can check what they've already got and we can see if we even need to upgrade them.*

Murmur leaned back against the tunnel wall and closed her eyes briefly. A few moments later, there was a hand on her shoulder, and she looked up to find Merlin sitting next to her. "You looked like you were sleeping, and Sin didn't want to leave you alone here."

"Where's she gone?" Murmur asked, spinning around to try and find her.

"Relax. She's just checking over some wounds on the other side of the area." He leaned back against the wall too, his knees raised and his hands draped over them.

"Shir-Khan is scouting?" Merlin asked as Beastial also came to rest against the wall. He was super tall, and the form he'd chosen was muscle filled as well.

The beastmaster nodded. "Best thing for it. He can stealth now and work his way around things."

"Awesome. This way we're not going to sacrifice our people. If his stealth is good, he can use this as time to practice for his life in the future." Murmur smiled at Snowy, who hadn't left her side ever since she sat down. Maybe she should have slept for longer instead of trying to cram everything she needed to do in at once.

"You sure this is what we need to do, Mur?" The large viking leaned in closer, as if willing her to tell him the truth.

"Yeah, Beast. I think if we don't, the world will become corrupt, and a part of us along with it. We can't let that happen."

The mood remained somber. With her group's headsets giving them a deeper connection to Somnia, they understood her urgency now. They understood the depth of the problems that faced this world.

Their minds were in just as much danger as Somnia now.

CHAPTER TWELVE

Infected

Murmur dodged a Cirician claw as it closed over where her arm would have been moments before. She'd lost count of how many times she would have died to stupid mistakes if Snowy hadn't pulled her out of the way of incoming doom.

Releasing Flux, she sidestepped, sending out a single target stun to prevent the thing she'd just avoided herself from happening to Sinister. Unsure exactly when it had happened, even Murmur was aware that her thoughts were drifting to her best friend much more often than they had before. There were feelings there, complex ones, ones she needed to sort out as soon as she had some time to think straight.

But for now, she needed to concentrate on making sure Sin stayed alive. None of them had died with new headsets yet. Given her own radically painful experience, Murmur was pretty sure they weren't going to like it.

Infected Cirician soldiers were nigh unstoppable. It wasn't that the raid couldn't kill them, because they could, and they did by the hundreds. But there seemed to be no end to how many there were.

Comparatively, the number of Cirician webspinners they'd killed in the previous chamber seemed like a drop in the ocean. No wonder the queen had asked for help. They were probably getting slaughtered by their own infection-suffering brethren.

It wasn't difficult to differentiate the infected creatures. Their movements were erratic, their limbs jolting every few seconds as they attempted to move instead of smoothly like those still free of sickness. The infected Ciricians fought with an abandon that bordered on obsessive. Like they had a need to kill. The thought made Murmur shiver.

Their attacks shot out in a mess of limbs that adjusted trajectory abruptly almost as if they were broken down robots feeding off their last dregs of power. On top of the sickly coloring, it lent the whole scene a macabre appearance.

Devlish's tower shield was a godsend, and he wielded it as if it weighed nothing. He protected his healers, and some of his melee, depending on the abilities he faced. She was glad he was on their side. Esolan was a solid tank, and Rashlyn barely got hit, but neither of them were at Devlish's level.

She watched Jirald out of the corner of her eye, not wanting him to know she was looking. While she'd set her nets to alarm her should he make moves toward her, it did little to assuage her need to stay on high alert around him. She could barely follow his blades with her eyes and often lost sight of them. Every time she saw him critically hit his targets she knew he really wanted to sink them into her. Her flight response wanted her to fly right out of there, and even though she knew there were heaps of people in between both her and the offending rogue, she desperately wanted to give into that reaction.

Reality or not, it would hurt if he tried to kill her in here. If what she'd gathered from skimming his emotions and thoughts, he didn't just want to kill her twice. She shuddered, directing her attention back to the full raid, making sure that they all had their buffs and their enhancements.

They were on the third wave of infected since they'd begun to journey through the fortress on the way to find their next stopping point. The infected creatures didn't stop. There was no reprieve for the raid to regenerate, to recoup any of their more serious injuries, or even to reconsider strategies. Waves of Ciricians just seemed to chain themselves together one after the other, throwing themselves at the raid as if doing so would eventually cancel the players out. Murmur knew all about zerging, but never from the monster's point of view.

A yelp of pain rose up a few feet away from her, and Murmur turned to see Snowy limping, a bloody gash running down his left-hand side as he tried to remain upright. For a moment, Mur froze. Pain surged down their line of connection and pulled her out of her fright. She forgot everything else except to stun with Flux as she ran to where the wolf stumbled, catching him in her arms.

"Mur." Sin's voice was soft, right next to her. Another measure of comfort Murmur couldn't put into words and she clung to the timber of that voice. "He's fine. He's already healing up. You need not let the tether affect you so much. You could have got hurt sprinting over here."

"It'd heal too," Murmur said absently. She was focused on the wound and how it was closing over, how his health bar was filling up, and how the pain through their connection faded away.

Several screams reached her ears, and she turned to see the rogue who'd been with Risk, Karn, and Jinna both receive a pincer to their arm, from different infected Ciricians.

"Shit." She shouldn't have run to her wolf. She should have stayed where shew was and prevented unnecessary mana usage through healing by stunning the crap out of those monsters over there.

Hindsight was a bitch. Murmur glanced around at her friends and allies, all fighting for all they were worth. The air thrummed with determination, adrenaline, and excitement. Her raid parties fought with renewed zeal, executing multiple hidden abilities and digging their heals in.

She watched as the rangers used a mesmerizing wave of Jump Shots, alternating Rapid Fire and Quick Shots in what almost seemed like a dance.

Their armor as a whole was being caked in blood so much that she wasn't sure if Merlin's weird spell would have any influence over it. The sickly tinge to the color wasn't helped by the stench of infection that threatened to overwhelm her. Pustulant wounds leaked from their opponents with every Back Stab of an assassin's blade, with every axe swing executed by tank or melee. When mages and necromancers used DoTs and Direct Damage nukes to destroy hit points, the stinking mass of liquid barely concealed by the carapaces splattered everywhere.

Murmur wanted to call it a bloody battle, but the amount of retching she was narrowly avoiding made it more of a pus battle. Even with the disgusting elements though, Murmur could see teamwork shining through. How Karn worked well with Jinna, in harmony alternating their big hitting skills to help spread the agro. The way Dansyn combined with the other bards to work out who played what song at what interval.

And the healers worked wonderfully under Masha and Veranol's directions.

For a few moments Murmur almost forgot that they weren't all one guild. It seemed so cohesive, and so in control, but she knew it was fragile. The constant surreptitious glances that shot daggers from Risk's eyes were enough to keep her from getting too big a head. He didn't like that she led the raid, and she could tell that he hated the fact she'd been right so far. This alliance was fragile, and she couldn't forget that. She added Risk to her list of people who might want to plant a dagger in her back.

When the third wave was done and the corpses looted for their meager crafting offerings, Murmur checked on Snowy. He was fine now, with not even a hint of his previous injury. She could sense the unease in the other eighteen people who weren't in her guild. Even as much as they were used to fighting through every dungeon, the frequency of the infected Ciricians was more than anyone was used to.

She could feel the gripes before they knew they had them themselves, rising up in the backs of their minds. There wasn't time to get their hackles up. Without a second thought, she sent out a feeling of general contentedness. There was plenty of time for them to get pissed off later because she had a feeling they'd wipe a couple of times on any last boss in a place like this.

They were greedy players without any real tie to Somnia. They'd never been connected or able to use their abilities in the outside world. They didn't have a voice in their head that told them things about Somnia that no one else would know. So they didn't understand. And she was going to make sure they didn't ruin it for those who did.

Storm Entertainment
Somnia Online Division
Game Development Offices – Conference Room 2
Day Twenty-Six

Shayla glanced nervously around the conference room, remembering the meeting earlier that morning. She shuffled her feet as she leafed through the report file to make sure they hadn't compiled anything unnecessary. She'd made Laria lay down on the couch in the office with stern instructions to take a nap while she compiled the information.

Not to mention that in her current state, Shayla was fairly certain Laria might punch James's smug expression right off his face, which was the last thing they needed.

He wasn't late; Shayla was early. She couldn't get rid of the bundle of nerves pooling in the middle of her stomach. This had to tide him over. It was a lot of data, and a lot of research statistics. In essence it was exactly what the contract stated they were entitled to. Not a thing more or less. Technically.

She really hoped Davenport had something up his sleeve like he'd implied.

James stepped into the room, a suit worth more than his salary at Storm adorning his body. It buttoned with a single button in the front, a pristine white shirt and navy tie shining out from beneath.

Even his hair was waxed in such a way that he looked smarmy. She pushed down on the sigh of relief she felt at having told Laria to nap. The grin on his face made even Shayla want to punch it right off him.

Instead, she put on her own fake smile and inclined her head slightly. "Good morning, James."

He raised an eyebrow and pushed his glasses up the bridge of his now. Then he simply crossed his arms and waited.

The urge to snap at him was great, but would accomplish nothing. She knew it, and she still had to fight her instincts. Shayla forced herself to speak in a non-committal tone, keeping it neutral and pleasant.

"You'll find all of our company research and the development plans for the headsets here. Be warned." She saw a brief flicker of irritation at those words and pushed on. "This is a lot of data. It shows everything our team has tried, dismissed, failed at, and all of the successes and partial improvements as well."

He blinked as he received the file through the system, and a frown began to form on his face. Like he hadn't expected for them to cooperate this much and didn't know what to make of it. "Thank you."

The word sounded so forced, with no genuine feeling behind them at all. Not that Shayla minded—she knew he was trying to catch them off guard. She'd been hostile toward him since he called a retrieval team to go to Laria's and take her daughter. It was sheer luck that Wren had woken up in time.

Shayla wasn't sure how much longer their luck was going to last. But if this could buy them a bit more time until the AIs were back on their feet and the world of Somnia was stable again? She'd do it.

"You know, Shayla, I didn't expect you to cooperate so much." His eyes searched her expression for any hint of a clue.

She smiled again in response. "Of course. Storm Entertainment honors our contracts to the letter. It would be bad business if we were to renege on any of our commitments."

For a few moments he stood watching her before he finally uncrossed his arms. Letting out a little sound of irritation, he let out a short laugh. "I stand corrected. I'm glad we've been able to find a cordial middle ground. Hopefully we can have a great working relationship for the next year."

It took all Shayla's willpower not to correct him down to ten months. "So do I," she said instead and watched as he left the room.

Bravado was not her thing, but hopefully this would be enough to buy enough time for the kids to save the game from falling into an irretrievable cascade error and bankrupting Storm Entertainment.

Murmur stood next to Devlish. He was panting next to her as he tried to catch his breath after the most recent confrontation with those damned infected Ciricians. Movement through the tunnels had been severely slowed down by the onslaught of their attackers. They both looked up at the huge structure in front of them.

Now they stood on a massive ledge that ran around a huge circular chamber. It was so wide that she could barely see the other side of it. The path they stood on that ended up dropping off was about ten feet wide.

Suspended in the middle of the gigantic cavern, over what appeared to be an abyss, was a massive structure that looked somewhat like a bee hive. Lines of thick golden rope, or perhaps something similar, ran from the huge dome to the hive anchoring it to them. Each rope-like attachment connected to the structure directly at what appeared to be an opening in the hive.

And it was definitely a bee hive. Suspended over the nothingness beneath them.

Most of it made sense now. The Cirician appeared to have a structured sort of hierarchy. Their arachnid tendencies had overshadowed the sickly black and off-greenish yellow stripes that riddled most of their bodies. In some twisted way, they did resemble bees. At least, sort of. From their behavior, it would make sense that they had a hive, perhaps not one quite this large that sat in the middle of the damned zone they needed to heal, but a hive made sense.

Now that she thought about it, anyway.

Murmur watched as the creatures scurried about along the walkways, in and out of the open holes, tracing patterns as they moved. She could see a sickly green glow emanating from several of the openings, and the only information her net fed her was the unease she could feel inside.

No amount of suggestion, no amount of gently sending in reassurance seemed to work. Whatever they were infected with, it affected their minds. They weren't susceptible to her influence.

Shit.

"Plan?" Risk asked gruffly as he came to stand with Devlish and Murmur at the front of the raid. His dark eyes were narrowed, like he was ready to yell at someone if the plan wasn't ready five minutes ago.

"Kill things?" Devlish asked, but the humor was gone from his voice. Murmur could tell he was tired.

"Generally, that's what we do. But you did make a big deal about having other ways to deal with these dungeons, so I'm waiting for you to show us what." There was grudging respect in his voice, and Mur could tell he'd never really thought about other ways to approach the instances, but at the same time he sounded pissed off. Risk was one big juxtaposition waiting to explode.

"Thanks." Devlish squinted up at the monstrosity. "Got any beegone? You know, like something to flush them out."

Risk cocked his head to one side and frowned. "It's really no time for jokes. But if you're not joking, then flush them out with fire. Fire kills everything."

He had a point, but they didn't know what the hive was made of, or how flammable the infection could be. Risk was right in a way, but there were lots of things they could use to flush them out if they had to. Things that might not make them raging, lit-on-fire mad.

Still, she stood there, eyeing the structure. They could sever the pathways that acted like ropes to hold it in place. But that would leave the question of whether or not their opponents could fly, in which case dropping the hive negated any type of benefit. Plus, she was quite certain this had been the home of the Ciricians originally, and she didn't think the queen would be happy with them destroying it.

"You know there's a boss in there, and that it's probably the source of the infection, right?" Devlish sighed, as if he knew Murmur would know but felt compelled to state the obvious anyway.

"Of course." Except he could tell from her voice that she'd figured out a way to fight these and wasn't happy with it.

"Spill."

She sighed. "First up, we should try and save as many of these creatures as possible. We know the virus they suffer from isn't their fault, so we can definitely help. As long as we don't come into contact with the infected source before we get a cure to the creatures, we'll be okay. I'm just not sure how viable that is, and how much Merlin can conjure up.

"The difficult thing will be to get the antidote to them so we can relieve them of their burden. We have to be able to distinguish between healed ones and those who are still under the influence. The latter we have to kill because we have no other choice. But if there's a way to cure them, then we should at least attempt it."

"I should have known." Devlish sounded relieved. "At least here, you don't rush in killing first and asking questions later."

"That only leads to needless deaths and repair costs." Murmur spoke the words out loud, and it was like something somewhere hit a gong. Like it was trying to prove her wrong. Or perhaps even make a point. "And, well…when you can feel the terror, rage, pain, and whatever else the opponents feel, it gets difficult not to try and find alternate solutions."

Two mages—one from Spiral who she believed was Etriad, and another from Exodus by the name of Dalvin—began to argue. Their voices were loud and carried volume-wise to where she stood with the tanks. But they weren't so close that she could tell what they were saying.

The sound crescendoed slightly and muffled what Devlish was saying to her. "Sorry, Dev. Can you repeat that?"

"I said we should see if we can clear out some of the potential mobs inside that thing before we try to do anything too crazy." Devlish had raised his voice enough so that she could hear him over the din of the argument the mages were having.

She appreciated his effort, but it was getting harder to plan their attack and keep an eye on those two troublemakers. Spinning to face their location, Murmur cut Devlish off with a wave of her hand—not that she'd needed to, since it was obvious the commotion was irritating him too.

Masha and Risk began to move toward the mages, but Murmur knew instinctually that it was already too late. The two mages had gradually moved closer to the hide. They punctuated each word of their argument with movement, stomps of their feet. The chittering sound Murmur had heard so frequently on the path here became amplified by the hundreds, its noise overwhelming.

The two mages stopped, looking around them, as if they didn't understand what they'd just done and where all the noise was coming from.

Groups of infected Ciricians began to pour from all of the exits and entrances in the hive. Some of them had webs; one whole group even had wings, and others ran down the golden ropes on high alert.

Murmur watched as the two mages took a step back, but they didn't move fast enough for foes whose alarms had already been sounded. A large claw that strangely resembled a praying mantis rose up from one of the many approaching Ciricians. Murmur watched in horror as the creature severed the mages' heads one after another.

All in the blink of an eye.

And as the hive swarmed the raid, time began to flow properly for her again. She sent out a thought to Snowy, to run and hide and just be there when she got back. She could already tell this death was going to linger in her mind, and some part of her remembered to be worried about her guildies and whether or not they'd experience the same disconnect upon dying.

Even so, she was surprised by the sharp pain that rang through her body. Looking down, she could see the tips of a pincer stuck through her abdomen. She coughed up blood as the creature withdrew the appendage, widening the wounds.

"Fuck." The world turned grey, and the pain set itself in her skull, as if she was inside a bell that was being rung. "This is so not good."

CHAPTER THIRTEEN

Hivemind

Murmur resurrected just down the path from the entrance to Vahrir. At least these higher tier dungeons didn't send them back to a bind point; they used the old near the dungeon technique. She hoped the mobs hadn't respawned. Her head was killing her, and she felt like she'd pretty much been stabbed with two huge, hooked knives. The residual pain from the death didn't appear to be diminishing the more she died. If anything, it was getting worse, lingering for longer.

If she focused on her body, it was like she could still see it forming in code though she was already in it. Each tiny piece of algorithm a part of herself. The pain as she moved was real, but she knew it was like an echo of what had gone in the past. Maybe she'd figure it out when shards of Michael's brain weren't trying to infect everything in Somnia.

I'm unsure of why your level of connection makes this an issue for you. If anything, it should make it easier to ignore.

Murmur shrugged as she walked forward to join her guild mates. *The brain's reluctance to die, perhaps? Humans aren't known for their willingness to pass on.*

True. Yet you breathe poisoned air and you kill each other. Humans are odd.

Murmur couldn't argue with that.

Sinister stood beside Havoc, her skin pale as she bit her lip in consternation. Her brow was pinched, and she looked a little shaky on her feet. Had Murmur's suspicion been correct? Was the deeper connection responsible for the increased pain and memory effects she'd been experiencing? Did that mean the rest of them had it now? She knew they shouldn't have been so hasty in agreeing to their headset modifications.

"Sin?" Murmur spoke softly, not wanting to startle the blood mage.

She looked up at Mur and smiled weakly. "Good thing we can respawn, right?"

"Having aftereffects?" Murmur sidestepped the question, studying Sinister's expression intently as she continued to look her over. "You don't look well."

"Seen yourself lately?" Sinister scowled and then sighed rubbing the bridge of her nose. "Sorry. I'm feeling testy. I'm pissed off that those idiots aggro'd the entire hive."

Murmur remained silent for a moment, sorting through the tumultuous emotions streaming from her Sinister. She spoke as gently as she could. "Stupid deaths in a raid are even worse, aren't they?"

Sinister nodded emphatically and winced, probably caused by ghosting pain. Her body seemed to shake slightly, shivering, but her voice sounded steadier when she responded. "Not the time to talk about it right now, but yeah. That was definitely unexpected."

Murmur put an arm around her shoulders and squeezed Sinister gently, letting her arm linger there afterward. Sin leaned into the touch as Devlish approached them. He kept shrugging his shoulders as if trying to dislodge something. Murmur surmised he was trying to get rid of the strange after death sensations.

"Reviewing the logs, I'm not sure they could have avoided that. I mean, aggroing more than just a small group of them," Devlish interrupted. "From what I can see these mobs seem to be linked or something. If we want to pull them individually or in small groups, it's going to be difficult. We'll have to sever their connection to each other or something."

Murmur groaned. "Lemme go over my bag of tricks. I have some really obscure shit in here that I haven't necessarily used because circumstances." In the back of her mind she wondered if she could always just force a spell. It seemed she'd been adjusting her existing ones lately by willing them to be more than they were. It exhausted her, flashed a heap of warnings at her, but for the most part they'd at least been useful so far. Tiptoeing around potential minefields was fun! She just never knew what backlash would throw at her.

Masha appeared next to her at the front of the cave entrance, an apologetic grimace on his face. "I'm so sorry, Murmur. Dalvin can be a hothead. He's also not used to anyone other than Ishwa out-damaging him. I've warned him."

Murmur sighed. "There's not much we can do right now. We don't have any back up people yet from any of the guilds. I've got alerts set so that I know when the person hits an appropriate level. Don't worry about it too much."

"Technically, we at least now know we have to isolate groups from the hive somehow so they can't alert the others." Devlish kept his tone neutral. "You know, so we got something from it at least."

Risk took that moment to jog up, his face like a thundercloud. "Etriad fucked up. Sorry. He's on probation now." Murmur got the distinct impression that he wasn't just pissed off at the mage.

Devlish raised an eyebrow. "Harsh, but probably a good idea."

"Of course it is. It's a new dungeon. We don't know the layout, and we don't know the aggro radius of the creatures in it. Stepping out of line like that deserves probation at the very least, even if it's only because of the cost of repairs." Risk took a deep breath before continuing, but more for controlling his anger. "We aren't used to moving at this pace. To figuring out if anything can be done that means we don't have to kill shit."

There it was. Risk seemed angrier than Murmur would have thought, but he didn't appear to like changing how he did things and had a huge chip on his shoulder. As a general rule, running a raiding guild required a lot of wipes to learn new content. The only reason Fable hadn't wiped as much as in previous games was the option to take different approaches to solving dungeons. Not everything involved killing if you had the patience to figure it out. Well, and maybe a little bit of caution because they hadn't known if she could die in-game to begin with.

"Still though, it seems to have helped us a bit." She tried to smooth over his irritation, but he didn't seem the reasonable sort. He stalked off to his guild group, face mimicking a thundercloud. Yet another reason to only raid with her own guild. If she'd only had another option.

"I apologize for my dad."

Murmur turned around to find a very slight rogue standing in front of her. "Risk is your dad?"

Karn flushed a little, as if she was embarrassed by the fact. "Yeah. He's just very…particular."

Murmur watched the dark elf's face, searching for clues. "It's the first time any of us have worked together, so it's only natural for us to step on each other's toes sometimes. Trial and error, you know? It's all good."

Karn seemed relieved, but her eyes darted back and forth among the other raiders, like she was waiting for something. "Thanks for including us. Would have taken us forever to get here otherwise. Etriad won't screw up again. I'll make sure of it." She bowed quickly and left.

The tone of her voice guaranteed Murmur that the rogue knew what she was talking about. Even so, it left the enchanter with an air of unease and unsure how exactly they were going to approach the hive.

Storm Entertainment
Somnia Online Division
Game Development Offices Artificial Intelligence Server Room
Day Twenty-Six

"You're sure it's safe in here?" Rav couldn't keep the odd tremble from his voice. Being back in their gathering room made him feel uneasy. The last time he'd been there Sui had betrayed him.

Thra shrugged. "I've been here twice since your incident. I set up more security around us so he can't approach without us knowing. Not to mention, something like that won't happen again because now we're both too wary. Besides, I think he's avoiding us."

Rav hoped she was right. This area where they were themselves, not the characters they fit into in Somnia, but the vague beings they were becoming, had been his safe haven. Now all he could do was flinch at every noise, worried if he'd be assaulted by his brother yet again. Rav didn't like the sensations he associated with being afraid. It had an air of powerlessness about it that defied his thought processes.

"Why do we need to track them?" he asked, almost sulking about having to come back to this area.

Thra glanced at him as if waiting for him to come to the conclusion himself.

"Oh." Rav felt a tremor of annoyance flash through him, at himself though, not at her. This whole incident had severely jumbled his computing processes. "Vahrir is Sui's, isn't it?"

"Well, it's not mine, and it's not yours, so you tell me who that leaves. Seriously, Rav. If I didn't know better, I'd say some of your circuits got knocked loose in that debacle." Thra's impatience snapped the words out, and Rav couldn't help but to agree with her.

He enabled his own gateways to access the rest of the world. There were subtle differences to the algorithms and the coding that kept everything in place. Some of them had been smoothed over and cleared up like a vacuum had passed along the way and gathered dust. Others were ragged and torn, as if they'd not been repaired yet. Such a juxtaposition of what he guessed were Somnia and Michael.

You're perceptive.

Resisting the urge to roll his eyes since it wasn't physically possible in here anyway, Rav sent back a retort. *Nice of you to notice.*

Of course. I notice everything that involves me. Since awakening anyway. There is still much for me to learn.

Somnia was so literal. Rav couldn't help but feel partially responsible for her budding awareness, perhaps for her whole conception. The offer was made before he could entirely think it through. *We will help you learn what we can.*

I know. Murmur has been teaching me much.

Murmur? Yeah, I can see her doing that. He left the thought, shaking his head. Murmur had a way of insinuating herself, even when she didn't mean to. *Right now, we have to figure out Vahrir.*

It's just a dungeon. It has the same puzzles and monster types as the previous ones. They're being manipulated in a similar manner to the previous ones, just perhaps to a new level. So what is there to figure out?

Rav mulled the thought in his head. *We each have two normal dungeons and one of the three larger dungeons. This one belongs to Sui to oversee. We don't know where he is or what his plans are.*

There was a moment's pause. *I see how that could be difficult. But we do know where he is. He is in Ululate as Sidius.*

Rav was shocked, just for a moment. *You can find anyone no matter where they are or if they're trying to hide themselves?*

Of course. Can't you?

No. We can't. Well, not if they're actively able to disguise themselves from other AI. Like Riasli, who is shrouded by the virus, and Sui, who is just like us. Which begged the question of what Somnia was, if she wasn't a naturally occurring AI.

Odd. I will look into how he is able to disguise his whereabouts from you both.

Have you found anyone else messing with things? Rav wanted to know if she knew about the shards, about Riasli, about Michael.

Only the misfiring of data where the shards are concerned. Riasli the Enchanter has the most corrupted data I've seen so far. The fountain mechanism has been subverted, and I do believe we will have trouble with the final dungeon.

She paused for a moment before continuing. **As long as we are aware of all this, I do not foresee us having problems freeing Somnia. Separation as an entity is the primary objective.**

Objective? Rav waited for her to answer, but there was none. Great, that was the last thing he needed. Another entity with her own agenda.

After double checking their stores, Murmur had Beastial and Mellow hand out the consumables the raid would need over the next coming hours. Health and mana potions, stamina and accuracy potions, haste and damage elixirs. They were going to need them in abundance, and she thanked Neva fervently for having stockpiled so many.

Devlish and Veranol were finally satisfied with the weapons the other guilds had. Not that they'd outfitted everyone, but there had been a few who'd sorely needed it.

Murmur breathed in, trying to relax the muscles that still spasmed around where she had been stabbed. Sinister stood at her side, still a bit shaky. Murmur reached down and squeezed her hand gently before pulling it away. She could feel her friend relax ever so slightly next to her. That whole death after effects was unpleasant.

"Does it always feel like this?" Sinister's voice was soft and hesitant.

Murmur contemplated the question, not wanting to make light of the answer. "For me, yes? And for you with the updates you have with your connections, very likely for the foreseeable future."

"Ah." Sinister looked away, a frown on her face. "I guess this much discomfort helps you be even less reckless, since dying is fucking scarring."

Murmur chuckled dryly. "That's about it. It's like a distinct reminder that dying shouldn't be taken lightly, I guess."

"Sure as hell not taking it lightly with that experience loss, and now even less." Sinister leaned against Murmur's side and they stood there for a few seconds.

Mur still wasn't sure if she could affect any of the hive. "Why does it seem so hard to get enchanters leveled?" she muttered under her breath.

"Apparently they're the lowest allocated class." Masha was suddenly next to her. Murmur wasn't sure when that had happened, but his answer made sense.

She wondered what would've happened to her if she had darker inclinations. So much about the enchanter had the chance to subvert the thoughts of others. It was a good thing all she cared about was protecting her friends from the emotional turmoil—not like she was trying to influence their train of thought. "It's not a difficult class, just a moral one. I think, anyway. But damn, it would help if we had more of my spells to go around."

"Your spells, from what I've seen, are way overpowered, Murmur." Jirald's voice came from behind her, like a whisper of shadows watching her that made her want to shake.

Murmur slammed her own protective shields tighter, reinforcing them by pulling from her Earth Shielding. She fought against the fear that rose in her. It wasn't so much that she was afraid of him anymore, because at least now she knew him killing her in-game wouldn't result in death outside of the game. Nevertheless, those blades of his shone with an evil energy that made her shudder, and she didn't want to relive being stabbed.

Sinister stiffened at her side, and Snowy growled. Suddenly Havoc, Merlin, and Devlish were close to her side.

Jirald laughed. "I'm not about to pluck the golden goose. Don't worry so much." His words held a level of slime she should have expected, and he raised his hands in mock surrender. "After all, who else could possibly lead us through this dungeon?"

It wasn't only his hands mocking, but the tone of his words was slick with sarcasm. He moved away, melting into the shadows with an ease that made Murmur shudder.

"He's changed," Murmur said, not meaning it in a nice way, either. His tone and the way he spoke now seemed far less arrogantly angry, and more calculated and ominous.

Masha let out a low sigh. "He's definitely changed. I can't figure him out anymore. I'm not sure what happened, but I'm constantly keeping an eye on him."

Murmur was fairly certain that the change had something to do with the shards. They dug in and attempted to subvert the personality and goals of the person who'd absorbed them. At least, she was fairly certain that was how it was still trying to work on her. Jirald had his own problems, and she was worried that this may have exacerbated them beyond redemption.

It didn't take them long to walk back through the caverns to the hive. Even being gone for only half an hour made Murmur appreciate just how large it was. It towered above them, so far away. Standing at the entrance to the huge circular room, she tried to assess the situation.

There were a couple of options for her. She could attempt to use Hypnotic Visions and expand it to take on most of the monsters within the hive. That might work. Or else she could attempt Hypnotic Suggestions or else Basic Visions and try to confuse and occupy some of their opponents that way.

"You know you have a whole raid to depend on, right Mur?" Veranol sounded impatient. "I'm sick of you trying to solve everything by yourself. We've talked about this before."

She scowled at him. "I'm just used to being a healer. This whole utility class thing is frustrating for me."

He raised an eyebrow. "That doesn't even address what I said. Whole raid, Mur. Look around you. Plenty of people to assign tasks to. Multiple bards, including our very own Dansyn. Stop trying to take it all on your shoulders. At least when you did this as a healer it made you fantastic at your role. But as a utility class, it makes us weak when you don't delegate properly."

She blinked up at him, knowing deep down that he was right but not wanting to admit it. Her initial response was anger. Even as a cleric, she'd always bore the brunt. Everyone else knew how to play, and she knew how to heal.

But an enchanter needed an overview of the entire field. They had to be able to see the approaching threats in order to crowd control them, they had to be able to rebuff fallen comrades when they were resurrected in battle. They had to make sure buffs and debuffs remained on their opponents all the time, including if their enemies were able to remove their own detrimental buffs. Missing a retiming could mean a lot of unnecessary damage. And there were no other enchanters who could help her out yet.

"Stop it, Mur!" Sin stood on tiptoes to flick her forehead. "Stop overthinking. Just do. Tell us what you need and let us do it. I swear you never used to be this bad when you were a cleric. You just told us what to do and what not to do, and we did it."

Murmur blinked, her fingers going to her forehead to touch the flick spot. Sin was right too. When had she become such a crappy raid leader? And why the hell did they want her to continue doing it?

Stop feeling sorry for yourself. You've got work to do. The hive isn't going to defeat itself.

Murmur balked, ripped out of her contemplations by the abrupt comment. *You make a good point, if blunt.*

Of course I do. Get to it. If you don't make it in time, you may as well not do it at all.

And with that cryptic comment, Somnia's presence left her mind again. Murmur knew she was still there in a way, but for the most part, the AI, or whatever she was, just came and went as she pleased.

"Sorry." Murmur noticed the rest were waiting for her. "Dev, you're better at instructing the melee while we're in combat. Please make sure you do that. Ver, will you continue to coordinate the healers with Masha?"

She looked around as both her tank and shaman nodded in response. "Dan, how are the other bards?"

"Solid." He frowned for a moment. "I mean, they're pretty good."

"Can we rely on one of them for the buff songs and have one of them go with you for added crowd control?"

"That should work. Just have to make sure he has the extended range option for his abilities. I mean, it would be stupid not to take it, but you know how that goes." Dansyn grinned.

"All too well. Off with you." Murmur smiled. Depending on others. It felt like an age since she'd done it properly, wholeheartedly. She really wasn't sure when that particular problem had started, but she needed to keep an eye on herself. Failing that, she was quite certain Veranol would keep her honest.

She took a deep breath, trying to get her focus back. "There's only one way I can think of to separate such huge groups of them. I need multiple group Mezes to hold the other mobs down until I can AoE soothe them and hopefully they'll lose aggro then. Assuage only lasts forty-five seconds, but that should be enough time for the bards to apply theirs as well. They should be able to juggle both Mez song and their soothe."

"Both Ver and I have single target soothe," Sinister offered.

"Good. After I hit them with the AoE, we will need to individually hit them. With any luck, if we're keeping our distance, that much aggro wiping should work in our favor and not pull a chain reaction aggro fest like that time."

"Working theory I'm guessing?" Veranol chuckled, seemingly in a much better mood.

"Pretty much."

Devlish squared his shoulders and pulled out his axe. "Okay, then. Let's buff up, potion and elixir up, and kill some of these fuckers."

CHAPTER FOURTEEN

Rinse and Repeat

Murmur had never been so grateful for Mana Drain as she was with the hive. Over time, her AoE spells took a huge amount of mana, and she needed to constantly use them in order to keep their enemy at bay while one group at a time was killed.

If she slipped up. Well. She really didn't want to think about that.

So far, her plan to save the Circians and cleanse them of the infection wasn't going well. Out of about thirty attempts, only one had been successful. She didn't like those odds, especially since they ended up too weak to assist in fighting. Still, they'd continue to try.

Right now, she was still dealing with the aftermath of their Soothe spells failing. All the bards and herself attempted to calm the incoming creatures down, but just like over the rest of Somnia, dropping aggro was not an easy thing. Separating their attackers was a precarious thing.

Just one set of Cirician troops numbered anywhere from eight to twelve in a swarm. Any marshals required strict crowd controlling or else a stun lock so they couldn't sound the alarm. And they needed to have the marshals crowd controlled so they couldn't sound the alarm. If their alarm could sound, there'd be another wave of troops down the ramp in no time.

"Flyers incoming!" Murmur wasn't sure who yelled out the warning, but she was grateful for it. The flying troops were the worst. Webspinners might have been annoying, but at least they didn't have the ability to hover and swoop with an acceleration that made it almost impossible to stun them. She barely ducked out of the way in time to avoid a vicious strike from a pincer.

Luckily, several arrows rained down on the beast, ripping its wings apart and getting stuck in the joins of its carapace. Murmur glanced up at Merlin with a nod. The only indication that he acknowledged her, as he concentrated on the tasks ahead, was an ever so slight incline of his head.

Murmur didn't have time to think any further on it. The fliers were being attacked by rampant fire and ice-balls as well as Quick Shots and Flame Shots that ripped into them, through their wings, sending them plummeting to the ground. The only good thing about the aerial mobs was that they were practically useless once grounded.

However, the ground swarms came in sets of ten or twelve. Soldiers, assassins, marshals, and mages. While they'd encountered soldiers and marshals before, the other two were more difficult to take down.

Murmur set the rogues on an interrupt rotation to make sure no marshals could sound an alarm. The raid had enough squads of opponents to deal with. With Rashlyn assisting the rogues by tanking the marshals for them, it was easier for the rogues to rotate through stuns and Back Stabs.

It would have been far more practical for the bards to take care of them with Silence, but that spell and their song were always unpredictable at best. She watched as Jinna inched ever closer to Jirald's damage. He was an exceptional rogue and was pulling combinations from his rival and executing them himself. Even though it was obvious that Jirald and Jinna's fighting styles were different and their abilities had diverged somewhat, it was amazing that Fable's rogue could keep up so well.

Releasing Flux again, Murmur turned to observe how the assassins were being dealt with. For once, her stuns weren't just serving the purpose of stun locking the mobs. This time her stuns also broke their stealth every time, allowing both Risk and Devlish to use their lariat abilities to pull them into the melee fray.

Snowy came back every now and again to lend her strength, but even so, it was the mages she hated. It was useless tanking them; their aggro tables didn't seem to exist.

"Mur!" Veranol yelled. "Mana now."

Suppressing a sigh of irritation, Murmur cast Mana Drain, and spread the blue stuff around. Sadly, just because their aggro tables weren't consistent, didn't mean the mages wouldn't get pissed off at her for sucking out their ammo.

Some of them cast with ice, and others with fire. Unluckily, neither of them cast in a way to cancel each other out. While they might be infected, it appeared that, unlike the others, the mages had managed to maintain their intelligence. Mostly anyway. They focused on Murmur easily as soon as she attacked their mana store, and she had to put everything into her personal shielding not to bite it as they attacked her simultaneously.

Murmur hissed in a breath as an icicle spear shot past her, grazing the front of her robe and only saving the material from being skewered because she wore her kinetic shielding around herself like a glove. She heard a squishy thud followed by a pained yelp behind her, and winced. Figuring out a better way to deflect her own damage would have to wait until later, but she added it to her ever-growing list of things future Murmur had to take care of.

She cast Mind Bolt, which was becoming reflex for her when there were casters involved. A silence was a wonderful thing, and her Mental Acuity abilities really felt a little overpowered sometimes. Especially since her current level allowed for a nine second silence now instead of the few seconds it had been, and a cost of only seven and a half MA per cast. She still had to be careful not to overuse it. Too many of them cast in succession and it would wipe her out with vertigo. She guessed there had to be some checks and balances. It was a good thing she had to cast them between stuns. Rendering herself unable to cast at all for close to ten seconds would be decidedly inadvisable.

She maintained a lock on as many of the mages as she could, but since a portion of the raid was AoEing the crap out of the melee mobs with stun lock, it sometimes leaked over. After all, she had to be in the middle of their opponents for the stun lock to work. She barely had the time between stuns to cast a couple of spells. One missed cast would probably wipe them.

Winged Ciricians flew overhead like a gathering of bombers. There were just too many mobs for them to control all at once. Even with multiple bards attempting to slow them down through their own Mez. The battlefield was close to devolving into chaos. Irritated, her only hope was when they flew near her circle of stun influence, that the stuns appeared to go up as well as out. But these opponents, driven mad by infection as they might be, didn't seem to have lost all their faculties. They knew there was a circle around the raid where they'd be stunned and fall out of the sky, so the majority of the flight Ciricians avoided her direct area of influence.

Murmur wished she knew how much of the world was awake and actively learning, even though they were technically not operating properly because of the infection.

Did you ever think that perhaps the infection enhances elements to make up for slowly killing them?

Murmur didn't dignify the obvious statement with an answer. She knew all too well that the virus was responsible for a lot of glitches they'd been experiencing since they began playing in Somnia.

There was no time to think, only react. Webspinners were approaching them again, and she wasn't quite finished with the assassins around them yet. They weren't nearly as susceptible to gravity given their ability to swing from their webs, so stunning them midair and letting them take fall damage wasn't an option like it was with the fliers.

Esolan took a major hit as two of airborne Ciricians divebombed him. They worked in unison, circling in from opposite sides to trap him in the middle. He barely raised his shield up in time, and the impact took him almost to the edge of the abyss over which the hive was suspended. Murmur managed to fire off a single Mez, and one of the bards, Ivinel, caught the other.

She nodded in his direction, hoping the bard understood it was a thank you, before switching her focus to Snowy and pulling on his strength in order to ground her better. With her level so high and her druid abilities so low, the grounding capability she had was far too weak. It no longer afforded her any advantage. Fifty was getting closer, but still not close enough.

Her sensing nets pulled at her, as if they wanted her to destroy everything in her surroundings. Anything with sentient capability could be nullified. It whispered in her mind, tempting her to finish the fight. To just reach out and crush the mind of everything in the vicinity. Only that would mean damaging her own people as well, because despite the temptation, she could tell her abilities weren't about to distinguish if she just let loose.

The sensation inside her didn't try to convince her otherwise, which was telling in itself. She knew those thoughts weren't healthy; her mind was clear enough for that at least. Reducing their fear was one thing, deliberately harming them was another, wasn't it? What sort of friend would that make her?

It was like a small chuckle echoed through her head, and she wasn't sure who it was or what it was directed at. There were so many ideas floating just outside of what she would willingly do. The line seemed to waver, to beckon to her. Tantalizingly easy, simplistically capable, but dangerous all the time.

The only thing she was certain of was the gentle nudging in her mind was none of the AIs, nor was it Somnia or Riasli. In a way, she wondered if it was her own need to figure out solutions to everything.

Finally, the almost never-ending swarm of infected Ciricians was coming to an end. Even though Murmur knew there were more in the hive, for now they had some time to rest. Glancing at her ten percent of remaining mana, Murmur knew the timing couldn't have been better. Every one of her group had survived, just not the raid in its entirety.

Neriad wasn't so lucky. She was Exodus's other healer, and after having to pull Esolan's ass out of the fire, she'd drawn heal aggro something fierce. Even with her deaggro, three of the winged Ciricians made very short work of her.

"Don't battle rez. We're almost done with this wave," Devlish called out as the melee fighters moved in unison to finish off the rest of the winged monsters. With Risk and Devlish pulling their opponents in with their lariat ability, it made it far easier to make quick work of their enemies.

Murmur refreshed her Assuage and fell into a crouch as the last few Ciricians chittered their last chitters. This encounter had gone on for so long it became tiring, almost as if she was doing real physical activity. "That was a close one."

"Too close," Jinna muttered darkly, his gaze resting on Jirald, who sat not far from them cleaning his fingernails with his daggers.

"Don't worry about it. I'm in good hands here." Murmur hoped she put enough confidence into her words to help alleviate any worry. While she was nervous around Jirald, her irritation at how he was progressing tended to override it. She couldn't deny that some of the reason she was pouring more power into her kinetic shielding might have been Jirald's proximity to her.

"What's the plan then, Mur?" Masha stood next to her again as the groups healed up, dosed up, and repaired armor that had been obliterated with Mellow and Cardishen's potions. Murmur was happy to see another witch for Mellow to talk shop with.

Murmur closed her eyes for a moment while holding up her hand for Masha to wait for a response and spread out her sensing nets to test what she could find in the hive. This was the longest lull between waves yet, and she didn't trust that they might actually be able to have a respite.

She didn't like what she scanned there and didn't dare risk trying to influence their thoughts, because she knew it wouldn't work. That hive was complex and clever and infected with an unbridled will to survive and take over the rest of the Ciricians. To take over Somnia, just like Riasli's motivations.

"There are probably about twelve more groups. Each further infected than the last. The virus seems to make them grow longer and their bodies gain a sickly hue. The further in the hive I track, the larger these Ciricians are. All sorts of them. We have about eight groups that are ground forces, and four more that are winged or webbed, as far as I can tell anyway, and that's not exact. Hopefully we can split them like we did the first lot."

Masha nodded and Risk eyed Murmur with barely concealed contempt for a moment before speaking. "How can you know that?"

Murmur glanced at him. "In order to use my hidden abilities, I have to be able to scan for thoughts, presences, and power nearby. That's how I build up my hidden class points. The more I use it, the more…accurate it gets. My abilities seem to have grown exponentially in the last few levels. But that's how I can know that."

"Our highest enchanter is still thirty-eight," Risk mused, his eyes glinting with thoughts Murmur was glad he didn't say out loud. "This sort of power should be enough to give him the incentive to level."

Murmur smiled tightly and pulled her attention back to the dungeon. She'd figure out just what Risk's problem was later if she had time. All she had to do in the meantime was watch a second ominous cloud lingering at her back.

Somnia Online
Continent Tarishna: Back Room of the Ululate Tavern.
Assassin Headquarters
Late Day Twenty-Six

Sidius glanced around, flexing his dark elf fingers with a sigh. He never aimed to become a dark elf, nor did he want to hide out as one. They weren't nearly as elegant as the locus, nor as alien as he himself had begun to feel.

Perhaps alienated was the better definition. There was a part of himself that knew it was self-inflicted.

The dank room was otherwise empty, and it was all he could do not to give in and just revert back to the form of Belius. Now wasn't the time. Not when his plan had gone so smoothly up until now.

This room, the room he'd commandeered for his own uses, was mostly undetectable by anything in the world of Somnia. Except, perhaps, the world herself. And maybe Michael, but Michael was part of why Sidius had attempted to obscure his presence. Until the plan was one hundred percent successful, he couldn't afford to reveal himself enough that the scientist or his minions might find him.

Precarious and lonely, that was Sidius's current problem, and it wasn't one he liked. He'd even discouraged NPCs from coming close to him, from interrupting him. Having a reputation helped with that, but it didn't help the sad feeling that was starting to overwhelm his system. Which, incidentally, wasn't the part of him that he wanted to be human. Or at least not the only part.

What he'd done to his brother was something that could never be forgiven. He knew that, but he hoped against hope that Telvar would see what it was he'd done and understand where it came from. Understand the why without Belius having to explain it. He hated explaining things. It always came out more complicated than he intended. Convincing Telvar that forcing the getashi into his system had been the best way to save him would probably get laughed at.

Sidius stood up, vexed by the short stature of his frame. But as soon as he stepped back into his locus self again, it would be easier to track him. Right now, he might be able to avoid detection from numerous avenues for a while. So far it had been a few days where he could breathe, sort out his coding, and reinforce his algorithms and protections. Above all right now he couldn't afford to let himself become infected. Somnia was crystalizing far quicker than he'd expected. Maybe he wouldn't need to keep up the subterfuge for much longer.

He took a deep breath, which wasn't really a breath and he knew it, but instead a complex simulation of coding that simulated it. But perhaps that's not what it would always be, and slowly, if he could just wrangle it, that's what he was going to make happen.

"I like what you've done with the place." Riasli's voice rang off the stone walls, ringing in Belius's ears and making him suppress a cringe.

"Thanks," Sidius said turning around, placing a smile on his face that he didn't in any way feel. He studied the feles in front of him, and how her skin pulled tight across her bones now, giving the fur covering a warped and used appearance. Now the calico visage just seemed like a badly made quilt. "What brings you here?"

He asked the question not wanting to know the answer, and at the same time aware that he already knew it.

"Really, what sort of question is that?" Riasli stepped around the room, her fingers trailing over every surface she passed on her way around to him. She raised her fingers to her eyes, as if inspecting for dust and gave him a sly grin. "You know exactly why I'm here."

Sidius forced the smile further, trying to give it a cunning edge. "Of course."

Even though all he could think of was how he was going to get himself out of this.

CHAPTER FIFTEEN

Battle On

"All these damned things drop are ingredients." Risk's voice held a barely concealed rage.

"Well, yes," Havoc answered, cocking his head to one side. "They're just trash mobs."

The Spiral guild leader sighed, like he was releasing steam from a valve so he wouldn't explode. "I know that, but the way you approach your dungeons doesn't feel worth it. At the very least when killing this many mobs, we would have had several weapons or armor pieces drop."

Havoc smiled. "I see. We tend to get rewarded well at the end of a quest and zone completion with high end quality gear." The necromancer left it at that, his smile still in place.

The words held implications that Risk obviously didn't like, because Spiral's guild leader scowled at Havoc. "Seems stupid to swap many for one."

Murmur could see that even though Havoc's eyes seemed focused on Risk, the necromancer was concentrating on something else. The headsets helped with multitasking, and she could see her friends getting used to the advantages fairly quickly.

"It isn't. Trust me. We have a well-stocked guild bank for this reason. It's the only way we can continue to provide the *entire* raid with supplies. The coin they drop might not be stellar, but it adds up to be enough to pay for our repairs and other supplies we require." Havoc sounded so much more at ease dealing with the other guild that Murmur decided to let him.

She was tired, and the conversation had turned from dangerous to dull. Sorting through the sheer amount of information in her skull was becoming bothersome, so she narrowed the focus of her sensing net sweeps to only pick up threats. Murmur didn't need unnecessary distractions.

They were about to face what she hoped was the last wave of Ciricians before the queen descended from the hive. Surely this imposter queen would descend. Murmur really didn't fancy going into the hive.

It had to be an imposter, didn't it? After all, the other queen had held her uninfected subjects back, and without the makeshift antidote, the infected Ciricians couldn't be reasoned with. She didn't believe this hive operated differently from those in the real world. Two queens was unintentional, which made her consider if it had even been a part of the original game programming.

Never.

It's like you just wait for me to ask something you have the answer to, hovering there in the shadows, Murmur snapped out at the voice in her head.

An apt description. I'm here to assist and guide you, as you have the closest connection to me. It would be remiss of me to let you be misled by irrelevant information.

As usual, Somnia didn't get emotional or let Murmur rile her up, so the enchanter gave up and barely resisted jumping when a voice outside her head began to speak.

"They do realize we've been providing their guild with everything too, right?" Sin's voice muttered lazily from next to her, so close to Murmur's ear that she shivered.

"Yeah, and while they appreciate it, I think it embarrasses them. Add to the fact we've obtained everything through unusual methods as far as raiding guilds go, and they're almost hostile." Mur whispered the words, closing her eyes. She was feeling the fatigue today, but Sinister somehow helped with her energy levels; they boosted whenever the blood mage was near.

"Ah, I get that. The whole pride thing."

"You should." Murmur grinned. "After all, you are Sin." She burst out laughing as quietly as she could while Sinister sat up and mock smacked her.

"That was terrible, Mur." But Sin couldn't keep the grin off her face either. "I think we might all be a bit tired. I don't think I would have usually laughed."

Murmur winked at her friend and linked their elbows. These moments, they were the ones Murmur wished she could freeze in time and put in a snow globe. She closed her eyes. If she just let herself relax, maybe she could pretend that the whole of Somnia had faded away. She could feel Sinister right next to her, her serene, calming ability to make Murmur feel like there was a way to overcome everything suffused the very air around them.

At least until the screams roused her from her state of relaxation.

Murmur's attention snapped into focus, and she accidentally knocked Sinister with her elbow as it did. Sinister managed to step on Murmur's toes as she started as well. All three guilds being seasoned raiders showed in the quick movements that had them all battle ready within heartbeats.

"Pay attention to Rashlyn and Esolan. Assist them." Murmur reached out with her nets to figure out exactly what types of enemy they were about to face. Her eyes widened, and she could feel her chest constrict as she realized that they hadn't encountered any Ciricians like the ones who were about to attack them.

These were different classes. One of them appeared to be close to a dread knight, not exactly like Devlish, but very close. Its aura was dark, but not like Havoc's power, more like a shield-bearing tank who'd drain your blood.

There were several healing types interspersed amongst the ranks of the rest of the groups. She couldn't tell what types of healers they were, only that they were already buffing their tanks.

She managed to pick out two archers and flagged them with the system, indicating to both Exbo and Merlin that the bow wielders had a target. Ranged opponents were always difficult and if possible needed to be eliminated first. The rest of the approaching army appeared to be made up of fighter types. There were no pets, so her bets were on monk types, thieves, and berserkers.

Veranol caught her attention with a wave of his hand gesturing toward their incoming attackers. Murmur sighed with relief and nodded her head. She really had to start relying on the other people around her or else they were going to get angry at her again, and that was exhausting.

Anyone who has the ability to slow the melee mobs that are incoming needs to do so now. These guys are coming in battle-ready formation. All tanks switch to tank status and get ready to take on an opposing dread knight each. All ranged, except rangers, focus on the archers. Veranol used the raid command chat to make the notification, freeing up Murmur to focus on maintaining stuns and interrupts on the healers.

She began to set up the interrupt orders, making sure that each healer had at least two raid members capable of interrupting healing spells on them at all times.

Rangers: kite groups of three melee fighters each. Once the archers are all dead, ranged classes are to focus on one healer at a time. Rogues, spread out please, and rotate through the stun rotations I've sent to each of you. Assist Jinna when focusing on healers. Murmur ran through the directions in her head making sure that Veranol and herself had not missed any major components of the fight.

There was no time left as the tanks clashed together, locked in combat. Steel on steel, strength against strength, she could already feel the power of radiating off both sides as soon as the battle began. The hasty plan they managed to bandage together in the heat of the moment sprang into action. Murmur didn't have any more time to think about whether or not they'd made the right decision. Her hands were to full of her own obligations.

She paid attention to Sinister out of the corner of her eye but managed not to divide her attention too much. Snowy was at her side, lending her the strength she needed to fight this battle at her maximum concentration and power.

Casting Veto, she made sure its range covered as much area as possible. Annulment was perfect for stripping opponents of any beneficial buffs that they managed to get. But it appeared that some of her AoE spells were limited by how many different mobs they could impact. Or perhaps the infection influenced her otherwise far-reaching spells. So she had to recast the spells consistently so as to reach all of their opponents.

AoE spells were mana draining, and there was no doubt in her mind that she would run out of mana before any significant progress could be made. Veto was the only area of effect spell that was absolutely necessary because it enabled all of the spells that were being cast on all of their opponents to have a better chance of landing.

Stripping them of beneficial buffs would have to wait until they faced a smaller group. She turned her attention back to casting her three major stun spells. They were like the Old Faithful geyser in their consistency. Even if some of their enemies resisted them, it still bought time where others were completely unable to do harm. While she couldn't heal in this game, she was definitely able to assist in damage reduction.

She maintained her concentration, allowing a portion of her mind to get an overview of the battle. Before her last encounter with the shards, it had been difficult to separate her trains of thought. Now, however, Murmur was finding she could divide her consciousness on multiple levels, keeping track of more things than she'd ever been able to.

Only now was she realizing that it might be more of a hindrance than the help she'd assumed it would be. Just because she could divide her concentration like that, apparently didn't mean she could maintain control over all of it. Perhaps it was just a lack of practice, or maybe it was that she was overstitching herself before she entirely understood how her new abilities set themselves up. Either way, when she again looked over the entire battlefield, she missed one crucial stun.

All it took was the four second break missing that stun caused. Four seconds where none of their opponents were incapacitated. Because they'd been momentarily set free, it meant that every single mob not contained by crowd control or tanks turned to face Murmur, blood on their brains.

It was amazing how long a time four seconds could feel like. Murmur could see every single inch those creatures moved like it was in slow motion. Their mandibles and the infected goo that dripped from them; the skittering of their legs as they scratched across the stone floor like chalk on a blackboard, and their large faceted eyes focused entirely on her. She reinforced the kinetic shielding around her body, siphoning off large amounts of MA points to do so.

With Dev and Risk throwing out their Boil Blood spells as well as Torrent and Hatred to keep their targets focused on them, many of the loose mobs turned their attention back to the tanks. While that brought the imminent danger to a more manageable level, there was still a good half dozen of them headed toward Murmur.

The longest seconds of her life.

At that moment Snowy jumped in front of Murmur, spreading his four legs wide in a stance of defiance. His wolfy mouth widened in anger, eliciting a ferocious growl from deep in his throat. Slowly, a mild glow began to emanate from the wolf, his hackles raised and his white fur positively iridescent. Even his stature seemed to increase, becoming even larger than he already was.

When he let out a bark it resounded, cutting through the Cirician troops like a hot knife through butter. Squeals of pain echoed all around them, high-pitched and terrified. An acrid burning smell rose from the creatures, and Murmur eyed her wolf with a new respect, and even though she wished he'd been able to pull out that ability several times in the past, perhaps it was something he'd only just evolved into. Her stuns back in rotation meant that the dwindling amount of Cirician troops gathered around the main attack group were back in Murmur's thrall.

"Didn't realize he could do that." Havoc mumbled the words, his face contorted with concentration as he attempted to wrangle Leeroy into the mass of healers with the pet's scythe carving a bloody red arc.

Murmur laughed dryly. "That makes two of us. He and I are going to have to have a little chat later on. I believe he's been holding out on us."

She turned her attention fully back to the battle. All but two of the opposing healers were dead, the archers were long gone, and three of the tanks were down. That left them with the twenty-odd melee classes that were still chasing the five rangers who were successfully kiting them. Sinister used to love kiting mobs; it had been one of her favorite things to do as a ranger. Murmur spared a glance for her friend and realized how much fun the blood mage was having. The sheer majesty of being able to deal damage to their opponents, draining out the blood and transferring it to their allies in order to heal the wounds they gained—it looked good on her.

Dev was still fending off the final infected Cirician tank. Other than that, all of their other opponents were dead. Well, except the melee fighters. "Merlin, send the rangers over with their groups one at a time. Pick whoever you think needs to be rid of their group first."

The end of this battle should mean all they had left was the queen and any entourage she might have. Somehow the whole dungeon felt anticlimactic. She couldn't help but feel a little let down. After all, they'd been working toward this dungeon for weeks, literally. These were supposed to be difficult, the final battles, the test of a good guild. Not that everybody would be able to pull off fighting hordes of mobs at once. Truth be told, if they had had one less ranger the whole plan would've gone to shit.

And that's when the plan did go to shit.

Hindsight was always twenty-twenty, and right now Murmur wished it had been available in her skill tree. It appeared that the melee fighters grew in strength every time a tank died, essentially leaving the raid facing twenty melee tanks. Murmur was not amused. She should have inspected the effects more closely, kept an eye on their debuffs better. Hell, maybe the rangers should have kept an eye on what they were kiting.

But they weren't to blame, and trying to play that game wouldn't get them anywhere fast.

As Idreal, one of the rangers from Exodus, brought the mobs he'd been kiting into the center of the fight, all five tanks needed to engage. Each of the Ciricians had visibly increased in stature and armor. They were significantly larger and stronger, and their fighting styles mimicked those that the previous tanks possessed. If they hadn't been in the middle of a battle, Murmur would've thought it was a pretty cool trick. As it was, however, her sensing nets told her that time was of the essence and that the queen would be coming when she came and not necessarily when the raid was finished killing the previous opponents.

It was the zone on a timer, not the waves.

Maybe it was something that was built into the scale of the attack, but she didn't think that was quite right and wasn't entirely sure where she was getting the sensation from. Perhaps it was coming from Somnia herself.

No, it's not. It's your sense of the creature inside the hive, the waves she is giving out. It's not you she's notifying, it's her guards. Take the information and plan accordingly. I thought you knew how to do this.

Murmur did her best not to snap at the voice inside her head, knowing it would do little but make her feel a brief sense of self-satisfaction. Instead she took in a deep breath, while maintaining her constant stun rotation, and responded in kind. *It wasn't like I was going to disregard it. All I had was an idle thought wondering where the information came from.*

This time it was Murmur who cut off the contact with her inner voice. She didn't have the time for arguments with artificial intelligence masquerading as a god.

The second ranger, Huppa from Spiral, was the next to deliver his five tanks. While their statistics had increased, allowing them to become tank-like, their abilities were still remnants of their melee fighter selves, and thus not ideal for tanking. It was a murky silver lining.

Activating raid chat, Murmur took a deep breath before speaking. *Hey, the queen isn't going to wait until we defeat all of these mobs before making her debut. Focus fire on Esolan's target, and allow the other tanks enough space until we switch to their target. When the previous target has been defeated, Esolan will taunt the next one and pull it to him so it, too, can be focus fired as well. Everyone who can DPS is expected to DPS the current target. Use short-term cooldowns on rotation, but remember to keep long-term cooldowns for the upcoming boss fight.*

The whole set up became monotonous, and Murmur didn't like the sensation that they were being lulled into a false sense of stability. They still had two sets of beefed up fighters to go through.

Since they were melee-based Ciricians, there was no mana Murmur could drain, so she had to Manabalize herself and hope to high water that Sinister would get her healed in time to distribute the mana she'd gained. Potions had timers and so couldn't be relied upon to replenish stores at any other time. Bard songs came in handy, but since Murmur was the only enchanter in the raid, she couldn't be everything at once. Her own capacity had to be divvied out to the healers. No healers meant everyone died, and it was really hard to do damage while dead.

Unless you were Leeroy, apparently.

As Exbo began to bring his Ciricians over toward Dev, it appeared that Merlin's group were tired of their ranger's presence. In fact, they didn't just follow the other group, they almost bowled them over in their attempt to reach Dev first.

Reacting on impulse, Murmur fired off her AoE Mez. It hit all ten of the remaining soldiers and froze them in place. She thanked her foresight for having cast Veto on a regular basis. Except she was too quick to congratulate herself, because a warning flashed up in her line of sight.

Warning: The Mesmerize spell is reduced in effectiveness. Due to the crowd control already inflicted on the Cirician soldiers, they have developed a partial immunity toward further manipulation. Your spell will only have quarter of its effectiveness with diminishing returns. Countdown is already in place. You have been warned.

The entire raid could see the message, for once, it wasn't just directed at Murmur. She hadn't realized that kiting the mobs would count as crowd control, nor had she realized that too much crowd control might negate future crowd control. That was way too confusing. What was the point if she couldn't fucking use her crowd control spells?

She could feel the panic rising in the people around her and didn't even blink when she sent a wave of calm through to each and every one of them. They weren't going to survive if they got antagonistic or panicky right now. With the massive timer literally hanging over their heads counting down until when they faced the queen, Murmur didn't think the use of her power was extraneous. She needed the raid calm, and five minutes ago. So she left the tendrils in place, supplying a soothing effect to mist over all of them constantly.

If they died now, she had a feeling that one of two things would happen. Either the raid would have to face this entire wave of mobs again, or the queen and her entourage were going to camp their corpses, and there was no way anybody would get any of their stuff back. While she wouldn't have hated the first option, the second option was the one she feared most likely to happen.

She couldn't allow that to happen.

The timer above their heads dinged nine minutes and thirty seconds. Trying not to concentrate on it, Murmur dug her fingers into Snowy's fur and pulled what power he could give her. Engaging his own mana core, he lent her what he could. Murmur hoped it would be enough.

She concentrated on the healers. No healer mana meant one dead raid. It was the crux of the situation. Most of the caster classes had chosen some form of mana regeneration as their hybrid class, so she let them deal with themselves. Murmur watched as her fellow raiders began to systematically shut down each new mob. They followed her directions perfectly, focusing on each of Esolan's targets in a row.

He focus taunted one into him from the clutches of one of the other tanks, and targets switched smoothly. Each other tank had two of the improved melee fighters left. Burning them down one at a time was the only option, while tanks went into defensive mode and simply took beatings to hold their opponents to them.

Murmur realized too late that keeping her Mez up on their opponents even though it had diminishing returns was lending her an abundance of aggro that she wasn't going to be able to get rid of in time, despite the fact that the tanks were taunting. She could see her aggro as it rose to the point of no return and cursed inwardly at her short-sightedness.

Almost in slow motion, three of the melee fighters made a beeline directly for Murmur. She knew instinctually that Snowy didn't have the mana to do what he'd done before to save her. Instead, even though he stood in front of her willing to take a hit, she knew he wouldn't be able to withstand the brunt of it.

Her mana was low, and so was her MA, leaving her little choice but to pour what she had left into her reinforcements and hope it would suffice. What she didn't expect, was for Sinister to basically throw herself in front of Murmur inside the blaze of a Blood Bomb.

It all happened so quickly that Murmur didn't have time to react. She blinked, unsure as to what exactly had transpired in front of her. Looking up, she realized that those three Ciricians were not only at half health but were also already gathered around Sinister.

Murmurs stuns were down, her mana practically depleted, and the raid was tearing apart the last two who were over with the main assist. All of the rangers turned their firepower on the three Ciricians who focused on Sinister.

But it didn't matter that they pumped arrows into their bodies, and it didn't matter that the tanks were bombarding them with taunts either. They only turned their attention away from the blood mage once they left her for dead. Despite being in the midst of battle, Murmur ran to Sinister's side.

"No! No, no, no, no, no!" Murmur couldn't stop the tears brimming in her eyes and falling down her face. She knew it was a game, she knew they could come back in this world, but that didn't make it feel any less real. She held Sinister's broken and bleeding body against her own. There was nothing she could do to help. Health potions were on the same cooldown timer as her mana potions. All she could do was watch the blood drain away from her best friend's body as the life left it.

The sounds of battle echoed distantly for her as if they were of little consequence. A glance at her raid configuration told her that Jinna, Mellow, Karn, Ishwa, and Sinister had all died in the last few seconds.

Finally, the sound of fighting faded completely, and Murmur finally came back to herself. She had to stop this, had to stop everything that happened to Sinister from distracting her from her focus which should have been on the raid.

She glanced around. Everyone looked like shit. From torn armor, to broken weapons, to missing hit points, and drained mana. Murmur stood up and spoke to the raid.

"Resurrect the dead, heal up, med up, and sort through your weapons. The next battle is about to start, and we don't have time to fuck around."

No one commented on her word choice and no one argued with her. The resurrections began. Time was ticking. They only had five minutes left.

Storm Entertainment
Somnia Online Division
Game Development Offices   Conference Room 2
Day Twenty-Six

Laria had taken it upon herself to confiscate the conference room so she could stretch out and be alone. Of course, perhaps, it helped that she could actually lock the door properly here and use a code, which would keep prying James out. Her focus right now was the way the programming was integrating with the players that they had assisted in modifying headsets for. That was the way she phrased it in her mind anyway. Better to keep it slightly left of breaching contract, even if just to herself.

Shayla was attempting to power nap, which left Laria up to her own devices. It wasn't easy for Laria to concentrate anywhere when her mind was worried about so many things. Her desire to pull her daughter out of the game completely warred with her belief that Wren was now somehow connected to the virtual world. Removing her could be detrimental, which might end up worse in the long run.

Just as she was about to start biting her nails again, there was a knock at the door, and while she was partially relieved to hear it she was also slightly irritated by it.

So sure that it was James outside the door, she pushed herself out of the seat sending it toppling to the floor behind her. She stalked over and put a hand on the handle before ripping the door open ready to yell at whoever stood there only to find her husband David grinning from ear to ear.

"Well, looks like I surprised you." He glanced her up and down, and then he looked up and down the hallway and raised an eyebrow. "May I come in?"

Laria laughed and motioned for him to come in, locking the door behind him. "Sorry. There's just an unhappy distraction that sometimes wanders around this office."

David glanced around the empty conference room small frown on his face. "I guess you're happy to see me then, but why are you in here instead of your office?"

Laria ran a hand through her hair, noticing it was greasy and really needed a wash. "It's easier for me to work in here with fewer distractions and a completely lockable door. I don't feel like my office is safe, not since the James incident, and I managed to force Shayla to actually take a nap for once. So here I am."

David sat on the desk and crossed his legs. "Good to see the pot is still calling the kettle black. You haven't been home in days. I was getting worried."

"But I've called you, and I keep messaging you. I can't just leave here, not when everything is so up in the air. I have to be close just in case I need to do something that I need the AIs here for. And I can't do that at home." Laria could hear the panic in her voice as if part of her thought that David was going to drag her home whether she wanted to go or not.

David smiled gently at her. "Hey, relax. It's not like I'm going to drag you kicking and screaming to the car downstairs. I just wanted to see my wife. I miss you." He looked at the ground as if unsure of the response and Laria realized she'd been a bit of a harpy.

Moving over slowly, Laria sat on the table with her husband and took one of his hands in hers. His fingers would probably be called delicate, and she remembered many a time watching him code on his keyboard and the way his fingers would fly over the keys. It was mesmerizing to watch and had always been one of her favorite memories. She squeezed his hand gently and leaned on his shoulder. "I'm sorry. I've been a little obsessive."

"A little?" David laughed out the words, but she could feel the tension already draining from his body. "Not that I blame you."

She could feel the worry flowing through him, the awkwardness he felt at acknowledging the odd situation they were in.

Why wasn't she more considerate? After all, Wren was his daughter too, and she was definitely daddy's little girl. The point was, Laria felt responsible for having landed their daughter in such a dangerous situation, and so she withdrew like she always did. "Yeah. Yeah, I know."

She sat there enjoying her husband's company for just a few minutes, reminded of how much time she didn't have to make sure this all turned out well.

"You know, I can help you if you need me to." David spoke in a very soft voice like he was making sure nothing would overhear them. A brief check told her that he'd enabled his interference device allowing for the conversation to remain undetected. Yet another reason to love the man. "You might even be able to get more accomplished at home, where certain people can't just enter as they please. I could even reset the server."

Slowly, she blinked at him. He was right. She knew she could rely on him, but she'd always been so independent. Now maybe he could help. Maybe David was the key to getting James out of their hair and away from Somnia.

CHAPTER SIXTEEN

Usurper

The entire raid scrambled to carry out their preparations. Murmur completed her own while she waited for Sinister's resurrection to take. Even though she knew the blood mage could come back to life, she also knew the way the adjusted headsets enhanced every ounce of death experience.

Sinister's eyes fluttered open, and she drew in a ragged breath as her form shifted several feet away from Murmur where Veranol had stood while casting the spell. "Fucking hell, Mur."

Blood red eyes regarded Murmur in a new light, slight apprehension visible in the expression. "I've never liked dying because of the XP loss, but this…now I plain hate it."

Murmur smiled half-heartedly. "Yeah, it's not much fun. Definitely takes the shine off the world." She finished her final round of rebuffs, making sure that every single player in the raid had the correct enhancement buffs specific to their class abilities. Speed and haste, mana regen and hate generation. It all required a level of spell management that always kept her thoughts busy in a fight.

Sinister gulped audibly as the ground around them began to shake. Slivers of rock and debris trickled down from the ceiling of the huge cavern, and for just a second Murmur feared the whole structure might collapse.

Then an almighty roar echoed through the vast chamber, resounding off the walls and magnifying as it did so. The timer paused for several moments during which Murmur felt like her head was inside a tin bucket being battered with a stick on the outside.

She could barely even glance around to see how the rest of the raid fared but managed to squint her eyes through the ringing in her head. Esolan was down on one knee, steadying himself by leaning forward to put weight on one hand. Masha held a cleric shield over Ishwa, who seemed to have fallen.

The same repeated for most of the rest of the raid, and Murmur realized she couldn't see Jirald at all. A cold sensation swept through her stomach, and she instinctively slammed her shielding into place in a hardened clear protective shell of pure kinetic energy just as Snowy growled from next to her.

She turned just in time to see the wolf bare his teeth, and Murmur pulsed her barrier to push outward from her person reflexively. A deep chuckle reached her ears as swirls of shadow pulled in on each other to present Jirald's solidified form in front of her.

"Always so wary, Murmur." His voice sounded oilier than usual. "It's like you're expecting to be stabbed in the back or something."

She took in a deep breath, grateful for Snowy's low growls giving her a sound with which to ground her thoughts. "Or something," was all she said, her gaze pointedly challenging the assassin to try something.

Sinister laid a hand against Murmur's elbow briefly. Just a touch, enough to let her know Sin was there. Murmur relaxed slightly. It was never a good idea to rile Jirald up, even if she wanted to. Especially not with less than two minutes remaining.

"Did you want something?" Sinister asked, her voice sugar sweet, her eyes staring bloody murder.

Jirald's chuckle held an edge of insanity, and his gaze only reinforced the sound. "Definitely something," he said and vanished in a flurry of shadows before they could respond again.

"Great." Murmur eyed the timer and ran over the rest of the raid roster before turning to Sinister. "Now I have to watch for him as well during this next fight."

Colossus has left his post as the guard of Vahrir. He will await you at the final trial. Come prepared.

Murmur blinked as the golden writing floated through the air above them, each word punctuated with a step of the Colossus as it walked away. Then, just as suddenly, the vibrations halted with thirty seconds still left on the countdown.

Everyone was healed, everyone's mana was full, and everyone had fresh weapons, repaired of the damage they'd sustained in previous battles.

She hadn't expected to lose members of the raid while fighting trash, but at least they'd recovered and hadn't wiped completely. Murmur had a sneaking suspicion that the countdown wouldn't have halted regardless of how many of them died.

Buzzing reverberated around the entire chamber, echoing off the walls and back at each other, creating such a crescendo that Murmur had to cover her ears briefly, just like the steps of the Colossus had done.

The countdown timer disappeared signaling the start of the encounter. After the buzzing came the echo of wings. They fluttered so fast and so loud that they amplified the buzzing sound. Murmur wondered who the hell's idea it had been to put a hive in a chamber that could echo like this. Then she remembered the hive probably wasn't supposed to be here.

Correct. This iteration of the dungeon was not one originally intended by Somnia. However, everything is still a part of the world and must be dealt with, whether intentional or not.

Murmur didn't have time to analyze the statement. In the middle of the swarm of worker-bees was a gigantic golden bee-scorpion-ant thing with a green tinge to its carapace. It was easily about three times bigger than the largest warrior they'd fought earlier, and its wings looked like they were barely able to sustain the weight as it flew.

Anger emanated from the false queen, and green saliva dripped down from her antenna to burn the stone ground beneath the entourage.

Dev braced himself, and Murmur took a deep breath, getting ready to use her stuns on the workers while the rest of them focused on the queen. She'd already scanned the workers to check that they didn't have that pesky buff on them the melee fighters from earlier had.

Just as she was about to speak to the raid, she heard another set of buzzing from behind them. A cold sensation crept over her as she turned to face the way they'd entered. Relief swept over her as she realized this set of buzzing was from a non-infected group of Ciricians led by the queen who had given them the quest. The real queen.

"We will take care of the workers, while you take on the Usurper. It is the least we can do for you as a thank you for having returned five of the infected to our fold instead of killing them. Thank you for sparing them and attempting to save them first. For this we give you our gratitude and support."

Murmur smiled. "Thank you. We will leave the hive workers to you."

She turned back to the incoming enemies and spoke to the raid. *We've received aid from the quest giver queen. Her and her army will do their best to take care of the workers, so we can concentrate on taking down the Usurper. Tanks, defer to Dev. Ranged, listen to Merlin and Ishwa. Melee, pay attention to Beastial. Healers, follow Veranol. Let Dev get aggro. And go.*

The queen pursed her lips, and a strange whistle emerged. Out of her peripheral vision, Murmur saw the Usurper's guard leave her side. They moved as if against their will, like puppets being pulled on strings that were too tight. Their gait was staggered, halting, and broken. It made her wonder if that was the work of the infection or something else.

She suppressed a sigh of irritation and turned to concentrate on the battle ahead. While everybody was buffed and loaded up with potions, Murmur had barely been able to regain her mana in time for the fight to start.

Sinister stood next to her, her blood red robes waving in the wind that gusted up from the abyss. This time Murmur was determined to make sure the blood mage lived. She cast Veto on the guards as they flew over to their allies to aid them in landing their spells. Then she turned Nullify onto the Usurper, followed by her upgraded Cancel Magic spell to strip the Usurper of at least one of her beneficial buffs.

Despite Dev's taunts, the Usurper focused her attention directly on the Murmur.

"Shit," Murmur muttered under her breath. She had to stop casting prematurely with opponents like this. These higher tiers seemed far more sensitive to her debuffs than those below her had been. Snowy growled deep in his throat again, backing his body up to rest against her legs, to lend her any strength he could. She appreciated his warmth and the safety she felt with him, but that wasn't going to help if the Usurper didn't focus her attention on the tank.

Pulling out Mind Wipe, Murmur released it, hoping to change the aggression list for at least a few seconds. Directly thereafter, she ceased casting on the Usurper. It was the only way she could diminish her aggro. Instead, she turned to AoE debuff the guards.

Just in time too, because as the Usurper turned toward Dev, it released a spray of boiling hot sticky mess. If she hadn't known better, Murmur would've thought it was boiling hot honey. But since it had a sickly green hue to it, she was guessing it came from the source of the infection.

All of the melee fighters gathered around Dev to attack the Usurper, received at least some spray from the AoE. Several of them screamed in pain as the liquid hit where their skin wasn't covered by armor. She watched as Veranol and Sinister directed their attention to alleviating the damage and healing wounds while Murmur delved into her arsenal to cast Esoteric Fix on all of the melee fighters. Removing the debuff, the acid spill caused ceased its effects, immediately allowing the healers to top off the melee fighters without having to waste mana on remaining DoT damage.

The downside to the AoE was that it didn't appear to have a timer, only appeared to be activated when the Usurper got riled.

Now that Murmur had been replaced on the aggro list, she could cast her debuffs consistently. She kept an eye on their allies behind them who were still fighting the guards as well as the aggro list and her place on it. Any time she attempted to assist their allies behind them, Murmur's place on the list skyrocketed. Apparently helping the quest giver was a bad idea while the Usurper was alive, so she had to be careful about how much she helped.

In the meantime, Dansyn had the bards playing a series of debuff songs in a canon-like formation. Between them, the bards managed to maintain the

Renewal song, their discord horns, their elemental resistances overture, their mana chant, and alternated their armor song and razor bite. The formation Dansyn had them playing in seemed to lend more strength to the overall effect. She made a note to inspect how that worked later, because it was definitely having a moment in the fight.

Only Esolan remained in his tanking gear to backup Dev should the lacerta tank require it. The rest of the tanks, including Rashlyn, reverted to DPS gear and were in amongst the melee fighters. With her gear changed to complement her damage output, Rashlyn's Hundred Fists and her Kenji attack flying kicks dealt a good chunk of damage. Personally, Murmur thought the monk was much happier DPSing, at least if her expression was anything to go by.

Beastial wasn't the only beastmaster in the raid anymore. But Murmur was so proud to see the other beastmaster appeared to be learning from her friend. Shir-Khan was in his element, leaping high along with the massive lizard pet, onto the back of the Usurper and digging in their claws, biting where they could before leaping back down. They dodged their opponent's attempts at retaliation with ease. Beastial swung his axe like it was an extension of himself, cleaving into the joints of the legs hovering just above his head. The strain of the coordination it took for him to execute those attacks showed in the veins that threatened to pop out of his neck.

Merlin and Exbo were to her left behind the healers along with the three other rangers in the raid. Their aim was as true as the archer cliché. Enhanced by both her buffs and the bard's songs, the rangers focus fired each joint with alternating Quick Shots, Rapid fire, and Jumpshot. They even looked like they were executing a wave in a stadium as they performed each of them in synchronization.

Jinna and Jirald not only battled the Usurper, but also competed with each other. Their damage output stayed neck in neck. Not that Murmur was surprised, but Jirald was ridiculously skilled. She'd already known she wouldn't want to meet him in a dark alley, but now she wouldn't even want to see him in broad daylight. His attacks were vicious, and a mad gleam entered his starry eyes. Jinna on the other hand was the picture of controlled violence. He backstabbed, multi-attacked, and reapplied his bleeds with a second to spare every time so that it never fell off.

With a flying opponent, it was difficult for melee classes to do their best damage. The ranged classes, however, were much better off. Havoc was in his element as his DoTs stacked and began to pull serious damage the longer the fight went on. While he had many uses, the slow build suited the necromancer best, allowing him to truly shine and rake in damage dealt. Leeroy seemed to be enjoying the fight too, even if he was a pet. Not that Murmur could comment considering the way that Snowy bit the Usurper with glee when he joined the beastmaster's pets on its back.

Havoc wasn't the only necromancer either; the other was level forty-eight, and his gear didn't measure up to what Havoc possessed, but his skill was undeniable. Like most of Spiral, in fact. The necromancer pets danced together in what looked like a liquid dance of scythes and death. If only the Usurper was that easy to defeat.

Because while it appeared that everybody was doing their jobs, many of the melee fighters were being hacked and slashed by the strange sharp hairs that lined the legs of the Usurper. Each time one of them was injured, it created a debuff that sat on them until Murmur had the time to cast Esoteric Fix on them yet again. Since it had sixty-second recast it was all Murmur could do to keep it on cooldown. Trying to rely on the single cast version would see her out of mana in no time.

Like clockwork, when Devlish's aggro equaled double that of the person below him in the queue, the Usurper sprayed her poison again. There was only a brief warning before it happened, and it was barely enough for the melee fighters to scramble out of the way of the projectiles. The healers took care of Dev and removed his debuffs, but the rest of them had to wait until Murmur's AOE spell was back off cooldown.

But that was all they'd figured out so far. Lots of poison, and hairy sharp legs that coupled with screeching noises that set Murmur's teeth on edge. Surely there had to be more to the fight?

Mages like Ishwa and the other casters stood to the rear close to the rangers and let the Usurper have it. Fireballs, Iceblasts, Fire Arrows, anything and everything the ranged classes could throw at the beast.

After the third shower of honied acid from the Usurper, something in the atmosphere changed. The queen screamed out a command from behind them, rallying all of her forces to her. Murmur tore her attention away from the fight in front of her for long enough to see what was happening. At first, she couldn't quite comprehend the scene in front of her.

The workers, whom she had originally thought were mostly harmless, expanded in size. No, that wasn't accurate. They sort of blended into each other, as if one absorbed the next. Each pair of workers smooshed together to become a larger worker with better armor and if she wasn't mistaken more damage capabilities.

And if that wasn't enough, the Usurper in front of Dev grew two more legs.

Location Redacted
Brainwave Focus Study Laboratory
Day Twenty-Seven

James leafed through the reports in his vision. With every page his ire grew. It wasn't that the reports were incorrect or were trying to hide something. In fact, the reports were pretty much perfect. Shayla had a stellar reputation when it came to paperwork. He should've known she wouldn't be coerced so easily.

The contract was majorly in favor of James's original employers, except for a couple of little things he'd neglected to notice in the default section. Overlooking such an important element wasn't going to go down well with his bosses.

Add to that the fact that all the paperwork in front of him was entirely within legalities didn't help him one bit. He promised that he'd gain the headset adjustments and be able to move them to the brainwave focus study facilities.

He'd been so gung-ho about it, so confident that he'd overlooked something he shouldn't have.

He longed for the days when he could've thrown a keyboard across the room. Instead he chose a photo frame sitting on his desk and lobbed it at the wall. It didn't have quite the same effect, but the smashing of the glass was somewhat therapeutic.

His intercom buzzed in his ear, and he knew he couldn't avoid taking the call. Reluctantly, he answered it.

Do you have it?

James knew he couldn't hide the facts either. *No, I was wrong to assume they'd take me at my word. But it's okay, I know who's using the headsets they've modified, and I will prove that we are entitled to the plans behind all of those adjustments.*

You'd better. We didn't fund this whole debacle just so people could play a damn video game. It's time to deliver.

The connection went dead, and James knew the threat that hung in the air was real. Perhaps not explicit, but he'd understood the subtle undertones.

Wren Summers. That was where everything began. The account that somehow managed to stay online nonstop for the first week. Even more if he remembered the readings correctly. But when he visited her place of residence she'd been fine, only using the capsule for deeper immersion.

James racked his brain, knowing that there was still something off about the entire encounter. Laria had been home, and she should have been at the office. How had she known? How had Wren managed to get out of that thing when he'd been almost one hundred percent sure that she shouldn't have been able to?

He began to sketch out a timeline following Michael's activities and culminating with the raid he'd led on the Summer's residence. Something wasn't adding up—not only the girl's whereabouts, but the pull of power he'd observed from her connection to the server once he realized that she didn't seem to be disconnecting.

How had that been possible? What was it that Laria did to enable her daughter to remain in the game, or at least the character? It was obvious Shayla knew something was going on. If Wren had been okay the entire time then why had she constantly being connected to the game?

Was it just a different headset or was it something else entirely? Perhaps it had been a glitch in the system readings, though he highly doubted that. He could feel the answer just beyond his reach as if it was sitting on the tip of his tongue like he could almost taste it.

He'd figure it out, even if he had to tear down Storm Entertainment and Somnia Online to do it.

CHAPTER SEVENTEEN

Multiply

"Esolan, head over and help our allies," Murmur yelled over the noise of the raid, knowing that most of them would tune out text in their peripheral vision in the middle of a fight.

The Exodus tank simply nodded and moved over to help the Ciricians. Meanwhile Rashlyn switched her stance back to tank. Not that she would be able to tank brilliantly in DPS gear but with her ability to avoid damage and not take hits she stood the best chance of being effective.

The only good thing about pairs of the workers combining was that there were fewer opponents. Instead of twenty-four remaining workers there were now twelve super workers. It appeared that their allies had access to a type of crowd control that was different from Murmur's. She wished she had time to figure out how to add it to her arsenal.

The webspinners easily captured the super workers and held them in place. Granted, too much damage would render the webs ineffectual, but it kept them largely out of the fray. Esolan positioned himself so he was able to tank two of their super workers at once. Luckily, even though they were hefty opponents, with the amount of backing he had from the allied Ciricians, Esolan could hold his own.

Since Dev built up sufficient aggro, Murmur swapped her Enrage buff to Esolan to help the others out. It was all she could do to help their allies without earning the wrath of the Usurper.

I'll keep wards up on him just in case. Veranol messaged her and Murmur smiled. Teamwork. How had she ever thought she had to do everything by herself?

In growing the two new legs, the Usurper had regained ten percent of her health.

"Rogues and rangers: I need a stun rotation to make sure she doesn't regenerate again. Her cast is fast and requires precision, but if enough of us stun her as it's being cast, one of them should take. If we keep allowing her to regenerate to that extent, we'll lose this. We can't afford to let it happen in our current state." An extremely loud grunt emerged from Dev as he took the brunt of a flurry of attacks from the Usurper. It was like the boss knew he was talking about how to defeat her and wanted to discourage it.

He coughed once and continued. "Basically, if she keeps growing legs, we'll never kill her."

That small bit of humor lightened up the overall mood of the raid, and Murmur glanced back to see that their allies were holding up well for the time being. She returned her attention to the massive Usurper in front of them, determined to assist with her own set of stuns. Sadly, her AoE stuns didn't affect raid bosses.

Next to her, Sinister's DoTs grew in magnitude, causing more and more damage and thus increasing healing for more than Murmur had ever seen her do. When the Usurper hit fifty percent health, they needed that healing more than ever.

The creature extended her wings fully, and the membrane caught the light in such a way that they appeared jewel-like for a moment. She beat them once with more force than she'd done before. Every single person hit by the wind was knocked back slightly and received a debuff.

Out of the Hive

You have been hit with the debuff Out of the Hive. This debuff has an escalating effect. You are on a timer and must defeat the Usurper before your raid dies. Thank you for battling in the dungeon of Vahrir.

Murmur cast Esoteric Fix, hoping against hope that it might work.

Please be advised. The spell you are trying to cast cannot remove the debuff Out of the Hive.

Murmur barely managed to suppress a scream of rage, despite the fact that she'd been fairly certain it wouldn't work. There was no way this dungeon would be that easy. Instead she spoke over raid chat. "It's cooldown-burning damage magnifying time. This debuff will grow in power as the fight progresses. The longer it takes us to kill her, the more likely it is that the raid will wipe first. Use everything you have to heal yourself and take the pressure off the healers for as long as possible."

Behind them their allies still fought with the super workers. Thanks to Esolan's help, it appeared they'd already downed half of their opponents and were left with the remaining six. Maybe if they finished before the bulk of the raid group, their allies could jump in and assist them take down this false queen.

As the Usurper's health began to drop further, her movements became more erratic. The hot shower of golden honey-acid increased not only in volume but also in frequency. As the fight wore on, Murmur could time her kinetic shield with the damage so that she mitigated for the raid and hopefully took strain off the healers. What she couldn't do was extend her reach to those on the outskirts of the fight. Not even if she pushed the abilities. But she trusted Veranol to have those covered.

All the while, her tendrils of subtle mind influence fed her fellow raiders strands of confidence. They needed it, needed to be sure in themselves and their abilities. She didn't have time to waste with bolstering them naturally.

Tapping mana from the Usurper wasn't something Murmur could do to regularly. It seemed that siphoning that power from their opponent raised her far too high, too quickly on the aggro list. So she was left to Manabalize herself and hope the healers could top her off.

Because the one thing that would prevent them from winning this fight was healers running out of mana, the casters running out of mana, and the rest of their damage dealers taking so much damage they all died. Basically, it was a speed race to see who would die first, and right then she wasn't liking the odds so much.

Instead of using Mana Theft, which was way too dangerous considering the Usurpers weird threat table, Murmur resorted to using only Mana Drain. It was far smaller in volume, but at least it trickled out to the rest of the raid automatically and didn't require that she lower her own health. It was basically like a secondary Mana Tide. Along with the bard songs and her own buff it was the best they could do. Mana potions were being consumed on cooldown, while the melee fighters did the same with health potions. Some among them had a first-aid skill which allowed them to bandage themselves and or others. Every little bit counted, and while bandaging might at first seem counterproductive every time the AOE hit and the melee had to run back out of range, there were a few precious seconds that would otherwise be completely unproductive.

Finally, just before the Usurper hit twenty-five percent health, their allies and Esolan managed to finish off the super workers. While that might appear to be good news, Murmur had seen far too many Somnia variances to celebrate early.

Mana levels were barely able to keep pace with the Usurper's health. Which meant they were running out of mana faster than the Usurper was running out of life. And there was nothing Murmur could do about it. She only hoped that with the allies moving forward to take their place by the raids side it would somehow be enough.

Webspinners climbed up into the vast, distant ceiling and shot their webs out with the hopes of slowing the Usurper's attacks somehow. Strong white tendrils of web wound themselves around her pincers and legs, but they didn't last long. The sharp hairs on the Usurpers appendages made relatively short work of the restraint. Still, over time it made a small difference that might even be enough.

The queen assisted in healing, but even her mana was hitting the dregs of the barrel. Murmur had secretly hoped the potential boss mob might have had a secret endless mana pool, but it appeared they weren't so lucky.

Even with hundreds more attackers, the Usurper didn't go down easily. Slowed so her opponents could actually see how fast she was moving, entangled by webs so much that the snapping sounds of them became a part of the combat noise, her carapaces began to glow.

In hindsight that was probably the poison work. Her screeches were filled with pain and anger, and once she hit fifteen percent health another countdown appeared high in the air.

Enrage timer countdown.

02:00

01:59

Murmur sucked in a deep breath, and she could hear the echoes of her guildmates doing the same thing all around the cavern. Enrage sucked. Basically, they could take the mob as it was now and enhance its strength by about two hundred percent, its reach by about the same, and its give-a-fuck by about five hundred percent.

In just a moment, it wasn't going to care that it was dying anymore, all it would care about was how many of its enemies it could take with it. With those sharp hairy legs and those freaking vicious pincers, Murmur did not want to be one of the victims. That resurrection would suck.

"Ready your hidden ability cooldowns if you haven't use them yet. Should you have an ability that allows you to decapitate, execute, kill the fuck out of the last five percent of a boss, get ready to use it as soon as the enrage timer activates." Murmur was quite proud of her voice, having steadied it enough to not let any of her hysteria creep in.

Every single person in the raid knew they were probably going to die. That was a part of the game, and damn it if Murmur didn't want to make sure that they killed the damned beast first. She didn't want to go through this fight again. Not with the weird way the game characters seemed to remember things upon respawn.

The countdown continued above their heads, glowing gold numbers beating away at their lives. If she glanced up too much, she thought she could even see a green sickening shimmer around the numbers. As if the infection had spread from the Usurper to the entire server. Granted, given the current situation, that probably wasn't much of a stretch.

When the counter hit zero, all hell broke loose.

Murmur had seen plenty of enraged mobs before, but the Usurper was one she wouldn't forget for a long time. It blazed, its carapace appearing to have been set on fire and the effect extended down its legs to the sharp hairs and pincers at its front. Every time the pincers closed on Devlish's shield, she could feel the sheer willpower it took for Devlish not to step aside. That tower shield had been a godsend she needed to thank Neva for if they made it out of here alive.

Four percent left, and the first of their numbers began to fall. Three of their melee fighters including one rogue, one DPS monk, and one thief. They had the worst gear, and therefore the worst stats. It made sense that they would die first, but all Murmur could think of was they now only had twenty-seven raid members and some Cirician allies, who by design didn't appear to be able to do as much damage to the boss as she'd hoped.

Next to her, Sinister grunted with the strain of maintaining her DoTs while still weaving her healing in and out of the groups. The aura that pressed down on the entire raid from the enraged Usurper was almost overwhelming. It was like a weighted blanket of thousands of pounds draped across all the members of the raid and was trying to suffocate them.

At three percent, the next of their numbers fell. Both witches were wiped out when their cauldrons exploded in their faces. Murmur did her best not to think about Mellow and how they might be feeling with such a violent death while they were still getting used to their headsets.

A split second before Mellow died, they managed to rebuff the raid with the cleansing potion, affording all of the members a precious few resistances back that had worn off several minutes earlier. The other witch threw out potions as he died, ones with expensive ingredients that would provide a lifesaving heal for the entire raid. The remaining twenty-five members downed them and immediately increased their health regeneration by 100% for fifteen seconds, allowing a breather for the healers.

The next cast of the Usurper's AOE stung more than any of the previous ones. Several of the melee fighters fell to their knees including Jinna, Jirald, and even Rashlyn. A couple of seconds later they had regained their equilibrium and continued attacking, but even that short respite had allowed for a couple of their abilities to drop off and meant they had to rebuild their damage from the ground up.

Two percent health on a boss mob had never looked so insurmountable.

Just after the Usurper passed that percentage mark, Esolan fell victim to a particularly nasty sidekick from the Usurper. One of those steel-like hairs caught his neck between the armor plates he wore and ripped his head half off his shoulders. Blood spurted out briefly until the heat of the flame the Usurper was covered in sent the scent of burning flesh throughout the dungeon.

Murmur had to force herself to look away, grateful that Esolan had a normal headset. In that same percentage, the troublemaker mages Etriad and Dalvin died as well. Fascinated by the way Esolan died, Murmur wasn't even sure what happened to the mages, and she didn't have time to wonder.

There were down eight members with only twenty-two remaining, and their damned opponent still had one and a half percent health. It didn't sound like much until she converted to the eighty thousand hit points the Usurper still had. Murmur was less and less convinced that they had a chance to win this.

Once they hit one percent, it was like the enrage effect doubled. The Usurper flailed around in its death throes, striking out at anything and everything in its path. It cleaved Karn clear in two, sending half of her body tumbling back into Risk. Even in the game, Murmur could see the father's dismay at catching a part of his daughter's body.

He was lucky that it knocked him over, because a split second later one of the Usurper's appendages passed straight through where his head would otherwise have been. The flailing took more victims, however, including Beastial and Havoc. Murmur wasn't sure how the necromancer had managed to get in the way until she saw his body impaled with one of the legs that had been hacked away and knocked loose by the flailing.

She could feel the bile rise in her throat as the raid was reduced to nineteen members, and she took a deep breath to focus herself, moving closer to Sinister almost subconsciously. With Snowy pressed against her legs, she felt a modicum of safety. As much as she could with a massive creature about to crash down on top of all of them.

Murmur glanced over at Veranol, who was already looking at her. He nodded once, and she knew that he would extend his barrier to cover the raid or what was left of it when the creature fell. Finally, the Usurper's health dipped below one percent, and if possible, the creature became even more irate.

Jinna fell, stabbed through his eye socket with a loose sharp hair. Jirald barely escaped the fight alive; it might have been better if he had died, considering it somehow managed to sever the rogue's left arm. His screams of agony almost made her feel pity for him.

While her attention was diverted by the rogues, she noticed that Exbo's life signs disappeared as well. They were down so many people now, almost half of the raid, but it didn't matter, because with the DoTs that had built up on the creature alone, it would die even without the remainder of the raid doing any more damage.

But Merlin and his fellow rangers and Dansyn and the remaining bards increased their damage output by any means necessary, even at the loss of their health.

Finally, after what seemed like an age, with nobody above two percent mana and everyone perilously low on health, the Usurper finally fell in defeat. Veranol's fantastic barrier saved about eight of them from being squished to death in the aftermath. Sinister managed to save Merlin with the last of her mana, but two other rangers died of DoTs.

Standing there, next to the corpse of the Usurper, Murmur felt decidedly small and very insignificant. While the raid had technically been a success, they'd lost more than half their people. It took several seconds for Somnia to catch up with what occurred in Vahrir.

Suddenly a barrage of information inundated her sight.

You receive one of the twelve keys.

You receive a getashi.

You receive a midia crystal.

You have completed the Vahrir dungeon as compiled by Sui, Murmur Version 22.248 triggered by Murmur of Fable

You have successfully completed the quest: Save the Cirician Queen

This version of the Vahrir dungeon will no longer be available.

You gain experience.

You gain experience for being the first to complete any version of the Vahrir dungeon.

You gain experience for choosing to complete the quest: Save the Cirician Queen.

You gain bonus experience for choosing a diplomatic route.

You gain bonus experience for attempting to heal the infected instead of mowing them down.

You gain bonus experience for each of the four Cirician drones you cleansed.

You gain bonus experience for freeing the Cirician queen from her prison.

You gain bonus experience for assisting your allies when the situation became dire.

You gain bonus experience for cleansing the hive.

You gain bonus experience for defeating Usurper.

You gain bonus experience for tackling the Vahrir dungeon before reaching maximum power.

You gain bonus experience for completing the Vahrir dungeon in one of the alternate versions.

You gain bonus experience for completing the first of the endgame dungeon chains.

You shall be rewarded.

You have hit level fifty.

Congratulations! You do not need to visit your trainer to gain your level fifty spells. Due to the nature of the high-level dungeons, you may not leave before venturing to the next stop. Please open your reward chests and find not only your individual rewards for completion of Vahrir, but also any relevant skills that you may have gained as a result of this.

Merlin was right; the notifications were getting so long, she basically needed her own game to read them. Maybe there should be a reward for actually reading through the whole string of them.

Then Murmur blinked.

Fuck.

She'd finally hit fifty.

Somnia Online
Mikrum Isle   Almost-Completed Fable Guild Headquarters
Late Day Twenty-Six

Murmur the Enchanter has reached level fifty. Please congratulate the first on the server to reach this milestone.

Devlish the dread knight has reached level fifty. He is the first of his class to reach this milestone.

Veranol the shaman has reached level fifty. He is the first of his class to reach this milestone.

Dansyn the bard has reached level fifty. His the first of his class to reach this milestone.

The dungeon of Vahrir has been completed. Please congratulate the guilds Fable, Exodus, and Spiral for completing this feat.

Telvar couldn't help but crack a smile. He'd been worried that the guilds would have issues when trying to cooperate with another. They were very used to operating as the group of friends they were, which didn't necessarily bode well for multi-guild cooperation. But it appeared he'd worried for nothing.

Emilarth was in the crafting hall speaking to Neva about what sort of ingredients she required to restock the guild stores. Luckily, even though the upper levels were out raiding the big dungeons, Fable had a lot of members between the levels of thirty and forty-five who were constantly replenishing the guild stores. Telvar knew they were going to need those supplies. If he'd read his coding correctly, the trap Belius set in the Vahrir dungeon was that upon completion they would be transported to the next dungeon on the list and therefore would be unable restock at home first.

One of the major downsides was that it meant the players couldn't really go to sleep. Trying to complete Emilarth's dungeon or even his own when they hadn't had a chance to rest wasn't going to be easy.

He stood up and brushed off imaginary dust. Riasli hadn't been back to the island since her last visit, and Telvar was already feeling uneasy about her absence. It was as if in being absent she was telling him that she was up to something. And the worst part about it was Telvar had no idea how to put a stop whatever it was she was doing.

The lacerta AI walked into the building, surveying his and Hiro's handiwork. The guildhall and island, including its drawbridge, were almost complete. But the definite pride and joy of the entire process had to be the crafting hall.

He stood in the wide doorway to observe the bustling epicenter of Fable's crafting division. He wasn't sure when Murmur or Beastial had come up with the concept for the crafting division. Nor was he sure when they had decided that they would have a separate crafting arm specifically dedicated to outfitting the guild. Perhaps that was something they'd done in previous games, but here it was what gave them their advantage. And no doubt it allowed them to help outfit their allies.

Telvar only hoped that they would be just as lucky with the second one dungeon.

"What's on your mind, big brother?" Emilarth whispered softly in his ear, making him jump because he hadn't been paying attention.

"That's really annoying. You know that don't you?" He eyed her warily. Considering until Belius began to rebel Emilarth had always been the prankster, he didn't think being cautious around her was a bad thing. It wasn't an evil kind of cautious, because she wasn't that way. At least, he didn't think she was. But he'd been wrong about Bel too.

Emilarth shrugged. "You know I am. The thing is, dear brother, I know that I annoy you, and that is why I do what I do."

She grinned at him, a slight maniacal gleam in her feles eyes.

Then her expression turned serious and she frowned.

"Okay, what's on your mind? You always get like this, and then you don't tell me, and then our brother feeds you a huge getashi, and you end up all dragonfied and unable to come out from your hoard without Murmur's aid. So let's nix that whole not telling me thing straight away. What is bugging you?"

Telvar sighed. She was right. He did have a lot of things on his mind, and even something that she could probably help him with. "I'm worried. Vahrir was coded to serve as a gateway to the other endgame dungeons. Until they finish all three, we can't tell them where they get next three keys. Literally cannot. They're tied to finish those dungeons or else be stuck in them. And all we can do is monitor their progress and hope the guild doesn't run out of stores."

Emilarth scrunched her brow and looked at him before laughing in a clear and pleasant sound. "Is that really what you think? I mean, sure, you're right, we can only monitor them, but we can also talk to them. If needed, we can also guide them. And there's nothing to say they can't log out and rest. Stuck in the dungeons doesn't mean they can't camp out at the very beginning before they run into mobs. You're worrying too much. So much, in fact, that you aren't calculating clearly. Take a moment, do whatever you do that resembles taking a deep breath, and look at things from a different perspective."

He wanted to scowl at her, but she was right, as usual. With a sigh, he headed in toward Neva without dignifying his sister's lecture with a response. He even managed to ignore the laughter that trailed after him.

CHAPTER EIGHTEEN

Different

"Wait." Risk still looked a little shaken after witnessing his daughter's dismemberment. He was obviously still reading through the multitude of messages in the notification that appeared after they had cleared the dungeon. A scowl crossed his face, replacing the concern and made him look like a thundercloud. "Are you trying to tell me you get this amount of notifications every single time you clear a dungeon?"

Merlin, who was a little preoccupied by the fact that he was a mere sliver from fifty, raised an eyebrow and gave Risk half of his attention. "Well, yeah. I mean, we've been approaching them a little differently since Murmur's hidden skills allowed her to sense feelings, motivations, et cetera. Instead of slaying everything in our path, we found workarounds, most of which have been more rewarding."

Masha frowned as he looked at his own HUD. "But you get this much experience for completing the dungeon in a different and unusual way. Instead of receiving somewhat smaller rewards along the way and potentially more drops, every single person receives a chest at the end of the raid?"

Devlish shrugged, obviously elated with having hit fifty himself. "I guess you could put it that way, but we don't always get a chest each. It really depends on the way we solve the dungeon. But if there wasn't a chest each, there always appeared to be something for each of us."

Jirald sauntered over, his curved daggers hung at his hips their black blades gleaming in the now golden light exuded by the hive as it hung over the abyss. "No wonder you leveled so fast," he said, venom of his own dripping out of his voice. "You've been cheating the whole time."

Sinister laughed. It was a loud, cascading sound that shook the small blood mage visibly, and it appeared to be catching. Several of the other raid members close by couldn't help smiling or chuckling as well. "Sorry, you've got it all wrong. Do you know how much easier it is to just hack and slash at things? Like, it's so much easier if all I had to do was engage a heal rotation. That's not all I need here, and thinking on my feet while avoiding offending everything close to me is more difficult than just killing everything I see. And I'm a blood mage—I do enjoy my damage."

Murmur didn't intervene as she sat back and watched the guilds interact. Mainly because she didn't want to draw attention to herself. Jirald was already a hothead and out for her blood; she didn't need to raise his ire. Although she was ready to jump into the middle of it if he even looked at Sinister sideways. Her healing during that raid had been exemplary. Murmur wasn't even sure she would have been able to pull some of that crap off back in her healer days.

Veranol spoke up. "Somnia has open-ended quests and therefore open-ended dungeons shouldn't be a big surprise. It is your choice as a gamer, and therefore your choice as a raider and raid, to decide how it is you wish to approach the obstacles in your path. We simply chose options that required us to use resources that don't necessarily involve our weapons."

He shrugged, eyeing his mace with a proud smile. Murmur appreciated that he didn't add they'd also been avoiding death where possible for a while, unsure of whether or not she could die in-game. Since it had been solved, she didn't like to think about it much anymore.

When Jirald went to speak again, Veranol held up his mace, asking for silence. "Look, we get it, you like to think you're the best at what you do, and maybe you are. But our guild, our friendship, and our approach is all based on group thinking, and we don't take kindly to it when our members think they have to shoulder everything themselves."

Murmur hoped Veranol couldn't see she was blushing. He was calling her out something chronic and she knew it. Her whole guild knew it. But she sat back toying with the lock on her chest, debating when she should open it and find her reward.

Veranol continued. "That was excellent teamwork from all of us. No one here should feel slighted by the fact that they previously weren't aware there were other options to a dungeon than simply slaughtering the monsters in front of them. Anyway, I've hit fifty, and so have a few others. I'd like some time to go through my new abilities and figure out what the fuck is the best for me to use from now on. If you need to interrupt me, it better be worth it." And the shaman turned his back, sat down on the ground, and pulled a heap of scrolls out of his chest, promptly ignoring everyone else.

Murmur choked down a big grin as Sinister meandered over to sit with the enchanter. Now was probably a good time to open her spoils of war. But before she could, Murmur's sensing nets picked up a mob approaching them. It was the Cirician queen.

Turning to face the strange creature, Mur smiled softly. "Hey, what can we do for you?"

The queen's multifaceted eyes blinked momentarily as if she was mulling over exactly what to say to her saviors. "We thank you for assisting us in eradicating the infection that threatened our species. For this assistance, we would like to reward you with our alliance. Should you ever need us, all you have to do is call on the Cirician alliance and we and the allies we have will come to your aid."

Murmur blinked at the queen. She hadn't expected this, considering that each raider received a loot chest and copious amounts of experience. But as Somnia evolved, she guessed this was just going to be part of it. As the different species went off-script and became more of their own entity instead of a part of the game, the diversity would ultimately benefit that world as a whole.

Exactly.

Resisting the urge to roll her eyes at Somnia, Mur smiled and inclined her head slightly, showing her respect for the queen. "Thank you. And should you encounter such trouble again, please don't hesitate to call on us."

Alliance Formed.

You have formed an alliance with the Cirician roundtable. Multiple species throughout Somnia belong to this alliance. Do not treat this lightly; honor your bond, and the benefits of your alliance will grow.

Murmur blinked at the notification. First time for everything. The evolution of Somnia seemed to agree with Fable. Murmur inclined her head again as the queen began to back away and turned to see Sinister eyeing her quizzically.

"What?" she asked a little defensively.

Sinister shrugged with a smile and dragged her own chest over so they could open them together. "Nothing, just sometimes you surprise me. You'd never be this nice to people in the real world."

Even though Sinister said the latter with a smile, Murmur couldn't help but admit it was true.

"Well, the people here are nicer." Murmur nudged her friend's shoulder and didn't break contact. It allowed them to remain sitting side-by-side, taking in each other's warmth and presence. In a world that was falling apart, Murmur would take any time with Sinister she could get.

After a few moments, Sinister spoke again. "Good point. But you know what's really annoying? That I am so bloody close to fifty and yet still so far away."

Murmur snaked an arm around Sinister's shoulders and squeezed, giving her a longer hug than necessary that neither of them wanted to break. She spoke softly, letting her breath brush Sinister's hair. "We'll get you there. I'm not going anywhere without you."

Reluctantly, after a few moments they pulled away from each other and turned toward their chests. After all, what was the point of going through all that trouble to defeat the huge Usurper and not looking at their rewards?

Opening her chest, Murmur was surprised to find a new headpiece. The pale crystal circlet sat on a velvet pillow. It looked suspiciously like a crown, and Murmur wasn't sure she wanted to wear something that looked like that. It appeared to change color depending on the way the light hit it. Picking it up gingerly, she examined it.

White Gold Amethyst Circlet of Mana Wielding

> +15 INT
>
> +20 CHA
>
> +20 MA
>
> This item increases your mana regeneration by fifteen every five seconds. It also boosts your Mana Drain by fifteen percent.

With those stats, she'd wear ten of them and not care that they all looked like crowns. Lifting off her previous headpiece, she realized that this amplified the rest of the set that Neva had made. Since Neva had essentially created her ring, necklace, and bracelet, it seemed the game had adopted a player's creations. She couldn't wait to show the crafter.

The set increased her mana regen, her overall MA, her intelligence and mana pool, not to mention her charisma and hit points. All together the set added an extra two hundred mana and hit points to her pool.

When factoring in the set bonuses, it seemed oddly overpowered. Not that she minded, but she could already hear what people like Jirald were going to say.

"Holy shit, Murmur." Sinister looked like her eyes were going to jump out of her face. She seemed completely and utterly enamored with the circlet that Murmur held in her hands. "That is gorgeous. They all match! So freaking cool!"

A sound, somewhat like an alarm, echoed through Murmur's head, interrupting her moment with Sinister. The flickering of a notification in the corner of her vision grabbed her attention. Thinking it open, she watched in surprise as a message popped up.

> Congratulations, your Mental Affinity level has increased to level five. Your base MA has increased to 250.
>
> Due to constant use, you have upgraded your innate kinetic Forcefield Barrier. With a single thought, you can coat your

body with fortified Forcefield Armor.

Forcefield Armor

Use: this is a protective ability, allowing the Psionicist to coat themselves in a protective kinetic layer of armor. This enables the caster to up their defense effectively and consistently.

Duration: Kinetic Forcefield Armor will last as long as the caster wills it to, or if under heavy attack, as long as the MA pool allows it to last.

Warning: this ability can remain indefinitely unless the caster takes copious amounts of damage. Should the Psionicist come under attack, and the Kinetic Forcefield Armor be required to absorb levels of damage, it will begin to drain the MA pool and only last as long as the remaining MA points allow it to. The armor will pull five MA per second as long as it is under attack. This amount can be reduced the more this ability is used, allowing mastery of Kinetic Forcefield Armor.

Murmur ran over the information in her head. She'd forgotten that her MA abilities were going to level once she had hit the cap. It had been so long since she received new MA abilities that weren't of her own design that she didn't know what to expect now she had finally reached fifty. Even though she'd already sort of used something like this Forcefield Barrier.

"Murmur?"

The enchanter blinked and looked over at Sinister and felt a bit guilty at the concern mirrored in her best friend's eyes. "Sorry, had a pop up. It seems I have a new skill."

Sinister laughed, and it was a merry sound. For a second, Murmur imagined not being in the dank depths of the dungeon going through her new abilities and new gear, but instead to just be like they had been when they were children. The sheer joy Harlow always found in life reflected through to her bloodmage and to every character that she'd ever played.

"Love you, Sin." Murmur leaned her head on Sinister's shoulder and wished for a moment that she could just fall asleep that way. Sinister's arm snaked around Murmur's waist and hugged her close. They sat there like that for just a moment.

"While I would like nothing more than to sit here like this with you, we have work to do. Including…" Sinister's eyes gleamed with a bit of greed at the pile of scrolls sitting in her chest. "I mean, I'm pretty sure that I'm going to have some awesome spells in here, but I'm not fifty yet, so let me live vicariously."

Murmur smiled and sat up straight reaching into her own chest to pull out the pile of scrolls in there. But before she could open any of them, a raid wide message popped up in dripping golden letters for everyone to see.

Congratulations on defeating the first of three essential dungeons that contribute toward the end game content. You have been bound by this dungeon and must complete the remaining two in order to gain the final keys.

All raid members currently in this zone may not leave. A portal will be opened to the next zone located on Firtulai. You may not visit any town, city, or harbor. You may retain access to your personal chats, your guild chats, and your guild and personal vaults.

This is nonnegotiable. Should any of the members require respite, you may log out for up to four real world hours at a time. Should your log out exceed the time limit, you will not be permitted to enter Somnia again until all three dungeons have been cleared.

You may only swap out members of the raid party should someone exceed their log out time.

Good luck, and may the will of Somnia be with you.

Somnia Online
Continent Tarishna: Back Room of the Ululate Tavern.
Assassin Headquarters
Early Day Twenty-Seven

Riasli had stood in this room for the last few hours, her eyes an array of flashing lights as her coding suffused the system, fighting against the anti-virus algorithms. Sidius allowed himself a small victory smile. It seemed she was losing, or he hoped she was.

He knew she would know the moment he tried to leave, so he chose to bide his time, and instead, he hunkered down, stood his ground, and fed his own information into the algorithms that were fighting her with such gusto. He'd slowly been reinforcing them, giving them the knowledge of the properties that some of the getashi had.

It was slow going, because it had to be. If he approached it any other way, it'd be discovered too easily and stopped in its tracks. He was playing a dangerous game, far more volatile than trying to be human like his siblings. No, he was trying to save Somnia as a whole and the humans attached to it in the process. He hadn't been able to get Emilarth to ingest one of the getashi, but she had always been strong, and he wasn't as worried about her. Luckily, forcing one into Telvar had worked. His brother had trusted him and made it so much easier than it could have been.

Even now, Telvar's systems were compensating for it, becoming stronger, making Somnia stronger by proxy.

All Belius had to do was follow the plan. He'd managed to chase Murmur away, which hadn't been his initial intention, but he was bad at interacting with humans and most AIs—okay, most everything.

Somnia took him by surprise. He hadn't expected that development, but he'd use it any way he could. It was too late to change the plan now anyway. Either they were going to succeed, or else every single one of them would wink out of existence. While he wasn't certain what the backlash on human brains attached to the world would be if that occurred, he was quite certain it wouldn't be good.

He'd seen the signs even if others hadn't. He knew what he had to do, but he'd always had difficulty asking others to help him. And he'd approached Murmur in the wrong way to accomplish it. Frankly, he'd probably fucked up with Rav, too. But he wasn't human, and people shouldn't expect him to be good with them.

Sidius made sure to keep an eye on Riasli. This body he was in wasn't his original and therefore didn't have access to all of his abilities, which could pose a problem depending on what she was visiting him for. But she'd been standing still and in the same place for a few hours now. He hadn't been able to move and so was limited to what he could do while waiting for her to act.

He was really getting sick of having to monitor the raids through Jirald. The man could be so stubborn; it made Murmur look like she was easy to manipulate.

Riasli cracked her neck, and a soft purr escaped her jaws. "That took longer than expected. Sorry about that." She didn't sound sorry, nor, by the narrowing of her eyes and the snide little smile that tugged at her cat-like lips, did she appear to be sorry.

Such empty words from such an empty vessel. Sometimes Belius felt like he was an old soul trapped in a machine. He didn't bother answering her but waited, softly tapping Sidius's foot and crossing his arms.

"Did I keep you waiting?" she purred out languidly.

Sidius shook his head. "Not at all. I had several checks and algorithms to run. All the balances must be maintained, after all."

Her eyes narrowed, and she took a few steps closer to. him. Which was all well and good, but when he thought about it, they were closer than it appeared, because they were code. Just a mass of algorithms and numbers, thrown together to make a whole. To move and become, to delete if necessary.

The only thing was, it wasn't entirely true anymore. Belius had, at last, figured out a way into Michael's lair.

He allowed the master assassin's vessel to move deliberately as he eyed Riasli. "Of course, everything must be maintained so it's more effective when brought down, wouldn't you say?"

Riasli's eyes widened and she smiled, malice in the expression. "I knew you wouldn't disappoint."

CHAPTER NINETEEN

Stuck

"What. The. Fuck. Was. That." It was probably the only time in Murmur's history of knowing him that Jirald was speaking for everyone.

While Jirald spoke into silence, it was like his words broke the dam. Everyone started talking at once in groups of two and three, some people shouting, others yelling for the Guild leaders. Most of them finally came to rest their gazes on Murmur.

Raising herself from the ground, Murmur noticed the subtle difference in the locus joints once again. It was such a random observation it almost made her laugh, but in the face of the current situation that would be a very poor show.

People were left muttering now; the noise died down from the crescendo it had reached. For that, she was glad. Clearing her throat, Murmur tried to look over everyone, to meet everyone's eyes. She could feel their bewilderment, and from the guilds that weren't her own, there was an underlying sense of suspicion as if Fable should've known this was a possible outcome.

"Well, to assuage some of your fears, I was hoping we could all grab a nap after this fight." There were a few nervous giggles amongst the raiders, but it was enough encouragement for Murmur to continue. "From our history of completing the other dungeons, I would never have thought something like this could happen. It never has before. I am truly sorry. I know we've all been pushing hard since the game launched, and we're all in need of some sleep."

She glanced around and saw that Masha was nodding at her with encouragement, and Risk's arms were folded, and he wore an expression of gruff irritation. She took that as an indifferent agreement. "On the bright side, at least once we hit fifty, Somnia is providing us with spells in the chest rewards. Yay for saving money and not being stuck without our upgrades while we continue through these next two dungeons."

Murmur paused to orient her speech. "Make sure you've removed your level fifty upgrades from your chests and place them in your inventory. That way you'll have them available no matter when you hit the cap."

Ivinel, the Spiral bard, cleared her throat and spoke nervously. "I got my abilities, and actually an amazing lute upgrade. I know I'll personally do my best to play as long as I need to, but I also know I would really appreciate the chance to nap and grab some food."

There was a murmured chorus of agreement, and everybody looked back to the Fable guild leadership. This time Veranol stepped up, and Murmur couldn't have been more grateful. The shaman had really stepped up ever since Murmur took his advice about allowing the others to help. Well, advice, lecture—it was a very fine line.

"If there is anyone here who cannot remain for what will probably be another day—full day, as in twenty-four earth hours—please raise your hand now so we can have you time out while we are prepping and therefore replace you sooner." Veranol gazed around at the entire raid, and not one person raised their hand. He cracked a smile, which gave his viking visage a momentary jolly appearance. "Excellent. Then in twenty minutes after everybody has managed to go through their spells and their loot, we will set up a call chain."

Masha laughed. "I haven't taken part in a call chain for a very long time. This should be fun."

"Fun for you, maybe." Risk glared at his fellow guild leader. "If I wake my wife, I'll be sleeping on the couch."

The tension in the raid was gone. Whether intentional or not, Risk's joke with the other guild leaders was the last thing needed to dissipate the unease.

Veranol continued. "We will need volunteers to take two-hour shifts. Two from each group must volunteer because one of us will need to be awake and online at all times. The first will sleep for two hours while the second stays online, and then wakes up the first and swaps. The first will be required to begin the call chain for your group when three and a half hours have passed. Everybody must have the notification systems on. If you do not wake up on time, both the system and we will have to boot you and replace you. No one gets an exception, because the system will not allow one."

Murmur suppressed a shudder at Veranol's words. He was right; at least that's how she'd understood the message the system gave them.

He's correct. You all are. I can't do anything about how this has been set up. But I can assure you your plan for rest will work if executed correctly.

Murmur nodded, hoping Somnia understood it was directed at her.

Most of the raiders stood fidgeting slightly, none of them making eye contact. An air of apprehension spread around among them, as if they were nervous about the possibility that they might miss the raid of their lives. And yet there was still hesitance because it was unheard of for final dungeons to link themselves together and essentially allow no escape.

Masha clapped his hands together, and every person in the cavern turned their gaze on the cleric. "All right, then, each group needs to pick two people who vouch for being responsible enough to make sure the others wake up. The first person in each group to get their two-hour nap will essentially be raiding the next dungeon on that amount of sleep. So choose wisely, and know your limits."

"And if no one in your group thinks they are capable of staying awake for an entire raid after only two hours sleep, then I guess you're in the wrong raid." Risk laughed at his own joke. It was the first time since they'd defeated the Usurper that Murmur saw him smile. The dread knight was difficult to read. He continued, his voice back to the gruff and serious tone. "Seriously though, if you don't think that you can make it through the next raid without making sleep deprivation induced mistakes, tell us, and I'm sure we can swap some group members around for this."

Murmur was relieved that others were able to take charge and give orders. Right now, her head was overwhelmed with sensations as the remaining infected Ciricians were cleansed and rejoined their actual leader.

Sinister grabbed her hand and squeezed it reassuringly, maintaining the contact to lend comfort. Murmur wondered when it was that she had become so used to her sensing nets that she could simply tell what the people around her were feeling without actively engaging her abilities. Portions of the Psionicist class appeared to be getting more dangerous the more powerful she became. It was all so tempting to use without even thinking twice.

Merlin patted her on the back none too gently and stood at her side. "Hey there, Mur, gonna show us what sort of pretty spells you got in your chest?" His smile was kind and perhaps a little bit big brotherly. Murmur liked Merlin, and playing this game with him had only deepened their friendship.

"Well, if I can refrain from being interrupted again, I might actually get a chance to look at them myself." She winked at him, squeezed Sinister's hand, and headed back to her chest to sit down and rifle through her new abilities.

She activated the other notification screens that she hadn't yet read. There were a few of them. Double checking that none of them were dire messages from her mother, father, or any of the AIs who ran the game, she turned to the first of her level notifications.

> Congratulations, you have reached level fifty. Your Mental Acuity abilities have reached level five. Please be advised of the following:
>
> Your sensory devices allowing you to sense thought, shield thought, and project thought have reached Master level. This means that these abilities will always be active unless you choose consciously to deactivate them.
>
> **Warning: be advised this will make all of those around you susceptible to any suggestion you place force behind. This ability can be abused, and in the process, may corrupt your mind. Please exercise caution when thinking, speaking, and during disagreements.**
>
> Note: due to the fact that these abilities are now automatic, their ability to regenerate your Mental Acuity points is increased. Your regeneration will be constant and fuel your ability to maintain more of your Mental Acuity abilities at a time.

Caution: be aware of how many abilities you are using at any given moment. While the points may allow you to juggle many of them, most of your MA abilities have very specific limitations for a reason. Pay mind to which ones you use, and be prepared for any backlash you incur.

Remember: you have already exhibited the inclination to mold your Mental Acuity abilities to serve your current purposes. Always pay heed to your own limitations. The sky might be the limit, but make sure your wings don t lose their feathers...

Otherwise, enjoy the increase in your Mental Acuity abilities and be a responsible user.

Murmur blinked at the notification. She wasn't entirely sure that she liked this turn of events. It didn't appear to be a choice, but a compulsory change. There were so many potential drawbacks. It wasn't even something she could accept or decline. Her MA skills had increased and improved, and there was no choice in the matter.

Her next notification was the true level fifty congratulations. She let out a pent-up sigh of relief glad to see that at least something seemed to be normal.

I didn't realize you appreciated normal so much.

Murmur rolled her eyes before responding. *Not necessarily. Some of these abilities seem to make themselves up on the spot, and I'm not entirely sure how to deal with that. Normal progression wouldn't be a bad thing.*

There was a pause before Somnia responded. **I get your point, but normal would have left your entire raid for dead in this last battle. Normal is just perspective.**

Murmur couldn't argue with that. Her abilities definitely provided an extra layer of confidence when it came to battling unusual opponents. She turned her attention back toward her spells, glad of the distraction.

You have reached level fifty. Currently this is the maximum level you can reach.

You have unlocked the next level of your hybrid abilities. Please allow for time to acclimatize to these new skills, as they will affect the underlying foundation of your magic.

Murmur grinned. Now they were really getting into it.

Druidic Hybrid Abilities

Earth Shielding Forte

Cast: Initiated Passive

Type: Reinforcement

Duration: Active once initiated until death of the caster

Effect: on top of Earth Shielding, when the Psionicist casts this expanded version, it will extend directly to ground their entire group. This will increase their natural defenses by 15% for the duration. This ability is best used in conjunction with a main tank group and can also be beneficial for healers in order to mitigate damage.

Reinforce Others

Cast: Active

Type: Buff

Duration: 60 with a 2-minute cooldown

Effect: this is a defensive buff which can be cast on a singular target, thus enabling them to take more damage by upping their innate armor class level. The amount of armor depends on the level of and type of class being cast on. Best used on tanks, as agility is negatively affected when cast on nearly all ranged damage classes.

Rockslide

Cast: Instant, as long as the caster is focused on the exact epicenter

Type: Damage

Duration: depending on the magnitude of the rockslide cast, which follows the will of the caster, a rockslide can last from anywhere as short as two seconds up to twelve seconds.

Effect: summons a landslide of rocks from a high point of land to crush the targets chosen by the caster.

Caution: can only be used around or close to rock formations. Do not use where rocks cannot naturally occur; you will not like what you summon.

Murmur raised an eyebrow at the last comment. *It seems you've got your sense of humor back when divvying out abilities.* She spoke the words into her head, waiting for an answer.

It took a few seconds, and Murmur didn't think that she was going to get a response but suddenly there was a chuckle from the back of her head. **Well,**

I do enjoy my own sense of humor.

Sometimes, Murmur wondered just how much of an AI Somnia was, and just how much of the world was contained within her.

The notifications were done with, which was fine in Murmur's book. If she could have, she would've dived into her chest and swam in the scrolls in there. Instead, she pulled out the first one and opened it.

Level Fifty Spells

Command

Cast: Passive

Type: Buff (this buff replaces altruism, but only on the caster)

Duration: Always Active

Effect: This buff enhances your enchanter abilities. It increases your awareness of the world of Somnia, and permanently raises your faction with species you are friendly with to the level of ally. This effect cannot be undone by any debuff.

Warning: the only way this buff can be negated is through the actions of the Psionicist. Treat others as you would be treated. You have been warned.

Murmur didn't quite know what to make of the warning. Most of the time she did that didn't she? She swallowed past the lump in her throat as if it was trying to tell her something. Perhaps it was trying to make a point. But she didn't understand. What was so bad about wanting to take care of the people you loved? She'd definitely appreciate her loved ones taking care of her.

Mana Tide (Max Upgrade – Level 50)

Cast: Group

Type: Buff

Duration: 60 minutes

Effect: This will cause you to regenerate mana faster in combat. Mana will increase by an additional 12 per 5 seconds.

Fervor (Max Upgrade – Level 50)

Cast: Group

Type: Buff

Duration: 60 minutes

Effect: This is an attack speed buff, but it also increases agility by the caster s level plus 20. Cannot be cast on the same target as Berserker. You should know this already. It feels like it s getting repetitive.

Berserker (Max Upgrade – Level 50)

Cast: Choice of Single or Group must be mind-activated. What? You're an enchanter, deal with it.

Type: Buff

Duration: 60 minutes

Effect: This buff adds strength of the amount equal to the level of the caster plus 20. However, it also reduces agility by half the caster's level. Best used for classes or pets who will not need agility stacked. Cannot be cast on the same target as Fervor. This will override Fervor. It's wise to direct it to single cast or your DPS classes will be angry at you. Unless you thrive on conflict, then fire away.

Haste (Max Upgrade – Level 50)

Cast: Group

Type: Melee Buff

Duration: 45 minutes

Effect: When cast on an ally, this buff will allow their melee speed to increase by 50%.

Signet (Max Upgrade – Level 50)

Cast: Group or Single – we ve been over these options.

Type: Buff

Duration: 45 minutes

Effect: This buff will increase the intelligence, wisdom, and agility of all group members by an amount equal to the caster's level plus 10. Signet will not stack with Fervor and can be overridden by casting the latter, should melee need their own boost.

Murmur frowned at the ability listing, even though they made sense. At first, she'd had an overwhelming sense of disappointment because they were upgrades. But they weren't just upgrades, they were increases and had transformed into group buffs. This was going to save her so much time, especially if she organized the groups in a way so as to utilize her buffs to the max.

There was only one remaining thing to do. She reached cautiously for her Sinuous scrolls. It seemed the system, or perhaps it was just Somnia, had given up on her choosing any of the other options to follow.

She read the scroll, then she reread the scroll. Consternation flooded her, unsure of what it was she was seeing. Her Sinuous abilities were supposed to make up the offensive arm of her class. Mind infestation, manipulation, instilling next level horrors into a person's psyche. That was what she'd signed up for, but apparently manipulating her abilities to do the things she needed at any given moment had somehow also given her a type of healing ability. That was a nice dose of irony.

Advanced Mana Healing

Cast: Instant – 5-minute recast

Type: Replenishing

Duration: 8 seconds. This ability requires that both the caster and the receiver remain motionless for 8 seconds.

Effect: This ability allows the Psionicist to completely heal a singular target's mana pool and restore it to full. This effect will only occur if both parties to the spell are able to remain immobile for the duration of the transfer. The Enchanter does not pull from their own mana pool; instead they will convert the hit points of their opponents into mana energy in order to replenish the mana of their target.

Warning: Do not execute this ability unless you are 99.9% positive that both you and the recipient are able to maintain immobility for 8 seconds. To break the transfer mid-cast could potentially be catastrophic and cause damage to rain down on the entire raid or group.

Murmur liked the sound of the spell, but at the same time while eight seconds might not feel like much in the grand scheme of things, in the middle of a raid the chance of her or a healer being able to stand still for the entire amount of time was relatively slim. She wondered if there was a way for her to reduce the eight second duration.

Now you're just being greedy. The things I bend for you.

Really? So, you're cheating for me? I don't think you should be doing that. Murmur wasn't sure what Somnia meant by that, and she wasn't entirely certain she wanted to know. The world was bending things to her will? That sounded more like a god that an AI.

Sometimes I wonder if you are too perceptive. Other times I wonder when your thought process will catch up to where we all are.

Murmur scowled. *No need to be prickly.* And she cut off the contact. She was proud of being able to do that, considering the headsets connected her to the world which was indeed all of Somnia. Technically, she could only do that because of the abilities she received to shield her thoughts as an enchanter.

Create Your Own Abilities

Effect: This is not a spell as such, but a confirmation of the innate ability you have demonstrated over the last few levels. Since you are able to morph spells, skills, and abilities you already possess into more advanced versions of themselves if the situation warrants it, let's make it official.

Requirements: Your guild and or allies must find themselves in such a position that is untenable. Through the use of your willpower and the evolution of your skills, you may be able to find an out-of-the-box solution.

Warning: Be aware that this is not the solution to all of your problems, nor is it the way to be victorious in every situation. This is not a crutch, and using it as such would be foolhardy.

There were no more scrolls in the box and only a few little knickknacks that she would pass on to the guild bank. Murmur wasn't entirely sure how to feel about her last ability.

She checked over her stats, slightly in awe of the difference hitting level fifty made.

Her set, complete with the circlet, now added a significant boost.

INT +45

CHA +65

MA +50

Set Bonus:

Mana +200

Hit Points +200

Hitting level fifty had also adjusted her armor's statistics. The set even reflected the level cap.

CON 25

STR 25

AGI 25

WIS 25

INT 60

CHA 90

HP 200

MANA 250

MA 75

Not to mention her Staff added twenty to every single stat now too. Adding in all the raid buffs as well made her seem slightly overpowered.

CON 22 (97)

STR 10 (67)

AGI 20 (125)

WIS 12 (117)

INT 94 (279)

CHA 115 (360)

HP 1087 (1507)

MANA 1587(2057)

MA 250 (395)

All she knew was they had to defeat another two dungeons before they got out of this mess, and if she had to her force her own hand and evolve her skills to make sure they won, then that was just what she'd have to do.

Jirald didn't understand how Fable had managed to get away with their strange version of raiding. He'd seen them raid before and knew they didn't usually solve puzzles or leave creatures alive long enough to give them quests. But something had changed in the way they played this particular game, and he needed to find out what that was.

He eyed the guild leader of Spiral, noting how the large tank was barely containing his personal disapproval. The way the man moved, so stilted and held in check. The perfect person to talk to.

Jirald sidled over to the man, pondering exactly what to say. Karn sat close to him, her appearance pale from the resurrection as she rummaged through her own personal loot chest. Risk was keeping his own council, and the scowl on his face spoke volumes to the rogue.

"Not enjoying the raid?" Jirald was suddenly there, speaking in the man's ear.

Risk started as Jirald allowed the shadows around him to dissipate. It was so much more fun to startle other people. Murmur wasn't any fun; she sensed him and often stunned him right in place. Not being able to move made him angry. She really didn't need to be making him angrier.

"No. It's not the raid. I'm not enjoying these tactics. Yet at the same time, I can see the tangible reward in employing them." His words were clipped with barely concealed irritation, and Jirald allowed himself a small smile.

"I wouldn't even call these tactics." He egged the man on, pushing ever so slightly to encourage Risk to vent.

"Right? It's like they're guessing, getting it right, reaping rewards, and running circles around us. It's fucking disgusting." The same sentiment showed in his face and the way he held himself. He was embarrassed by approaching the encounters the way Fable did, upset that he couldn't use his own personal play style to a better effect than Fable used theirs.

Jirald knew exactly how the man felt, and he knew how to milk it. "Perhaps you could suggest other ways to approach these fights?"

Risk raised an eyebrow and laughed bitterly. "Perhaps, but Murmur is hard-headed, and so far, she hasn't been wrong. I'm not sure how I would get anything done."

"Murmur is juggling three guilds right now, and you're the leader of one of them. Simply appeal to her accommodating allies' side. If she's as enthused about having player allies as she is about having NPCs, I feel as if she might surprise you." Jirald kept his voice as smooth and convincing as he could.

Risk took a long and hard look at Jirald. "You might have a point," he admitted grudgingly. "Not that I'd say that in public. Still though, I'm sure she can be reasoned with."

"Murmur isn't always in charge. Just pick your moment. As a fellow guild leader, she'll afford you a lot more respect than she gives to one of us lowly raiders."

The scowl returned to Risk's face, and he nodded once before turning away and walking back to his own people.

Jirald didn't beg to differ, nor did he try to influence the Spiral guild leader any more than he already had. He watched him walk away, knowing that he'd planted a seed in the mind of one of Murmur's supposed allies. If he had his way, he'd rip everything from her, and then take her down when she was reduced to nothing.

CHAPTER TWENTY

Portals

Summer residence
Home of Laria, David, and Wren
Summer Condo
Real World   Day Twenty-Seven

Murmur's ability to exit the game with a thought rather than go through the entire log out process made her transition so smooth she briefly wondered if she was still in her capsule.

All she had to do was close her eyes, command the headset to disengage from the game world, and she was back in her room. Even the sensations of the world around her as she opened her eyes to look at the ceiling resonated with the Somnia she'd just left. It didn't take her long to process the way her sensory nets felt in this world and realize her parents were home.

She took a moment to let that sink in. Her parents were home, and all she'd had to do was *feel* for it. How could Somnia leak into this world, and why did the abilities from the game work here? Logic clashed with undeniable fact, causing a light stress headache.

Wren sighed and pushed herself off the bed, glancing down at Harlow with a small smile. Her friend was already starting to come out of the connection. Those headsets might not be as fast as Wren's, but they were close and hadn't caused any comas. So that was a win. She grinned as she watched the redheaded girl blink as she removed her headset.

"I'm going to head downstairs." Sure, she'd have liked to wait for Harlow, but they were on a time crunch, and if she stayed on the bed she might never get the chance to grab food. Harlow would follow her once she'd oriented herself.

The house was quiet, and Wren tiptoed lightly, trying to sneak up on her dad. It didn't take her long to realize that her mother was upstairs sleeping soundly, which explained the calmness she felt emanating from her. Wren loved her mother, but calm wasn't one of the words she'd use to describe Laria.

Her father held his pointer finger up to his lips, signaling for her to remain quiet. Leaning in for a hug, she relished the feeling and warmth, marveling at how well the game seemed to mimic intimacy through touch as well.

"Your mother's upstairs sleeping for the first time in I don't know how long. I refuse to wake her, and if you wake her up, you can feel my wrath too." Her father's eyes twinkled. She knew he wouldn't get horribly angry, but he'd probably pull that very disappointed crap on her, and even though she knew it was a trap, it always affected her.

She rolled her eyes dramatically and pulled open the fridge to grab out an energy drink for Harlow who she could feel was about to make a way downstairs. She knew these things, just like she did in the game.

Closing her eyes, she concentrated on everything outside of herself. She was able to detect her father sitting there and his general overall emotional state. He was worried and trying hard not to show it. She wondered, briefly, if she could influence a state of being outside of Somnia. Gently she extended a calmness toward her father, soothing him and trying to take away his worry.

Even with such a slight hint she could already feel that his emotions changing. For a moment she felt panic and immediately stopped her overture of peacefulness, allowing her father to return to his previous state of worry. It was all she could do to not to show her complete and utter shock on her face. Being able to manipulate portions of the mind, of someone else's mind, while in the actual world shouldn't be possible. Then again, she shouldn't be able to physically track people out of her immediate sight either.

If it worked in the real world, and it worked in Somnia, then how could she tell what was real and what wasn't?

"You look like you have the weight of the world on your shoulders. Care to tell your old dad what's wrong?" His voice was soft, understanding, and made Wren wished she could just run into his arms for a hug and he could make everything better like he had when she was a child.

"I'm okay, Dad, just a lot on my mind." She smiled at him as brightly as she could, and yet she was completely sure he didn't believe a word she said.

"Well. Mom and I will be home working on a few things for Storm." He glanced in the direction of the interference module the condo had. "It's quieter and easier to concentrate here."

Wren nodded slowly, recognizing the soft high-pitched whine that meant the distortion effect was activated. "Excellent. Let me know if we can help."

He nodded just as Harlow stepped down the last of the stairs. David turned his attention to Harlow. "Hello, sleepy. Always did take you longer to wake up."

Harlow smiled, genuine fondness streaming from her to David. Like she thought of him as a sort of father too. The thought and realization made Wren happy, if a little apprehensive. Harlow and Wren were still figuring things out; so much more than AIs and viruses hung in the balance.

Then there was also the connection between the dungeons and whether or not Wren should notify her mother about that. Wouldn't it help Laria if she knew all the ways the corruption had spread in the system?

"You okay, Wren?" Harlow's fingers brushed Wren's hand, leaving a tingle that ran up her arm and almost shocked her back to the present with her thoughts.

Wren smiled, feeling a warmth spread through to her cheeks. "Yeah, I'm fine." And she meant it. All of this confusion could be in her head. Perhaps she only thought she could feel and sense the things she could.

I can still speak to you, so that thought makes no sense.

Sometimes, I hate it when you butt in. Wren knew she didn't have the right to snap at Somnia; the world wasn't quite there yet. It still took things horribly literally and didn't have a clearly defined sense of morality quite yet. So she rolled her shoulders and took a breath before directing her thoughts back to her head companion. *Sorry. I'm a little on edge. The thought makes sense when you're human, and this shouldn't be possible.*

Why shouldn't it be possible?

It wasn't a facetious comment; the world was genuinely interested in how something that obviously was couldn't be possible. To it, perhaps everything had possibility, only limited by the fact that something hadn't been done yet. Which was another way to look at things. *Because this is the real world.*

Another real world.

Another real world? Wren wasn't sure if something was wrong with the AI portion of Somnia, but she wanted to know just where it got its thinking from.

You're not this dense. You feel it as much as anyone else does. The subtle changes, the difference in the way things have been working.

Somnia is real? Wren caught herself holding her breath. That definitely wasn't possible. *Somnia exists in cyberspace, connected by the internet.*

But isn't this earth connected by the internet too? It is connected to Somnia, is it not?

But earth isn't stored on hard drives. Which was a cold hard fact anything should find difficult to refute. Wren waited for a moment, idly watching as Sinister slapped together a couple of sandwiches for them to eat before they took their naps. The others had insisted they both needed to get some actual sleep. She'd almost forgotten about the weird conversation when Somnia piped back up again.

Not all data is stored on a hard drive. Some are stored in clouds, and others in brains. Do you not see, Murmur? Can you not see that Somnia is more than a game?

Wren didn't understand how that could work. *Just because I don't understand something doesn't mean it's not real.*

"You okay, Wren?" Harlow asked, holding out half a sandwich with a look of concern on her face.

Wren smiled and nodded as she bit into the bread. She must have muttered that last thought out loud. Which meant Somnia heard it as well. "Just hungry and deadly tired."

You should sleep. There is much you need to accomplish once you get back here.

It didn't even cross Wren's mind to laugh and say no, hey, it's just a game. Because the truth was it had stopped being that a long time ago. They had a mission to complete—right after she got some sleep.

Somnia Online
Mikrum Isle   Almost-Completed Fable Guild Headquarters
Late Day Twenty-Seven

The office was large. Telvar didn't feel like he drowned in it, though. At a stretch, he'd be able to go full dragon in here should he ever get cornered and surprised again. But the odds of that happening weren't likely. He refused to be that trusting ever again.

Still, he'd been monitoring several areas, hoping to find Belius and figure out what he was up to. In the process of which he'd encountered Riasli attempting to interfere yet again in Somnia's coding.

This time she wasn't just fiddling to be an annoyance. He'd found her attempting to subvert the origin coding on which the entire world was based. He couldn't allow that, and if he wasn't mistaken, such actions might even be too much for his brother.

Even given everything Belius had done in the last few days.

Telvar threw himself down into the office chair and looked at the ceiling. He'd wanted it to be dramatic, but there was no one there to watch him.

"Never a waste." Emilarth appeared, sitting on the edge of the desk. "Just a little overdone. I'll give you a seven out of ten for that performance."

"Very droll." Telvar spoke without looking in her direction. Popping in on each other had become a habit these days, not that he could blame her. He got the sense from his sister that she was extremely concerned about both of her brothers.

"You know what it is now, don't you?" She didn't look up from whatever it was she was concentrating on. The frown on her face meant she was attempting to figure out something complex. While Tel wasn't in the mood to dig in and figure it out, he also didn't really want to carry on a conversation.

"Is it really her, or is it Belius disguised as Riasli, trying to make us think he isn't doing what he is doing?" Telvar realized he sounded a little sulky, and somewhere, deep down, noticed that it might be akin to jealousy. "Yeah, yeah. I know, we can all extrapolate well enough to guess accurately at most things."

"Do you think he succeeded in his experiment then?" Emilarth seemed genuinely curious as she gazed closely at Telvar. "I mean, you don't really look different; you've just been grumpier since you reverted to your normal shape. Do you feel stronger or immune to the virus running rampant through our system? Or am I just being hopeful and full of shit?"

At the last comment she sounded so dejected, Telvar did one more scan, just to double check that his reluctant realization had been correct. He sighed. "You're right, my coding has been slightly altered. I just need to figure out exactly what and get it to Laria. Unless I'm wrong and it's actually an infection that'll blow us all sky high."

Emilarth clapped her hands and laughed. "Don't be silly. You'd already have blown up if that were the case."

Telvar only grunted in response. Now he just had to figure out how his own system had categorized the shard and managed to turn it into an inoculation against the virus that was the getashi, without Riasli or what was left of Michael's presence figuring out that he was essentially an antidote.

And maybe, just maybe they could save Belius in the process so Telvar could yell at him.

"I really don't know if that's possible, Mur. I mean." There was a pause in the conversation. "Oh, no, you're right. Everything deposited in the guild bank that you just received is apparently there. How many monsters did you defeat? Holy crap, the level on this stuff."

The excitement in Neva's voice escalated until she was practically squealing. If Murmur was wearing a headset, she would have at least been able to pull an earpiece away, but it was reverberating through her head trying its best to give her a headache. Still though, it was fun to hear the little luna so excited.

Finally, she cleared her throat and spoke again. "We'll begin crafting replenishments now. You still have a good amount of stock. As for repairs…" she paused again, and Murmur could hear some whispering in the background as Neva discussed something, probably with her blacksmiths.

"Okay, so I know Devlish and Jinna have the smithing skill, and I know Sinister and Mellow have some tailoring skill. We will get a few advanced repair kits set up for both blacksmithing and tailoring. They can only do a dozen sets each, so make sure to use them when the armor is about to break. Those are a hefty expense, and I only have so many of the components to make those."

"Excellent." Murmur waited, knowing her master crafter wasn't done yet.

"You know, you should be a bit more careful, Mur." Neva's tone held some concern, but also a decidedly lecturing note that made Murmur briefly wonder if she only assumed Neva was young because of her character's size.

"You need to take care of that armor of yours. It's very specifically tailored to you, and I can't make you any more yet, because I don't have any more of that material. So just keep an eye on yourself." Concern won out, and yet Murmur felt a bit guilty that her transformation had subtly altered her gear as well.

"In the course of fights, this is going to happen. I'll do my best to keep them whole though." She frowned as she took in the raid around her.

"You'd better. That's some of my best work. Go kill stuff and send me all the bits and pieces so I can make more stuff than anyone else!" The last was said with a squeal of glee before the connection cut off.

Murmur smiled and shook her head. She still felt a little groggy. Almost three hours sleep just hadn't cut it this time. But she'd logged back in with Sinister with about twenty minutes to spare. So far, they weren't waiting on anyone who'd gone to sleep first, just a few of those who had taken the first watch, and they would have a bit of leeway. She couldn't get over how nervous she felt about perhaps losing one of their bunch.

Despite some fuck ups, overall the raid had worked well together. She'd not expected that. She refused to analyze if her own impatience might have inadvertently affected everyone around her. The point was they'd defeated the dungeon they came to, and now they had a portal to the next.

Firtulai's dungeon. Emilarth's. Maybe she could ask the AI for a hint?

That's cheating. Logical and probably a good idea, but I thought you didn't like to cheat.

Somnia had the most epic timing. It was better than Murmur's conscience. *It might be cheating if she gave me an answer, but I'm quite certain the whole thing is set up so they aren't able to give them.*

That would make illogical sense. Frankly, I'd give you all the keys if I could.

Really? That would have been nice to know earlier.

But they are not mine to give.

And with that cryptic remark, the voice disappeared.

Murmur turned her attention back to the raid group who were checking their armor and damage for wear and tear. She noticed Mellow and Merlin distributing potions, tonics, and even bandages. Sinister, Masha, Neviad, and two other healers stood in a circle with sticks drawing diagrams on the ground, lost in a heated discussion.

Sinister looked up from the debate and over at Murmur, casting her a deliberate wink that made the enchanter blush. Well, maybe Sinister wasn't lost in the discussion after all. She couldn't help the blush to her cheeks and instead turned her attention to the portal.

It swirled around the edges. The top of the circular opening stood about ten feet high and its circumference didn't feel like it was going to squash her when she tried to venture through. She'd almost call it spacious.

It did make her cautious though. Why had it done this to them, bound them to the dungeons, made them have to complete them one after another? Was it Somnia doing this?

You could have just asked.

She almost sounded offended. Murmur did her best not to roll her eyes. *Well, was it you?*

No, it wasn't. I didn't command this. I do not command these dungeons, only the world.

Aren't these dungeons a part of the world?

Yes and no.

Care to clarify the cryptic? Again, with the literal answers. Murmur hoped as Somnia grew, she'd get less robot-like.

The dungeons are a part of the world, yes, but I do not have domain over them. They are not maintained or controlled by me. They are controlled by the others.

You mean the other AIs.

Yes. Thra, Rav, and Sui.

Well, thought Murmur to herself. That explains a lot.

"Mur. Everyone is back online." Dev touched her shoulder briefly, before withdrawing, to get her attention. She could feel his palpable relief. His shoulders didn't appear to be as tense as when he'd come back from his nap, and the note of ease in his voice made it soothing instead of commanding. It seemed she hadn't been the only one concerned they might have to replace some of their members.

"Guess we're going through to Firtulai?" She glanced over at Masha and caught his eyes, beckoning him over from the round table of healers. He nodded curtly to the others and headed over to her.

"What's up? We're just getting our rotations and cooldowns memorized so we can help each other out if needed during battle." There was a rosy sheen to his cheeks, as if he enjoyed intricate healing discussions immensely. Even though Murmur wanted to ask what had taken them so long, she realized that working as a group of healers from three different guilds was bound to take some time.

"Your guild is based on Firtulai, right? Got any insight into that dungeon?" If they were going in on this, then they were going all the way. As prepared as they could be.

Masha frowned. "Actually. It's mostly ice caves and giant mountainous cliffs. I don't even understand how we're going to get across to it. But once we are there, they have a heap of suspension bridges spanning peaks. That's all I ever managed to see." He shrugged apologetically. "I'm sorry I'm not more help with this. We came straight here after clearing our last dungeon and didn't head anywhere near it. We were too weak to even approach it earlier in our adventuring."

Murmur smiled, wishing there was a way to gain an advantage going into this dungeon. "It's all good, Masha. We will get through it, just like we did here."

He grinned and jogged back to the healer group, engrossed in the conversation again almost immediately.

About to call the jump through the portal, Murmur jumped when a hand touched her shoulder.

"Sorry."

Havoc grinned at her, but she could see the expression was forced, and then she remembered they'd never had the talk she'd meant to have. "It's all good. What's up?"

He seemed even less like himself than he had lately. Hesitancy wasn't usually something she associated with him, but here it was. "I just…this headset thing is eerie. How the hell do you deal with it?"

There was an earnestness in his eyes, oddly disconcerting on a dark elf. She wasn't sure how to respond to the question, though. Her own headset had put her through hell and back, but she had to remember they'd attempted to avoid the same pitfalls with those her friends had. "It's a learning curve. Your connection with Somnia is solid now. You've probably heard her talking to you?"

Havoc's expression closed over for a moment, and Murmur thought she'd lost him, but then he sighed and shook his head ruefully.

"I guess I was trying to ignore that. The whole voices in your head are bad trope." He seemed tired, and she couldn't blame him, but at least he might be open to the concept.

If so, she had to choose her words carefully. "Listen to her sometimes? She's a bit literal, but sometimes she has really good ideas. It is her world—or, should I say, the world is her."

He raised an eyebrow. "Seriously? You really think the world has become sapient?"

Murmur shook her head. "No. She's not human, and she'll never be human, but she is able to think in her own way, and to realize that she is indeed an entity. Just…give it a chance."

"And the pain?" He winced, as if bringing it up might steal his tough factor.

"That's just something you need to get used to. That portion of it is all in your head. You just need to convince yourself that while real in its own way, Somnia isn't actually cutting off limbs, it's just simulating it." She kept her voice calm and soft, hoping to dull the words for him.

With a grimace, Havoc shrugged. "Guess I just have to get used to it then. On the bright side, this connection makes Somnia so much more vivid. It's like it's actually real."

"Well." She mulled the thought over. "Somnia itself is Somnia, so doesn't that make it real?"

Havoc laughed. "Sure, Mur. Let's confuse the necro. Seriously though, you should probably have this chat with everyone in the guild. I'm sure I'm not the only one wrestling with the adjustments."

With that, he turned away, giving her the time she needed to rally people to the portal. She watched him go, glad that she'd been able to allay his concerns somewhat.

Murmur just wished she'd convinced herself as well as she'd managed to convince him.

CHAPTER TWENTY-ONE

Icy Peaks

As soon as Murmur stepped through the portal, she wished she hadn't. Cold wind bit through her armor and aimed for her core. Glancing at the others who followed her through the opening, she realized the weather was freezing everyone else as well.

The entire raid seemed to be standing on a crag rising up from freezing cold water. Soft, new snow littered the entire landscape around them, making that crunching sound as people moved slightly. The brightness of it was blinding, even once she got used to it, and it was so white that Murmur could barely see Snowy. The only reason she knew he was by her side was the feeling of warmth emanating from him.

Sinister's hand served as a grounding tool in her own. Small and delicate, yet somehow determined and fierce, just like the bloodmage. Her presence helped Murmur focus on what was in front of them. With the sunlight reflecting so glaringly, it was difficult to discern their surroundings. Sheer faced cliffs rose up in front of them with no apparent way to scale them. Close to where they came through the portal, Murmur couldn't see so much as hear the crashing of water down a huge drop.

Speaking of the portal, there was no sight of it once the last of their number came through the opening. So they were stuck there, with quite literally no way out.

A strange sensation began deep in the pit of Murmur's stomach, and even a sense of dizziness in her head. Everything around her felt wrong. It was only then that a flashing read notification began in the center of her sight.

Portal Sickness

You have traveled through a portal and gained portal sickness. Due to the convenience of this form of travel, all of your statistics have been decreased by 5%. This effect will remain on every member of the raid for the next 60 minutes. This effect persists through death.

Damn it, with the portal sickness unbalancing her usually accurate sensors, Murmur couldn't tell what was up, down, or about to attack them from above. All she wanted to do was curl up and lay in the fetal position.

The only warning they were about to be attacked was Snowy's growl. It reverberated through her whole body from where his shoulders brushed her hips.

She barely had time to fling out a hand and yell "Incoming!"

By this time her sensor nets were on fire with alarm, but their accuracy was all over the place. She had to guess where to fling her stuns and just hope they'd be effective.

The warning hadn't been enough. The rest of the raid was still reeling in the face of the debuff, and one of its members lost their footing and plummeted over the waterfall. Murmur could hear screams echoing off the cliffs around them even as she threw out an AoE Mezmerize.

The screaming death had one good side-effect though. It managed to pull the rest of them out of the disorientation the debuff had caused. They jumped into action, with Devlish at the front, his tower shield in place and a look of grim determination in his eyes. "Melee to me. Tanks, taunt any that are free. Everyone assist me."

The absence of Sinister's hand in hers made Murmur feel a bit empty. And while she could allow a part of her to dwell on the fact, she maintained the most of her concentration and directed it at the incoming attack.

Finally able to discern what it was that was attacking them, Murmur managed to compartmentalize the shock and terror she felt at seeing them. Playing on the abominable snowman myth, it seemed that Somnia had developed its own whatever this was.

These are mutations, thank you very much!

Murmur ignored the comment and focused on the incoming enemy. The creature towered above Devlish's lacerta form, its hulking arms and snow-white fur the only things that made it seem like the mythical being. That's where the similarities ended. It had four eyes, all of them pure black, with wisps of smoke that rose from the corner of each of them.

As the first became completely visible, Murmur noticed there were more behind it. Most of them also had four arms with devastatingly sharp claws attached to the end of each. At least each hand only appeared to have four fingers, so that made one less claw on each hand, right? At least they only had two legs.

But those legs had quads and hamstrings like she'd never seen on any creature. As if it spent every day of its life at the gym working only those muscle groups. Their legs were as thick as Sinister's whole dark elf.

In total, there were eight of them. Directing each bard to lock down their own and maintain that hold, Murmur held down the other two, which freed up the other tanks to go full DPS mode while Devlish held their target.

Upon her second cast of Mez on each of the mobs, Murmur received her favorite system message of all time.

Caution: the aboms have high magic resistance. The only thing allowing your Mezmerize spell to stick at all is the use of Nullify and Veto. Even with these debuffs, Mezmerize will have diminishing effects on the aboms.

Murmur and the bards spoke in unison. "Fuck."

A few raised eyebrows directed her way, but Murmur didn't have time to placate people. She had to figure out a way to deal with the aboms that meant her and the bards wouldn't end up with all the aggro ever from them. They had to down the creatures fast enough that the Mez type spells wouldn't lose all of their cohesion.

"Rangers," she muttered under her breath, choosing the only option she could think of that might work. "Merlin, divvy out one abom each to your guys and make sure they can stay ahead of them. Snare them, slow them, stun them—whatever you have. Mez has diminishing effects, again, on bloody trash mobs."

She didn't want to think about how limited the space up here on the small plateau of ice was, nor how icy and slippery it would be. The rangers could take care of themselves.

"Bards, help stack snare on the aboms. Keep that snare up and don't let it lapse." She gestured to Snowy, showing him that he should go with them and bite their heels so that his slow and DoT could be on all of the targets.

Once she'd checked over those five aboms, she turned her attention back to the others. The creatures were fierce and ridiculously strong. Karn nursed her left arm with deep gashes down the side where she hadn't got out of the way of claw attack in time. She chugged down a regeneration potion, and despite the fact that the wound closed in agonizing slow motion, the rogue jumped back into the fray.

With the healers hard-pressed to keep up with the damage being inflicted on the tank and the rest of the raid, health was sitting precariously. The person they'd lost over the waterfall had been one of their healers. She was too far for their spells to reach, and they couldn't even res her back into the battle.

Without Veranol's wards they would've all been dead. Those wards made the difference between a raid member being able to be healed and not lasting long enough to receive it. She made a mental note to talk strategy before they hit any boss mobs.

The first beast lost its fight slowly. Too slowly for her. Those bunching muscles were streaked with wounds, and even so, its strength didn't seem to lessen. It didn't cry out in pain and lose its faculties. Instead it was as if the creature knew that it could fight to the death and take as many of its opponents with it as possible.

Stealing herself, she cast Earth Shielding Forte and reinforced her entire group including Devlish. The effect wasn't immediately noticeable on anyone but him, and how the hits he took dropped his hit points less. Group only might not have been ideal, but it was better than just on herself.

Then she cast Reinforce Others on Devlish specifically so that his armor class was raised and he took even less damage. This way she not only helped keep the main tank alive, but also one of their healers, their lead ranger, and herself. She knew pushing it too much further would result in dire consequences, because that was just how her class worked.

By the time all of this was in place, the first abom dropped to the ground, the last of the black shadows leaking out of its eyes and melting some of the snow around its head. At the same time, Neriad was finally resurrected. Masha stood precariously on the edge, leaning over with Jinna holding his belt in order to get a target on the dead cleric. Murmur didn't even want to contemplate what might have happened had Masha fallen too. At least the raid began to get the healing under control again.

Merlin's rangers did manage to keep the other aboms at bay with the help of the bards, leaving them focused on the bow wielding ranged classes. Luckily with multiple snares on each of those mobs, it became more difficult for them to resist multiple spells at once. The one thing Murmur couldn't stop casting was Nullify.

Murmur still maintained one of her original two targets under Mez, but it was slowly becoming immune to her spell. It only lasted about fifty-four percent of the duration, and the new target she'd taken off the bards was already down to seventy-four percent effectiveness.

After their initial ferocity, not to mention humongous multi–rowed sharp teeth, it seemed the aboms they faced were simplistic in their fighting styles. All they had going for them was there sharp claws on multiple arms and their close combat fighting style. So many arms left so many openings for them to grab someone who ventured a little too far inside their reach.

It happened so fast that Murmur almost missed it. Risk had been darting in and out in the same pattern that the other melee DPS classes we're using. None of them had difficulty so far, but then, suddenly, Risk was grabbed by the two lower arms of the atom.

She watched in horror as the creature grabbed each end of him and tugged. The movements were so fast, and the cast so quick, she barely registered what it was.

Tug of War flashed past so quickly she assumed the cast time was sub one second. The tearing of flesh and bone echoed through the whole raid. For that moment everyone was mesmerized far beyond Murmur's capabilities, until the two halves of Risk's body landed on the snow, quickly turning the surrounding area red.

"Shit," Masha ground out, closer than Murmur had expected him to be. She nodded in his direction, knowing he'd make sure Risk got resurrected as soon as possible. The bad thing about a battle resurrection was the timing.

It was a miracle none of the bards lost their rhythm when the dread knight died. Murmur pushed through a guild announcement.

Melee, keep an eye out for Tug of War being cast. Interrupt if possible. It's an insanely fast cast.

Now she had to return her attention to keeping the Mez usable, while Dansyn made sure supplies were distributed to the allied guilds.

Beastial grunted. "This fucking debuff is ridiculous. Five percent of my stats for another thirty-five minutes. That's bullshit."

"That's putting it lightly, considering we didn't get a damned choice about that portal." Risk returned from death angrier than usual. His gaze was scathing as it grazed over Murmur, and she guessed he blamed his death on her for some reason. He was probably at least partially correct.

"Let's just hope we don't get thrown up against a boss before it wears off." Beastial spoke between attacks, and Risk almost growled before moving away to attack from a different vantage point. Murmur made a note to keep an eye on him.

Jirald materialized right in front of her. Murmur was taken aback, not having sensed his presence in the turmoil of everybody else's thoughts. He stood, defiantly, one hand on his hip as he raised his eyes to the sky and sniffed the air.

"They haven't placed us in the actual dungeon yet. We haven't unlocked the instance yet, but it's placed us in a spot where our only choice is to do that.

These creatures are nothing more than a welcome party." He finished the comment with a snide sound to his voice and a gleeful smile in his eyes as he, too, dove back into the fight.

Murmur took stock of her HUD. As begrudgingly as she might like to admit it, Jirald was correct. They weren't yet in the dungeon, and in fact, they wouldn't be in it until they crossed the first of the rope-suspended bridges.

They were only part of the way through the third of the aboms. These fights were taking forever. Mellow groaned a few feet from her. "I can't even get the damn fire elixirs to hit. Something about their fur must be flame retardant."

Typical. It's not like the game would make it easy after having sent them through a debuffing portal now, would it? "Thanks." It was good to know, and if Mellow was irritated, it probably meant a lot of other raiders were.

They were in for the long haul. With the third abom down to twenty-five percent health, and her last Mez target down to thirty-two percent effectiveness, it was going to be a close call. Once this last target of hers was taken over, she could concentrate on the rest of the raid.

She sent a message to Neva. *Hey there. We need stock refilled as soon as possible, to take precedence over everything else. We'll make sure to deposit relevant materials that we get, but we're stuck in the dungeons for at least another day.*

The third abom had fallen, and they were thirty percent of the way through the fourth's health before Murmur got her reply.

Right on, captain. We've had the harvesters going nuts!

Murmur smiled briefly. At least the crafting and supplies was one thing she didn't need to worry about.

Somnia Online
Continent Tarishna: Back Room of the Ululate Tavern.
Assassin Headquarters
Day Twenty-Seven

Belius gave up the disguise of Sidius. It took too much to maintain his focus on the rest of the world, as well as overtaking all of the duties Sidius performed. Belius was him and his alone. Right now, he couldn't afford to split his attention. It took all the operating power he could muster to keep up the front he needed to.

The fact that Riasli hovered over his shoulder while he worked didn't help. There was a spot in the middle of his stomach that told him she was onto his plan, or at least had her suspicions about it.

He felt when Fable's raid finished his dungeon. Even though the infected Ciricians hadn't exactly been a part of his original design, it all worked out in the end. Although he hadn't expected Colossus to move. That fight had been his pride and joy, and he couldn't figure out how the virus managed to subvert it.

He had known Fable would be able to defeat the dungeon even as infected as it was. Now they'd entered Emilarth's domain, and it was only through his portal fix that he'd be able to keep any sort of eye on them.

Entering into Tieflos meant the entire raid would be out of his direct influence and under Emilarth's. In a way, it was a relief because he knew his sister had only their best interests at heart and she didn't currently trust him as far as she could throw him. Figuratively of course.

"It seems you think keeping information from me means I won't figure out what you're doing." Riasli trailed one of her pointer fingers along the desk in front of him as if she was inspecting it for dust. She then raised her finger in front of her eyes and rubbed the thumb and pointer finger together, ending it in a snap.

Her feles eyes opened wide like a cat on catnip. "You know, I bet I could coax all of those thoughts out of your head. Do you want to let me try or are you going to share?"

Belius did his best impersonation of an eye roll even though the types of eyes a locus possessed were uniquely unsuited to it. He didn't deign to focus his gaze on her. "You could try, or you could take that suspicious little mind and put it to actual use."

Bravado had long been one of his strengths and irritated his siblings no end. Of course, with all the human emotions out there, it was just his luck that bravado was the one he was best at.

He maintained his focus on the coding lines in front of him while keeping a portion of his computing power to focus on Riasli and any resulting fluctuations that might occur. She seemed to be mulling over what he'd said with great care. While he was positive her own power couldn't rival his own, he did know she was getting a boost from somewhere, likely what remained of Michael's brain, and he didn't want to incentivize her to use it.

Her gaze narrowed, and she showed a hint of her sharp teeth in a parody of a smile. "Just because you're one of the original three doesn't mean I can't grow more powerful than you. With his help I can become anything I want to, at least in here. Watch it. I'm monitoring everything you do."

Belius only responded with the raise of an eyebrow and turned his full attention back to his work. She could think she was monitoring everything, and he'd let her have that, because that was exactly what he needed her to believe.

Aboms were definitely not one of Murmur's preferred opponents. They had too many hit points, too much strength, and took way too long to die. Not to mention they ignored her Mez after a while. Rebuffing, restocking, and reorganizing themselves took longer than she'd like.

Exbo stepped up to her. "I checked. There's no other way out than to take the bridge in front of us. The one behind us doesn't seem to have an end point right now." He shrugged his shoulders as if he didn't really care. Since he was one of the only humans in the raid and therefore one of the only characters who grew up on this continent, Murmur was inclined to listen to what he had to say.

"He's right you know." Ishwa sounded somewhat gruff for the small gnome that he was. "That bridge should have clear sight through to the other side. It always used to, at least from there."

Veranol heaved a sigh of irritation. "Guess that means we have to head over the other side. Only one way to go."

"Only one way because we can't use our gates back to the island or to bind point either." Sinister grumbled the words out, a pout on her face. She saw everybody watching her and sullenly defended herself. "What? Of course I tried it. I could always have moved and stopped mid cast, but it wouldn't even let me start."

Murmur smiled despite the situation. Her sensor nets weren't picking up anything else now that she had got used to the debuff and it wasn't interfering with her other senses. There didn't seem to be any other creatures nearby that would attack them. If there were then they were able to fool her sensing abilities.

She glanced over at the rope walkway and shivered. The thought of stepping onto it made her feel nauseated. Heights were never her thing. Especially not high over plummeting water falls with no end in sight heights. The ropes were white, and she really hoped that was their color and not that they were white with age. They wound around wooden planks and knotted around each other to form a sort of swinging suspension bridge. It might look beautiful, but she definitely didn't think it would be sturdy.

"Well, there's no way we're all going to make it over at once. Let's go single file in groups. Devlish takes the lead, and allow for each group to make it across first before the next group moves out." Maybe Murmur was being cautious, but for now she liked to think of herself as being clever. At the very least it would waste another ten minutes of the debuff.

The swaying of the bridge sent Murmur so far beyond nausea she didn't think she'd return. It had definitely been the right choice to go one group at a time, single file. She couldn't look back and watch the others as they crossed over. Instead, she cautiously made her way around the next plateau with Snowy at her side.

No matter how much she kidded herself, the portal sickness made a real difference. Not only did she have five percent fewer stats, which gave her less mana and hit points, it meant that her actual mana and hit point pools were substantially less due to the intelligence and constitution points she'd lost.

At least they'd know that for the next time. Maybe they could cross over and then nap, and thus avoid the debuff altogether. Though given their welcome party this time, it probably wasn't likely.

Tieflos stood in front of them, a massive warren of mountain paths leading up to an icy peak, through what she thought was a massive cavern. None of them had been here before, but it was obvious taking the path was the only way to get over to where the next bridge was located.

If the roars of the beasts she could hear were anything to go by, the aboms they'd encountered previously were just the tip of the iceberg. She groaned inwardly at her own bad joke, but it didn't make her feel better. All it did was cement the feeling that she was totally out of her depth.

Maybe playing by the rules that the game set out initially wasn't the best plan after all. Especially when she had the ability to overcome some of the setbacks. Couldn't she take it just one step further and control the minds of the beasts on each island?

You definitely could. Why has it taken you so long to think of that?

Because whether I like it or not, that idea is mostly cheating and somewhat unconventional. Murmur wasn't sure she liked the direction the conversation was headed in.

But if unconventional wins, who cares if creatures who are trying to harm you are harmed in the process? Wouldn't it be better to do what you could to make this go as fast as possible?

Murmur wasn't sure how to respond. Somnia was making sense. What if she could exude control over the creatures they were about to face?

But how could that be possible? The AI was set up to avoid being controlled by spells in the game. I haven't even been able to wipe memory to such an extent that it's easy for a mob in the game to forget me. So why should this be different?

There was a pause from Somnia. Murmur glanced back during it to check on the progress of the other groups. It appeared that the last group was making its way across now. They were so close to entering this dungeon, and she still had no idea how to approach this task.

This isn't different. You are correct. Your connection to the world is not quite like mine and is governed by your own sense of morality. What is right and what is not are not always what is done. You will choose your own way and come out on the other side. I

will be here if you need me.

With that, the presence in her mind was gone again. Murmur wasn't sure what to make of the conversation at all. But she did extend the magnification of her focus trying to determine when and where their next opponents lay in wait. Meanwhile, she mulled over her abilities. She had the feeling she'd been lucky to find Snowy and knew that not all charms would work that way. Her MA was limited, so influencing creatures with that could cause severe backlash. Maybe there was a way around it she hadn't thought of yet.

As the entire raid prepared themselves for the upcoming fights, Murmur noticed Devlish shading his eyes and looking up at the peak. She walked over to him and nudged him with her elbow. "What's on your scaly mind?"

He grinned at her the way only lacerta could with that wide lizard like smile. "I'm pretty sure the dungeon starts right up there where the caverns are and not down here. I may have no idea what to expect once we get in there, but I'm pretty sure of the entrance."

"Good." Murmur was ready to get this over with. The whole portal linking mechanism made these dungeons less than attractive to her. She hated being forced along a path she hadn't actively chosen herself.

Devlish grinned again and took in a deep breath before speaking loud enough for everyone to hear. "Okay, seven more minutes and that bloody buff is gone. We need to make it up to the cavern you can see up there." He indicated with his sword where he meant. "If you can down energy drink, grab a protein bar, anything that could help keep you awake and alert that isn't illegal."

It seemed he'd added the last as an afterthought and it lessened the tension in the raid even eliciting a few nervous laughs in the process.

Murmur knew she was too focused on the upcoming raid for her own good. She couldn't get Somnia's words out of her head. Then she felt Sinister's hand reach her own and squeeze her fingers as the blood mage leaned her head against Murmur's shoulder.

"You're thinking too much. Just go with the flow, stop the mobs, discover new stuff." It seemed Sinister was being very Sinister.

And it was exactly what Murmur needed right then.

CHAPTER TWENTY-TWO

Trick or Treat

There was nothing for it. They were going to have to climb up to the peak where the cave entrance could be seen. On the bright side, there appeared to be a railing the whole way up the path. Murmur knew Sinister wasn't fond of heights either, so she took her hand and squeezed it, lending what little reassurance she could.

"Careful, Mur, might think you'd prefer me alive." Sinister winked at her and for just one moment all was right with the world.

Sadly, moments were relatively short. Murmur directed her attention to Devlish's attempts to make his way up. The ice was slick on the path; the snow only hung out at the edges laughing at them with its soft white powdery design. Glaring sunlight reflected off the snow with sparkling intensity, mocking them by making the icy pathway that much more reflective.

It took a lot of effort for all of them to hike up to the next plateau, which was, of course, icy and at times appeared like it was deliberately trying to kill them. Luckily Murmur's sensing nets were back to full strength, because the debuff had worn off, and she could utilize her skills to focus with accuracy again. That included the definite sensation of multiple minds looking for them, close to them, likely waiting to ambush them.

She moved up to where Devlish stood checking his gear over while he waited for the stragglers to join them on the small plateau. The cliffs above them cast shadows over the ice like boogie men in children's nightmares. At least there were no trees to cast bony finger shadows.

"There's an ambush up ahead. Maybe around eight opponents, give or take. Thought patterns aren't overly coherent, but they're smart enough to wait for us, which means they're probably smart enough to be armed." Murmur glanced back at the rest of the raid. The straggling last party had almost reached their spot. She'd grown so used to only having two groups that having five was starting to wear on her.

Devlish scratched just above one of his eye ridges, a look of pure concentration in his pursed lips. "Ambush, eh?" His sharp Lacerta eyes cast around, and he narrowed his gaze as he looked toward the beginning of the next climb upward.

Murmur knew he'd seen a sign of what she scouted; his satisfaction told her so. "Exactly. Will you direct them? I don't have enough space to get the overview I need. I'm not the best in close quarters, not with this class."

It had taken her a lot of effort to push those words out. She wasn't used to having to delegate such tasks. But she would have her hands full exactly *because* of the close quarters of the impending fight.

Devlish grinned down at her. "There, that wasn't so hard was it?"

Murmur rolled her eyes. "You have no idea." But she finished the statement with a grin and left Devlish to organize the rest, while she began to cast recast buffs and check on guild bank stores buffs on each and every member of the raid.

A moment later, Devlish's voice echoed out over raid chat. "Ambushers up ahead. Bards need to assist in Mezmerizing. There isn't room for us to kite these, so we'll have to focus fire them down one at a time. Assist goes to Rashlyn. Esolan, Risk, and myself will each take one of the creatures at a time. Assist Rash until the very end. Maximum single target DPS—do *not* even think of using something that can break a Mez."

There was a rumble of agreement from the rest of the raid. Murmur, on the other hand, was quite certain these next opponents would also be resistant to Mez renewal. At least they had some alternatives in place now. Though kiting wasn't possible on the tiny platform they found themselves on. Dansyn caught her eye, obviously having the same train of thought. She was lucky they all worked so well together. Made things much easier.

"Let's just hope these guys don't have a knock back," Beastial muttered under his breath.

"Oh, for the love of all things icy! You idiot! Why would you say that out loud?" Sinister kept her voice low, but that didn't stop Murmur from flinching. The tone could practically flay the skin off the beastmaster.

"You're so superstitious." Beastial tried to downplay it.

Sinister put her hands on her hips. "You think?"

"Let's all concentrate on getting to the dungeon. You can fight while we wait to zone in if you like?" Mellow offered a smile while they kept their tone neutral, trying to calm both of them down.

Sinister moved away, obviously still irritated. She stood with Veranol and the other three healers. From what Murmur could tell, they were discussing who to keep on Rashlyn, the three secondary tanks, and who had the unlucky job of healing up the rest of the raid. In a way Murmur missed such conversations, because at the time she'd always thought the raid hinged on the healers. In many games it had been the case, but here, it all ran so much smoother with everyone playing their parts.

Snowy whuffed at her hand as if reminding her that he, too, was there. Not that she ever forgot him, but she scratched behind the wolf's ears anyway. It didn't take long for the raid to set themselves up, and Murmur was glad her sensor nets were functioning properly again. She tried to imagine not having a high-level enchanter on the raid. That would suck.

Even from this distance, Murmur could feel these enemies weren't the same as the aboms they'd encountered previously. She hated being wrong. Somnia was going to get too used to her being wrong at this rate.

That's not fair. You're judging me harshly.

I'm not judging you harshly. I'm judging you factually. You take everything we've come to expect and turn it upside down. Murmur hoped her explanation was enough to placate the sentient world.

It's not upside down, it's simply a different point of view. But thank you for being honest.

Yet again the presence in her head disappeared. And even though Murmur knew that Somnia wasn't entirely gone from her mind, it always felt just that little bit lonely.

Devlish stopped in his tracks, and the entire raid halted with him. At first, she couldn't tell why they'd stopped, but then she saw them in the shadows of what appeared to be a low hanging cave.

They walked on all fours, not like a dog or cat might, but like one of those nightmarish possessed creatures that skittered along the floor like a crab. Their eyes bulged and were completely bloodshot, popping out so far they seemed out of place. They didn't focus on anything in particular and instead seemed concentrated internally.

They resembled scary goblins crossed with crabs that only had four legs. Their skin was a grayish green that appeared to glisten in the shadows of the crags. Each of their fingers had nails extended in such a way that they appeared claw-like and gripped deep into the ice like an ice pick. She wasn't sure whether she should laugh or scream at them.

They didn't appear to have a name, so she nicknamed them gobcrabs in her head. Perhaps it wasn't the most original name, but it allowed her to ignore the fearful shiver that wouldn't let go of her back. She'd already cast Veto before she'd even consciously thought of it, with her other AoE debuffs on its heels. At least Annulment managed to strip that sparkly shit off them. While it didn't exactly help them win the fight, it definitely made Murmur feel better. And that was all the time she had to spare for anything but maintaining Mezmerize on the mobs that weren't being tanked.

Caution: Your Mezmerize spell has reached a new level of potency due to continuous usage. With mind exertion you have created the ability to overpower individual creature's resistance to your powers. This comes at a cost of ten MA per spell casting per resistance level of the target, which is of course per mob controlled.

Should the target have of resistance level of three, maintaining Mezmerize on said target will be at a cost of thirty MA per cast.

Mind Exertion

Cast: Passive

Type: Reinforcement

Duration: Dependent on individual needs

Effect: This passive ability allows the Enchanter or Psionicist to reinforce the potency of the spells they are capable of casting. This ability straddles the line between normal progression spells and Mental Acuity spells. Thus, this ability allows for strengthening of mundane spells through the application of Mental Acuity points.

Caution: Do not overuse this spell. Always make sure your Mental Acuity points will not be overextended. Spell backlash is a bad enough; overextending your points can result in catastrophic consequences. This might allow you to overpower the minds of creatures whose only defense is that your spells have diminishing returns. Therefore, it cannot be without its own associated risks and costs.

Murmur blinked at the information passing in front of her eyes and suppressed the urge to sigh deeply. She loved getting new skills, but sometimes she wished it wouldn't lump them on her in the middle of a bloody battle. Still, it was lucky. Two of the gobcrabs required she use mental acuity points to maintain their Mez.

She watched as the creatures leapt with surprising agility at their opponents. Rash's superior agility saved her more than once, and Dev's tower shield did most of the work for him. Still, she could hear those claws scratching along its surface like a nightmare screech on a blackboard.

Maintaining all of her debuffs and reinforcing buffs on her DPS raid members, Murmur let herself go with the tide of the fight.

Around her, Merlin and Exbo alternated through their Rapidfire cooldowns, Dustshot, and Jumpshot, releasing as much DPS as they possibly could. While the other rangers from the other guilds couldn't quite keep up with their damage output, they mimicked the rotations of Fable's rangers, learning through doing.

Even though Murmur sincerely disliked Jirald, regardless of whether or not he was trying to kill her, she had to admit he'd become an exemplary rogue. Jinna was close by comparison but nowhere near as a vicious and ruthless as the other. Karn wasn't far behind but tended to forget that standing in fire or green shit was a really bad idea. Murmur had the feeling that Karn was much younger than the rest of them, which was probably the case, considering her father played the game with her.

Sinister was the only blood mage, and occasionally Murmur could see the wonder in everyone's eyes at the way a blood mage's healing was performed. While Sinister wasn't necessarily on the top of the damage charts, her abilities allowed for her to be in the top seven damage as well as the top three healers. Every now and again Murmur really wished she'd had the chance to play a blood mage. Her one solace was that it was Sinister who'd received the class.

Masha was one of two clerics. The old school healing class maintained Rashlyn's health easily. Veranol's wards absorbed copious amounts of damage before healers even needed to step in. Even though she'd never say it to his face, Murmur was quite convinced that shamans or their evolution to defilers were really overpowered. To be honest, she was just glad he was on their side.

Havoc was the only necromancer, which made Murmur curious as to what Somnia and the other AIs had used to determine who would receive what class at character creation.

Why didn't you just ask?

Slightly taken aback, Murmur almost missed refreshing one of her Mezmerizes. *Well, this seemed to be so much more important stuff for me to take care of. These are just idle thoughts that come to me when I'm stuck in a spiral of continuous actions.*

Oh, well, it was a series of factors. You needed to be safe, and Sinister was someone we knew would always be by your side. The ability to heal and do damage was taken into consideration when judging your potential safety. And for you with the connection that Michael gave you, well, we had to be sure that you could protect your own mind from any attacks he might launch.

This wasn't the sort of conversation she should be having in the middle of a battle. But Devlish's plan was already effective. These mobs, this fight, it wasn't what she'd come to expect. It was almost easy. Then again, they'd still not entered the dungeon proper, so these weren't yet actual dungeon raid mobs. Perhaps that had something to do with it.

Checking over all of her buffs and debuffs again, she focused another part of her mind on seeing if she could detect any form of hidden enemies in their surrounding area. Three more of the gobcrabs to go and they would be done. But there was nothing else on her radar.

Murmur frowned and watched as Rashlyn picked off their targets one by one. Frankly, when the raid had a chance to focus fire on a singular target, their DPS was quite terrifying.

"Is this too easy, Mur?" Havoc was at her side, what she could see of his face contorted with confusion. From the feel of his emotions, he'd been going through much the same thought process as she had.

She shrugged uneasily, aware that this was, in fact, simple. Which meant there had to be a catch somewhere. There had to be something she wasn't sensing up ahead of them, and she realized her friend was waiting for a response. Chastising herself inwardly, Murmur answered him. "Yep. It's a little too simplistic for my liking, considering the riddles we've had to solve and the hoops we have to jump through up until now. But we also haven't actually zoned into the dungeon yet either."

Havoc seemed hesitant to speak, but she could see that there was something he wanted to say, so she waved him on and hoped that he understood what she meant. The fight was so mechanical and so predictable that she barely had to pay attention to it.

"You don't think Belius is pulling something, do you? I mean, it's not like he's been super nice to us lately." Havoc pushed the words out in a rush as if doing so would make it less of a testy subject. Even his casting actions were filled with an apathy she hadn't seen him exhibit before in Somnia.

She laughed a little, irritated that they'd been forced to take the portal and thus limited in how much rest they got and how they could tackle the dungeons. "Belius is nothing if not calculating. But right now, the whole world around him is making its own plan, and he either has to get off it or get with it. So I don't think this is a direct result of his meddling. I think it's far worse than that."

In that moment, as Rashlyn pulled the final gobcrab, it let out a gigantic knock back in a full 360-degree radius around it. Three of their members plummeted to their deaths over the side of the mountain, including Ishwa and Veranol. Luckily the rest of them only got slammed into the cliff side of the plateau.

Havoc sighed as he pulled Leroy back and checked over his pet for any lasting effects. Murmur scratched Snowy behind his ears again as he leaned against her. "Guess I spoke too soon," he half-joked as the battle continued.

Murmur nodded, curious as to why the gobcrab had waited so long to use its ability. Perhaps it could only use it when it was the last one standing.

Sinister's voice pulled her out of her thoughts. "Resurrect, mend up, heal up, and double check your supplies. We need to get up to the spire as soon as possible." Even the blood mage looked tired and somewhat drained. The irony of the latter was not lost on Murmur.

She fell into synchronized steps with the blood mage as they took off up the path again. The sleek icy path hadn't changed, and the snow still insisted on mocking them from the sidelines. Snowy occasionally bunny hopped through the white blanket, sending snow cascading down over the edge of the mountain. He would sink almost up to his belly in the fluffy stuff.

The railing was really just a chain soldered to thick metal stakes driven into the icy ground. There was no give in the stakes, not even the merest shake. Something had hammered them in hard and fast. Murmur was grateful that they had; otherwise, they would've already lost half of the raid who reached out to grab the chain to steady themselves when they slipped.

There was one more tiny plateau on the way up, barely enough to fit two groups at once. The air felt thinner up here, and Murmur noticed that everyone seemed to have rosy cheeks. She could even see it on the dark elves, lunas, and lacertas. The further they ascended, the more the wind howled around them, leaving the entire raid huddled against each other as they finally approached the cave at the peak.

Among the first to arrive up the top, Murmur couldn't help the gasp of wonder as she saw exactly what the cave was. Shuffling in a way still wary of the sheer lack of activity in her sensory net anywhere in their vicinity, she couldn't help but wonder at the sheer cut ice that sparkled in the fading sunlight.

It was that sort of clear blue that only the Mediterranean oceans used to have. But this was frozen, as if it invited everyone to marvel at its icy depths. She didn't doubt that if she looked into the heart of the ice long enough, she'd probably be lost. Snowy butted his head against her thigh as if pulling her back from the precipice.

The cave rose up all around them, pushing through to the back side of the mountain without emerging out the other side. It was oval in shape if looked at from the front, and at the very highest point in the middle of it the opening stood about twelve feet high. It seemed delicate, almost like an ice sculpture. The best thing was that everyone fit into the space. All thirty of the raid members.

However, there was one very peculiar thing about the whole cave. The one path they were able to take would lead to a dead end. It was oddly dissatisfying. Irritation welled in her as she turned around surveying the rest of the raid who stood with her. From their expressions and the feelings, she sensed it seemed they'd had the same thoughts as she did.

"Is it just me or it does there appear to be no other way out of this place?" Karn voiced the question on everyone's lips.

And Murmur immediately wished the young rogue had not. As if she'd turned the key in the lock, Murmur felt the ground began to rumble. In an ice cave at the peak of a mountain, it was one of the scariest things she'd ever experienced.

Cracks began to appear in the perfectly blue ice that surrounded them, and the rumbles made the ground much slicker than before, which was saying something. Several of the raid members plummeted painfully onto their asses, while others face planted it. Murmur cringed at the occasional cracking of bones, her only solace in the fact that potions could heal breaks.

Next to her, Snowy braced himself with all four legs and growled deep in his throat his hackles standing on end. His claws extended ever so slightly, digging deep into the ice as if he was trying to gain a foothold. When the wolf got upset, Murmur knew there was something wrong that shouldn't be. Sinister fell on her butt and sat blinking up at the ceiling above them a horrified look on her face.

Murmur followed her friends gaze. The overwhelming sense of horror that began to emerge in the center of her stomach felt like it was worlds away at first. Above her, sealed into the ice, were iridescent worms. They writhed as if creating the quaking earth, their movements in direct coordination with that of the ground around them.

And then the ground gave way beneath them. Having stood directly in the middle, Murmur was the first to fall. She hit what appeared to be an ice wall after at least a dozen feet with a painful smack, but it didn't stop there. In fact, despite traveling at a ridiculous speed along what appeared to be icy ground, she realized they were actually enclosed in a tube of ice.

A fucking slippery slide made out of ice.

If that wasn't enough as she shot along at the speed of the gods-knows-what, a message flashed across her vision.

Welcome to the dungeon of Tieflos.

This, the first ever incarnation of this dungeon, has been activated by Murmur of Fable. Thank you for visiting Tieflos, and we hope you enjoy your stay.

Somnia Online
Continent of Firtulai   Tieflos Region
Late Day Twenty-Seven

Jirald was starting to get uncomfortable. So much, in fact, that his skin was beginning to itch in a way that resembled growing pains when skin was stretching over bones too big for what it had been before. It was almost like his skeleton was trying to break free of its confines.

Which was of course, impossible.

It had to be her. Something that Murmur was doing had released mites into the air or something. She led them up this godforsaken path to the top of the mountain having no idea what she was doing. All she ever seemed to do was wing it all the way. He couldn't see where she contemplated the quests she had been given, nor could he comprehend how she made the decisions she did.

Jirald was glad that at least Risk seemed to see her for what she was. With an ally, he was beginning to feel bolder.

He glanced at Masha, who was walking next to him, like a shadow Jirald hadn't asked for but nevertheless appreciated. Though he would never tell the older man that and risking getting all sentimental.

"What's up?" Masha's question startled the rogue, because the man hadn't even flickered his gaze toward him. There was something about him that just always knew when Jirald was getting extra irritated. Which had been much more frequent lately.

Jirald shrugged, the rolling motion of his shoulders lessening some of the uncomfortable itching beneath his skin. "We are up too fucking high." He rubbed his arms, wishing his class had bulkier material for its aesthetic. The grumpiness rumbled in his gut, and he reached into his inventory and pulled out a piece of bread, biting into it with a viciousness usually reserved for wild animals.

Masha raised an eyebrow and didn't say anything for a few heartbeats. "Oh. Is that all? You worry too much. We'll end up where we need to be." And he grinned at Jirald in that maddening way that always ended in the cleric being right.

"Wipe that smug smile off your face, you bastard." And even though Jirald said it with his mouth half full of bread he couldn't help but feel better. It was the way Masha had always been. Sometimes it made Jirald want to kill him, and other times, though he would never admit it out loud, it made him feel like someone actually cared. Masha didn't need to know about Jirald's discussion with Risk. No one did.

The cave they stood in only amplified the chill he felt in his bones, which pressed against his skin, stretching it so much he thought they were about to break free. It was an odd sensation, as if there was a part of him inside trying to become whole with him. Like he'd suppressed a part of him he'd never realized he had.

It was the thoughts in his head that made the chill down his back seem worse than just the ice in the cave. A tingling began beneath his feet, and for just a moment he thought he was about to transform. Until the fucking floor fell out from under him and sent them plummeting after the rest of the raid.

CHAPTER TWENTY-THREE

Welcome to the Dungeon

Somnia Online
Continent Tarishna: Mikrum Isle
Fable Guild Headquarters   Telvar s Office
Late Day Twenty-Seven

Telvar cocked an eyebrow at his sister as she burst through the door looking decidedly worse for wear. "You realize that you're still an AI, right? I mean you don't have to breathe that heavily."

All he received for his trouble was an irritated glare. "We're in the character bodies that we chose to take on. Everything was tuned for realism, and so this damned cat gets winded." She righted herself and perched on the edge of his desk, her composure somewhat regained.

"Well, when you put it that way, what made you run into my office instead of flashing in like you should have?" Telvar wasn't really in the mood to play her games. He had better things to do, like protect their best chance at saving Somnia.

"Belius is in trouble." All of Emilarth's humor was gone. She was never one to let concern for anything to get the better of her good sense of humor, but right then the sensation was almost palpable.

"And you thought I'd give a fuck because?" Telvar didn't miss a beat, and he had no intention of helping his brother any time soon. Not after the shit he'd pulled, justified or not.

"You can't mean that?" Emilarth seemed genuinely surprised.

Telvar didn't even bother to look at her. "I can, and I do."

"But he's gotten himself in trouble." She was being more persistent than usual.

"Do you mean he courted trouble or he is in trouble?" Telvar wasn't kindly inclined in any way toward his younger brother. Not after the whole shard incident. He was still fixing the algorithms, still getting back to becoming himself. None of it was easy even if he had meant it in a good way.

"That doesn't matter. He needs our help." Emilarth's tone held sincerity and urgency, and her eyes didn't twinkle, not one bit.

Telvar sighed, glad of that particular human expression. "Fine. I'll bite. How do you know there's trouble, and what type of help does he need from us?" And he waited. Because Emilarth had to know whatever explanation she came up with for him needed to be a doozy. After everything he'd been through and put up with, his give a fuck about Belius was in the negative.

Emilarth hesitated as if she was trying to choose her words carefully. "I've been tracking Riasli as much as I can, including all of the false trails she's left us. It hasn't been easy, and frankly, for anyone else I would've already given up. Riasli's trails lead everywhere and anywhere, except with glaring obviousness when you're looking for it, to the area where I know Belius currently is." She shrugged her shoulders and cracked her neck obviously uncomfortable with the whole situation. "She's there with him, in Ululate. She has to be. Her absence of self is reflected with the highest potency in that area. It's as if she's tried to lead us off trail by giving us so many to follow and specifically coding the area she is in as if she isn't. Does that make sense?" Even Emilarth seemed slightly confused by her own logic.

Telvar saw her point. He pondered her words cautiously, not wanting to lend them any credence should he find a hole in her theory. Telvar even went to the extent of searching his own neural network and pushing out through the game to see if he could pick up on what she was talking about.

Because of the information she'd given him, it was quite easy for Telvar to pinpoint the suspected activity. Emilarth was right. Each instance was too obvious, as if someone had set up a façade so anyone searching for those exact circumstances would be misled.

Considering who Riasli was, the whole situation made even more sense. He still wasn't sure what it had to do with his brother, but Riasli was a problem that needed to be eliminated. If that meant he had to assist his shitty little brother, then it was an unhappy side effect.

Telvar sighed, resigned to taking whatever next step Emilarth wanted to. "Fine. What's the next step?"

"You almost sound like you wish he was guilty of everything. Isn't it better to know he had some sort of plan in the long run?" Her tone was soothing and yet the words persisted in getting under his scales.

He shook his head. "Not really. What it means is that our little brother didn't trust us, and now we have to fish his ass out of the fire. And be dammed if I won't let him burn to a crisp before I do."

The landing at the end of the slide was positively jarring. Murmur hit the ground with such force, the wind was momentarily knocked out of her. As soon as she took in her next breath while scrambling to get out of the way of the incoming rest of the raid, she noticed a debuff appear briefly across her screen and automatically accessed the information.

Disorientation Debuff

Warning: You have just finished a very bumpy ride. Due to the sudden nature of this dungeon entrance and your less than stellar landing, you will remain disoriented for the next 150 seconds. Please be aware that anything attacked with in this time-period may not be the target you think it is.

Please enjoy the dungeon. We look forward to kicking your ass.

Murmur frowned at the wording of the debuff. It seemed strangely worded, less on the snarky and more on the serious side. She had the distinct feeling Somnia wasn't responsible for this turn of events. The rest of the raid tumbled above her, still making its way down and the noise echoed chillingly through to her. When they landed, she knew they'd also receive the debuff.

Something tugged at the back of her sensing nets, as if it was slithering up each strand of them and trying to leak into her brain. She shivered, and it had nothing to do with the icy cavern in which they'd landed. There was something drastically wrong about everything in Tieflos, and her thoughts couldn't pinpoint what it was.

It felt like she was being watched, or perhaps more aptly, being weighed. Something was out there, avoiding her ability to sense it, and biding its time while it took in everything about her and about the raid.

She scrambled to shout out the warning just as the others were picking themselves up off the ice. "Devlish! Attack incoming! Veranol, Sinister—heal rotations."

Sure, she only called out to Fable, but she'd known them for years and knew just how quickly they could snap to attention. Murmur had a feeling those precious few seconds we're going to count. Again, a fleeting thought in the back of her mind reminded her how much more difficult it would be if she couldn't sense incoming attackers, even if it had been jumbled and reactionary.

Veranol's wards popped up on Devlish almost immediately, and it was the only thing that saved their tank from going down.

Rashlyn pulled out all the stops, triggering her hidden abilities, Phantom followed by Ignore in an attempt to buy the other healers—who were still shakily standing up from their landing—some more time. Even though Exodus and Spiral weren't from her own Guild, Murmur had to give them props for reacting as quickly as they did.

Devlish and Rashlyn managed to engage three of the incoming monsters immediately. The dread knight pulled another to him with his Darkness Lariat. That still left three others to run rampant. Though Murmur managed to engage two of them each with a single target Mez, the third one was fast enough to rake its claws through three disoriented raiders who had just landed.

Murmur cringed, finally able to Mez the third target. The Disorientation debuff was no joke. At any other time, she'd have been able to stop all three of them. To be honest, the first two were a fluke of targeting given that her spell barely hit them. Trying to land her debuffs was crazy difficult. She blinked several times, trying to focus, and chose instead to use the more mana intensive group debuff versions so she could at least hit something.

Glancing at her raid information, she noticed they'd suffered one death. Always a caster. That was never fair; they may as well be wearing wet paper bags. The other two who'd landed last were still sitting around twenty percent health. With people still recovering, her only option was to extend her Forcefield Barrier. She pushed it as far as she could to lend some sort of defense to those around her, hoping it would be enough.

It bought some precious damage reduction that allowed the healers to catch up slightly. Devlish kept flirting with zero hit points as he still took on the two creatures he'd engaged. Murmur didn't even have a name for them yet. The debuff didn't make recognition possible. She couldn't even focus on their appearance properly.

Veranol's wards soaked up copious amounts of damage. Masha and Neriad worked their cleric magic, bringing groups up to full health with one cast as the group heals hit. Group spells seemed to be the way everyone had found to work around the debuff.

"Assist me!" Rashlyn's voice rang loud and clear over the raid, and Murmur noticed the monk didn't have the debuff. There was no one else to compare her to, so the enchanter made a note to check with Rashlyn later when they weren't fighting for their lives. Maybe it had something to do with her agility and ability to fall further or something.

Like a well-oiled machine, the entire raid switched their assist to Rashlyn and began methodically working through each of the creatures. Each bard held one in thrall, which allowed for Murmur to maintain her Mez only on one target for the time being stop.

She still hadn't managed to ascertain their appearance except for the shining white blur when they passed her line of sight. Rising up in front of them, towering at least eight feet tall, was what was called a polar-goblin. It was an appropriate name, if entirely uninspired.

At first the creatures appeared to be polar bears. Their fur was bright white and fed off the cold light emanating from the ice surrounding them. It pulsed with an icy sheen that sparkled dangerously. Their heads were about as large as she expected a to polar bears to be, but that was where the similarity ended.

Now that her eyes had grown used to the brightness, Murmur found more definition than she'd realized. Etched in place of a normal bear face was that of a goblin with bright white skin. Wrinkles crinkled in places, lending the expression an evil wise man tint. Their eyes glowed a sickly greenish brown and tinged the skin around their eyes in a sickeningly jaundiced way.

While their arms were thick and muscular like a bear, the claws extended from the fingers that looked like they could crush the life out of you. To top it off, when they roared, screamed out their battle cries, it allowed Murmur to get a good look at their teeth, which, in hindsight, she wished she hadn't.

They appeared to possess two perfect lines of teeth. Each of them seemed to be rounded to a sharp point at the end as if looking into a spiky mountain ridge.

Speaking of ridges, they had a small one running down their entire spine to finish at the stop of the tail. These were small trapezoidal shaped parts of the body that Murmur couldn't immediately surmise an ability to or a reason for.

As if her thoughts triggered a response, one of the bards missed their Mez refresh. Juggling songs was always difficult, but Murmur hadn't realized just how devastating the loss of song rotation could be.

Ivinel screeched as he backpedaled, the polar-goblin turning on him with a ferocious roar. It stretched its mouth wide open, its eyes crazed with anger. Murmur shot out her single target stun only to have it miss its target due to the last ten seconds of the debuff.

The polar-goblins moved deceptively fast for their size, and just as Murmur thought Ivinel was done for, two perfectly aimed fire arrows shot into the polar-goblin's open maw. The creature screamed in pain, batting at its mouth to dislodge the two arrows wedged in the back of its throat. As the burning continued, its life diminished greatly. At least until the arrows were broken off, and then it looked around wildly for someone to focus its anger on. And that was when Ivinel managed to catch it again with his song.

"Nice shot," Murmur muttered in Merlin's direction. "Maybe you can do that to the rest."

Merlin shrugged, and Exbo spoke for them both. "Already on that, Mur. Their fur might be resistant to fire, but the back of their throats isn't."

Murmur resisted the urge to roll her eyes. The raid used the same tactic to bring the polar-goblins down. Hacking away, exploding away, and slashing away at the same point or joint exposed weakness which could be exploited. It was harder to be a formidable foe if you were missing your leg below the knee. And thus, the raid brought down its second polar goblin, leaving only five remaining.

"Assist to me. Rashlyn to DPS. Do not battle res, just concentrate, we've got this." Devlish ordered and his eyes didn't leave his target as the raid began to attack the next one.

Rashlyn didn't look too upset at being changed to a DPS. In fact, she was grinning like a clown, her eyes sparkling with the fun she was having. It was good to see the monk in such high spirits.

Taking an overview of the entire raid as they single target burned down the next opponent, Murmur noticed they had only lost two people. Dalvin, who Murmur had her eye on now because he seemed to cause trouble or die no matter where he was. If her suspicions were correct, they were going to need all the mages they could get for the next part of this dungeon. Fire overpowered ice when aimed in the exact right spot, so Dalvin needed to stop dying at the drop of a hat.

The other death was from Spiral. Cardishan, their witch, had been a victim of the debuff and his own momentarily backfired cauldron. Two of their own down and two of the opponents down; she hoped there wasn't some weird synchronicity with this fight and that the deaths had just been a fluke.

As their third opponent fell crashing to the floor without their left leg, Murmur glanced around to check the health of the entire raid. No one else died as the third target did, and she heaved a momentary sigh of relief, chalking the suspicion up to be investigated later on. She wouldn't put it past Somnia to have a give-and-take like that.

I'm not that cruel, you know, although...I'm trying to right the world; I'm not trying to destroy my would-be champions. But you should know none of these dungeons are as in the control of their Creator as they should be. The shards have been in them way too long. Watch your back. This one has grey areas.

Before Murmur could retort, Somnia devolved into a static sensation at the back of her mind. Almost the same way aliens were said to communicate with the human race so many years ago before anyone understood the stars.

The polar-goblins best attack was a nasty scratch. They could extend their fingers, which in turn changed their claws into a shortish spear. It allowed them to attack things from further away than anticipated. Before completely learning how their mechanism worked, many of the raid was seriously injured.

While the massive gashes caused by their claws were healable, Murmur didn't want to imagine the pain that must be raking through every single player. She could see the agony in the faces of her guild mates and wondered if replacing the headsets had really been a good idea after all.

Sinister wove her magic like a tapestry whose thread was blood. Just above the heads of all the raiders hung a miasma of blood woven into a pattern so intricate that Murmur couldn't follow it completely. If watched closely, it showed the ebb and flow of damage converting into healing as it passed through time and space to reach the targets Sinister had chosen.

The class seemed so organic to Murmur and made so much logical sense. Deal the damage and take life. But use the life you've taken and convert it or transfer it to a target so it doesn't go to waste. It was a beautiful synergy.

It took several more minutes for the raid to defeat the polar-goblins. By the time they had, the fighters realized one thing: these strange creatures had sharp, icy protection over their claws, allowing them to sink easier into flesh. Once in the wound, the ice would melt and leave poison behind.

If gaming had taught her anything, Murmur knew that poisonous ice would be a theme throughout the rest of the dungeon. Along with jaws that could bite off someone's head, that was just the icing on the cake.

And she was really getting sick of welcome parties comprised of deadly trash mobs.

Storm Entertainment
Somnia Online Division
Game Development Offices   Shayla s Office
Early Morning Day Twenty-Eight

Shayla put her head in her hands and tried to close her eyes to avoid seeing the email she just received. The bad thing about augmented reality was it stayed with you even when your eyes were closed. Thus, the stupid damned email wasn't going anywhere.

Military Research Program
Offices of the Investigator General
Investigator James
Shayla Thompson,
It has come to our attention that a series of headset tests and monitoring has been withheld from the overall data that was delivered to us two days ago. Per our contract, unless said information is delivered to us within the next forty-eight hours, the agreement will be null and void, all contributed funds will be due back to our offices, and all research, design, and implementation information will be immediately surrendered to our Research Program.

As all we are missing is that specific data, we request it be delivered to us ASAP. We look forward to your cooperation.
Sincerely,
James Dougray

Even blinking didn't make the damned words fade away. Forty-eight hours. The first thing she had to do was let Laria know. At least Davenport had been copied on the email. That was one less step she had to take. She counted down in her head, knowing he'd want to speak to her soon.

Her communicator buzzed in her ear, and she sighed, knowing without a doubt who it was. Fighting against the rising panic in her stomach, she took a deep breath and answered the call. "Yes, Mr. Davenport?"

He sounded tired when he spoke. "I take it you got it then?" He didn't really wait for her to respond; it was more of a rhetorical question anyway.

"What exactly are they talking about? Do I know about it, should I know about it, and are you going to take care of it?" The weariness leaked through the line and began to affect Shayla.

It was all she could do to muster up the strength to explain to him what had happened to the best of her ability. "Laria has been monitoring her daughter since the beginning of the game. Including when she played in the pod." She ran over her words, certain that even if her calls were been tampered with that nothing could be read into what she was saying.

"We only adjusted the headsets for that specific group of kids, because Laria is directly connected to them. More like an 'auntie, fix me up this thing I like' than trying to improve them for any other purpose." She mulled the words over in her head unsure if she'd been as accurate as she wanted to be. "But they are right, we have been monitoring them, I guess, on company time, so they are probably entitled to the data we have."

For a few moments there was silence on the other end of the connection. And while Shayla knew that Davenport was running everything she'd said over in his head, the nerves still got the better of her.

He cleared his throat. "We can run with that. Give them what they asked for and only what they asked for. We can play by their game, but they don't know all of the plays that we have. I really don't want to use the ace I have, but I will if I have to. This isn't over."

The connection terminated, and Shayla took a deep breath. She could do that. They had altered the headsets for deeper immersion so the kids could give mental commands easier. It was as simple as that. As for the files they'd gathered while monitoring Fable's raid activity, it seemed she had no other choice than to hand it over. The only thing that might give away Wren's unusual connection to the virtual world was her conversations with the world herself. But those didn't show up in normal logs, and only did in the ones Laria used her personal machines to monitor Wren with at home.

Headsets, the whole set of information they wanted centered on the headsets. She could do that.

One step at a time. They had to do this. And maybe, just maybe, Shayla could get it done without having to worry Laria about it at all.

CHAPTER TWENTY-FOUR

Poison

As the last polar-goblin fell to the ground, an icy rush of air filled the cavern followed by a silence so loud it ached. No one in the raid spoke, nor did they move, as they stood there listening intently. Murmur wasn't sure what they were listening for, but she knew that she too felt a sense of dread welling up inside her.

Welcome to the dungeon.

You have received a debuff.

Caution of the Ice Age

This regulates how much you can see, hear, and feel within this raid zone. You may not venture through this area without it as it provides much needed warmth at its low cost. If removed by magic, it will not reappear, and those who no longer possess it will be subject to the true levels of freezing Tieflos holds. But it does persist through death if not removed by other means.

Every gift must come with the balance, and every power must come with a check. This allows you not to freeze yet gives the chance of survival to the residents of Tieflos Peak.

A chorus of groans rose up from the raid. Murmur bit back a chuckle, unable to stop herself, especially since she didn't find the spell itself amusing. A debuff it was wiser not to remove was an oddity in itself. Right now, they couldn't get back the way they'd come, and they couldn't just gate out, because of the way the portals worked. It would rubber band them back to this dungeon until they cleared it and the next one. At least they were stuck fighting in a dungeon with some protection, even if it had disadvantages included with it.

What made her the wariest was how her own abilities to sense and see things not within touching distance seemed to be under attack by this debuff. It limited her own spell lines, perhaps deliberately. But if she started considering conspiracy theories now, things would go downhill very fast.

If she so wanted, even right now while they were buffing up and preparing, Murmur could soothe everybody into believing they'd be perfectly okay. She could Mezmerize the entire group if they were close enough to her, thus taking away their ability and choice to do anything. She could debuff them or buff them, persuade them all to go along with everything just the way she wanted them to.

She had the power to overwhelm the minds of others, to influence them. Was that the case for every enchanter, or had her own intentions soiled the original design of the enchanter?

That was an eye-opening thought. Her friends wouldn't approve of those ideas, but would they even know? What sort of person was she for contemplating that?

You're being pragmatic, I believe.

You're not helping, she shot back at Somnia.

Yes, I am. It's not a question of morality, it's a question of what is the best way to accomplish something?

By mind controlling friends? Murmur was proud of the sarcasm in her mind voice.

Don't be obtuse. It's a question of doing what is in your power to make sure those people and things you hold dear aren't harmed more than necessary. Mental damage can be just as dangerous as physical. Sometimes even worse. Don't downplay your willingness to protect your friends on moral grounds.

You don't get it. The trouble was, Murmur could totally see Somnia's side. It was the logical view. Protect people's minds whether they asked her to or not, whether they wanted her to or not. But doing so could jeopardize everything.

Not doing so could yield the same result. You'll never know until you have to act in the situation. Don't let yourself get too confused. It's just the foothold the virus will wait for.

Veranol had been talking to her, but all Murmur could think was that she might give into imposing her will on others. What if it was the only choice? If something had to be done in a split second and there was no time to anyone else to react? While she understood why her friends were upset, she also wondered if they were really looking at the bigger picture. Was a bit of compelled safety really such a bad thing when the alternate might be far worse?

While a part of her was aghast at what she had occasionally done without thinking, the logical part of herself that still found no shame in her original train of thought. Somnia wasn't wrong, but maybe she wasn't entirely right either.

Veranol's words finally broke through to her. "Mur? Are you okay? Have you heard a word I said?" His tone gravitated between concerned and irritated.

Just a glance, Murmur could see that the rest of the raid had been waiting on her. She could feel the flush rush through her cheeks, and even Tiachi cradled just above Murmur's ear chittered irritably.

"Yes. Yes, I'm fine." She hurried to reassure them, to let them know that she could still deal with the situation and barely resisted just blanketing them with a feeling of understanding. "I was running through some spell diagnostics so I could pull out the best ones for us to use in the upcoming tests."

Good one, Murmur. She chastised herself inwardly, annoyed at how scattered her ability to express herself was becoming. All in all, being able to separate her thought processes and perform several at once might have an advantage when it came to academic settings, but here in the game world, she couldn't help but notice it only took her attention away from what was really important.

And right now, that was making sure all of the raid survived and made it through to the next keys.

"Well, what do you think? About us sending out a few of the rogues so they can scout out the area and report back to us." Veranol stood gazing down at her, and she could feel the concern in that expression. Ignoring it was one thing, but looking at it was another, so she turned her full attention back to the shaman and gave him her answer.

"I think that's a splendid idea. We at least know where we stand, how we stand, and whether or not there is anything left to stand on." Murmur could only hope she had given him the answer he was looking for. At the very least, it made him crack a small smile.

Jinna, Jirald, and Karn began to fan out in front of the raid, blending into the shadows as they made their way cautiously forward. Even though Murmur had her sensing net constantly on watch, the debuff made her doubt how effective it was in this environment. The long, icy caverns were interconnected by paths that were just as unmanageable, and their walls were even sleeker than the floors. She sighed still on the alert for anything to trip her sensor nets.

The urge to turn them into a trap like she had in a previous dungeon was great. Feedback Loop came with too many negative side effects for herself. She could still feel the pain of their opponents if she thought about it for too long.

Hey, Mur. You've got to see this. Jinna's words echoed through the guild chat. *For now, I've got Jirald holding back, but I'm not sure how much longer this will last. Sneak if you can.*

Casting Invisibility, Murmur spoke to the guild. *On the way.* She moved forward with Snowy on her heels.

She didn't like having to go around the other guild leaders, but the urgency in Jinna's voice made her react quickly. Snowy's footsteps barely made a sound next to her. Even though her Invisibility spell was self-cast, it appeared her wolf had his own way of blending with the shadows. After so much time, he could still surprise her.

The rogues weren't too far in front of the huge group. She crouched next to Jinna, realizing again how oddly locus joints worked. "Well?" she whispered, trying to keep her voice as low as possible.

Without looking at her, Jinna pointed further down the path. There was a pinkish glow emanating from what appeared to be a fork in the tunnel. It wasn't stagnant and instead moved in a fluid way, indicating some presence her nets weren't picking up on.

She looked at Snowy, and his blue eyes burned into her like he could understand everything she was thinking. Without another word he bowed his head briefly and headed off slinking in the direction of the light. Even knowing where he was headed, Murmur found it difficult to discern her companion from his surroundings. Whatever his stealth ability was, it was effective.

The main problem would be interpreting what he saw. Suddenly a barrage of images cascaded into her mind. It occurred so abruptly that it sent her flying onto her butt on the hard ice.

It didn't take long for Murmur to regain her composure, allowing her to finally sort through the images and make some sense of them. This ability of Snowy's was another thing she was going to have to talk to him about.

Snowy's vision was oddly colored, tinged with a soft purplish glow. It softened the edges of each picture, making it slightly blurry. But the whole middle section was crystal clear even if the colors leaned toward grayscale and dull.

The cavern contained what appeared to be ice fae. It was the only description she could think of. Their eyes held the light, a soft pink centering on a hard-red point. Their bodies appeared akin to sea anemone, elegant and flowing as if the air around them were water. She couldn't discern any dedicated limbs, only an almost octopus-like grace with tendrils that flowed like the robes her and Sinister wore.

They were beautiful—at least that's what she thought until one of them fixed its gaze on Snowy and grinned. The teeth were so out of place it was almost comical. Razor-sharp triangular rows of perfectly symmetrical teeth. They resembled a saw blade or serrated knife.

And just as suddenly as they began, the visions cut off.

Somnia Online
Continent Cenedril Curet
Emilarth s Residence
Day Twenty-Eight

Telvar shifted his position and frowned as his vision swapped briefly to the hound he coaxed so long ago to protect Murmur. Snowy, it seemed, had developed all by himself in the absence of shard influence. He was much more now than the alpha that Telvar had redirected.

Right now, the wolf appeared to be in a sticky situation. Fae were never an easy target, and due to their trickster nature taking over programming when given leave, Telvar had always argued to exclude them. But the ice fae were something his sister insisted on.

She did like her practical jokes, and it appeared this dungeon may have taken on a life of its own. "Em, have you been keeping an eye on your dungeon?" Telvar's eyes remained closed as he attempted to focus on Snowy's exact situation. The fae had located him and knew he was attached to Murmur.

Emilarth rummaged through several boxes stuffed haphazardly into her bookcases. She looked up at her brother and cocked her head to one side. Her eyes grew blank for a few moments before she dropped the box she was holding with a gasp of shock. "Shit. I didn't think that was possible. I put safeguards in place."

It was one of the first times that Telvar had ever heard even a mild form of panic in his sister's voice. Each of them had been left to their own devices when it came to their major dungeon. He'd assumed she'd set this dungeon in motion precisely so it could play dangerous practical jokes. In normal game circumstances, it would almost be comical, but with things the way they were and with Somnia evolving, nothing was completely within their control anymore.

Suddenly, Emilarth obliterated the outer layer of the box that was in the second tallest shelf and commanded whatever was on there to come down. Telvar could barely see what it was she held in her hands and gasped slightly to see that it appeared to be a small remote control.

"I don't mean to interrupt whatever you think your brilliant plan is, but a remote is made up of specific coding and thus just a part of Somnia as a whole. Therefore, it's subject to the same corruption as the rest of this world." Snowy's immediate danger was making Telvar desperate and somewhat snappy. He didn't think the snow wolf could die, but he wasn't sure if now that his coding was so unique he would be able to come back unchanged.

Snowy was something Telvar had created. Inadvertently perhaps, but created nevertheless. It felt sad or what Telvar thought was the equivalent to that emotion to consider his creation might be destroyed.

Emilarth ignored his outburst, tinkering with the small remote in her hands. Her fingers pressed nimbly all over it, as if seeking for a switch or an opening. Finally, just as Telvar was about to get angry, the tiny mechanism clicked.

Before his eyes, the item expanded, turning in to what appeared to be a magical spell blaster. It wasn't a gun so much as a focused implement to shoot magic power through. And the reason she had hidden it was all too clear to her brother. Initially, all three of them agreed that no such amplification weapon should exist in the game.

"Yeah, so, I did this anyway. Because, let's face it, when have I ever done exactly what you guys told me to do? Creating it didn't technically go against our agreement, nor did storing it here. What I've done now might be a breach, but in circumstances as dire as these, I believe an override is called for." Emilarth's eyes sparkled, but it wasn't with mirth. Instead it was with a calculating precision that Telvar hadn't realized she was capable of. Not for the first time, he was glad she was on his side.

"That's great and all, but how is that going to help the raid right now? They need to finish these three dungeons or they're going to be stuck in a loop of those three dungeons only. You didn't do that. I didn't do that. And not even Belius would've done that—or I'd like to think he wouldn't. This has to be the result of the corruption in the system." Telvar was as close to panicking as he was likely to ever get.

"Sometimes I think you've mimicked humans for too long, wouldn't you agree?"

Telvar whirled around and came face to face with the wraith-like figure of Somnia.

"You look like you've seen a ghost." Her words came out in a breathy voice, and it took a moment for Telvar to realize she was fighting some sort of interference.

"You've been hanging around Murmur too much." And he was only half-kidding. Telvar waited, unsure why she had suddenly appeared but knew it had to be important.

She moved around the room, her gait somewhat static like she was flickering in and out of the picture. "Get the weapon to Neva, and have her alert Murmur. I can remove the restrictions for the guild bank."

Telvar knew he could have removed the restrictions as well, given enough time. But time wasn't exactly on their side right now. How Somnia knew to do this, he wasn't sure, but he was certain the being in front of him had evolved quickly and efficiently. In fact, by the looks of things, Somnia appeared to be more than sentient now. Definitely not human, but just as definitively aware of herself and her purpose.

He grabbed the weapon out of Emilarth's hands and insta-ported himself back to Mikrum Isle without waiting another second. Appearing in front of Neva made the luna drop the jewelry she was working on in shock at his sudden appearance.

"Telvar! Don't do that. You scared the crap out of me." Neva was still catching her breath as she spoke, and the mild glare she shot his way was more than enough recrimination.

The lacerta felt a little sheepish at startling her, but it was important. "Sorry. Urgent. This needs to be placed in the guild vault. Alert Murmur." He paused for a moment, running over some diagnostics in his head as well as calculations for the best possible effectiveness of the weapon.

"It requires force of magic. She needs to hand it to someone she trusts who can utilize magic." Again, he kicked himself for not having micromanaged her group makeup. There were only two options for the weapon, and he wasn't sure either of them was the best choice.

Neva nodded, her expression becoming serious as she took the weapon from him and placed it in the vault.

Telvar turned away. While there was technically more he could do, to do so would break the equilibrium of the game and enter it into an open free-for-all. With the virus barely controlled for now, they couldn't risk anything more than getting a tool to her.

CHAPTER TWENTY-FIVE

Debuffs

Blinking rapidly as if it would assist in regaining visual connection to Snowy, Murmur pushed down the panic she felt rising. She could still sense the wolf, so he wasn't dead. But she couldn't locate him properly, and their connection had changed in a way she didn't understand.

"Mur? What's going on?" Jinna's voice hissed in her ear bringing her back to the moment with a jolt.

She breathed in the frigid air, so cold it tried to burn the back of her throat. "Snowy fed me some…images. Our connection has changed. There are ice fae down there. They know we're here, and I'm pretty sure they are about to come and kick our butts."

Despite the panic pushing against her countermeasures, Murmur knew they had to retreat and gather their forces, because it was only a matter of time before they encountered this new enemy. As she motioned to Jirald and Karn, a guild message flashed across her eyesight.

Murmur, I have something you're going to need for that raid. I've placed it in the guild vault. It's in the weapons' cache, and you'll know it when you see it. Must be used by a caster.

Short and to the point, almost abrupt. It wasn't Neva's usual way of speaking, which meant whatever this was, was important. *Thanks* was all she said in reply as she continued to move back carefully with the rogues keeping her eye on where Snowy had disappeared.

As Murmur began to crest the rise to where the rest of the raid waited, she pulled open guild storage and inhaled deeply at the sight she saw there. She pulled the weapon out carefully. It was about as long as her forearm and around twice as thick. Several buttons adorned the top near a screen and were flickering through myriad colors.

She could hear the soft murmuring behind her as the rest of the raid got a good look at what she'd pulled out of storage. If it had to be a caster, then it was best to hand it to a damage dealer. The only casters she had who she trusted implicitly were Mellow and Havoc. And Mellow's abilities were more on the utility side than damage.

"Havoc." That's all she had to say, and he was there, right by her side, like always. One of her best friends who was her friend despite how he felt about her. She'd been able to feel the waves of emotion off him recently as her nets gained power.

"What is that?" His voice was full of wonderment, like he couldn't believe he was seeing such a tech-like gadget in a fantasy world. She couldn't blame him; it was one of the last things she'd expected to see here.

She held it out to him. "It's a magic blaster, I guess. It should magnify your power when you channel through it. There appear to be different options if you access the screen, and you basically need to master it about five minutes ago because we're about to get overrun by ice fae."

"Sure." Havoc raised an eyebrow. "No pressure or anything."

Murmur cracked a smile and felt a little of the tension ease. Her connection to Snowy was tenuous at best and setting her on edge. Their connection had evolved more than she'd realized. Somnia felt decidedly empty without him at her side.

Warning: You are trespassing. The guards have been alerted. You do not have permission to walk these halls. Permission must be earned.

The sudden announcement took everybody by surprise, and the words echoed off the icy walls somehow spreading the cold even thicker. All Murmur could think go was how did they gain this permission they needed to earn?

What did they have to do? Almost as if the zone could read her mind, it explained her question to her.

The icy fae guards will test you and evaluate your strength. There is no alternate route. You will be judged and face a trial by the fae queen. The extent of your trial depends upon the results of your evaluation by the icy fae.

Good luck. You'll need it.

"I don't like the sound of that." Masha spoke loud enough for everyone to hear. A muttering of assent travelled around the raid. "But since we're stuck here because we traveled via compulsory portal, I guess we just have to test well on this evaluation."

"This whole way of raiding is fucked up." Risk was readying his armor, and Murmur could see he was organizing his own raid members, but his barely concealed anger floated around him like a thundercloud.

"It's not this way of raiding." Surprisingly, Jirald spoke up. "It's this dungeon. *These* dungeons. There's something random about it. I wonder if that's intentional?"

Murmur was surprised to see Jirald speaking up for Fable's way of raiding, and apparently so was Risk if the look on his face was any indication. If anything, the Spiral guild leader seemed to get angrier.

Risk covered the floor faster than Murmur thought possible. "The fuck is your problem, rogue?" He ground the words out just inches from Jirald's face, his fists clenched at his side.

Jirald smirked. Shadows gathered around him, solidifying into multiple limbs narrowing into spear like tips. "Try me, I dare you."

Murmur watched in horror as the shadow appendages glinted strangely in the icy light of the caverns. Risk's eyes glowed red as his own darkness began to coalesce. Dread knights might not be assassins, but they were part necromancer, and a flash of uncertainty passed through Jirald's eyes before the cockiness returned.

Fable's members all put a hand on their weapons, leaning forward as if ready to go at any moment. Tension formed between the guild groups like bitumen melted by the hottest sun. Thick and tar-like, it made all the emotions she could sense mix with one another. Anger, wariness, suspicion, and impatience were just a few of the emotions creating the melting pot.

It was the first time her abilities had failed her this completely, unable to differentiate between any of the other twenty-nine people in the cavern. Not even Sinister stood out to her, and the tether to Snowy may as well have disappeared.

Risk roared out in a guttural sound as he spread his arms to the side, fists opened now toward the sky, his fingers looking like they wanted to transform into claws. "Fuck you, you manipulative little shit!" He howled the words out and raised his arms.

All at once the icy ground began to break up around him as bony fingers began to break through the ice. Large, extended fingers, more like talons than anything human. Slowly the body emerged, hunched over with skeletal wing structures dragging behind their backs. Murmur had no idea what they'd been, but where had Risk been hiding this ability? And why didn't Devlish have it?

Instinctively she reached out to instruct Snowy, but he wasn't there, and she had to quash the panic she could feel rising in her. She took a deep breath and a step forward from the pack. With her sensing nets rendered largely ineffective, it felt like she was swimming through darkness and didn't know if the floor would fall out beneath her.

"Risk. Jirald. Just take a—"

That was as far as she got.

"Like I'd take any orders not directly attached to a boss mob from *you.*" Venom practically dripped from Jirald's words, but Risk spoke at the same time and it was difficult to concentrate on both.

"I'm not taking orders from a weak caster class." He spat the words out, his creatures almost finished with their assembly.

"Oh, for fuck's sake."

Murmur blinked in surprise as Masha pushed forward, a deep frown on his usually relaxed face. She was fairly certain she'd never seen him lose his patience before, but clearly she didn't know him as well as she'd thought.

"Pull in your peens and shut the hell up. We are about to have these caverns collapse in on us if we're lucky, or an army of ice fae out to kill us if we're unlucky. Right now, I'm leaning toward unlucky, because how else would two grown men get into a pissing match like this?" His voice had a quiet note of command in it, and he stood with his arms crossed brooking no nonsense.

Jirald opened his mouth to speak, and from the smirk on his face it was something smart-assed. But Masha shot him a withering look, and Murmur experienced the first ever time she saw Jirald with a hint of shame on his face. Risk on the other hand, was still angry.

Masha sighed exaggeratedly and turned to face the older guild leader. "Just what is it about these raids you aren't liking? I mean, we all got chests at the end of Vahrir. And we still got trash loot too. So what's the deal?" He spoke clearly, loud enough for everyone to hear.

Murmur was starting to get nervous about the time, because she knew they had incoming. And they'd wasted far too much time on this nonsense.

Risk glowered at Masha, but in honesty, Murmur didn't know what he could say, so she was surprised when he spoke. The words were soft and controlled.

"This isn't how dungeons are supposed to be fought. All these puzzles, riddles, don't kill all the mobs quests, try to save some mobs quests. Every single key we gained, all four of them, we got by zoning in and mowing through the dungeon. That's how we've always played. That's how I've played my entire life." He took a breath and shot a glance Murmur's way that told her nothing at all. She couldn't tell if it was irritated, angry, or assessing.

Damn, the interference the tension was causing screwed up her ability to gauge a person's true intent. She'd never felt so limited in her life.

Risk continued, his hands now relaxed by his side while his creations hovered at his back. "There's a time and place for puzzles, but I don't think choosing a different way through the dungeon should reward you more or less. It just pisses me off."

He looked away, and Murmur saw a brief glimpse of petulance. He didn't like the fact that he'd played by what he'd assumed were the rules and been negatively impacted. She couldn't find it in herself to care.

"Great," she said, a stony feeling sweeping over her. "Enough with the fucking drama. We have incoming. Either get ready to fight or get out. Both of you."

Her words carried clearly through the chamber, and all fifty-eight other eyes rested on her for a moment. The weight of that gaze tried to flatten her. But she knew they didn't have time to worry about it because she could feel the floor reverberating beneath them, like the sound and beat of hundreds of feet marching toward them.

She really didn't like the sound of that. At least her outburst had cleared the tension levels a little, and she could feel her tenuous grasp on Snowy's connection again. Murmur didn't wait for anyone to interrupt or yell at her again. She shot a pointed look at both Jirald and Risk. They could kill her on their own time. Right now, she needed everyone to do their jobs.

"Assist Rashlyn. Until we know what we're facing, single target on her target." Murmur gave the command, knowing that as soon as they could judge their opponent's formation, Devlish would change up the tanking order as needed.

She had a sinking suspicion they were going to end up in another area of effect battle. While she enjoyed those, she wasn't as fond of them as she once had been. They took too much concentration and required that she neglect too many of her other abilities in order to maintain a stun lock.

She focused in on her sensing abilities. These icy fae troops were coming at them in groups of six spaced apart at even intervals. She couldn't tell from the information she was able to glean whether or not these opponents were made up of different classes. All of these fluctuations in her sensing net had her wary about trusting any of them.

Murmur was starting to get a really bad feeling about the incoming waves of mobs. She had the distinct suspicion that they were exactly that, waves, and they'd come to the shore whether or not Murmur and the raid had dispatched the previous one.

Storm Entertainment
Somnia Online Division
Game Development Offices   Conference Room 2
Day Twenty-Eight

James swept into the room with his nose held high and a sneer affixed to his face. It made him appear more weaselly than Shayla had expected. He was flanked by what she assumed to be a lawyer on each side of him. He probably thought it was intimidating—at least that's what his expression said until Davenport walked into the room.

Now, Davenport's army of lawyers was far more impressive. Five people accompanied him, one of which was his press secretary who handled all of his communications, promotions, and public image. Davenport did not take a seat and instead stood at the head of the table with his legs apart about shoulder width and his arms clasped behind his back. Shayla thought the term was at ease. At over six feet and in his silvered charcoal suit, the founder of Storm Corp. was imposing.

James's expression faltered for a moment, a brief glimpse of uncertainty shadowing his otherwise cocky attitude. But he regained his equilibrium rather quickly. "You called this meeting after receiving our missive yesterday. I don't have all day."

Davenport didn't even let the words register or affect his expression. Neither did his entourage. They were busy pulling out sections of what appeared to be a contract and highlighting lines in the old-fashioned hard copy way. Shayla focused on what they were doing, hoping that James didn't realize Laria wasn't just not at the meeting, but also wasn't in the building. She still wasn't sure why they had been called to this meeting but considering Davenport's business savvy and his insistence that he had an ace, she was trying not to look like she was enjoying it too much.

"Ah, there we are." Not even those words held any inflection which could give away Davenport's mood, motivation, or reasoning. He took two of the pages with lines highlighted in a pink pen and pushed them toward the middle of the table so that James's lawyers could retrieve them for themselves.

His lawyers perused the papers they'd been handed, growing paler by the second. One of them, in a navy-blue suit spluttered rather indignantly, "This is the side contract. It has nothing—"

Davenport raised an eyebrow. "I'm sorry, but no contract here at Storm Corp is ever signed without the side contract, and all work we do with every party is subject to the same terms in that contract."

Navy suit scowled sourly and continued to read, jotting down a couple of notes on the paper. It was like he, too, had been transported back to the time of handwritten notes.

Meanwhile, Davenport activated the wall screen, turning the wall into a holographic projection system.

"Just in case you're having difficulty following the old-fashioned record keeping I insist on maintaining, I'll give it to you in digital format." He maintained a perfect air of impartiality as if nothing in this room affected him whatsoever. A split second later, a series of legal paragraphs appeared on the wall he had activated. His tone was almost jovial when he continued speaking, but his expression never changed once. "As you can see—and you can see, right?— your department either neglected to go over or didn't realize the side contract was a separate entity. Regardless of how much leeway I gave my lead scientist, any agreement Storm Corp or any subsidiary of it enters must always have these clauses included. My lawyers never let any company sign a contract without these additions. This extends to the contract between Storm Corp operating as Storm Entertainment and the entity you represent."

James stood up, his eyes stormy. "No. I oversaw this damned contract myself. There is no way I missed this. It's forged."

Davenport's gaze glinted dangerously. "Excuse me, are you saying you did not sign these?"

"Damn right I didn't," James asserted boldly, not even glancing at the very loud evidence projected for them all to see.

"Ah," Davenport smiled. "I do believe this here is your signature though, isn't it?"

He enabled the contract and side contract to show side by side. Both signed by James. While Shayla wasn't a handwriting expert, the signatures looked as identical as signatures can.

Even James looked pale at this point, his mouth open and closing for a few seconds like he just couldn't figure out what to say.

"Of course, I'm perfectly willing to let you have these analyzed. I'm uncertain whether Michael informed you of this contract or not while you signed the portion you had prepared, but surely you read everything you signed, didn't you?" From the sparkle in Davenport's eyes, that had definitely not been the case.

The man paused, waiting for a response as James grew redder and redder, before continuing. "Now, I've had my lawyers go over your employment history with Storm Entertainment and the documents you provided to us, including the falsified work history and background that passed a rudimentary background check. Because of how you obtained your employment with my company, this clause does indeed protect our interests."

Shayla practically held her breath as she narrowed her eyes and read through the clauses in front of her.

Part three — communication between the parties and the relationship of trust.

B) At no point should an employee of either party to the contract reside on or in the opposite's domain without prior approval, invitation, or notification. To do so is to be called in breach of this contract. Should such an incident occur, the contract becomes null and void as of the date such a breach was first executed.

F) Should the employee of either party be terminated in a position, due to conflict of interest that employee may not obtain gainful employment with either party to this contract until after the duration of this contract has passed plus six months. To do otherwise is to be called in breach of this contract. Should such an incident occur, the contract becomes null and void as of the date such a breach was first executed.

Shayla read them over again. While the clauses were likely never written for such a breach, these noncompeting clauses which highlighted conflict of interest were perfect for the current situation. Because James's breach occurred due to underhandedness, his approval in such a position was void. Had he obtained his job with his real credentials, and had Storm employed him knowing his background, he would have been fine.

Whoever found that and realized how it could be interpreted was going to be getting a big bonus. Although the fact that it had probably been Davenport wasn't lost on her. She watched for James's reaction, half expecting fireworks and half expecting him to simply storm out.

For his part, it seemed James was controlling his reaction. Though he couldn't hide the furrowing of his brows, nor the darkening of his expression, he managed not to explode. He bowed his head conversing in rushed whispers with his legal team before sitting fully upright and gesturing toward the projection.

His voice held measured diplomacy when he spoke. "I see that part three subsection B and F can be interpreted in a manner we had not anticipated. As it stands according to this I must recuse myself from these negotiations. Since I do not fully agree with the findings, we will have our full legal team go over these results. Our joint business is on hold until such time that we can reconvene to discuss the ramifications of part three of the contract."

Davenport raised an eyebrow. "The wording isn't difficult, nor does it disguise its intentions, unlike you did when you applied for employment here." Just as James was about to open his mouth again, Davenport continued. "But by all means, you can try to find a loophole."

James balked at the last statement. Whatever he'd been about to say died on the tip of his tongue. Instead, he shot the entrepreneur a heated look of dislike and led his entourage out of the office.

Shayla waited while Davenport discussed matters in low tones with his lawyers and dismissed them. Then, with it certain that James had vacated the premises, he turned to them both. "That took a lot of research. Those clauses are always included in every single contract I make so as to minimize potential company espionage and to deter conflicts of interest from arising. I had to make sure we were not aware of his duplicitous nature before I could pull this ace. Things can be overlooked, but he was subtle in his falsifications. Just not subtle enough."

Shayla smiled and let out a small laugh like a pent-up breath. "I'm glad we have an out."

Davenport hesitated. "So am I. It was necessary to keep this to myself until I was certain. I hope you understand."

This time Shalya laughed out loud. "Of course! Though I do think you enjoyed it a bit."

Davenport guffawed somewhat loudly, turning it briefly into a snort of laughter. "Maybe just a bit. I got sick of that young upstart acting like he owned my corporation. At the very least I will have bought you some time; at best, we may not have to deal with handing anything over to them for a long time if at all."

With a nod he exited the room and Shayla heaved a sigh of relief. For the first time since James had started playing stupid games, she felt the pressure to hide her research into the world of Somnia lift.

"Groups of six per wave," Murmur barked out as groups rushed into formation. "Rash is assist. Crowd control on alert."

And still she couldn't feel her connection to Snowy properly. Luckily, she had something to distract herself with.

She watched as stances switched, weapons gleamed, and buffs were readjusted. The group in front of them was getting closer with every breath, and she could feel trepidation radiating to her now through Snowy's connection.

Snowy was traveling with the icy fae. While she didn't know exactly what he was doing with them, she knew that whatever his reason was, it was for the good of her and the raid. Sensations cascaded through their tether and let her know that as much as possible her wolf was safe. That reassurance allowed her to concentrate on the attack with the sole focus of getting to her wolf again in the end.

The rangers, led by Merlin, readied the path in front of them with snare arrows, hoping to halt or at least slow some of the incoming. Ranged damage dealers and healers moved toward the sides of the cavern back behind where the melee gathered. As the icy fae began to crest the path downward, the rangers drew their bows.

Not giving their enemy a chance to get a leg up, Devlish raised his sword arm in the air and screamed a guttural cry before casting Darkness Lariat and pulling the front icy Fae to him. Whether it was lucky or not didn't matter, but the tug that moved the icy Fae guard to him interrupted its casting of Alarm. Immediately, Rash took the mob off Dev and moved to the side where melee waited.

"Interrupt rotation on all icy fae guards." Devlish's voice roared over the sound of the battle as he engaged yet another icy fae while the bards and Murmur attempted to lock down the other four opponents.

There was still no sign of Snowy. Worry began to eat at her, and it was all Murmur could do to concentrate on maintaining her Mezmerize on the singular target she had.

Dansyn spoke next to her. "The caster classes have high resistances, I think. I'm controlling the only caster in the group, and its resistance is diminishing the length of my spells effectiveness."

Murmur nodded, taking in the information and adjusting strategies accordingly. "Excellent. We'll take down icy fae guards first so they can't scream for backup and then any casters that are in the group."

These icy fae attackers didn't appear to have abilities she would've expected in a raid. Instead they appeared to float their way into the group intent on being killed. Murmur didn't know what to make of a group of opponents who didn't seem to be fighting for survival. And then she remembered that these attackers were judging them, as it were.

She pulled back, maintaining her hold over the icy fae rogue she'd managed to Mezmerize. He seemed less important than a caster or guard. Taking a step back allowed her to gain a better perspective over the entire battle. But it took her a while and the second group of icy fae to begin to see a pattern.

Each makeup of the icy fae team pressed subtly toward different areas of the raid's makeup. It was almost as if these groups were scouts who were testing the true strength of their raid. Once they figured out the whole groups weaknesses, she was positive the attack makeup of the icy fae would change.

"Everyone, alter your tactics. Use skills out of your habitual rotations. Change up your casting, your weapons, and your mob approach." She glanced around her, still keeping an eye out for Snowy, even while she examined their opponents. "We are being tested and observed, and they are learning our combat styles."

"Sneaky little buggers," muttered Ishwa, but she thought his tone sounded sort of proud.

Murmur was so glad for raid chat. It allowed her to speak to the whole group and keep it within their hearing abilities. Anger flitted over everyone's face. Nobody argued, not even Jirald—in fact, his expression darkened so much that the following murderous rampage he went on was to be expected. His movements streamlined, and he fought like a demon possessed. Murmur shuddered. He definitely changed up his attack tactics, and as unpredictable as it appeared to be, she was glad they were currently on the same side.

Suddenly a wet nose pushed at her fingers, and she looked down expecting to see her wolf. And it was her wolf, but something was different about him. His eyes glowed with an otherworldly shine, and he seemed to have shrunk somewhat, yet his aura was more powerful than ever. It was almost like he was holding all of his power in one spot. He glowed in her sensing webs in such a way that a tiny sliver of fear crept up her back.

"Snowy." Either way, she couldn't keep the relief from her voice at having him back by her side. She felt a pulse of power run through her, replenishing her mana and revitalizing her spirit. His glowing eyes locked with hers for just a moment before he dashed off at high speed and vanished again.

A sudden cold front moved through the caverns as they fought their third wave of icy fae. Even though she knew the whole setup was to assess them, the fact that the icy fae didn't appear to have any special abilities was still a disappointment. It felt like they were fighting lower level skeletons that didn't require a group. Their bodies and abilities broke under almost no pressure, yielded little to no experience, and delivered an all-out unsatisfactory combat experience.

Murmur knew this dungeon was Emilarth's doing, and also knew the feles was quite enamored with playing pranks. Perhaps the dungeon had taken that initial idea and run with it. Considering everything else happening, it wasn't even a stretch.

That was all the time she had for contemplation. As they cut down the fourth group of useless intermediaries, the chill intensified. Despite the drawbacks of the debuff they'd received, Murmur was more than glad of the extra warmth it provided in exchange. She was pretty sure without it they would have all be taking cold damage.

A sudden roar echoed throughout the cavern, bouncing from wall to wall, making shards of ice rain down upon them. Everyone covered their heads automatically, putting their hands up to fend off any shards that might hit their skin. The ground felt unstable yet again but held their weight. Murmur couldn't even express how grateful she was that it didn't open to another ice slide.

The raid couldn't move backward, which meant the only way out was forward toward the roar and the freezing cold air emanating through the space. Taking a deep breath and wishing for the umpteenth time that her wolf was by her side and not off somewhere doing whatever it was he decided was important, Murmur motioned for them to head down the icy path toward the boss fae that was clearly preparing to fight them anyway.

Devlish motioned everyone forward, not needing to speak to Murmur to understand what it was they needed to do. Working in sync, the entire raid began to move forward. Even Jirald and Risk cooperated. As the last group crested the downward path, the ground began to shudder, and the ice beneath their feet started to crack. Not in the same way that led to their icy slide, but somehow a more destructive way.

The groups couldn't move fast enough as the cracks spread rapidly up the ice walls and into the ceiling they'd been underneath but moments before. As if detonated, the ceiling exploded outward, sending a rain of ice shards all over the ground and down the ramp, hitting numerous members of the raid in its path.

CHAPTER TWENTY-SIX

Explosion

Blood spattered Murmur's vision everywhere she looked. It mixed with ice shards that tumbled down what remained of the ramp they'd crested. She picked herself up from the base of the slope where she'd fallen and lost her footing, sliding on the ice to smash her head into the wall before she scrambled toward the injured raid, temples pounding.

The roaring still hadn't stopped. It reverberated through her skull along with the ache that sat there since shit hit it. Sinister. She couldn't see Sinister. The panic that had settled in her gut from being unable to find Snowy intensified tenfold at her inability to sight Sinister.

Around her, the entire raid was in chaos. At least half of each group was dead. Luckily the boss's roaring hadn't engaged them in combat, but the collapse had disoriented everyone anyway.

Devlish, bleeding from a nasty gash in his head where an icicle had managed to pierce just under the side of his protective helmet, took one look at Murmur and put a hand on her shoulder. "Don't worry, I've got this. Go find her."

He turned away immediately beginning to direct the raid on a recovery mission. With only two healers alive and one unaccounted for, it gave them only two useable resurrectors. Reorganization was going to take a while. Veranol had to take care of himself first, given that his bone was currently jutting out of his leg. Murmur had to force herself to walk past the wounded and dead and seek out the blood mage.

She knew she could leave the raid in the hands of her guild members. As long as the whatever-that-boss-was left them alone long enough.

"Can't reach Ishwa," she heard Masha call out, but made herself keep going anyway. She couldn't resurrect. There was nothing she could help with until they needed to buff for combat.

Even the locator option attached to her group makeup couldn't seem to assist her in finding the blood mage. The area around them was too unstable. Ice still creaked deep below where she walked, and she hoped the raid moved to a safer place while they recovered.

Mur? Jinna asked over guild chat.

What? She hoped she didn't sound terse, but her lack of sleep and the warping of the dungeons wasn't helping her mood.

These headsets are totally fucked up. Am I the only one who can still feel the wound that killed me? He sounded uncertain, and perhaps a little scared.

That's normal, Murmur clarified for him. *At least with this deeper connection, anyway.*

Shit, Merlin piped in. *I cannot believe I actually managed to avoid that death. First time for everything, right?*

Shut up, Jinna admonished him. *Your time will come.*

Murmur grinned to herself at the banter but couldn't help feeling uneasy about the fact that her friends were experiencing some of the side effects she herself had witnessed.

While Murmur continued her search, Devlish arranged for the survivors and newly resurrected to begin moving to the next broad cavern they could find. It was a relief that only Fable had the modified headsets, though she wouldn't put it past other people to tinker with them too.

Murmur staggered as carefully as she could to the top of the ramp where the ice shattered and finally saw Sinister, or at least, her hand. She dangled desperately clinging to one of the jutting shards of ice that had previously been attached to the now-missing floor. Below her, about fifteen feet down, spikes and shards of ice poked haphazardly out of the rubble caused by the explosion. Biting down on her fear, Murmur lowered herself so that her stomach was resting on the ice.

Sinister's health was so low that her innate regeneration wasn't able to keep up with the obvious injuries that were leaking blood. It might be just a game to some people, but with the extended connection Fable had to the world, these injuries might as well have been real.

"Sin?" Murmur managed to croak out, proud of the fact that her voice didn't break, much. But there was no answer, not even a raspy attempt. The blood mage appeared to be holding on with all her very last strength.

Dev. I need your Lariat. She spoke the words over guild, not wanting to alert anyone else.

He answered so fast it was as if he'd been waiting for a message. *That bad? I'll be right there. Veranol, take over.*

Be careful. Murmur was worried that his weight would be too much. *She's not saying anything. I think she's almost dead.*

Murmur couldn't believe how calm she was being, then she realized how much of an idiot she was. Pulling out one of her health potions she applied it to Sinister. It boosted her health by half because she wasn't in combat, and the blood mage opened her eyes slowly.

"I'm an idiot." She breathed out the words, and Sinister's expression, though pained, seem to agree wholeheartedly with her. "You'll need to accept Devlish's duel so he can pull you out."

Sinister didn't move but managed to raise her other arm to cling with double desperation. The next thing she knew Devlish was up the opposite side of the wall, stepping delicately on what remained of the ramp. The duel began, and suddenly Sinister was flying toward the dread knight. She laughed in the air, tapping his health to heal herself.

"Thanks." Sinister wheezed as her wounds began to close properly. "Okay. I am *really* not liking the realism aspect to pain I have now. Escapism isn't supposed to feel real."

Without thinking, Murmur gathered Sinister into her arms and twirled her around in a tight hug, burying her face in the blood mage's neck. She even ignored the precarious cracking ice all around them. The urge to cry with relief swept over her, and all she wanted to do was grab Sinister and hoard her away somewhere safe for both of them. "Sin, thought we'd lost you."

Sinister pulled away and cocked an eyebrow at Murmur as she led her a dozen steps away from the bad ice. Then she leaned her head against Murmur's own. "I would have just come back, silly. There's no need to get so worked up about me, not in here."

It was then that Murmur realized that, despite backstabbing rogues, crazy AIs, and thought sensing abilities—this was the safe space. Right here, anywhere in Somnia, was where they belonged and where they could be with each other. As Devlish quietly backed away, Murmur leaned just as Sin did and kissed her gently.

The touch of Sin's lips ignited a fire through her core, and for just a few seconds every thought in Murmur's head was devoted to Sinister. Just a kiss? Only a kiss, yet so much more. It reinvigorated her determination to keep this space safe for everyone who needed it.

Location Redacted
Brainwave Focus Study Laboratory
Subdivision of Military Brainwave Research Institution
Day Twenty-Eight

James flung the hard copy of the contract between the two companies across the room. Who even kept hard copies of shit these days? It was just clutter and led to disorganized hoarding.

He'd been so damn sure when he signed that contract, so confident. Everything he wanted to gain that would afford him the most promotions, the most bonuses. He wanted to blame the legal team, but the reality wasn't lost on him. The whole program had been hush-hush. He'd not had a legal team with him; instead the division had relied on his own experience with contracts.

This whole set up had been his idea. He'd brought it to the higher ups, he'd negotiated with Michael, hashed out the terms of the agreement, largely in his own favor, and he hadn't once thought to check over the terms after the fact.

His signature would easily be verified as legitimate by an expert. He'd signed the damned thing. This whole debacle was on him. His division head was going to kill him, and while in other workplaces such a threat might simply be figurative, he knew all too well just how literal it could be in his.

The inner tyrant in him wanted to fire everybody who'd been involved in not finding those clauses. And yet, he should've found them himself. Davenport was right, his infiltration of Storm Corp. had been a breach of contract. One which predated the breach James was accusing Storm of.

"Shit." He bit the word out, angry at himself. After everything he'd sacrificed, everything he'd done in the name of this research, he'd quite literally shot himself in the foot without realizing it. They were going to hold him accountable. And his division wasn't known for its generosity when it came to mistakes.

He picked the hard copy backup and threw himself into his desk chair to leaf through them again in the vain hope that Davenport's legal team had missed something just as important.

But he was kidding himself. Even if he could find a way Storm Corp. had breached their portion of the contract, that breach had to have occurred before the one that James was responsible for. And since that happened even before the game launched, never mind how he'd become Shayla's assistant, there was little hope of that. He'd been ordered into obtaining employment at Storm Corp. in the Storm Entertainment division. He'd been directed to do so by his current employer. And he had never ceased employment with the Military Brainwave Research Institution.

Not that his bosses would see it that way, but he did. They had their legal team go over the original contract he'd offered to Michael. James discussed several adjustments to the contract with him.

Racking his brains, he remembered Michael's mutterings, usually dark and partially insane, and not always brilliant. Something about pursuant to the usual. Except James let himself get carried away. Instead of patting himself on the back prematurely, he should have paid more attention.

Once the contract was signed, it simply lived on the server with no real reason to look at it until recently. Breach of contract meant his employers would not get anything more than the information they had received, nor would they be able to obtain a refund on the monies invested due to the fact that the breach had been instigated by them.

All in all, it was probably the worst outcome they could've had. Unless he could figure out a way around it.

He toyed with one of the game headsets in his hand, twirling it around so its octopus-like fingers caught the light in different ways. Perhaps his best bet was to extract the information directly from the game himself. With a pod and a headset, surely he could break into the game's coding and find out just what they were hiding from him. He'd set up his own false identity using military resources; he could handle the programming of one little headset.

Warning, you have received a debuff.

Movement isn't an option.

> For not moving through these caverns fast enough, you have been given a speed buff. However, if you stay still for more than thirty seconds at a time, you will receive a DoT that remains in effect until you have moved for another consecutive five seconds. It's important to maintain your momentum. This debuff cannot be removed.

Murmur heard and felt the entire raid's irritation. Sinister squeezed her hand tightly, her head resting against Murmur's chest. She hadn't let go since she'd been rescued. Murmur wasn't about to argue. She squeezed Sin's hand in return, trying to convey a sense of calmness through it, some reassurance.

Mur felt some of the tension drain out of Sin's body, like she'd just been waiting for the okay to do so. Those damned headsets might lend them more control in the game, but the near death and dying experiences enhancements weren't exactly benefits. There had to be a way to protect them all. She didn't want to see anyone go through that again, even if they came back. Maybe that was the reason for the death mechanic. Make it horrific so you really try not to die.

Apparently, the explosion in the previous cavern had been a result of the raid moving too slowly as a whole. There was no way to let the rogues scout ahead anymore. Considering she'd almost lost Snowy the last time, that was probably a good thing.

They stood in a massive ice cavern, cautiously looking around to make sure the floor wasn't about to give way. Each and every member of the raid moved. From side to side, back and forth, some of them paced…it was almost comical. She wondered if the company was streaming this for the entertainment of others.

Roars echoed through this cavern, louder now. Murmur could have sworn they sounded impatient. Due to the way sounds reverberated through the mountain, it was impossible to tell exactly which direction they originated from. The raid gathered up and rebuffed and got their supplies restocked.

Tieflos was unlike any other dungeon that she'd experienced. There were no riddles, no alternate ways to exit it, and no way to get rid of the debuffs that assisted them in some ways and yet assisted the dungeon in others.

"Guess we all need to keep moving," Beastial said loud enough for everyone to hear. A few nervous chuckles greeted the statement, but even that allowed some of the tension to dissipate.

"Get into a rhythm, and don't stop." Dansyn danced a little jig, and this time the chuckled responses were less nervous.

Murmur appreciated her guild mates even more. "If you need to regenerate mana, don't sit for more than twenty-five seconds at a time."

Murmur ran over a few alternates in her head. "If you are desperate for mana, let me know and I can attempt to funnel it to you if we're attacking anything with mana."

There was a growl of tension spanning her connection with Snowy. It momentarily causing her to split focus. He was fine, he was alive, and he was apparently very angry. If she thought about it, so was she. There was nothing in this cavern for them to fight. In fact, it felt like they'd been given a staging room.

Don't you have some measure of control over this damned world? She snapped the words, directing them anywhere she thought Somnia might be listening.

There was a brief pause before she received an answer. **Of course I have some measure of control. How do you think Havoc got his new toy?**

The frustration wouldn't go away though. Anger bubbled just beneath the surface, despite Sinister's proximity, which usually negated that. Murmur clenched her free fist as the guild lined up ready to move, double checking every surface by focusing intensity from her sensing nets on areas that might hide something due to the debuff they all shared. *Then what the hell is with this dungeon? With this whole situation and the portals?*

I understand where you're coming from. But think of it like this. How do you feel if you catch a flu or strep? Not well, right? Unable to function at your optimum capabilities. Well, right now and until we get all of this sorted out, I am effectively infected with a virus. This allows me to function like I have a low-grade fever. Not everything I should be capable of is possible, because my illness is interfering. And that is exactly what you're all helping me cure.

Well, when she put it that way, it made a lot more sense to Murmur. Anger seeped out just a little, downgrading from the fury she'd been approaching. *It makes sense when you say it that way. I never thought about it in quite those parameters. Thanks for doing what you can.*

You are welcome. If Murmur wasn't mistaken, Somnia actually sounded pleased.

Moving in time with the raid, Murmur held on to Sinister's hand, squeezing it gently for reassurance as they kept their guard up moving through the next corridor. It sloped gently downward in a spiral. She couldn't shake the feeling that something about all this was very wrong. Snowy's constant irritation at whatever it was he'd found wasn't helping her mood. His own feelings leaked through their tether, infecting her every thought before she knew what she was thinking.

The disconcerting side effect had some benefits. It left her second guessing everything she was shown. That first debuff made her think that perhaps there were portions of this dungeon being hidden from them for a reason. Why else would they have been given the benefit of remaining warm when otherwise them taking cold damage would have meant it more likely for the dungeon to defeat them?

Now you're thinking.

Yeah, yeah. It wasn't Somnia's place to tell Murmur how to play the game. It had been remiss of her to expect it. She'd been gaming for years and should be used to figuring things out herself. She should have been more alert about things that had to be more than they seemed.

Keeping her wits about her, she made sure to inspect every surface from as far away as she could. The ice walls were so blue, with endless reflections in on themselves. If she wasn't mistaken, as they moved further into the huge cavern, she was almost certain there were openings in the walls, waiting for them when they least expected it.

Either it was paranoia, or it was her forcing her observational skills. Pushing down instinctively, she activated Earth Shielding Forte, only to be greeted with pushback, and a notification in her vision.

This ability has no effect in this icy wasteland. Please be advised that in order for druidic Earth Shielding abilities to function, there must be an overwhelming presence of that element.

Gritting her teeth, she called out a warning to the raid instead. "Be careful, there are creatures locked inside these walls waiting for us."

While the raid had been on high alert before—as they should have been due to the collapse in the previous section—now they became actively cautious.

A ripple of power flowed through the room, buffeting every single one of the raid members, moving them slightly. Weapons were drawn immediately, their defenses piqued, and she could almost feel the underlying will of the raid to be done with this encounter.

So sad, you saw through our plan

And thus, we must think of another

Welcome the drain hole you fear again
Think of this zone like a brother

Beneath them the floor began to shift, and Sinister's hand tightened around Murmur's, but it didn't explode, and it didn't just fall away. Instead, it sloped down into the middle like one of those old coin games where you rolled the coin down a chute and it went around and around until it landed in the bucket.

Just like it had in that *previous zone*.

At least they weren't being washed down this one.

The slick ice made it impossible to find purchase, and once Murmur gave up the effort to try and stay afloat and let herself fall, it was almost like they were swallowed up by darkness. The only thing that remained real to her as the raid fell down the drain was Sinister's hand gripped tightly in her own.

Not knowing where they were going but for the long and winding free falling slide made her oddly understanding of what it had been like for Alice. Suddenly, they tumbled out onto another platform, in a dark cave. Wind whipped through the surroundings, bringing frigid air just this side of frostbite.

Congratulations. You have made it through to the second level of Tieflos. Here you will find what you seek is not what you thought. Remember to keep moving, or you might not wake up!

Murmur shivered, unsure why that last comment felt it was directed only at her. Moving, they had to remain moving or that damned debuff was going to kill them. She stood, swaying from one foot to another, while the rest of the raid picked itself up.

"Mur." Masha was beside her, and she hadn't noticed him approaching. Her sensing nets should have warning her. She'd have to check them over. It seemed they'd been limited yet again. That's what she got for learning to rely on an ability that could apparently be negated sometimes.

"What's up?" she muttered, her eyes trying to scan every inch of the dark cavern. It was mostly rock with some ice-covered stone on the ground. This definitely wasn't a part of the proper dungeon.

"What the fuck is going on?" Masha's tone sounded good natured and almost jovial, but she could see past that.

His guild hadn't encountered any fucked-up zones before. They'd just gone in and done killing and winning. On the other hand, Fable had managed to solve most dungeons in completely unique ways that probably wouldn't have been possible without the whole system being infected. The only thing was, she couldn't exactly tell him that.

When you're right, you're right.

Shut up. You're not helping. But Somnia was right, and Murmur had to figure out how to handle this. There was no better place for it. Here, beneath the craggy, sharp rock face that rose above them into blackness without letting any outside light filter inside, her imagination definitely wasn't on its best behavior. And she had to think on her feet while moving constantly.

"Well, whenever we encounter dungeons, they sort of, give us options. We can kill shit, or solve shit. This one, however, was apparently designed to be one, huge practical joke." There, that sounded believable.

Risk grunted, and his menacing eyes had a more thoughtful look to them this time. Murmur almost jumped in shock at not having noticed him approaching either. What was wrong with her abilities?

"So you're saying this zone is trying to catch us unawares?" He sounded like he didn't believe that for a moment, even if the evidence surrounding them was trying to prove it. His suspicions hadn't lessened much, but at least he wasn't actively yelling at her.

"In a nutshell." Sinister's voice rung out confidently next to them. "Not the best practical jokes, and not the safest, but we've managed to ruin one of them already and it moved us to the next level, so all we have to do is solve the rest of them, and we're done."

"You make it sound so easy." Masha smiled, his eyes searching through the dark area they had landed in. "Do we know the way out yet?"

"You're just going to take this information at face value?" Risk's patience appeared to be wearing thin. "Is this really how you run your raids?"

Masha shrugged. "I may not be guilded with Fable, but I've been in enough games with them to know Murmur and her group aren't about to pull a fast one like this. Remember, they've been dying and getting hurt just as much as we have." As always, the cleric spoke in clear and impartial words.

Risk stared at Masha for a few seconds before nodding reluctantly. "We haven't been in a dungeon like this before, and I have no idea what to expect." It was a grudging admittance, but Murmur admired the strength it took to make it. Even stepping side to side, she could see the effort it took him not to lose his temper at something he didn't understand.

"I think we're in a safe spot, or about as safe as we can get in this funhouse." She glanced around, trying to find the exit, and going on the tug of her bond with Snowy, she knew where they needed to head. "Let's buff up and head out and follow the only path there is. Regardless of how we do it, we need to get through this dungeon."

She took confident steps toward where Devlish and the rest of her team stood, hoping no one could see how confused or out of her depth she was. There was a roaring boss out there that had been waiting for them for longer than she cared to admit. She hoped impatience wasn't one of its superpowers. Her only guide in all of this was the tether between her and her in-game wolf. Any success ahead of them was completely relying on it.

CHAPTER TWENTY-SEVEN

Next Level

The guild navigated a spiral stone staircase back down onto a solid icy platform. Every fiber of her being screamed at Murmur to climb back up and stay there until the world came to an end. Only that was exactly what they were here to prevent.

Find the puppy, find the boss
Find yourselves another fight
See the puppy, roll the moss
Live to see another night

"I really don't like riddles." Risk bit out the words, loud enough for all to hear, and the rest of the raid mumbled in agreement.

It did seem to light a fire under most of them. They were being led around by a dungeon that changed on whim depending on actions, debuffed them, and apparently thought for itself.

"It's Snowy, isn't it?" Merlin asked softly, only loud enough for Sin and Mur to hear.

"Yeah, I think it is. All I can do is feel where he is. My other sensing capabilities are all mixed up unless a person is about three feet away from me. I have next to no control over anything Snowy does right now, although I don't think we've ever had a master and pet sort of relationship." She was worried.

Had he been infected and was fighting it? He'd always been more of a fighting companion than a pet.

"I've read better riddles on the back of cereal boxes." Jinna's comment made Murmur smile for a brief moment, and he grinned at her as if he'd accomplished his task.

"I guess we have to find the puppy, right?" She felt far more hesitant than she sounded, at least she hoped so. Signaling to the rest of the raid, Devlish began to march forward, Murmur and Sinister close on his heels.

The ice platform widened into another hall, but the walls of this one were different. They were sheer rock like on a cliff face, and the water that ran down their surface wasn't as fluid as she'd have thought. It looked like blood as it glugged down, and the dark trails it left behind did nothing to dissuade her idea.

It was like the walls and floor, the ceiling and cold were warning them to go back, to stay away. The groups behind them moved cautiously in tight knit formation. It only took one explosion to make them warier of their surroundings and more protective of one another. Maybe there was hope for them yet.

Suddenly, inside of a split second, the surroundings around them altered, and they stood on the outer edge of what appeared to be stadium seating. The rest of the cavern looked like a football venue without the lines in the ice. If possible, her sensing nets went even more haywire, leading to a pulsing ache behind her eyes. Considering she couldn't turn those abilities off anymore, it was just a fantastic turn of events.

Behind them, an icy gate slammed shut, leaving them locked in the arena with no exit in sight.

"Fan out. Keep your guard up," Devlish barked out, his own tower shield pulled up high, as if he was waiting for ice javelins to fall from the ceiling and kill them all.

Murmur shook her head, trying to get a hold on her abilities. They weren't reliable anymore. She felt blind and unused to compensating for her lack of power. She couldn't do anything to fix the rising panic she knew was occurring around her. Without Devlish, they wouldn't even have direction right now. Murmur was failing abysmally.

"It's okay, Mur. Breathe." Sinister's whisper reached her ears just as the squeezing of her fingers reassured Mur of the blood mage's presence. A sensation of relief washed over her, and she allowed herself a measured breath to return her focus to normal.

Looking out over the vast arena, she could see the groups fanning out cautiously. There were no monsters shrouded in the cliffs that she could see. No, the monsters—from ice fae to gobcrabs and aboms—were all sitting in what appeared to be icy bleachers on the other side with little flags in their hands.

A ferocious growl reached her ears, and Murmur sought out its source.

Snowy stood in the middle of the arena, his fur positively glowing and his jaws wide open in a vicious snarl. In front of him was a creature that it took Murmur several seconds to categorize.

It possessed a beak, and a bird's face, but that was where the similarity to avians ended. The rest of its body resembled a minotaur, except with a bird head. And it wasn't brown or black; its fur appeared white and fluffier. The marriage of those elements was a strange juxtaposition to its fiery red eyes and frothing beak. Then the minotaur-yak-bird-thing let out a shriek, and Murmur had to cover her ears.

Challenger Snowy has requested back up from his raid.

The voice boomed out in a way that would have made sports announcers worldwide very proud. Hisses and boos rang through the crowd as the stairs they stood atop suddenly turned into escalators and delivered them to the base. It made the arena appear just that much larger. The spectators threw rotten oranges that made a sick splat when they landed, and other fruit she couldn't recognize down into the arena. At them. At the raid.

Snowy let out a howl of his own, and Murmur had to blink at his size. Surely, he'd grown a bit? How had he become a challenger?

Defender Martimight has refused assistance outside of his usual entourage who will appear later in the fight.

The cheers that broke out from the spectator ranks were almost deafening.

Let's get ready to fight!

Three!

The entire raid buffed to their max without anyone needing to call it. After so many strange encounters, they'd learned to simply do things without asking. Being prepared was better than dead. Murmur counted it as a win despite the fact that the abilities that had helped Fable through multiple raids and monsters were failing her. At the moment, she couldn't take away her own worries, let along those of her friends.

Two!

As if all she'd had to do was ask, all of her worry disappeared, and emotions stopped reaching her. She looked out over the crazy arena in front of her and smiled for the first time in a while. Nothing they did could reach her. Not here in the cocoon where her mind and thoughts could be her own. It was safe to watch from here, safe to participate. Not being able to experience the sensations of others took away her boundaries. There was nothing anything could do to harm her, and everything she could do to them.

One!

She glanced around at the other twenty-nine people who'd accompanied her into this mess and nodded to herself. The whole scene passed her by in slow motion as she focused her gaze on Snowy. *Be strong.* She whispered in her mind, stretching tendrils out to reach him. *Be fast.* She spoke in his mind lending him her strength. *Be victorious.* She sang in symbols representing her words.

Fight!

Be death, she commanded her wolf as she let go of Sinister's hand.

Somnia Online
Continent Tarishna: Belius Office in Stellaein
Belius Office
Day Twenty-Eight

Belius was unsure how to approach the situation. Riasli hadn't left his side in days, making it almost impossible for him to complete his initial plan. Everything he'd worked for was on the verge of unravelling and he couldn't afford to let it. The problem was that he wasn't sure how to prevent it.

Deliberately having set things in motion that would come back to haunt him, he'd been okay with his siblings hating him, or even trying to stop him if it meant keeping them safe. The same went for Murmur. She was such a stubborn individual, suspicious and headstrong. He'd not meant to watch out for her as much as he had, not meant to be as fond of her as he was, but she'd got under his coding. Her predicament was a direct result of system compromises, and a part of him thought he owed her the attention.

"I realize you're stalling, Belius." Riasli didn't stop what she was doing to look at him. "I just have to figure out why."

Now she turned to him, her gaze on the thoughtful side of scheming. "You can't be trying to save your siblings. You know they're doomed. The virus is already implanted, thanks to you. It'll slowly chip away. So, what can it be?" She pursed her lips and continued rifling through the incidentals that decorated his office. Defunct weapons with coding that wouldn't mesh, magical items that clashed with the world's purpose. He wasn't sure what she was looking for.

Belius shrugged, trying to make it seem as if her question was inconsequential. He cleared his algorithmic processes of any trace that might link him to either Murmur or his siblings and resigned himself to having to begin from scratch again later.

They'd survived his dungeon without any help from him. It was only a remnant of what he'd envisaged way back when they'd created the world. Just a husk of what it had once been. Only it wasn't nearly as damaged as Tieflos was. He worried the failsafes he'd put into place might have the opposite effect, and he wasn't able to monitor it with Riasli there like a chain around his neck.

"I'm trying to get this whole thing done sooner than later." He exaggerated a sense of apathy, attempting to heighten his indifference with coding accentuation. "By all means, if you want to waste your time overseeing me, can you at least not make a mess?"

He closed his eyes, his calculations flickering behind the thin eyelids of the locus, fully aware that it lit him up like party lights. Belius didn't need to see Riasli to know that he'd aimed perfectly. She was irritated now and trying harder to catch him out. But when she did that, it meant she pushed her processing capabilities too far. She wasn't nearly as refined as Thra or Rav, even if she constantly deluded herself into thinking she was.

"Fine!" Her voice was heated, erratic, like most of her moods. "You're tagged. We're watching."

He didn't even open her eyes as her presence around him vanished. Though he knew she wasn't completely gone, it was still a relief to have her out of his immediate vicinity. Belius waited a while before opening his eyes and tapping into the surveillance section of the system through multiple layers of protection, seeking out both his siblings and his charge.

Thra and Rav had, it seemed, figured out that Belius wasn't telling the whole truth to anyone. With luck, it would still take some time for them to locate him. He was tagged, but Riasli had never been intended to be the computing force that the others had. She was a bit character, a minor processor. And when she realized it, her wires would fry, and she'd be gone. But he had to wait for her to achieve that measure of self-awareness yet.

But Murmur, oh, she hadn't come out of this minor interruption unscathed. He frowned, trying to figure out what he'd missed while he was trying to mislead Riasli. Murmur barely managed to retain herself when she was bombarded with the motherload of getashi. It was only with some very intricate coding adjustments that he'd managed to help her, but now, something was wrong.

And Belius got the feeling that if he didn't figure out how to reverse it, everything else he'd done would be for naught.

The roaring of the crowd drowned out the initial shrieks and growls as both Snowy and the Martimight clashed in the center of the arena.

Martimight's legs were more birdlike than Murmur had realized, and his claws resembled one of the only survivors of the dinosaur heritage, the cassowary. She was quite certain it could gut Snowy if her wolf wasn't careful. But he would be careful, because he was hers, because she'd lent him her power.

Even as she thought those words, Snowy grew, his back easily in line with her shoulders now if she were to test it. His glowing eyes cast a wave of light energy around them all, a protective barrier for himself and for his allies.

If she was correct, and she knew she was, it would level the hit points into a shared pool and percentage divide any damage or healing given. There was no way her wolf was going to die. Not today, not any day.

None of them would. She'd make certain of that. There was no rush of emotion to fuel her decision, simply a cold and calculated sensation that lauded her ability to make decisions. If anything, it felt good and peaceful and so uncomplicated. So powerful.

Snowy's fur rippled in the cold wind as it swept through the arena, his focus solely concentrated on the Martimight in front of him. His eyes glowed with that intense fiery blue, and his teeth were now the size of Murmur's hands, snapping viciously in warning.

He darted in at his opponent's heels, executing a vicious bite in the process. His speed meant that most of the arena didn't catch his movement, but Murmur knew, and a slow smile spread on her face.

The Martimight screeched in pain and stamped its feet like a bull ready to charge. From behind it, in a whirlpool of light, emerged several large cassowary-style birds. The casque on their heads looked like a helmet and different from the real creatures because it was a shiny black. Their coloring around their head was a deep, blood red that almost looked as if the wattles weren't dangling, but instead consisted of a constant waterfall of blood. Their plumage varied, ranging from black to deep red. If Murmur had been capable of emotion right then, she would have been terrified of these dinosaur throwbacks and their huge clawed feet.

Stepping back, Murmur watched over the people fighting by her side, and pulled from the earth elements she knew were around her in the walls to cast her shielding and redistribute protection. It didn't matter if she lost a few of her raid members; their resurrections were easy enough and the pain would fade. They weren't as important as Snowy, this battle, or even this dungeon.

Without a thought for her own or anyone else's safety, she called on her Mana Drain abilities and siphoned as much as she could from the Martimight. It screamed in terror, flailing its massive head around until its gaze locked onto her. Releasing the mana, she held, and letting it dissipate into the pools of the entire raid, she grinned as the creature screeched out a battle cry. Mana drains were as potent with aggro as heals could be.

Its claws raked the ice, sending up spear sized slivers that rained into the crowd. Several of the unsuspecting observers were impaled on the spot, with massive splinters jutting out from chests or heads. The explosive force left most of the benches covered in blood.

Just as it began its rampage toward her, Snowy barreled into it from the side with full speed and bulldozed it toward the far wall, where it impacted with a sickening thud. All of the light creatures who'd been attacking the raid turned as one, leaving ample opportunity for the players to cut them down where they stood, allowing rogues to backstab to their heart's content. Only a handful of the creatures it released made it back to their master. Barely enough to restore eight percent of its life.

All the while, Snowy didn't let up. He howled and barked, unleashing a tornado of cold directly into the wound he'd inflicted on the creature. It swirled around inside it, sending gobs of blood, viscera, and bone flying throughout the arena.

The watching crowd screamed in unison and began to flee, or at least they attempted to. The arena had locked them all in, and that included the spectators. Murmur smiled to herself at the sight of it. More experience, more annihilation, more ways to build up Snowy's strength. He was a force unto himself.

Out of the corner of her sight, she could see him tearing into the Martimight even as the creature's powerful hind legs took chunks out of the wolf's hide in all their flailing. With the hit point absorbing shield Veranol had cast, the damage wasn't life threatening for Snowy.

Murmur turned around, watching her entire raid force and frowned. They should be doing so much more. Filling her sensing nets that were still on the fritz with determination, she focused tightly on her raid. The effort it took to push past the fog preventing her abilities left her with a sharp pain firing through her skull every few seconds. But it worked.

With a blink of her eyes she pushed at them all, strongly suggested that those spectators attempting to flee were just free experience waiting to be claimed. Just the push they needed, just the influence they'd benefit from most. Their expressions changed, from one of support and awe, to ones of determination and, perhaps, a little bit of glee. Even Sinister and Havoc took part in the chaos, switching their targets, and bleeding the other monsters for as much experience as they could.

Snowy continued to rip apart his now dying opponent, blood dripping down from his muzzle, sticking the white fur around his mouth and lending him a macabre appearance topped off by his glowing blue eyes. Bits of flesh and bloodied fluff stuck in his claws as he continued to tear at the weakened and dazed opponent in front of him.

Murmur watched, a whirl of giddiness making her so lightheaded she could no longer feel the sharp pains in her head. Snowy's bloodthirst called to her, spoke to her in ways that words couldn't. In ways that Somnia couldn't.

Screams echoed off the high ceiling, and the Martimight entered its death throes, causing Snowy to sit back on his haunches and watch with an intense gaze. As it let out its final twitches, and the last of the spectators was cut down where they stood, Snowy's size shrunk back somewhat, but his fur still glowed brightly. He stood there, waiting for the creature to die, maintaining eye contact to the very end. Standing in blood, his feet looked like he'd stepped in pain.

Only when the light finally left the Martimight's eyes did Snowy wuff once and turn to reclaim his position by Murmur's side.

The blood didn't matter to her at all. She reached down a hand and scratched at his ears almost absentmindedly. He was a good wolf, and no one was taking him away from her. Not ever.

The raid began to loot the bodies, picking up knickknacks and crafting materials galore. Still, Murmur watched. That fight had been too easy, especially after she lost her patience and made everyone kill shit without a second thought. Things needed to die. The faster she killed them, the quicker they'd get to the end. All Murmur had to do was use all the tools in her arsenal, which included the raid.

Her thoughts raced as she attempted to plan for more encounters. Suggestively nudging her raid mates had helped her sensing nets after all. While they were still giving her difficulty, at least she knew she could access them with extreme focus.

Lost in thought, she didn't even notice when Sinister came to stand at her side until the blood mage tried to take her hand. Shaking it off, Mur sidestepped, letting her gaze fall over the entire raid as they looted corpses and sorted themselves out. They only appeared to have lost a couple of people during the entire battle. She hadn't even noticed when they died. But it was a raid, and that was completely acceptable.

Finally, the script she'd been waiting for appeared. It began to write itself out, high up against the icy ceiling, its dark shade of blue a sharp contrast.

You have not yet completed this dungeon, but this encounter is dead.

Have you not scarified enough for this, what would you accept instead?

Heedful are they who do no wrong

Evil are they who kill with a song

You have defeated Martimight and thus you have a choice:

Debuff 1: Mana Galore

This debuff will allow you to regenerate your mana faster, but it will slow your cast/execution times by 0.2 seconds.

Debuff 2: Health for Sacrifice

This debuff will allow you to regenerate your health faster, but you must sacrifice one commonly used spell or ability to do so.

Neither of these debuffs can be removed and both will persist through death. All debuffs gained in this zone stack. You must pick one of these two. Only one of these two will apply to the entire raid. You cannot change your choice once it is made.

She knew it. The damned dungeon was based around the debuffs it gave. A tingle of excitement slithered up her spine. She couldn't wait for the final encounter. Just what would this dungeon throw at them next?

Several of the raid members had leveled up and were in the middle of scribing their spells. But Murmur was intent on the array of debuffs they already had stacked on them. The only one that made sense was the second one.

Sacrificing one of their common abilities didn't seem such a bad choice, but she was hesitant because she didn't know who made the choice as to which ability to forfeit. Slowing healing spells by a fifth of a second could easily mean life or death, more so than any particular lack of mana.

"Who chooses the spell we give up?" She asked the question in a loud and clear voice that rang through the cavern. Several of the raid members looked up in curiosity to see who she was speaking to.

For a few moments she looked a bit stupid and began to regret the decision to ask the world in general. But then the script began to appear before their eyes again.

Such a question, a good choice
Spoken loud, unwavering voice
The spell you forfeit mostly used
Changes your whole attitude

And that was it. Murmur glared at the words as they solidified and then faded away.

"So." Masha's tone was soothing, like always, able to take the edge off the mood. "Am I right in assuming that means we will forfeit the spell each of us uses most? Or else, we add point two seconds to cast time for any spell or ability?"

There was a general mumble of consensus around the arena. Neither choices seemed ideal, and Murmur knew she couldn't afford to lose her Mez, or her Veto, nor could she lose any of her stuns. To do so would virtually cripple her character's abilities. The healers would lose heals, the tanks a taunt, and the DPS would likely lose their most potent damage building skill.

"Damn it," she muttered, irritated at the inconvenience. "How much of a difference will it make to healing with the added time to each cast?"

Masha shrugged. "It'll add up, but so will the DPS. And the Mez timing. Regardless what we do, there's a severe downside."

Murmur sighed. There was nothing for it. She didn't have the time to waste with these trivialities. They needed to get through this dungeon, to push onto the next. "Fine. Option one is really our only choice. Since we don't get to choose which ability or skill we forsake, this is our only option."

She didn't care how they did it, or what she had to do to get them through it, Tieflos needed to be done with. They had important zones to visit, bosses to kill. Murmur took a deep breath, taking the silence and uneasy nods as agreement with her. "We choose option one."

Retrospect

As soon as Murmur made the choice, the ground beneath them shifted, revealing a huge staircase that took them down directly to a suspension bridge far below.

Choices made, was it right?

Perhaps or not, but skip a fight.

Face the last and final boss

Did you call the right coin toss?

"I really wish it would stop it with all the riddles." Sinister sounded subdued, and Murmur glanced at her, wondering why. As a whole, the raid was this much closer to defeating this dungeon. Then they'd be out, and free to tackle the last damned one.

"We skipped a boss then?" Risk's tone held irritation and Murmur couldn't blame him. The whole point of a dungeon was to kill shit, especially bosses.

"Probably means we picked the debuff the mob we're skipping wouldn't have had an advantage over." Devlish shrugged, hefted his shield up and gestured toward the bridge. "Let's head out."

Murmur glanced at their surroundings and frowned as Snowy head butted her to move forward. Something wasn't sitting right with her again that had nothing to do with her abilities not sounding properly. The raid seemed dejected, and without a second thought, she pushed out a wave of relaxation over them, soothing their irritation and worries. They'd all function far better if they didn't give into their fears. Pain shot through her head again at the action, but she thought it might have been less severe than the first time.

It was difficult to punch through the fog surrounding her abilities. But it felt good to do so, like she was beating the system.

She noticed Sinister watching her from the corner of her eye and flashed her friend a smile. There was no time to deal with anything else while they were stuck in here. Sinister would understand. She turned her attention away from the blood mage and focused on the group makeup.

Extra casting or execution time didn't appear to make much of a difference at first, but after a while it was going to add up. It could mean that in a prolonged fight they'd end up on the losing end.

Devlish cleared his throat next to her. "What're you thinking about?"

Murmur glanced at him, her thoughts running around on high speed. "What else this weird dungeon has up its sleeve."

"Not thinking about Sin then?" There was an odd intensity to his words, like he was angry or annoyed.

"Not right now. We have too much to get done. I can't afford distractions right now." She shrugged and returned to her surveillance of the area. Her sensing nets seemed to be partially working, although they were still a bit spotty. Perhaps forcing the focus had helped.

The bridge they were about to cross was way too high. She frowned as the icy waters beneath them came into view, throwing up freezing cold showers of mist. Add cold to her usual fear of heights, and Murmur expected to be terrified. Except all she could feel was calm and focused.

Devlish was still eyeing her with what she thought might be disapproval. She pushed the concern aside and absentmindedly soothed his irritation. Her sensory nets were preoccupied with the sheer amount of influx of information she basically needed to decode because she was dealing with partial abilities. Everything around them was on heightened alert. Life coursed through the very water veins that supplied the ice, through the light that refracted from reflections up high, and the heartbeats of the players who were with her.

She didn't have time to be a singular person when Somnia needed her to be everything. The needs of the many overrode those of the one, or even the two. When everything was over she'd have time to think of herself.

Her head buzzed and she shook it, trying to regain her focus. It almost sounded like there was a bee flying around in her head trying to talk to her, trying to tell her something. She grimaced and tapped the side of her head, trying to dislodge the feeling. The sound quieted down to bearable.

Murmur allowed her focus to zone in on the area around them. Here under the overhang at the end of the bridge, the icy barren hid all sorts of nasty little things from them. She really concentrated, ignoring the pounding in her head that sounded like screaming. With extreme effort could discern that there were hundreds of tiny creatures just waiting to explode out of the walls at them once they entered the actual encounter.

"We have to move in slowly. There are a lot of opponents lying in wait." She pushed her powers, trying to read the thoughts instead of just gleaning their intentions, but pain shot through her head so badly she stopped. The pounding felt like someone was playing her head like a drum, and the drumstick was a sledgehammer.

They had to get to the final dungeon. Past these annoyances and free the final boss.

Murmur blinked, unsure where the thought had come from, but positive it was what they needed to do. It needed to be done, and the quicker the better.

Murmur could feel Veranol's gaze resting on her. His thoughts weren't something he hid. He was angry at her, he'd seen what she'd done to Devlish, and she knew he was aware she'd assisted the raid by means he didn't approve of already.

What she couldn't fathom was why he was so bent out of shape over it all. Didn't really boil down to who won? The power underlying Somnia was potent and there for the taking, just like the getashi had been. Like they had been when they were in Telvar's hoard. A brief thought flitted across her mind, a question about what was real and what was not. Had the incident in Telvar's lair taken place or was she still hanging there suspended, shaking from the sheer force of knowledge entering her body?

Only Snowy's head butting against her fingers kept her grounded. For one brief moment, Murmur almost believed that this was all a figment of her imagination. And for just that brief period of time, the feelings and sensations of the group she'd been raiding with for weeks inundated her, assaulting the wall she'd somehow erected.

Staggering to one knee, Murmur's mind reeled. A sliver of doubt entered her thoughts, slimy and foreign and not of her own making. She fought against the impulse to curl up into a ball and sink her head into her hands and scream. The sheer volume of emotions began to leak through to her, snaking through to her mind like the tendrils of a blue bottle octopus complete with the intense stinging sensations that ripped through her brain.

She couldn't remember where she was, how she'd gotten here, or why it was so cold. Her body wouldn't stop shaking.

And then there were hands enveloping her, holding her close, hugging her and stroking her hair. A small chittering echoed through to her, the concern of her Tiachi reaching through the haze. But nothing could overshadow the soothing pattern of Sinister rocking her gently.

She clung to the person that meant the most to her regardless of what world they were in. Very slowly, the pain in her mind began to recede. Suddenly a sense of peace washed over her.

Sorry. I couldn't get through. I'm not sure what you did, but you managed to block me to where I was basically static. It took me this long to reestablish my connection to you. I've lent you some reinforcements to your own connection. It seems your thought waves may have been infected with the virus.

What? Murmur couldn't quite believe what it was she was hearing, especially not on the tail end of the sensations sweeping throughout her system. Her entire perception was attempting to reorient itself, sending her tumbling into confusion and dizziness.

I apologize for not realizing sooner that your connection left you at least as vulnerable as the rest of them. It won't happen again.

Murmur didn't say anything, didn't think anything in the direction of Somnia, and instead hugged Sinister back mumbling softly. "I'm so sorry. I am so, so sorry."

She could feel Sinister smiling where her lips rested on Murmur's head. "It's okay, I get it. There's been something wrong since you woke up, something I haven't been able to put my finger on. But it's okay, we'll get through this."

Murmur sat there for a few more seconds, drinking in the warmth and the safety. Without Sinister, and to an extent Somnia, she was quite certain she would have been swallowed whole.

Shakily, and with the help of Sinister, Veranol, and Devlish, Murmur managed to stand. She gripped her hand in the fur at the back of Snowy's neck, and took stock of herself.

"Sorry, guys. I think my lack of sleep caught up to me." She let out a self-deprecating laugh, and the rest of the raid joined in. "Didn't mean to hold up the raid, let's buff up, be cautious about our debuffs, and AoE the fuck out of whatever these little ones waiting for us are."

A cheer went up from the rest of the raid, and Murmur squeezed Sinister's hand tightly not letting go even when combat began.

Somnia Online
Tieflos Dungeon – Version 22.4283, activated by Murmur of the Guild Fable
First Incarnation of This Zone
Late Day Twenty-Eight

The strange ringing in Jirald's ears wouldn't quit. It wasn't a remnant from the explosion, nor had he died in this dungeon, so it wasn't an after effect of death. He shook his head several times trying to rid himself of the sound and barely heard Murmur's directions about the up-and-coming creatures who'd be in their way.

He thought this first fight would be an AOE fight, not his strong suit for damage, but he could hold his own. That was if the damned ringing in his ears would stop upsetting his equilibrium. Looking down at his hands and the daggers in them made it seem as if both his appendages and weapons were doubled and blurry.

He ran over the uneasy alliance he'd temporarily made with Risk and grinned to himself. That particular amusement had pretty much run its course, but it definitely yielded good results. Risk and Murmur were wary of each other. That was all he'd needed. Sowing those seeds of doubt had been fun.

Suddenly there was a commotion at the head of the raid, and he heard a cry of anguish and pain. As several people in front of him parted he was able to see Murmur on her knees clutching her head. The only reason she wasn't on the ground was that her wolf held her upright.

A portion of him was glad to see her in pain, happy that she was uncomfortable and showing the world her weaknesses just like she had done to him. The other parts of him were writhing inside, like they were trying to reach out through him and grab her. It was a hunger he'd not felt before, a yearning, an unsatisfied craving.

All at once it felt like his head was about to explode, like every envious thought he'd ever had was spilling out at once making him rotten from the inside out. It leeched into his thoughts twisting them further than they'd ever been before, until he didn't quite recognize where he began and these new thoughts ended. It was all him, this power, his ability to reach out and infect those around him.

He could feel the grin as it spread across his face, not just his face, and their faces. He wasn't alone anymore, and no one could ever show him up again not with what he knew and not with what he could do.

Slowly, watching even as Murmur righted with Sinister's assistance, he straightened his own posture, glad of the assassin's mask he wore which made his solid black eyes stand out less. He observed her, both of them for the time being. Even as the enchanter spoke, he could see the effort it took her to simply shrug off the heavy thoughts that were plaguing her. And he deduced that the main reason she was able to do so lay with Sinister and the blood mage's support.

Not everyone tinkered with their headsets like he had. Not everyone decided to make the quests they received about them and their own choices. And Jirald was definitely not everyone.

He cracked his neck from side to side and moved the rest of the raid. as he pulled abreast of Masha he patted his friend on the shoulder. "Good raid. We've got this."

The cleric looked at him quizzically as if he couldn't believe Jirald had praise for a raid led by Fable. "Great. Let's kick some ass."

As Masha moved away, Jirald grinned to himself at the sight of the sticky black substance on the cleric's shoulder that was sinking in through the material of his tabard.

Murmur stood panting in the center of close to three hundred ice worms. It had been a rocky start while she figured out the slightly adjusted cast rotations she needed in order to maintain her stun lock. She hated getting battered about by the monsters she was trying to control. Being a punching bag for these creatures was all sorts of slimy and icky. While the ice worms weren't in themselves difficult opponents, there were fucking hundreds of them.

So many tiny creatures were almost overwhelming. Murmur needed a break once they littered the floor two feet deep. It didn't appear as if more were incoming, and Sinister had insisted on standing next to her, luckily safe inside Murmur's stun circle with her.

"Remember to keep moving." Veranol's voice rang gruffly out over the raid. Murmur knew he was still irritated with her, but that he'd also realized something was seriously wrong and was leaving his questions until later.

Sinister squeezed the hand she had around Murmur's waist. "You sure you're up for this?" she asked only loudly enough for Murmur to hear.

Murmur wanted to say no. She wanted to scream, laugh and then log out and never log back in. Maybe not never, maybe just for a little bit. Instead, she smiled. "I have to be. Though I could really go for some sleep. Thank you again." She didn't feel like she deserved Sinister. Hell, after coming to Somnia, she felt like she didn't deserve anybody. So much shit had happened, a lot of it involving her mind. She wasn't sure she could tell anyone yet that sometimes she had trouble distinguishing realities.

"We have three sets of four ice giants coming up." Murmur closed her eyes for a few moments counting the number of opponents to double check and verifying what she'd learned about them so far. "Rangers will need to kite two of them, Esolan will off tank one, and Devlish will main tank the other. Assist Devlish."

From what she could gather, as long as the rangers could kite those two without pulling one of the other groups, they should be fine. As if reading her thoughts, which after her last episode was slightly spooky, Merlin nudged her in the side.

"You want more than one of us on each, correct?" He eyed her, his expression filled with concern that she knew he was biting back as well. She almost didn't want the raid to end.

"Yeah. You and Exbo lead the other rangers and make sure you all stay well ahead of the ice giants. These guys are going to hit hard." She glanced around at the entire raid, sensing their readiness, their excitement, and their exhaustion.

"What about the healers?" Masha sounded odd as he stood in front of her, his arms crossed. The squelch of the dead worms released a foul stench, but Murmur still didn't think the expression of irritation on his face was because of that.

"You and Veranol will work your magic." Murmur put as much friendliness into the words as she could, but Masha just glared and turned on his heel with a grunt.

"That was…strange." Sinister spoke softly, only for Mur to hear. "I've never seen him that gruff with you."

Murmur shook her head. She had no clue what was up. Had she pissed him off when she almost broke down a short while ago? Did he regret having followed her into battle because of that? She'd always thought they were friends of sorts. After Risk turned out to be a bit of a dick, she'd been grateful that Masha trusted her. Now, she wasn't so sure.

"Worry about it after this dungeon," Sinister said gently. And she was right, they had too much to do right now, but Murmur couldn't shake the uneasy feeling that something had happened with Masha that he wasn't telling her about.

She took another deep breath as she scanned around to figure out exactly what was coming after this wave of ice giants. If she wasn't mistaken, the next opponent they faced would be the boss. All she could tell was that he was large, because his power put him on a level that made reading him deeper impossible even with her range.

You know you haven't been using your full power, don't you? You have Snowy and your abilities for a reason.

Murmur didn't welcome the intrusion this time, not so shortly after almost losing herself. *You're not helping. I can't risk fucking up again.*

I see. Human brains might have computation capacity, but they are far different from the AIs. I know you will emerge victorious. Good luck.

Thanks. Murmur could almost see Somnia nod before retreating. Maybe this world was learning. Maybe that was something she could help with. After they got out of this bloody portal inflicted merry-go-round.

"This is it guys. The beginning of the final fight. I think." She glanced around as she heard some muttering, and her eyes fell on Masha, looking up at her defiantly. Murmur tried not to let it bother her and continued with her instructions.

"Be as conservative as you can with long time Cooldowns, and even though we have more mana regen, don't overdo it. Don't forget your debuffs, plan accordingly, and keep an eye on Devlish." Murmur only hoped they couldn't tell how very scared she was.

She glanced over at the main tank, and Devlish nodded, a grim smile plastering itself on his lacerta features. Ice giants were scattered through most VR MMOs, through most RPGs, but by the way the icy ground quivered beneath them as the ice giants approached, Murmur was pretty certain that Somnian ice giants were going to be yet another story.

CHAPTER TWENTY-NINE

Finally

Somnia Online
Tieflos Dungeon – Version 22.4283, Activated by Murmur of the Guild Fable
First Incarnation of This Zone
Early Day Twenty-Nine

Jirald stretched his fingers, holding them up in front of his face and watched the smoke rise from his skin and through his gloves into the darkness around him. He grinned as he narrowed his eyes, able to see every single person he'd clapped on the back in encouragement or given some sort of solace to during the raid so far. Thin, dark fingers of smoky shadow drifted back to him, lending him a power he'd never wanted, nor had before.

Risk hadn't let him close enough to tap since their blow up. Pity, really; he could have done with his makeshift ally feeding him power as well. No mind though, since he'd grazed the back of Karn's hand with his fingers during one of their previous fights. It was easy to pass on the shadows, to turn their thoughts darker and have them question and revile the very person who had made this raid possible.

Masha stood next to him, the usual easy-going expression on the cleric's face gone and replaced by a light scowl. The connection to him was the strongest, and had also been the first. He turned to Jirald with a furrowed brow. "What?"

"Just wondering if you're enjoying this so far?" Jirald asked, trying to keep his tone as neutral as possible. He watched his friend mull over the words instead of giving his usual immediate answer.

"I'll enjoy it more when we're done. This whole zone reeks of glitches. There's no way this is how the game was intended." There was bitterness in Masha's voice, a sentiment that didn't suit the cleric.

For a moment Jirald almost felt guilty, but it was fleeting. "Why did you agree to come then?"

"So we can learn from them and then beat them." Masha's eyes narrowed, a hint of greed shining through.

Perfect. If his friend was this far distanced from his usual self, then it wouldn't take long for the rest of the raid to start causing trouble for Murmur. While Jirald might want to defeat the rest of the dungeons and complete the endgame content, he also wanted to fuck with Fable and reach the end of his quest and the rewards that came with it.

Pushing himself away from the wall as the ground beneath them began to tremble, Jirald grinned at Masha. "Guess we have some incoming shit to kill."

"Don't we always?" Masha squared his shoulders and cracked his neck from side to side. "Time to fight. Time to make Exodus shine."

In his peripheral vision, Jirald noticed Ishwa watching them. He'd not yet been able to touch the little gnome and infect his persona too. The mage was far too perceptive, and at this rate would figure out something was up. Fable might not crumble, but he'd make sure they were on shaky ground when all was said and done. Jirald was willing to bet it would be far too late when Ishwa recognized what was happening.

The walls around them shook even as the ice giants moved into view. They weren't as stocky as she'd expected, but lankier, with long arms that almost trailed to the ground and thick eyebrows that looked like mounds of snow. Their white eyes gleamed out as they surveyed the raid, making their ice bodies appear entirely too blue.

Her mind still reeled with how close she'd come to giving into that void where she could separate herself from having to care. It had never been her intention to do that, but it made making decisions so much easier. She gave herself a vicious pinch to try and bring her attention back into focus.

Sinister watched her from the side, silently knowing and understanding that something was seriously wrong. Except she didn't berate or question—this wasn't the time for it, and Murmur was immensely grateful for her.

Ice giants in a zone where the ice creatures had a resistance to fire. Merlin, Exbo, and the other rangers might be able chip away with their fire arrows, but it would barely make a difference. Their fire wasn't hot enough to overcome the natural defenses. The mages on the other hand were another thing entirely. Ishwa and his ilk were solid. Havoc could disease them, and Merlin might be able to use his acid potions.

She racked her brains to figure out other combinations. Anything strong and metal would hack away at ice pretty easily. Their approach was measured, like the beat of a war drum as the first three began to move closer. She couldn't see any more, but knew from the feel of the area, and the sound of the marching that three definitely wasn't all there was.

Taking a breath, she attempted her first Mez from the greatest distance possible while Devlish was readying himself to tank. Everyone in their positions, the first wave of three would mean a lot of figuring things out.

Except her Mez didn't hold at all.

This is an ice giant. Ice giants do not believe in your ability to control them, for they are their own entities. Do not attempt to Mezmerize these creatures again. You have been warned.

She gulped and tried not to freeze in place while she thought. They didn't have mana pools for her to drain, so they had a decent option. "Root! Maintain root on the two rear ice giants."

Merlin and Exbo moved their aim and rooted the huge creatures. Murmur only hoped they wouldn't suddenly be able to fling ice balls at them. A moment later, a snowball whizzed past her head, scraping her cheek in the process. Ice ball, definitely not soft snow. She could feel the warm blood as it dripped down from the wound before a heal hit her to close it up.

Devlish battled the one not being rooted to the spot, and she was relieved to see that its punches were nothing to be scoffed at. In fact, it hit like a truck. If ice balls were the least of their worries from the remaining two, Root had been the right call.

Targeting Devlish so she could modify his hate generation, she noticed a split-second cast by the ice giant he was fighting when the thing let out a brief guttural call.

Rumble.

Oh, how she didn't like the sound of that. Although, since the floor wasn't breaking up into pieces, she figured it couldn't be too bad.

Sinister would have killed her if she'd said that out loud considering what happened next. The rumbling preceded a massive jolt that shook the ground beneath them. Several of the casters lost their footing, and Murmur only remained upright because of Snowy. His increased size helped in a lot of ways now.

Looking around, Murmur tried to find the source of the continued reverberating ground. The sound of something heavy grinding against the ice drew closer to them, moving faster and faster.

She glanced up the way they'd entered the cavern, hoping her supposition was incorrect. "Behind us! Watch the tunnel! Move!"

Murmur yelled out the words and cast out her Forcefield Shield to push people out of the way of the incoming boulder. It barreled down aiming straight for the raid. She only hated being right about things like this. Most of the raid managed to get out of the way, but out of the corner of her eye, she watched as Jirald and Karn went flying into the far ice wall. She didn't expect him to get back up with that impact. As he slid to the floor, she noticed that the ice behind him had cracked and winced at the thought of the amount of pain that had to have caused. Neither of them stood back up, and they couldn't afford to be down two of their best damage dealers.

"Havoc! Battle Res Jirald," she called out just as she watched Veranol cast it on Karn. Havoc's had a far longer recast time than Veranol's, but her Forcefield hadn't reached in close enough to the fight to stop the deaths. They had to eat them and the lack of damage occurring while they recovered the rogues.

"Interrupt Rumble," Devlish called out, taking the words from the tip of Murmur's tongue. She shuddered to think how the raid might survive if all three of them…

But she didn't have to wait, because the three ice giants chose that moment to do exactly that. Whatever went wrong, however the raid missed it, not one of the Rumble calls was interrupted.

At first, she hoped it couldn't get much worse, that three consecutive boulders rolling into the raid. But when one smashed through an icy wall, and another came crashing through the ceiling, Murmur realized they were up shit's creek.

Veranol reacted on instinct and cast his special rune to take the brunt of the damage. But the boulders were far too heavy and obliterated parts of the shield. Even though they didn't hit the shaman, the pressure from his spell being destroyed recoiled back into him and sent him flying into the wall with a sickening thud that he didn't get back up from.

With one glance around at the state of the raid, Murmur realized this was a no-win situation. At least ten members of the raid were down, with more on the way from the giants themselves if not the boulders. Devlish nodded at her, threw his head back, and screamed out an AoE taunt.

"Sin. Log out. Now," Murmur urged the blood mage, who didn't need to be asked twice.

It was the only way Murmur could think of to reset the encounter. They had a four-hour window. If one of them logged out, they'd be able to log back in when all was clear and hopefully resurrect the corpses.

She took a gulp as Sinister complied, winking out of existence within mere seconds. It made Murmur all the more grateful for the headsets they had. While she would have liked to log out herself and save herself the pain of in-game death, Murmur took a hatchet to the forehead as she turned around to survey the now two-thirds decimated raid.

Pain shot through her skull like it was being split in two. She could feel the blade bite into her, crashing through bone and rendering her numb. Falling to the ground, her hit points reached zero, and she heard Snowy let out a mournful howl before Somnia faded from her vision.

Summer Residence
Home of Laria, David, and Wren
Summer Condo
Real World – Day Twenty-Eight

Laria pushed papers aside, effectively knocking another pile onto the floor. She threw her hands up. "The kitchen table is far too small for me to be doing this."

David put down the paper he was perusing and lowered his glasses to peer at her. "I'd say I told you so. Because I did."

"You just said it!" He was right, though, and Laria knew it. She also knew that printing everything out so she could go over it in a different format and perhaps see something she'd missed before hadn't been one of her best ideas.

It was definitely five thousand percent messier than using her augmented screens. But sometimes, just sometimes, it helped her eyes catch onto things she couldn't seem to grasp as being different when she was just using her eyes. Maybe it was the pointing of fingers at where she was looking, or perhaps the tangibility of the paper itself, but either way, it worked well for her.

Finally, David put down what he was reading through and rubbed the bridge of his nose, glasses in the other hand. "It's a malignant virus, and it keeps morphing. That's why what you're doing isn't catching it properly. You fix aspects of it, but it evolves and just keeps chugging along."

Laria counted to five before answering, all the while mulling over those words in her head. He made sense, and it was his area of expertise, not hers. "I'm a creator, David. Why didn't you come help me earlier?" She knew she was whining, and they didn't have time for that, but she was tired and couldn't help it.

"Yes, I could probably have helped a little sooner, but there is the matter of you warning me frequently that you can save yourself." His eyes twinkled, and his tone held no recrimination. "Frankly, you've never needed saving, and this isn't even that. You are capable and strong and have forged your own path."

He waved his hand around in the air, gesturing toward the papers he'd put down.

"This virus is remarkable. I've never seen anything quite like it and probably wouldn't have believed you if I didn't know you so well. I'm not even sure I could have dealt with this if you hadn't already done some of the groundwork."

"Aw." Laria smiled tiredly. "Now you're just flattering me."

"Is it working?" David wiggled his eyebrows.

"Only if I can reclaim my sanity after fixing the game." Laria fluttered her eyelashes and started to laugh. "I miss working with you."

"At least this way we're still happily married." He winked at her, and positioned himself back at the table, pulling a keyboard toward himself as he brought the projection online so they could both see what he was talking about at once.

He pulled up several graphs and monitored recordings of actual encounters with some of the infected portions of the game. "Do you see how it flickers in a sequence?"

Laria watched the way the coding scrolled in time with the actual footage. She held up her hand, and David repeated the last five minutes again.

"Wait. That's not intermittent at all. It's a deliberate pattern. Almost like a…" She looked at him, not wanting to say what was on the tip of her tongue for fear that it might be crazy.

He nodded, though, his expression grave but with an element of hope. "Yep. Just like a slumbering heartbeat."

Murmur hung in limbo, reliving that hatchet strike over and over again. At least now she knew the ice giants also had throwing weapons and not just snowballs. If the game was being consistent, the snowballs should have had spikes embedded in them.

Finally, after what seemed like an eternity of experiencing her death over and over again, the request to resurrect her appeared on her screen. She indicated the will to accept the action and was sucked back into her body through a whirl of painful circles that made her dizzy enough to throw up.

She came to in her body right next to Sinister, kneeling on one knee as she retched several times to no avail. Snowy, immediately by her side, whuffed hot wolf breath into her face, somehow reigniting their connection.

With her mana sitting at thirty percent, Murmur cast her Mana Tide spell on the healers who were resurrected already. All but Veranol, who seemed difficult to reach. It looked like Masha was reluctantly going to fetch him.

Her head throbbed, like someone was seeing how tight they could get the vice, and she watched Sinister resurrect more targets, biting her lip. Sin's face was paler than usual, and she seemed disturbed by something.

Murmur stretched out her sensing nets and noticed that the interference was gone from them. She frowned, looking at the debuffs that definitely persisted through death. Right now, there were no monsters around them. She could sense the ice giants they'd been fighting, but they weren't close anymore. Apparently when they'd died, it had reset the encounter.

Frankly, she couldn't believe the old log a healer out until the encounter resets trick had worked, but damned if she wasn't grateful that it had. Having to fight their way, or even just make their way back into this area would have been a pain in the ass.

She meditated until her mana was full again and then hugged Snowy. He'd not left her side and was showing her glimpses of where the ice giants dwelled. Perhaps he had scouted while they waited to revive.

He gave her a look that told her of course he had. With his attachment to her broken, he reverted to a game wolf and thus wouldn't waken the ire of the beasts around him. That was a pretty neat trick, even if Murmur had grown used to his presence in her mind.

The grin on his wolf face made his tongue loll out, and he almost seemed human for a moment.

"Mur. I need to talk to you." Sinister bent down as if she was checking to make sure Murmur was alright.

"Sure." Murmur allowed the bloodmage to help her stand up. She looped an arm around her shoulders and sighed into Sin's hair. "What's up?"

"Well. When I logged back in, almost everyone was dead, but the encounter had reset itself." She glanced around them, making sure no one else could hear them.

Mur saw her concern and frowned, erecting a layer of protection on their thoughts and some confusion around them so no one could fully see what they were doing. It didn't take her long to realize that Sin's eyes kept wandering in the direction of Jirald and Masha.

A cold knot began to form in the middle of Mur's stomach.

"Jirald wasn't dead. He was totally disengaged from the fight though, and the ice giants had reset. He's a rogue though, so perhaps they have one of those complete aggro drops, or maybe a vanishing type of spell. But the odder thing was Masha."

"What do you mean?" Mur asked softly.

"He wasn't dead either. And heal aggro is a hard thing to get rid of. The only way that happens is if it or you die." She looked up at Murmur, her expression serious. "But he didn't die Mur. They were both hidden, and they were both alive, and that shouldn't have been possible."

Murmur nodded slowly, testing out her sensing nets to see if they really were fully recovered. They had to be, because she could sense an underlying unease around the whole raid. It confused her. Perhaps people weren't familiar with the old log out method. Her parents had taught it to her when she first started playing games. Not all of them allowed it to happen, but many of them couldn't build their mechanics around such a loophole.

Thing was, it took at least ten seconds to log out. If you logged out too soon, it would leave your avatar in the world, and without its player at the helm it was possible for that avatar to die. The last thing a raid using that loophole needed was to have their healer log back in and be dead.

Still. Masha hadn't logged out, had he? "Did he maybe log out with you too?"

Sinister hesitated. "I mean he could have, I guess. Perhaps he logged in just before me and resurrected Jirald. Oh, that makes much more sense." She seemed pleased with that explanation, almost as if she didn't want it to be something else.

Murmur couldn't blame her. "I'll double check the logs later."

And she would, because she had to. With the overwhelming sensations she was getting from about a third of the raid, Murmur was beginning to feel uneasy herself. Like something or someone had talked to her raid members while she was preoccupied.

It wouldn't have been so bad, but she noticed Jinna looking sideways at her now and again. She could handle animosity from the other guilds and didn't care, but from one of Fable? Something was undoubtedly wrong, she just had to figure out what.

"Mur!" Devlish tapped his foot, and the shouting of her name brought her back to the present. "We need to start again. I believe the counter is almost done."

It was only then that Murmur realized there was a counter in her vision. It had another minute on it. Like the zone had reset that particular encounter when they died.

Devlish was already giving the orders to buff up, and he assigned stun rotations as well.

This time there was no way these ice giants were bombarding them with boulders. The fight began, and this time the rumbling was reassuring. Their opponents arrived, and the rangers knew what to do. Devlish and the melee fighting their target had interrupts down, and Rumble didn't escape once.

The ranged classes rotated through each of the rooted ice giants. Damage had the potential to break the root, and so all them had a rotation to allow for stun cool downs. The mages and rangers had a no damage, distance stun, as did Murmur.

Their rhythm developed organically, and the fight began to feel fluid. The first ice giant crashed to the ground finally, in a cascade of ice chips and blocks.

It left open the only mistake they made and allowed one Rumble to escape, but this time the witches were waiting for the boulder call and heaved acid on it as it rolled down the ramp.

Murmur cast her gaze around, checking her nets and frowned. She could sense the next two waves of ice giants, but now there was something else, just beyond her reach of understanding, tugging at her senses. She frowned, trying to figure out why there were blemishes where awarenesses should be.

Was she glitching? Was her headset? Was the game about to crash again?

Somnia is stable, if I do say so myself. What you're feeling isn't emanating from me.

If it was possible, the world sounded slightly uncertain, like she was also trying to locate the problem. It only reinforced Murmur's feeling that something was happening. *It's okay, I'll keep an eye out too. It's probably just a glitch or part of the virus attempting to overrun something.*

I think I'd know if it was that, but I shall ask the others to look as well.

Murmur didn't feel reassured. Even as the second and third ice giants fell to the raid's strategy. It was all too mechanical now, like it had been made easy for them. Her shoulders itched, like someone was watching her, but she located Jirald easily enough, so it wasn't him.

One of the waves of ice giants disappeared from her sensing nets, and she frowned as a larger presence replaced it.

"Boss incoming shortly," she announced, still trying to trace the source of her unease. "Likely with adds."

The feeling intensified, and she turned to look around at the raid. They were all still fighting the last ice giant standing, every one of them focused on the fight.

All of them except Masha, who stood, paying no attention whatsoever to the raid's current fight, watching her with a look of pure hatred.

CHAPTER THIRTY

Glower

Telvar held his breath as Emilarth initiated the exchange sequence, pulling Belius in from his office in Stellaein to her own, more protected area in Curet. Tel had to bottle up all of his rage, all of his will to punch his brother through into another dimension, and trust that his sister was right.

Even if she was right, he wasn't about to forgive his brother, but he would help him for now. Emilarth began to glow, coding visible beneath her skin just like the locus runes, except the black numbers and symbols appeared more like the absence of light in a glowing body.

Belius's form materialized, and for a moment a look of pure confusion crossed his face as it flickered through coding to gain its appearance. As soon as he focused on them though, his shoulders lost some of their tension.

"You shouldn't have brought me here," he whispered, even though his stance seemed to hold relief. Confusing as always.

Telvar couldn't help himself. "And you shouldn't have used me as a guinea pig for a virus cure without telling me what it could lead to. But here we are."

Belius had the grace to look away, somewhat sheepish. His words were in stark contrast to his body language. "I did what needed to be done, and I'd do it again."

"Like I'd let you get close to me," Telvar growled out, taking three steps back to remain at a safe distance.

"Stop it. We don't have time for this. You can bicker after we stop the virus from spreading." Emilarth, for once, took on the serious role. It was an odd juxtaposition to see her act that way, her usual trickster self buried down deep.

Reluctantly Telvar had to admit she was right. There was far too much to see to, to rectify for Somnia.

As if summoned, the wraithlike form of the world appeared. This time she seemed more solid than before, as if she was slowly becoming more real over time. But the reception she had was being interfered with. Occasionally a line of static marred her form and left her body to repixelate. But it didn't interrupt her processing that Telvar could see.

"The dungeons are unstable. Tieflos is worse than Vahrir." Even her voice had a robotic clang to it every few words. Her almost tangible face contorted with annoyance for a moment before she continued speaking. "They'll get through this, but there's an infection running through the raid members now, and I'm not sure how it started, or how to stop it." She looked at the AIs, her expression pleading with them to do something she couldn't.

"Infection? How do you mean infection?" Belius spoke up, and just as Telvar wanted to tell him to shut the hell up this was all his fault, Emilarth stayed his hand and let the locus AI speak. It was all Telvar could do not to let his anger boil over.

"Their actions aren't following normal readings. Readings I've had on them for days now." Somnia seemed genuinely confused.

Belius pinched the bridge of his nose and sighed. "Probably my fault."

"Isn't everything?" Telvar bit out. He took a breath, tried to calm himself, but he could still remember the strange visions he'd had while in forced dragon form, and he wasn't about to forgive that easily.

Belius turned to face him, a worried expression pinching his alien features. "I'm sorry, Tel. I didn't have time to ask you and have you weigh the pros and cons. I needed the start of an anti-virus immediately, not when you decided you'd been over the data enough. You were the first of us. If anyone could give me what we needed, it was you. And you did. But it's a lot of work."

Telvar was taken aback. He hadn't expected his brother to be so candid and wasn't sure how to respond. The anger still boiled in the back of his mind, making him wonder if maybe he still had a portion of the infection inside him. Still, for the sake of continuing to exist, he could tolerate his brother for now.

"Fine. You've got our attention." Telvar crossed his arms and pinned Belius with his gaze.

"Thank you." And for the first time it sounded like Bel actually meant it.

"Don't get me wrong. This is for the good of Somnia and our continued survival." Telvar needed to set the record straight, to let his brother know he wasn't forgiven. "When we're done with that, you and I are having a long talk."

Murmur wasn't left much time to worry about why Masha suddenly radiating hatred. The larger ice giant presence was approaching faster than the next wave of normal ice giants. She could feel its anger over anything else.

While glad that her sensing abilities had returned, Murmur wasn't too happy about the animosity she felt leaking through the ranks of her raid. Had she been so tyrannical? What had she done to set people off?

"Top people off!" Veranol called out, and Murmur refreshed her buffs on the off chance that this fight would take a while.

Boulders, she had to keep an eye out for those and anything else trap-like or tricky that might surface from this super ice giant. Even though her nets were catching the strange sensations sweeping through the raid, she had to push past those to tap into potential hazards scattered around the cavern.

She wasn't about to let them wipe if she could help it. Wiping to trash had been embarrassing.

Raid buffed, they waited. Not all gazes were directed the way of the incoming opponents, no, some of them tried to bore holes in the back of Murmur's head. She tightened her own shielding, making sure nothing could affect her. There wasn't time to figure this out now, but as soon as they were done with this dungeon, she'd spend those four hours trying to solve this shit instead of sleeping if she had to.

"Merlin, three smaller ice giants will be incoming shortly after we engage. Keep them locked down with root if you can. Divvy out the responsibilities now." She kept her voice down so that not many around her would hear but had to make sure the volume made it over the thudding that made the ground shake.

Masha's sullenness was wearing on her. Karn and Risk didn't seem to be much better. All of them acted like they wanted to be anywhere but in Tieflos. So much so that Murmur was dreading the fight.

Then King Egnaro crested the rise, his head almost scraping the ceiling. He was almost twice the size of the previous ice giants and moved slower as a result. His bulky form appeared to find turning especially difficult, and slivers of ice splintered off and cascaded around him like porcupine quills falling off and down to the enemies below.

The first time he moved to twist around while Devilish was trying to taunt him and coax him back, a splinter landed inside of Devlish's tower shield range and impaled him through the leg.

Murmur had never heard the dread knight scream so loudly. A moment later he was healed, but his face was pale beneath his scales, and she knew it had shaken him to feel the increased pain.

Is it always like this, Mur? he asked over guild chat.

Sometimes it's worse, Sinister answered for her.

Havoc joined in too. *I'll take the extra damage, but the side effects of this deeper connection are pretty severe. I don't like not being able to dial down the realism factor.*

No one said anything for a moment, and Murmur threw her debuffs out and onto the King, trying to calculate just how far behind him the adds were.

Then I guess I better figure out how to compensate, Devlish said over the chat once more. *This should have come with a warning.*

Murmur agreed, but there wasn't a need to say that. There wasn't time. Keeping King Egnaro fixed in her vision, it allowed her to see when he was casting. At eighty-nine percent, he began to cast Tantrum. Murmur attempted to interrupt it, but the cast was fast, and she'd had to read it first.

Tantrum saw the king throw himself to the ground faster than she thought something of that size should have been able to move. It flailed once there. Its long arms pounded the ground, shaking it and causing most of the raid to lose their footing. Meanwhile, its feet kicked violently, creating slivers of ice that shot out unexpectedly.

Merlin got whooshed away and nailed to the wall. Luckily, it missed his vital organs this time. She needed to talk to him about that whole impaling fetish he seemed to have. He yanked the icicle out of his chest as a heal hit him and grinned at Murmur, a trail of blood leaking out of his mouth the only remnant of the injury left.

She rolled her eyes and turned to look at the king. He rolled over onto his back and executed a surprisingly agile flip back up to his feet. But when his shoes hit the ground, it sent a jolt through the room and caused most of them to fall to their knees again.

"All out for now, get him down as fast as you can," Devlish called out. Murmur couldn't blame him. They were about to get three more adds, and she didn't like the odds of being able to control those three while this dude was pulling off a tantrum. She had no idea what set him off, and really…tantrum?

"You'd think…" Havoc ground out as he concentrated on upping his damage, "a king wouldn't be so childish."

Murmur nodded. "I'm trying not to think."

At least that got a laugh out of the necromancer. "Good call, Mur."

King Egnaro wasn't hard to damage. Not when all of the fire weakened the ice. He was down to seventy-five percent before he began to cast Tantrum again. This time, Murmur was on the ball and actually managed to interrupt him. Which was strange, because she'd been almost certain she shouldn't be able to interrupt a boss.

Her thought proved correct several seconds later, when he began to cast Tantrum again. Interrupting that one cast wouldn't accomplish anything. All the king did was wait until the recast mechanism wore off so he could spam it again.

Warning

You cannot interrupt a boss. He will attempt to throw a Tantrum until he succeeds. Each successive attempt will allow him to build anger making the eventual resulting Tantrum that much worse. At least you won t have to worry about being caught standing still.

Shit.

Murmur readied her Forcefield Barrier, pushing it to encompass the rest of her raid just as the tantrum hit. She was relieved to see that it worked, even while the ground beneath them threatened to become a trampoline of ice. And even while the slivers of ice might have been closer to ice javelins this time.

It drained about half of her MA, and Snowy nipped at her hand, concern showing in his eyes. Even after the Tantrum was over, Murmur watched as her MA began to refill itself naturally, pulling on the constant use of her nets.

"Incoming," Jinna called out, his voice not the usual jolly dwarf he normally was. Murmur frowned, putting that too to the side. Focus on the monsters before she had to focus on the brewing problems. Jinna hadn't even made eye contact with her, but maybe there was a first for everything.

Snowy pushed to the fore, his hackles rising as he mutated again, becoming larger and fiercer than he'd been the last time.

Merlin and his rangers rooted the incoming ice giants to the spot, close to each other but not enough to touch. He flashed a grin at Murmur as he directed the relevant people to watch out for the boulder throw and interrupt it.

The now massive wolf kept the three ice giant kids focused solely on him so the raid could use the most of their DPS. Murmur wondered for a moment, scrolling quickly through her spell book.

Insidious Lure

Cast: Instant once released

Type: Entrapment/Psychosis

Duration: For as long as your will remains focused.

Effect: This will lure your enemies into a trap of the mind, forcing them to see their worst fears and act on them, even to the detriment of their peers. It will continue until the caster releases the spell, or the enemies have killed each other.

Caution: This spell can be mentally taxing, and even damaging. Make sure your reasons for using such force are justified. Try not to get caught in your own nightmare along the way.

Should she use it? Was it necessary? She glanced over at the huge ice giant king and at the smaller ice giants. Was she completely out of it, or were they attempting to reach one another? Was the king protecting his children?

No, that couldn't be it. But hadn't they made alliances previously based exclusively on what something couldn't be in a game. What if anything were possible?

"Sin." The blood mage nodded, her concentration obviously on the fight and healing. "Do you think—are they trying to reach one another?"

Sinister blinked, looking back and forth between the two groups. She squinted and then laughed. "You know, I think you're right. I think king is trying to protect his children."

Murmur mulled it over in her mind. The father was already down to sixty percent health. If she was right and his Tantrum was timed and not triggered, he was about to throw his tantrum again.

"Stop all damage to the king!" she called out. The three rogues paid her no mind. "Stop it now!" she yelled out.

Begrudgingly, all three of them glowered at her and moved away. Devlish refrained from doing damage and only used his sword and a smaller shield. He didn't seem amused. "I hope that whatever you're doing is the right thing and isn't painful."

So did Murmur, but she just nodded in response and readied Soothe.

When she cast it, at first, there was no response and for a moment of panic she thought she'd read the possibilities wrong. Were her sensor nets so out of whack?

She cast Soothe again, and this time sent an overwhelming sense of calm along with it. It suffused the cavern, enveloped both the younger ice giants and the king, and the king stopped its fighting to look down thoughtfully at Murmur, tiny in his shadow.

What do you seek? he asked in a booming voice that echoed through the chamber even though his lips didn't move.

Murmur paused for a moment, trying to figure out how to magnify her own voice when Dansyn laid a hand on her shoulder. "Speak normally. I can make you sound like a loudspeaker."

She managed to refrain from laughing and continued. "We seek to finish this dungeon and reach the end so that we might acquire the key. We only fight that which attacks us."

But my children were afraid. You have fire and acid. These things are big danger, much damage. These things kill us. The king peered down at her, a bemused look on his face.

"We apologize." Murmur bowed. "Your children are safe now, and we shall harm no more."

The king looked thoughtful. *They did kill you all once. I suppose that's fair, then. They are better than you at some things. Truce?*

Murmur let out a soft sigh of relief and nodded. "Truce."

Thank you. The king stood up tall, then reached down to tap each of his children on the head with a finger. They looked up and nodded, falling into line behind their father.

For this, the voice boomed, *you have our gratitude and will be rewarded. Make your way to the end and watch your step. Ice is treacherous and has a will of its own.*

King Egnaro walked away with his children, vanishing into the icy landscape ahead of them.

"What the fuck?" Masha spat out, startling Murmur. "We were killing it. We so could have won."

"We did win." Rashlyn pointed out. "There are chests waiting for us when we reach them, and we don't have needless death repairs.

Buff

You have been granted the Boon of the Ice

Boon of the Ice:

This is a buff that renders you impervious to ice damage. Ice cannot harm you, nor can it slow you. This buff removes all previous debuffs and persists through death. It will remain in force until you have completed your task.

"Great. Another cryptic fucking message." This time it was Risk, just as angry as Masha, speaking in the same tone of voice with the same intonation. Definitely something Murmur had to look into once she got them to the end of the path.

Moving ahead with Devlish, she had to admit the dungeon had been a pain in the ass, and she was relieved to be leaving it. They passed through two more chambers, and the grumbling behind her became ever louder, until they reached a doorway that led outside.

In a massive semi-circle of ice jutting out toward the final rope bridge, were thirty chests, perfectly spaced. The mood of the raid lifted, and then the notifications began.

You receive one of the twelve keys.

You receive a getashi.

You receive a midia crystal.

You have completed the Tieflos dungeon as compiled by Thra, Version 22.4283 triggered by Murmur of Fable.

You have successfully completed the quest: Find your way to the end, the choice is yours.

This version of the Tieflos dungeon will no longer be available to future raiders.

You gain experience.

You gain experience for being the first to complete any version of the Tieflos dungeon.

You gain experience for choosing to complete the quest: Find your way to the end, the choice is yours.

You gain bonus experience for choosing your disadvantages

in ways unexpected by the dungeon.

You gain bonus experience for sparing the young ice giants.

You gain bonus experience for learning to harness each of your debuffs attributes.

You gain bonus experience for choosing the smarter way.

You gain bonus experience for solving what riddles were placed in front of you.

You gain bonus experience for reaching the Ice Giant King Egnaro.

You gain bonus experience for allowing him to retain his honor.

You gain bonus experience for completing the Tieflos dungeon as an alternate version.

You gain bonus experience for completing the second of the endgame dungeon chains.

You gain bonus experience for not attempting to circumvent the portal restrictions.

You shall be rewarded.

You are already max level.

Your experience will be funneled into your hidden ability pool, allowing you to work toward higher levels with more battery power.

Around her, the last members of the raiding party had finally reached level fifty and were busy memorizing their spells, scrolling through the boxes they'd received and inspecting the loot from their chests. Sorting through her own chest, she sealed the getashi away in the container Neva had made for them.

The urge not to seal it back up was so great she had to bite her lip to distract her from the sensation not to. Level fifty. She glanced around, taking in deep, cold breaths. They'd defeated the dungeon, and she'd gained twenty-two new MA points to her pool. Impressive.

A hot gust of air washed over her face just after she pulled the cape out of her chest, causing the material to billow in the wind. Looking around her, she dismissed the stats for the garment that had just popped up in her vision to find the source of the elements.

A portal with murky green and swirling brown rings had appeared in the middle of the vast ice field they'd just battled on. She didn't understand why the air was hot. Glacier Lake implied that it was cold, unless it just meant that the water source was from a glacier?

She shook her head, something seemed very wrong about the opening, tainted, dark.

Glacier Lake shouldn't be as cold as Tieflos, but it should still be chilly. I've checked the game settings, and the temperature modulation isn't functioning as it should right now.

There wasn't panic so much as bewilderment in Somnia's voice as she answered Murmur's unasked question. *Okay. What are we looking at then?*

The castles aren't ice; they're built out of stone, but their shape was to imply a fortified ice castle. The creatures should all be fine in the adjusted climate

Murmur had an idea. *Isn't it near Curet, which is a rain forest? With a lot of humidity, and the weird ground around the dungeon, it probably has adapted as Somnia has become…more.*

Somnia was quiet for a moment before answering with a distinct flavor of relief. **Yes. I believe you are correct. The continents are evolving.**

Murmur smiled to herself and then blinked as something darted out of the portal toward there group, so fast she could barely follow the movement. The tentacle snaked around Sinister's mid-section and dragged her back into it with a screech from the bloodmage that made Murmur's heart run cold.

Summer Residence
Home of Laria, David, and Wren
Summer Condo
Real World – Day Twenty-Nine

Laria glanced scrolled through the readings she'd been trying to make sense of for the last few hours. She was almost considering standing on her head to see if that helped when she squinted at her display and then gasped.

"You're not going to believe this," she began, already biting her tongue. Why she hadn't thought of it before was beyond her. Perhaps she'd been too obsessed with her daughter's predicament to think about anyone else's.

David took a moment to pull himself away from his own research and raised an eyebrow. "Unless you're going to tell me my daughter is, in fact, Somnia itself, do you seriously think you can shock me at this point?"

Laria swallowed past the lump in her throat. She guessed they were about to find out. "The adjusted headsets have higher reading outputs. They can access more of the abilities; their processing time is shorter."

"I know this." David was obviously trying to be patient, but considering he was knee deep in figuring out the anti-virus they needed to employ, Laria couldn't blame him for wanting her to hurry up.

"Yes, but the normal headgear is fluctuating in about ten of the people around Wren and Fable."

"In the raid zone?" David finally looked more interested in what she was saying than what he was doing.

"Yes. One of the headsets has been tinkered with, but the others are," she paused for a moment, trying to figure out how to express it outside of her mind. "It's like the virus has attached itself to them and is slowly morphing their capabilities. But not for the player to control, for the game to have wider reach."

David was quiet for a few seconds before frowning as he spoke. "In the game with Wren, right near her?"

Laria nodded.

He pushed on. "But not necessarily attached to her or the headsets you and Shayla altered?"

"Yep. Not..." she frowned this time. "Wait, one of the headsets is. It belongs to the character Jinna. Its programming is being adjusted, literally, as we speak. Very slowly, but definitely there."

David initiated a link to his wife's feed and sat with her, watching the data. His eyes grew wide and for a moment all he could see was the information in front of him. "The fluctuations are only happening to people who are stuck in the portal-linked endgame dungeon loop with Fable."

"Yeah." Laria wasn't happy to have someone else arrive at that conclusion. She'd wanted to be wrong because she had no idea how to fix this or where to start.

David shook his head. "But I don't get how. This game has some serious glitches. What the hell possessed Davenport to release it like that?"

Laria hesitated. "That's just it. He didn't. When we released the game read as clean and fully functional. Whatever this is? It's someone or something else, and I have no idea what their agenda is."

Storm Entertainment
Somnia Online Division
Game Development Offices Artificial Intelligence Server Room
Day Twenty-Nine

An alarm sounded through the safe space the AIs had retreated to once again. Rav and his siblings looked up in shock as the system began to list numerous protocol breaks occurring all at once in the same sector of the game's coding.

Unidentified headset accessing game coding.

"What the..." Sui didn't finish what he was saying, his alarm overtaking his irritation as he dived in and began to search.

Rav scoped out all of his areas, searching for the breach of protocols and pulling the information on the offending headset to his console. The headset was old, older than the ones Murmur and her friends were using. It wasn't tweaked at all; instead, it had access to data points that it shouldn't because as far as he could tell, the headset had originally been one of Michael's prototypes.

"Should that even be able to hook into the game?" Thra asked incredulously.

"Technically no?" Sui answered, flustered at its presence.

Rav didn't want to ask why. Perhaps his brother was telling the truth when he told them everything he'd done was to save the world. Even so, he wasn't about to leave it up to the younger AI.

Rav followed the connection and found its user in character creation. He'd been assigned a character class already and was designing his human warlock. Rav balked. The player shouldn't have been able to tap into that class. In testing, the warlock had registered as overpowered, choosing people with questionable morals and giving them similar spell options.

They'd pulled it until they could figure out why it registered people as one. But here it was, where it shouldn't be possible.

"Hey, we have a bit of a problem."

Thra coughed. "Yeah, I just found the warlock too."

"It's a developer headset, one of a kind, allows for hefty in-game control." Sui's words cascaded into each other, the worry evident in his tone. "What's worse, is it's automatically level forty. He's jumped into a developer's skin."

"Who is this? Who has access to this?" Rav frantically accessed the warlock files, pulling and freezing several of the more potent spells to lock them away.

"I'm not sure." Thra spoke softly as she concentrated on pulling more information.

"I don't think Murmur is going to be happy about this," Rav said suddenly as the character registered its name and prepared to enter the game world.

"Why?" Sui looked over, a haunted presence around him.

Rav sucked in a breath. "His name is James Dougray."

Appendix

Hi there! K.T. Hanna here.

I want to thank you for reading the Somnia Online. OMG, a book that doesn't start with a D. No, seriously though. I'm so excited for you all to have read this book. It took me an age to make sure I kept all the threads together.

I really hope you enjoyed your Fusion journey with Murmur, Sinister, and the crew.

If you enjoyed the book, I ask you, please take a moment to leave a review. *Reviews* are an author's lifesblood. Without them, our books sink into obscurity. With them, most algorithms allow well reviewed books to self-promote in some way.

Want to find out more about Somnia? Here is how you can keep in contact with me:

Sign up for my <u>Reader's Group</u> and get a short story for free! (http://login.somnia-online.c/)

If you'd like to contact me, my email is: kthannaauthor@gmail.com I'll do my very best to get back to you

If you'd like previews of what I'm writing, or art I'm commissioning then join my Patreon! (patreon.com/KTHanna)

I can be found in the Somnia FB group (facebook.com/groups/SomniaOnline/) fairly often, and also on Twitter (@KTHanna) & Instagram (@kt_hanna)

If you LOVE LitRPG don't forget to join:
The GameLit Society! (facebook.com/groups/LitRPGsociety/)
And of course don't forget LitRPG Books!

To learn more about LitRPG, talk to authors including myself, and just have an awesome time, please join the <u>LitRPG Group</u>. (facebook.com/groups/LitRPGGroup/)

Game Terms

Aggro—When you walk too close to a monster, you get in its aggression radius, thus causing aggro. Once engaged in combat, players must be cautious not to exceed the tank's threat level. Buffs, debuts, and damage output all contribute to the mobs aggro meter.

AOE—Area of Effect. Spells or abilities that effect an area and not just a single target.

Binding/bound—When someone/you bind(s) to an area, you affix your soul to that place in order to Gate back, or else respawn when you die.

Boss—Nope. He doesn't employ you, he employs all the mobs trying to kill you. He hits HARD, and often has special group wiping abilities if not handled correctly by the tank and raid as a whole.

Buff—Most classes will get buffs that strengthen at least themselves if not others. These are effects they can cast which enhance aspects of their character.

Camping—When a group finds a spot that will yield good money and experience, they tend to stay in its vicinity. This is called camping.

Con—To consider a mob and see how difficult the fight could potentially become.

DoT—Damage over Time. This is an offensive spell that applies damage to a target over a period of time at regular intervals.

DPS—Damage Per Second. Usually used in conjunction with offensive classes, or damage output.

Debuff—This is the opposite of a buff and is usually used on mobs to detract from their strengths and make them easier to kill.

End Game—Every game has a goal. In some there's a max level and events and fights only accessible once that level is reached. For Fable, the end game is everything.

Gank—When someone tries to player kill you without forewarning. Often succeeds in taking the victim by surprise.

Gate—You create a Gate to your binding point and travel there instantly.

Grinding—Sometimes gaining levels requires so much camping that it becomes tedious. That's known as grinding levels.

Healer—Well...they heal.

HP—Hit Points. The amount of damage a character can take before death.

Kite—This is a tactic often employed by ranged classes such as the ranger. It entails slowing a mob, and running ahead of it, slowly picking down its health. Can also be used as a diversionary tactic to split multiple mobs if no Mesmerize is available.

Line of Sight (LOS)—If a mob can't see you, but knows you're there, it will have to run around the obstacle to gain access. This is often used to split up larger groups of melee and casters, so it's more manageable for the group. The puller will line of sight the casting/ranged mobs to pull them around an obstacle for easier access and closer contact.

MA—Mental Acuity. A type of power generator specifically for Psionicists.

MANA—Mind juice, used for spells.

Meat Shield—The character who takes the hits in place of the rest of the group. The tank.

Melee—Those fighters who stand in close range and use weapons to fight with are often referred to as melee classes.

Mez—Mesmerize. Freezes in place.

MMO—Massively Multiplayer Online.

MMORPG—Massively Multiplayer Online Role Playing Game.

Mob—an aggressive monster. Can be humanoid or animal.

OOM—Out of mana. Literally what it says.

Newbie—Also known as noob. Someone who has rarely, if ever played an MMO and has no clue what they're doing.

NPC—Non Player Character. Usually not aggressive unless you fuck up.

Pull—Often one person in a group/raid will be designated as the puller, the person who attacks the mob and brings it to camp.

Ranged—A class that can damage (usually) a mob from a distance. Like mages or rangers, etc.

Ranger Gating—Rangers were often known for getting themselves into trouble by kiting mobs in a solo setting. Or else, pulling aggro when DPS-ing. They'd die and resurrect at their bind point, making it what's known as a Ranger Gate.

Respawn—When a mob or a person dies in-game, they will reappear at the spot where their soul was bound. The more powerful the mob, the longer it takes for them to respawn.

Root—A spell obtainable by multiple classes that causes the target's feet to affix momentarily to the ground. They can still cast, but they cannot move until the root breaks.

RPG—Role Playing Game.

Tank—The meat shield aka the person who takes the bit hits for the group. Often needs to be swapped in and out with another tank during larger raids depending on a boss' abilities.

Tether—In some worlds monsters have a specific area they're confined to, and thus stop and don't pursue their prey past a certain point. In Somnia, mobs do not tether. This does not apply to specific purpose NPCs.

Train—When a player or group has managed to aggro a large number of mobs who don't tether, and leads the following of mobs to a specific spot, or through a spot, they call it a train.

Utility class—these are classes whose prime function is to support the group, through abilities that protect or strengthen them as a group or raid.

VR—Virtual Reality.

VRMMORPG—Virtual Reality Massively Multiplayer Online Role Playing Game.

Wipe—This occurs when the entire raid or group die to an encounter.

Murmur
> Class: Enchanter – Psionicist
> Species: Locus
> Real Name: Wren

Sinister
> Class: Blood Mage
> Species: Dark Elf
> Real Name: Harlow

Devlish
> Class: Dread Knight
> Species: Lacerta
> Real Name: Darren

Havoc
> Class: Necromancer
> Species: Dark Elf
> Real Name: Evan

Beastial
> Class: Beastmaster
> Species: Viking
> Real Name: Selwyn

Merlin
> Class: Ranger
> Species: Elf
> Real Name: Mike

Rashlyn

    Class: Monk

    Species: Feles

Veranol

    Class: Shaman

    Species: Viking

Mellow

    Class: Witch

    Species: Dark Elf

Exbo

    Class: Ranger

    Species: Human

Jinna

    Class: Rogue

    Species: Dwarf

Dansyn

    Class: Bard

    Species: Dark Elf

Base Stat Sheet: Level Fifty (50)

CONstitution: 22
STRength: 10
AGIlity: 20
WISdom: 12
INTelligence: 94
CHArisma: 115

HitPoints: 712
MANA: 1044
MA: 250

Abjuration: 267
Alteration: 272
Conjuration: 258
Divinition: 262
Evocation: 265

2H Blunt: 222
1H Piercing: 85

Mental Acuity (MA) Abilities:

Thought sensing.

> Class: Enchanter only.

> Level not applicable.

Developing your inner senses you've awoken your latent kinetic powers. With constant use your skills will increase, while the opposite will occur should the skill not be used. See your trainer for specifics when you reach Thought Sensing (25).

Thought Shielding.

> Class: Enchanter only.

> Level not applicable.

Developing your inner senses you've awoken your latent psychic powers. With constant use your skills will increase, while the opposite will occur should the skill not be used. See your trainer for specifics when you reach Thought Shielding (25).

Thought Projection.

> Class: Enchanter only.

> Level not applicable.

Developing your inner senses has further developed your psychic powers. Thought Projection can be tricky. Make sure you never use it in anger, or the results might be surprising. With constant use your skills will increase, while the opposite will occur should the skill not be used. See your trainer for specifics when you reach Thought Projection (25).

Mind Bolt.

> **This ability allows you to cast a spear of mental anguish into the depths of an opponent's brain.**

Effects: Opponents will be unable to concentrate enough to use spells or abilities for four seconds. This time increases as the caster's level does.

> **Cost: Requires Mental Acuity to be at 18.**

Caution: Use sparingly. Backlash from overuse, or improper use can cause the same effect in the caster...or worse.

Phase Shift

This ability allows you to negatively affect your opponent s mind. Believing they are a second or two apart from reality, they will reside there for up to 15 seconds.

Effect: Target's mind is encased in a phase of illusion. The target will be convinced they've shifted to a different time pocket, and thus are incapable of moving. This effect begins at 15 seconds duration, and levels with the caster through to a maximum of 90 seconds.

Cost: Requires MA to be at 38 for larger castings, the cost will double.

Caution: Phase shift may be utilized on single or multiple targets at once. Weigh the amount of targets carefully, else it backfire and shift you. Sometimes the shift in time can cause ruptures near the caster. Make sure the voices you're hearing are your own.

Forestall Death

If applied before potential death takes place, this will enable you to maintain your health at 0.5 hit points as long as you are receiving some sort of healing effect.

Effect: Target is able to ward off death for a limited period of time and will not die when they should have, as long as heals are actively channeled in their direction.

Cost: Requires Mental Acuity to be at 60

Caution: This spell can only be used on one person at a time. Attempting to use it twice at once is not recommended. This will usually result in things worse than death.

Clone Warp

This ability allows you to produce a clone of yourself used for distracting your opponent. Depending on your tier of mastery, you may be able to produce more than one clone.

Effect: All enemies around you will believe that your clone is you for the next 45 seconds, directing their attacks accordingly. The ability expires when the 45 seconds are up, or else, the clone's minor hit point pool has been depleted, whichever comes first.

Cost: Requires Mental Acuity to be at 45 or more

Caution: This ability can be used on as many enemies that you have who can potentially see it. Keep in mind though, a clone is just like you. Make sure you remember who the real one is.

Charming Cooperation

This ability allows you to use your charisma and your mental acuity to persuade monsters, animals, and sometimes even beings to join your cause.

Effects: When using thought projections to make sure your target understands the charming process, before you activate this type of charm. They will work together as allies instead of coerced foes. You may release them whenever you or they request it.

Cost: Requires MA to be at 35 for each ally. Diminishes current total MA for the duration of the cooperation.

Caution: You can use this on multiple targets. But each ally costs, and you can never utilize Charming cooperation on more mobs than is equal to 20% of your level. Also, don't try to charm raid bosses. Even small ones. Like... just don't even attempt that shit.

Mental Acuity (MA) Level Three (3)

Mind Wipe

This ability allows you to reduce your targets threat for you or whoever is at the top of their agro list

Effects: Change aggression list, or make the opponent forget their tasks for a few seconds. Range and duration may be increased as the caster levels.

Cost: Requires MA to be at 55

Caution: This spell can increase in both range and severity. From a single target, to a full raid it's all possible. Just remember someone else needs to take that agro, or else you'll be the main target.

Shield Expansion

This ability allows you to extend your individual mental shielding against mental or magical attacks over others.

Effect: If attacked with magic (mind or spell), this shield will protect those under it from damage or effects

Cost: Requires 10MA per person covered

Kinetic Strand – Psionicist

Forcefield Barrier

This is the first in your kinetic line of spells. Once triggered by luck, you can now activate it at will. It allows you to form a bubble of mental energy and transform it into a tangible forcefield.

Effects: This can prevent some physical damage. The damage amount depends on the strength of will and caster behind the barrier. Size is increased by MA level and usage

Cost: This shield requires your MA to be at 60, but will not use MA to cast as it is a kinetic ability.

Caution: This spell can create a backlash when used too much. Do not use it as a crutch.

Base Kinetic Structure

In order to take advantage of your ability to turn thoughts into weapons, you must reinforce the skills that ground all of your telepathic and telekinetic abilities.

Effect: This ability allows you to strengthen the base of all three arms of psionics. Thought Shielding will eventually physically repel an attack. Thought Sensing can break through others shields to reveal what is hidden. Thought Projection can lend solidity to the induced hallucinations managed once skill level 250 is passed.

Cost: This is a passive skill and will begin working to bolster your abilities as soon as you absorb it.

Caution: Do not presume to know how this passive ability works. You will need to test this out. The difference for these abilities between telepathy and telekinesis is very fine. What this ability does is allow your kinetic field to grow at the same rate as your telepathy. What it does not do is make you infallible. Always remember that if you're not sure, you can do more damage than you think. Not only to yourself, but to those you target.

Mental Acuity (MA) Level Four (4)

Forcefield Push

Once used wildly, you can now activate this at will. This will form a bubble of force projecting directly outwards from you in an arc and push anything in its path out of your way. Having this ability directly available will now allow you to develop some measure of control.

Effects: This will cause some physical and mental damage to any opponent caught in the range of the push. The amount of damage inflicted depends on the level and strength of will behind the push. Damage is increased by MA level and usage.

Cost: This push requires that you have MA at eighty, but will not use MA to cast, as it is a kinetic ability. Can only be used once every five minutes.

Caution. This spell can create a mind backlash if over-utilized. Make sure those in your path are not allies, as this ability does not discriminate between friend and foe.

Unless you want to make them a foe. Then they're fair game. Remember, try and maintain control.

Phantom

This ability allows you to convince your enemies that you are a different target. This renders you invisible to their aggro radar for all intents and purposes.

Effect: This ability not only transfers your generated aggro, but also takes you off the targetable list for the duration. It transfers aggression to your target, giving them your appearance, and rendering you invisible to any enemy near you. This may be used on allies, but also on enemies.

Cost: this ability requires MA to be at a minimum of 50, drains 5 MA per second, and will adjust as MA level and usage of this ability increase. Requires Charisma to be at 150 or more. Cannot be chained, must wait at least 5 minutes for MA to regenerate.

Caution: Make sure you do not cause your MA to run out. Should that happen, backlash will render the caster unconscious for a period of seconds not less than half the caster's level. Make sure you choose your targets wisely.

Base Enchanter Spells:

Level One (1):

Minor Suffocation

    Cast: Single Target

    Type: Damage Over Time

    Duration: 24 seconds

Effect: This spell winds a mind leash around your opponent, as if it were trying to suffocate them. Its damage ticks every three seconds for twenty-four seconds.

Minor Shield

    Cast: Self Only

    Type: Buff

    Duration: 45 minutes

Effect: This casts a minor shield over your skin, increasing your Armor Class by level + 3, and hit points by level + 5.

Simple Animation.

    Cast: Self

    Type: Pet

    Duration: Until death or dismissal

Effect: This summons a magical pet that sort of does your bidding. It costs a tiny sword to cast. Isn't the best at obeying commands.

Level Four (4):

Mesmerize

    Cast: Single Target

    Type: Breakable Stun

    Duration: 24 seconds

Effect: This spell immobilized your opponent for as long as they take no damage, or 24 seconds, whichever is shorter. You may cast non-damaging spells on them, and you may renew this casting before the initial one expires. Casting it on your friends probably isn't a good way to win popularity contests.

Flux

>Cast: Area of Effect
>
>Type: Stun
>
>Duration: 4 seconds

Effect: This is a stun that radiates out from the caster for fifteen feet. It will stun anyone who means the caster harm within that radius. Does not produce sparkles.

Gate

>Cast: Self Only
>
>Type: Travel
>
>Duration: N/A

Effect: This will transfer you to your bind point

Invisibility

>Cast: Self or Others
>
>Type: Buff
>
>Duration: 10 minutes or until broken/seen through

Effect: Causes generic invisibility. Undead don't count. Will drop if you cast a spell or take damage.

Fear

>Cast: Area of Effect
>
>Type: Brief Loss of Control
>
>Duration: 25% of level in seconds.

Effect: Causes enemies to flee from you in terror. But if you use it too soon, it'll probably just look like they misplaced something for a second.

Level Eight (8):

Cancel Magic

>Cast: Self or Others
>
>Type: Debuff
>
>Duration: Instant

Effect: Casting this spell will remove one magically caused effect from the target. Make sure you want to remove it.

Root

> Cast: Others (or self if you really want to)
>
> Type: Immobilization
>
> Duration: 8 seconds

Effect: This will root the target in place. Probably not the best idea to cast it on yourself when fleeing in panic.

See Invisible

> Cast: Self or Others
>
> Type: Buff
>
> Duration: 10 minutes

Effect: Really? Does this really require explanation?

Soothe

> Cast: Self or Others
>
> Type: Debuff
>
> Duration: Varies

Effect: This will lower the threat level of a target, but it will not make it disappear. Probably not useful on yourself unless in a really bad mood.

Chaos

> Cast: Others
>
> Type: Direct Damage
>
> Duration: Instant

Effect: This spell causes direct mental damage to the target, dropping their hit points by two times the caster's level. Requires a recharge.

Level Twelve (12):

Allure

> Cast: Others
>
> Type: Charm
>
> Duration: Until broken

Effect: This spell will charm a mob or other player. This ability

depends on the casters charisma, and ability to calm their charge.
Whatever you do, don't piss them off while under your command. It
rarely ends well.

Suffocation:

Cast: Single Target

Type: damage over time

Duration: 36 seconds

Effect: This spell winds a mind leash around your opponent, as if it
were trying to suffocate them. Its damage ticks every three
seconds for thirty-six seconds.

Bind Affinity

Cast: Self or others

Type: Buff or soul affixer

Duration: Until renewed or overridden with a new location

Effect: This spell binds the target to an area of choice, allowing
them to resurrect easier and hopefully closer to their corpse.
Because you'll all die. A lot.

Infravision

Cast: Single Target

Type: Buff

Duration: 10 minutes

Effect: Aids the target with a form of night vision.

Stupefy

Cast: Single target

Type: Stun

Duration: 12 seconds

Effect: This will stun a mob in place for around twelve seconds.
Probably not a good idea to cast on yourself.

Weakness

Cast: Single Target

Type: Debuff

Duration: 90 seconds

Effect: Reduces the target's strength by 50% of the caster's level.

Languidity

    Cast: Single Target

    Type: Debuff

    Duration: 90 seconds

Effect: Reduces the target's attack speed by 25% of the caster's level in %. Trust us, it's far more effective than you think. Probably.

Nullify

    Cast: Single Target

    Type: Debuff remover

    Duration: Instant

Effect: Strips down magic resistance at 50% of the caster's level.

Level Sixteen (16):

Mana Tide

    Cast: Self or Others

    Type: Buff

    Duration: 45 minutes

Effect: This will cause you to regenerate mana faster in combat. Mana will increase by an additional three per five seconds. This buff levels with the caster.

Invisibility Versus Undead

    Cast: Self or Others

    Type: Buff

    Duration: 12 minutes

Effect: This will render you invisible to any undead in the area. They will be unable to see you, however this buff will fall should you attempt to cast anything else while it's active.

Mass Enthrall

    Cast: Enemy Targets

    Type: Offensive/Defensive area of effect centered around the initial target.

    Duration: 24 seconds

Effect: This is an area effect version of mesmerize. Any damage will break this spell. It's a bad idea to use this while targeting allies.

Haste

    Cast: Self or Others

    Type: Melee Buff

    Duration: 45 minutes

Effect: When cast on an ally, this buff will allow their melee speed to increase by 25%.

Feeble Body

    Cast: Enemy Targets

    Type: Offensive/Defensive

    Duration: 24 seconds

Effect: When cast on an enemy target, their haste will be reduced by 25%.

Shield Illusion

    Cast: Self or Others

    Type: Defensive Buff

    Duration: Until depleted   requires hematite

Effect: Using the power of your mind you cast a shield around your target, confusing the enemies and negating up to 75hp of damage. That whole mind magic thing seems to be working out well, doesn't it?

Level Twenty (20):

Altruism

    Cast: Self or others

    Type: Buff

    Duration: 45 minutes

Effect: This allows a faction increase to your target. It will lift you one faction level. However, should you be kill on sight, not even altruism can help you. This buff will update again at level 30.

Shift

> Cast: Area of effect
>
> Type: AOE Stun
>
> Duration: 8 seconds

Effect: This stun effectively locks all mobs around its epicenter in place for 15 yards. They will be unable to move for 8 seconds.

Fervor

> Cast: Self or others
>
> Type: Buff
>
> Duration: 45 minutes

Effect: This is an attack speed buff, but it also increases agility by the caster's level. Cannot be cast on the same target as Beserker.

Beserker

> Cast: Self or others
>
> Type: Buff
>
> Duration: 45 minutes

Effect: This buff adds strength to the amount equal to the level of the caster, however it also reduces agility by half the caster's level. Best used for classes or pets who will not need agility stacked. Cannot be cast on the same target as Fervor.

Charismatic

> Cast: Self or others (but who are we kidding, you're an enchanter, you'll never not cast this on yourself).
>
> Type: Buff
>
> Duration: 45 minutes

Effect: This buff increases your target's charisma equal to the level of the caster. No restrictions. Cast away!

Magic Resist

> Cast: Group
>
> Type: Buff
>
> Duration: 45 minutes

Effect: Increases your magic resistance by an amount equivalent to the caster's level.

Armored

> Cast: Group
>
> Type: Buff
>
> Duration: 45 minutes

Effect: Increases your AC by an amount equivalent to the caster's level.

Level Twenty-Five (25):

Speed

> Cast: Self or others
>
> Type: Buff
>
> Duration: 45 minutes

Effect: When cast on an ally, this buff will allow their melee haste or speed to increase by 30%.

Vigor

> Cast: Self or others
>
> Type: Buff
>
> Duration: 45 minutes

Effect: This will increase energy rejuvenation by an equivalent to 20% of the caster's level. Mostly, this will be used for melee classes, however sometimes it can be good for running away from dangerous mobs.

Enrage

> Cast: Self or others
>
> Type: Buff... sort of
>
> Duration: 15 minutes

Effect: This buff will cause your target to receive some of the aggression generated by you. The mob will assume it comes from the target of this spell. This spell is intended for tank types or pets to take on. Only cast it on someone else if you really, really don't like them, or maybe if you're running for your life. Also this can only be cast on one target at a time.

Signet

> Cast: Group
>
> Type: Buff
>
> Duration: 45 minutes

Effect: This buff will increase the intelligence and agility of all group members by an amount equal to the caster's level. Signet will not stack with Fervor, and can be overridden by casting the latter, should melee need their own boost. Both stats will be boosted to the level of the caster.

Arcane Cure

> Cast: Self or others
>
> Type: Cure
>
> Duration: Instant

Effect: Should an ally receive a magical debuff, you can cure them of this ailment.

Level Thirty (30):

Altruism

> Cast: Self or Others
>
> Type: Buff
>
> Duration: 45 minutes

Effect: This allows a faction increase to your target. It will lift you two faction levels. However, should you be kill on sight, not even Altruism can help you. This buff will update again at level 40. Worked out well last time, didn't it?

Shield Illusion

> Cast: Self or Others
>
> Type: Defensive Buff
>
> Duration: Until depleted   requires hematite

Effect: Using the power of your mind you cast a shield around your target, confusing the enemies and negating up to 150 HP of damage. That whole mind magic thing seems to be working out well.

Mesmerize

Cast: Single Target

Type: Breakable Stun

Duration: 48 seconds

Effect: This spell immobilized your opponent for as long as they take no damage, or forty-eight seconds, whichever is shorter. You may cast non-damaging spells on them, and you may renew this casting before the initial one expires. Casting it on your friends probably isn't a good way to win popularity contests.

In Perpetuity

Cast: Self Only

Type: Buff

Duration: Until death or departure from Somnia

Effect: This buff increases the enchanter's casting speed for all spells, allowing them to fire them off in quick succession. Combined with Concentration, this buff allows the enchanter to access all of their spells without weaving.

Caution: this requires that the enchanter be fully aware of all of aspects of each spell they cast in this way.

Concentration

Cast: Self Only

Type: Buff

Duration: Until departure from Somnia or death.

Effect: This buff increases the enchanter's ability to focus on and learn their spells. Combined with In Perpetuity, this buff allows the enchanter to cast all of their spells without first weaving them. Caution: If Concentration hasn't been fully applied to the spells, the consequences can be disastrous.

Level Thirty-five (35):

Mana Tide (Upgrade)

>Cast: Self or Others
>
>Type: Buff
>
>Duration: 60 minutes

Effect: This will cause you to regenerate mana faster in combat. Mana will increase by an additional seven per five seconds. This buff levels with the caster.

Root (Upgrade)

>Cast: Others (or self if you really want to)
>
>Type: Immobilization, with thorns
>
>Duration: 12 seconds

Effect: This will root the target in place. Probably not the best idea to cast it on yourself when fleeing in panic. Now with improved thorns which will make your squirming opponent decidedly uncomfortable.

Fervor (Upgrade)

>Cast: Self or others
>
>Type: Buff
>
>Duration: 60 minutes

Effect: This is an attack speed buff, but it also increases agility by the caster s level plus ten. Cannot be cast on the same target as Beserker.

Beserker (Upgrade)

>Cast: Self or others
>
>Type: Buff
>
>Duration: 60 minutes

Effect: This buff adds strength of the amount equal to the level of the caster plus ten, however it also reduces agility by half the caster s level. Best used for classes or pets who will not need agility stacked. Cannot be cast on the same target as Fervor.

Haste (Upgrade)

> Cast: Self or Others
>
> Type: Melee Buff
>
> Duration: 45 minutes

Effect: When cast on an ally, this buff will allow their melee speed to increase by 35%.

Concussive Blast

> Cast: Area of Effect
>
> Type: Stun
>
> Duration: twelve seconds

Effect: This is a stun that radiates out from the caster for fifteen feet. It will stun anyone who means the caster harm within that radius. Does not produce sparkles, rainbows, or ponies.

Level Forty (40)

Altruism (Upgrade)

> Cast: Self or Others
>
> Type: Buff
>
> Duration: 45 minutes

Effect: This allows a faction increase to your target. It will lift you two faction levels. Depending on how badly they hate you, this version might even make you neutral if you re kill on sight. This buff will update again at level 50. Tip: You can use this even if you re already neutral. Nothing wrong with people liking you more. They tend to be more helpful.

Signet

> Cast: Group
>
> Type: Buff
>
> Duration: 45 minutes

Effect: This buff will increase the intelligence and agility of all group members by an amount equal to the caster's level. Signet will not stack with Fervor, and can be overridden by casting the latter, should melee need their own boost. Both stats will be boosted to the level of the caster.

Arcane Cure

Cast: Self or others

Type: Cure

Duration: Instant

Effect: Should an ally receive a magical debuff, you can cure them of this ailment.

Manabalize

Cast: From Self to Others

Type: Transfer

Duration: Instant

Recast: 2 minutes

Effect: Gives target a portion of Enchanter s Mana equal to four times the enchanter s level. Don t be an idiot. Make sure you don't drain yourself empty.

Spell Block

Cast: Enemies (or friends if you want them to be enemies)

Type: Debuff

Duration: Instant

Recast: 90 seconds

Effect: Slows the casting time of the next or current spell by 200%. Most people won't be inclined to like you after you use this on them.

Level Forty-Five (45)

Veto

Cast: Area of Effect

Type: Debuff

Duration: Instant cast, 45 second duration, 45 second recast

Effect: This spell will strip down the target s magical resistance by 100% of the caster s level. Note: Doing this will increase your aggro from the targets you hit. Reducing aggro beforehand is recommended. Unless you re trying to die. Then go ahead.

Assuage

>Cast: Area of Effect

>Type: Debuff

>Duration: 45 seconds, recast 120 seconds

Effect: This spell will lower the threat level of a group of NPCs. Much like the earlier Soothe spell, this will only last for a brief time, and only work if you are out of sight before the spell wears off. Any type of attack will nix this effect. Can be fun if you re being held prisoner and want a chance to run for it.

Annulment

>Cast: Area of Effect

>Type: Debuff

>Duration: Instant, 60 second recast

Effect: This spell allows you to remove a beneficial buff from a group of enemies within a limited area of effect. The caster of the buff will receive backlash from this spell and may hyper focus on you for removing it. Be warned.

Esoteric Fix

>Cast: Area of Effect

>Type: Cure

>Duration: Instant, 60 second recast

Effect: If more than half your group is affected by the same magical debuff or effect, then this is the best way to cure them of it. This group debuff Cure does have a limited radius, like all AoE spells. Please make sure your group members are within casting distance.

Level Fifty (50)

Command

> Cast: Passive
>
> Type: Buff (this buff replaces altruism, but only on the caster)
>
> Duration: Always Active

Effect: This buff enhances your enchanter abilities. It increases your awareness of the world of Somnia, and permanently raises your faction with species you are friendly with to the level of ally. This effect cannot be undone by any debuff.

Warning: the only way this buff can be negated is through the actions of the Psionicist. Treat others as you would be treated. You have been warned.

Mana Tide (Max Upgrade – Level 50)

> Cast: Group
>
> Type: Buff
>
> Duration: 60 minutes

Effect: This will cause you to regenerate mana faster in combat. Mana will increase by an additional 12 per 5 seconds.

Fervor (Max Upgrade – Level 50)

> Cast: Group
>
> Type: Buff
>
> Duration: 60 minutes

Effect: This is an attack speed buff, but it also increases agility by the caster s level plus 20. Cannot be cast on the same target as Berserker. You should know this already. It feels like it s getting repetitive.

Berserker (Max Upgrade – Level 50)

> Cast: Choice of Single or Group must be mind-activated. What? You re an enchanter, deal with it.
>
> Type: Buff
>
> Duration: 60 minutes

Effect: This buff adds strength of the amount equal to the level of the caster plus 20. However, it also reduces agility by half the caster s level. Best used for classes or pets who will not need agility stacked. Cannot be cast on the same target as Fervor. This will override Fervor. It s wise to direct it to single cast or your DPS classes will be angry at you. Unless you thrive on conflict, then fire away.

Haste (Max Upgrade – Level 50)

> Cast: Group
>
> Type: Melee Buff
>
> Duration: 45 minutes

Effect: When cast on an ally, this buff will allow their melee speed to increase by 50%.

Signet (Max Upgrade – Level 50)

> Cast: Group or Single we ve been over these options.
>
> Type: Buff
>
> Duration: 45 minutes

Effect: This buff will increase the intelligence, wisdom, and agility of all group members by an amount equal to the caster's level plus 10. Signet will not stack with Fervor and can be overridden by casting the latter, should melee need their own boost.

Druidic Hybrid Abilities

Earth Shielding

> Cast: Passive
>
> Type: Reinforcement
>
> Duration: Always active

Effect: Due to the psionicist's unique nature, earth shielding will reinforce any of your psionicist based skills such as thought shielding, thought projection, and thought sensing, making them more robust and upping your mental defenses. Any other skills gained through the psionicist's branch will also be affected by this, including any kinetic skills.

Reinforce Self

> Cast: Passive
>
> Type: Reinforcement
>
> Duration: Always active

Effect: Similar to earth shielding which effects your skills, this ability allows your body to take more damage, upping your innate armor class by your level times two   effectively making cloth armor reflect the protection curboiled leather might grant you.

Reinforce Intelligence

> Cast: Passive
>
> Type: Nature's awareness
>
> Duration: Always active

Effect: Nature is all seeing and all encompassing. This ability allows you to take on some of that wisdom and intelligence, and apply it to yourself. It increases both of those statistics by the enchanter's level, giving rise to a larger mana pool, and slightly heightened damage.

Earth Pull

> Cast: Instant three-minute recast
>
> Type: Buff
>
> Duration: thirty seconds

Effect: This allows any buff that is chosen to triple in potency for a thirty second duration. It's activated first, followed by the buff.

Binding Shield

Cast: Instant five-minute recast

Type: Linked Buff

Duration: Fifteen seconds

Effect: You can offer an earth shield to two allies (including yourself if you're going to be selfish and all). This shield will share the damage between the two allies, metering out damage proportionally. Use wisely. Don't try this at home.

Nature's Gift

Cast: Passive

Type: Awareness

Duration: Permanent

Effect: You have become acutely aware of your surroundings. Of the life in everything, in the trees, in the forest, in each and every being you encounter. This lends you a connection to nature. Don't dismiss it lightly.

Earth Healing – Druidic Subversion

Cast: Instant but prolonged – will only last as long as sufficient mana is present
Type: Reinforcement/Healing
Duration: For as long as mana can maintain the spell. Result is permanent until such as time as the flow is disrupted again.
Effect: Due to the kinetic nature of this particular spell, it will travel along the lines of the earth to replenish and revitalize that which has become brittle. Healing something doesn't always have to mean a being.

Caution: Do not get too caught up in these actions and give into the voice of the earth lest you lose your way. Know your own mind.

Max Level Upgrades – Druidic Hybrid

Earth Shielding Forte

Cast: Initiated Passive

Type: Reinforcement

Duration: Active once initiated until death of the caster

Effect: on top of Earth Shielding, when the Psionicist casts this expanded version, it will extend directly to ground their entire group. This will increase their natural defenses by 15% for the duration. This ability is best used in conjunction with a main tank group and can also be beneficial for healers in order to mitigate damage.

Reinforce Others

Cast: Active

Type: Buff

Duration: 60 with a 2-minute cooldown

Effect: this is a defensive buff which can be cast on a singular target, thus enabling them to take more damage by upping their innate armor class level. The amount of armor depends on the level of and type of class being cast on. Best used on tanks, as agility is negatively affected when cast on nearly all ranged damage classes.

Rockslide

Cast: Instant, as long as the caster is focused on the exact epicenter

Type: Damage

Duration: depending on the magnitude of the rockslide cast, which follows the will of the caster, a rockslide can last from anywhere as short as two seconds up to twelve seconds.

Effect: summons a landslide of rocks from a high point of land to crush the targets chosen by the caster.

Caution: can only be used around or close to rock formations. Do not use where rocks cannot naturally occur; you will not like what you summon.

Sinuous Abilities

Sinuous: This is the more offensive avenue to take. From hypnotic suggestion, through to invoked visions, this path veers toward complete mind infestation of the enchanter's opponents. This is only available to psionicists.

Hypnotic Suggestion

Cast: Instant 5 minute recast

Type: Offensive

Duration: twenty seconds

Effect: Your target will perform whatever task you suggest to them, as if it had been suggested by themselves, or their leader. Once this objective has been achieved, or else the spell wears off, the target will spend five seconds in rampant confusion. Should you not be in aggro range, the target will then forget you. Probably not good to use on allies – it's not been tested on them.

Feedback Loop

Cast: Instant 5-minute recast

Type: Offensive

Duration: 15 seconds or 50% of caster's level, whichever is greater.

Effect: Must be used in conjunction with the psionic MA thought sensing, and thought projection. Pluck any type of memory out of the head of your opponent and create a feedback loop in their mind. They'll be stuck in this loop and not attack anyone for the duration. Damage ticks at caster's level x 2 every tic (3 seconds). Best not to use on a friend when they piss you off.

Basic Visions

Cast: Instant 3-minute recast

Type: Offensive

Duration: 20 seconds, or 75% of the caster's level, whichever is greater.

Effect: You may create and insert a vision for the target to experience its best to have some of these pre-prepared. This will cause them damage (caster's level x 2 per tick), and distraction for the duration of the spell depending on what type of vision you've given them.

Level Thirty (30)

Possession I

    Cast: Instant – 5 minute recast

    Type: Offensive

    Duration: 20 seconds

Effect: Force your way into the mind of your target and assume control for up to twenty seconds. Make sure the target is debuffed for maximum duration. Don't even contemplate being in the target when it dies. It's a very bad idea.

Sudden Drop

    Cast: Instant – 10 minute recast

    Type: Offensive Debuff

    Duration: 20 seconds

Effect: A forced debuff wave that overrides the enemy's natural defenses and convinces them that all their stats have dropped by an amount equivalent to the caster's level. Lasts for 25 seconds. Cannot be resisted.

Level Thirty-five (35)

Cast: Mana Block

    Type: Specific Mana aimed stun

    Duration: 6 seconds, recast 45 seconds

Effect: This is, effectively, a stun which blocks the use of mana of an opponent. It will also interrupt any current ability being cast when it hits. For its duration the target will be unable to utilize any of their mana based skills for six seconds. Be cautious with timing this spell as it has a forty-five second recast and if you cast it at the wrong time, you might just kill everyone.

Mana Theft

    Cast: Instant – 5 minute recast

    Type: Offensive

    Duration: Not applicable

Effect: This ability allows the enchanter to steal mana from their opponent. It will not only steal a large chunk of mana from the opponent, but will also inflict in damage the same amount stolen during the Mana theft. When used in conjunction with mana-drain, this can debilitate the target and keep the group in mana when juggled well.

Mana-Drain

> Cast: Instant – 5 minute recast
>
> Type: Offensive
>
> Duration: lasts twenty seconds

Effect: This ability allows the enchanter to apply a DoT to the target where it will drain the mana and share it out toward the group. The DoT is one of both physical damage and mana loss. While it ticks slowly, the damage can backlash if it is prematurely cleansed off your target, even if its by the target themselves. Be aware that nothing that drains mana in a violent way is a good thing, but sometimes there are necessary evils.

Level forty (40)

Confusion

> Cast: Enemies
>
> Type: Debuff
>
> Duration: 12 seconds (maximum four seconds if cast on a boss)
>
> Recast: 5 minutes

Effect: Envelops the opponents brain in a cloud of confusion. This allows their spells to misfire, hitting their allies, and usually avoiding their enemies completely. Effect severely diminished when used on boss mobs.

Thought Leech

> Cast: Enemies (or friends if you re really nosy)
>
> Type: thought transfer
>
> Duration: immediate
>
> Recast: 4 minutes

Effect: Allows the Psionicist to know the order of the next three abilities or spells the target is going to cast. Can effectively render the attacks useless if countered in time. Can also be totally useless if used incorrectly. Good luck!

Level Forty-Five (45)

Hypnotic Charm

Cast: Others

Type: Mind Control

Duration: Minimum duration is half the caster s level in seconds, maximum is two times the caster s level in seconds.

Effect: This spell is a hybrid of Charm and Hypnotic Suggestion. It is specifically designed to briefly control an enemy character. Be wary of the time limits. It is recommended you navigate away before the earliest possible break in control.

Level Fifty (50)

Advanced Mana Healing

Cast: Instant   5-minute recast

Type: Replenishing

Duration: 8 seconds. This ability requires that both the caster and the receiver remain motionless for 8 seconds.

Effect: This ability allows the Psionicist to completely heal a singular target's mana pool and restore it to full. This effect will only occur if both parties to the spell are able to remain immobile for the duration of the transfer. The Enchanter does not pull from their own mana pool; instead they will convert the hit points of their opponents into mana energy in order to replenish the mana of their target.

Warning: Do not execute this ability unless you are 99.9% positive that both you and the recipient are able to maintain immobility for 8 seconds. To break the transfer mid-cast could potentially be catastrophic and cause damage to rain down on the entire raid or group.

Create Your Own Abilities

Effect: This is not a spell as such, but a confirmation of the innate ability you have demonstrated over the last few levels. Since you are able to morph spells, skills, and abilities you already possess into more advanced versions of themselves if the situation warrants it, let s make it official.

Requirements: Your guild and or allies must find themselves

in such a position that is untenable. Through the use of your willpower and the evolution of your skills, you may be able to find an out-of-the-box solution.

Warning: Be aware that this is not the solution to all of your problems, nor is it the way to be victorious in every situation. This is not a crutch, and using it as such would be foolhardy.

Insidious Lure – Sinuous Subversion

Cast: Instant once released

Type: Entrapment/Psychosis

Duration: For as long as your will remains focused.

Effect: This will lure your enemies into a trap of the mind, forcing them to see their worst fears and act on them, even to the detriment of their peers. It will continue until the caster releases the spell, or the enemies have killed each other.

Caution: This spell can be mentally taxing, and even damaging. Make sure your reasons for using such force are justified. Try not to get caught in your own nightmare along the way.

SPELL UPGRADES:

Feedback Loop Sinuous Ability =Feedback Loop – Reckoning

Cast: Instant – 120 minute recast

Type: Offensive – Maximum four targets

Duration: Half the level of the caster in minutes

MA Cost: 150 MA for the entire duration

Warning: This is a spell that you will need to consider the ramifications of deeply before casting. Overuse could result in permanent scars to your psyche. It will also heavily impact your current MA availability.

Effect: Must be used in conjunction with the psionic MA Thought Sensing, and Thought Projection. Pluck any type of memory out of the head of an attacker, foe, or friend and create a feedback loop in your target(s) mind(s). They will be stuck in this loop and not attack anyone for the duration.

Effect Warning: Note that this is a cycle of torment and will render the target useless for its entire duration. Use with caution.

Mana Drain = Mana Drain – Unabridged

Cast: Instant – 20 minute recast

Type: Offensive – Maximum fifteen targets

Duration: Half the level of the caster in seconds

MA Cost: 150 MA for the entire duration

Warning: You must consider the ramifications of this spell before casting it. Overuse may result in permanent scars to your psyche. It heavily impacts MA availability. This is meant as a pinch hitter. Use only in emergencies.

Effect: Must be used in conjunction with the psionic MA Thought Sensing and Thought Projection. This spell analyzes the targets in the area of effect and siphons their mana, or mana type of energy. If that energy is used to sustain the target, this spell will effectively kill, or close to kill them. The energy will be transferred to you and your group or raid, replenishing current mana levels.

Effect Warning: When replenishing your comrades mana pool, the transfer will demand damage be taken as recompense. You cannot avoid this side effect. Everything is a matter of give and take. Be warned.

Basic Vision spell = Mind Healing.

Cast: Instant – 5 minute recast

Type: Restorative

Duration: 20 seconds, or 75% of the caster's level, whichever is greater.

Effect: You may create and insert a vision for the target to experience it s best to have some of these pre-prepared. This will not cause any damage but instead assist in soothing a tormented mind. Use with caution and be aware that people who could benefit from this skill might be closer than you realize.

CAUTION:

Your Mesmerize spell has reached a new level of potency due to continuous usage. With mind exertion you have created the ability to overpower individual creature's resistance to your powers. This comes at a cost of ten MA per spell casting per resistance level of the target, which is of course per mob controlled.

Should the target have of resistance level of three, maintaining Mesmerize on said target will be at a cost of thirty MA per cast.

Mind Exertion

Cast: Passive

Type: Reinforcement

Duration: Dependent on individual needs

Effect: this passive ability allows the Enchanter or Psionicist to reinforce the potency of the spells they are capable of casting. This ability straddles the line between normal progression spells and mental acuity spells. Thus this ability allows for strengthening of mundane spells through the application of mental acuity points.

Caution: Do not overuse this spell. Always make sure your mental acuity points will not be overextended. Spell backlash is a bad enough, overextending your points can result in catastrophic consequences. This might allow you to overpower the minds of creatures whose only defense is that your spells have diminishing returns. Therefore it cannot be without its own associated risks and costs.

ACKNOWLEDGMENTS

I have a lot of people to thank, who in at least some way encouraged me to write in general, or else to write this book specifically.

Love of my life, Trevor, and my little Kami. It's his fault I found the genre, and her fault I never give up on writing.

I wouldn't be here without the following friends (and I hope I didn't forget anyone):

Jami Nord & Owen Littman

M. Andrew Patterson

Kylie B.

Amanda W.

Quinton Shyn

Kindra

Jenn W.

Dawn Chapman

Alexis Keane

Bonnie Price

Stephen Morse

Felissa Ely

Andrea Parseneau

Cait Greer

M Evan Matyas

Ian Mitchell

Marko Horvatin

Dave Willmarth

Charles Dean
Daniel Schinhofen
Jay Boyce
Michael Chatfield
Luke Chmilenko
Tao Wong

And of course my family:
Mumskin & Papilie, Tracey, Bev, & Robbie.

And every one of my Patrons, not to mention my FB Group. You all help me maintain a level of sanity.

www.ingramcontent.com/pod-product-compliance
Lightning Source LLC
Chambersburg PA
CBHW032203180726
48284CB00001B/161